THE ANGEL
of
HIGHGATE

Also by Vaughn Entwistle

THE REVENANT OF THRAXTON HALL
THE DEAD ASSASSIN

THE ANGEL
of
HIGHGATE

VAUGHN ENTWISTLE

TITAN BOOKS

The Angel of Highgate
Print edition ISBN: 9781783295340
E-book edition ISBN: 9781783295357

Published by Titan Books
A division of Titan Publishing Group Ltd
144 Southwark Street, London SE1 0UP

First edition: December 2015
10 9 8 7 6 5 4 3 2 1

A CIP catalogue record for this title is available from the British Library.

Printed in the USA.

This book is dedicated to my wife Shelley,
my inamorata now and forever.

I

IN HOPES OF THE RESURRECTION TO COME

October 4th 1859, almost seven a.m. on a Sunday morning. God was in His Heaven. Queen Victoria was on her throne. And Lord Geoffrey Thraxton was prowling the pathways of Highgate Cemetery. Ectoplasmic mists swirled about the brooding mass of stone mausoleums. A ghostly winged form—a carved angel perched atop a grave— crooked a beckoning finger from the gloom. Thraxton ignored the summons and strode on, the fog cupping his face in its cool hands.

Despite the early hour and the somber setting, Thraxton was impeccably dressed in black frock coat and tight, camel-color breeches, a bright yellow cravat knotted at his throat, a gray silk top hat perched at an insolent angle upon his head. In one kid-gloved hand he gripped a walking stick whose grip was formed by a golden phoenix bursting forth from tongues of flame. The other hand, gloveless, stroked the cashmere lining of his coat pocket. In his early thirties, and of above average height and muscular build, Thraxton had a face that could have been said to be both handsome and noble, were it not for a certain weakness in the mouth, a hint of dissolution in the corners of the intense blue eyes.

In the still air, the only sound was the crackle of leaves underfoot, the rattle of robins in the berry bushes, and as the hour struck, the slow, dolorous clang of bells from the nearby Church of St. Michael's. To the south lay the city of London, an invisible but palpable presence in the fog, for the smoke coughed up from the sooty throats of its myriad chimneys left a bitter tang of sulfur on the tongue.

Highgate was arguably the most beautiful necropolis in the capital, with its mixture of Classical and Egyptian influenced tombs and mausoleums, including its most celebrated architectural flourish, the Circle of Lebanon, so named for the gnarled cedar that rooted at its center. It was a place for London's fashionable living to perambulate, as well as a final resting place for London's fashionable dead to await the Crack of Doom and the body's resurrection.

At this hour, however, Thraxton had only the latter for company. On a path leading to the Egyptian Avenue, he paused to contemplate the rain-worn face of a stone angel, its eyes cast downward in an expression of profound loss. At that moment, the bells of St. Michael's peeled a final stroke and fell mute, opening an abyss of silence wherein the world beyond the cemetery fell away, and the dead caught their breath. Then a sorrowful wail drifted from afar, faintly, as if all the stone angels of Highgate were weeping, but soon followed the rattle of carriage wheels, the jingle of horse brasses and the muffled thump of hooves on soft soil.

A rectangular shape loomed in the mist, gathering solidity until it materialized in the form of a hearse drawn by two coal-dark mares, their huge heads nodding with black plumes. Atop the hearse rode two funeral grooms in black frock coats with top hats draped in black crepe. Two more paced behind the hearse on foot, followed by four women in black mourning dresses, their faces darkly veiled. These women were the source of the weeping, which they interspersed with the occasional heart-cracking wail. At the rear of the procession strode two men dressed in daily attire but for the black crepe armbands that marked them as mourners.

The taller of the two was a handsome gentleman of about the same age as Thraxton with blonde curls spilling out from beneath his top hat. The fellow that walked beside him was a full foot shorter, barely into his twenties, and whose bowler hat and shabby jacket marked him as a domestic servant. Both men wore expressions shaped by the solemnity of the occasion, yet the servant's face seemed to bear a look at once both serious and supercilious.

The hearse clattered around the bend of the narrow lane and Thraxton stepped aside to allow it to pass, doffing his top hat in respect. Such a lugubrious display was calculated to instill a profound sense of loss and mourning in all who witnessed it, yet the sight of the hearse had served only to tease a faint smile onto Thraxton's lips.

The glass sides of the hearse flashed as it drew alongside and he caught a glimpse of the deceased—a young woman in a crystal coffin, her body swathed in a white lace death shroud of intricate delicacy.

As the solemn cortège trundled by, Thraxton's presence went unacknowledged by the slightest glance from either the funeral grooms or the wailing women. But the blond gentleman looked up as he passed, and for the briefest of moments his calm hazel eyes met and held Thraxton's.

The funeral procession carried on for another thirty feet and drew up next to a stone mausoleum. To gain a better vantage, Thraxton clambered up on the pedestal with the stone angel. Setting his hat momentarily atop the angel's head, he stood with his arms wrapped around its waist, his cheek pressed up against the mossy stone as he watched the melancholy scene from a discreet distance.

The lamenting reached its climax as the four grooms lifted the coffin from the hearse. Assisted by the gentleman and the servant, they bore it into the tomb upon their shoulders, and the mourning women wept after them.

It was over quickly. The mourners re-emerged from the tomb, minus the coffin, the groomsmen led the horses around until they faced the direction they had just come from, and soon the cortège passed by heading in the other direction. The funereal wailing softened into the distance. The hearse grew transparent, lost substance, and dissolved into the seething grayness. Thraxton retrieved his top hat, stepped down from his angelic perch, and sauntered toward the mausoleum.

A fresh wreath hung upon the bronze door, above which a stonemason had carved a grinning skull nestled amongst winged cherubs. Thraxton studied the memento mori as he stole a single white flower from the wreath and threaded the bloom into his boutonnière. He cast a casual glance first left and then right. The funeral party was long gone. Apart from the slumbering dead of Highgate, no one was about. The latch lifted beneath his thumb and a gentle push creaked the tomb door open. Thraxton slipped inside and swung the door shut behind him.

Inside the tomb, a profusion of candles burned here and there, their waxy scent muddled with the fragrance of white lilies scattered atop the coffin's crystal lid. He stepped closer. The flowers concealed the face of the deceased, so he swept them to the floor and peered in. What he saw made him catch his breath. The woman inside the coffin was beautiful and shockingly young, scarcely sixteen.

"My God," he gasped, "how perfect a bloom to have fallen so soon."

His fingers closed on the handle of the coffin lid. A gentle tug revealed that it was not fastened. The crystal lid was massive and awkward, but Thraxton heaved it off and set it down on the floor.

At last, he stood over the open coffin gazing down at the vision within. Despite the heavily applied white powder and red-rouged cheeks and lips, the woman seemed young, fresh and alive. The sight of that face, like a sleeping angel's, sent a tremor through him. To disturb such beauty seemed sacrilege, but after a moment's hesitation, he reached out and caressed the soft down of her cheek with his fingertips.

"The blush of youth still lingers on flesh grown cold."

As he traced the full, rouged lips with his thumb, a muscle in his jaw trembled.

"Surely Death, your new husband, would not be jealous of a single kiss on this, your wedding day?"

Thraxton leaned in and softly kissed the corpse's lips. They were full and pliant, and parted slightly as he drew his lips away.

"How sweet. Even in death. How sweet."

The shroud was fastened at the front by a number of delicately tied bows. He caught and tugged the end of the topmost. The bow silkily unknotted and the shroud fell open, revealing an alabaster neck and chest. The remaining bows soon surrendered to his quick fingers and Thraxton drew the shroud open to reveal small, firm breasts with taut, high nipples, the soft dome of a belly, a patch of golden hair between the thighs. In the shifting candlelight, the flesh seemed marble that had flowed waxen and set in the shape of an Aphrodite.

Thraxton's eyes drank in the sight. He realized he had been holding his breath, and now let it out in one deep, languorous sigh.

"Ah, pretty one, has a coffin become your bridal bed? Will Death be the first to take your maidenhood?"

Thraxton slid out of his coat and let it fall at his feet. His fingers tore at the buttons of his waistcoat. He yanked the fine linen shirt over his head in one quick motion, shedding several pearl buttons. By now, anticipation had tightened him into a throbbing knot, and as he peeled off the tight breeches he was already stiff and quivering in the chill air of the tomb.

Naked, he climbed up onto the bier the coffin was set upon and stared down upon the body in a state of greedy rapture.

"And now," he breathed, "a taste of the fruit new-fallen from the tree, before the worms can canker it!"

Thraxton lifted and spread the woman's legs, letting them dangle on either side of the open coffin, then slid in between. It was difficult to move in such restricted confines, but he squirmed his hips left and right, searching for an entry, until he slid in effortlessly.

"I will cuckold Death and add my little death to yours!"

As he began to thrust, the cold body moved rhythmically under him. The sound of his labored breathing filled the tomb, and the light of the guttering candles refracted through the coffin's crystal sides, threw grotesque, quivering shadows on the walls.

Outside, the morning fog was beginning to burn off under the weak September sun. The service at nearby St. Michael's had finished but a few minutes ago, and now many of those who had attended, gentlemen and ladies, couples with their children, were enjoying a stroll in the tranquil peace of the cemetery grounds.

Inside the mausoleum, Thraxton's thrusting had intensified to the point where the woman's head was softly thumping into the end of the coffin. It could have been a trick of the shifting candlelight, but it appeared as though the corpse had the slightest of smiles upon its lips. The dead woman's legs had slid down until the cold soles of her feet pressed on Thraxton's steely buttocks. Even more miraculous was when the corpse's eyes opened slightly and a singularly delicious giggle escaped the deceased's lips.

Thraxton laughed and said, "Was there ever a more lovely Lazarus?"

By now the pathways of Highgate Cemetery were busy with morning strollers and relatives come to lay flowers on the graves of their loved ones. The visitors now looked up in alarm and horror as the serenity of a Sunday morning was broken by the echoing grunts and moans of a man and a woman in the throes of sexual ecstasy.

Their macabre tryst completed, Thraxton collected his scattered attire from the floor of the tomb, while the woman put on clothes that had been tucked beneath the coffin's satin pillows. Dressed only in a white corset, the young woman let out a mischievous giggle as she tied the red silk bow that held up one of her knee-length white stockings. "You took your bleedin' time, Geoffrey," she said. "My bloomin' arse was freezin' in that coffin!"

Thraxton smiled as he cinched the silk cravat into an insolent knot at his throat. "Merely showing due deference and respect for the deceased, Maisy, m'dear."

She snickered at that. "Bloomin' 'eck. I don't fink wot you just done to me was the least bit respectful!"

"Nonsense," Thraxton corrected, slipping an arm around her narrow, corseted waist and pulling her towards him. "What greater respect can a mere supplicant show than to worship at the altar of Venus?"

Maisy's eyes softened at his words. "I know I'm nuffink but a common tart, Geoffrey, but when you says them things it makes me feel all special and bee-you-tee-full!"

Never taking his eyes from hers, Thraxton slipped two fingers inside her, then put them in his mouth, tasting the acrid tang of their commingled essences. He sought to share it with a kiss, his tongue probing the sweet cavern of Maisy's mouth. For a moment, she sucked on his tongue thrillingly. Perceiving her renewed passion, Thraxton felt his ardor rise again. But then Maisy dissolved, once more, into titters.

It shattered the illusion, reminding Thraxton that, despite the elaborate pretense, Maisy was merely a street girl he had purchased for a few hours' diversion. He broke off the kiss, gave her cheek a fond caress, and went back to pulling his clothes on. "And so you are beautiful and special," Thraxton said, digging a heavy coin from his pocket which he pressed into her hand. "And here's a golden sovereign to keep your beautiful arse warm in the winter."

Maisy, who had never seen much more than a shilling for herself in the four years she had worked as a prostitute, gasped at the largesse. "Thanks ever so much, Geoffrey! You are a proper gent you are!"

He grabbed her roughly and kissed her hard on the mouth, then spun her around and slapped her on the bare behind. "Now then, go, my child, and sin no more!"

Maisy rubbed her stinging right buttock and giggled effervescently. "My Gawd! You are such a card, Geoffrey. Really you are. You oughta be on the music hall stage!"

Thraxton paused in brushing a smudge of tomb dust from his top hat and threw his arms out expressively. "But I am, my dear. I am. And every day of my life is merely another act I must play."

While Maisy pulled on her dress, Thraxton sat on the coffin staring into the shadows, a thousand conflicting thoughts wrestling in his mind. He was given to moodiness, and now he felt a post-coital depression settling upon him, mixed with the vague sense of disappointment that always accompanies the indulgence of a long-held fantasy.

Maisy by now had finished dressing, and with her parasol and little lace-up boots that showed when she coquettishly lifted her skirts, could have passed for the local vicar's daughter out for a Sunday promenade. On her way out of the mausoleum she turned and curtsied to Thraxton. "Good day, milord," she said and dissolved once more into giggles.

The heavy door thumped shut and Maisy was gone.

With the closing of the door a waft of fresh air crashed into the walls and dispersed, churning with the heady scents of candle wax, flowers and sex. Thraxton moved about the tomb, extinguishing candles until only one remained burning. He stood close by, feeling its heat on his cheek, his face lit by the candle's amber glow. His eyes instead were fixed on the shadows that squirmed at the edge of the light. The candle flame shivered in a sudden draft that made the shadows lunge then recoil. Thraxton gazed into their shifting depths and sensed an invisible presence hovering there. When the hairs at the nape of his neck began to rise, he knew it had arrived. The Dark Presence. His old adversary. "Death?" he said, his voice a brittle whisper in the echoing silence of the tomb. "Can you hear me, Death? Yes?" He smiled. "Not today... not today."

Thraxton licked his fingers and pinched the wick out with a sizzle, and with no light to hold them back, the shadows of the tomb fell in upon him.

When Thraxton finally left the family tomb, he found the harsh morning sunshine jarring, the knots of politely smiling middle-class strollers an irritant. He wished to cling to his sense of gloomy isolation a while longer, so he turned away from the cemetery entrance and followed the pathways to the center of the necropolis, the Circle of Lebanon. The fog here had yet to lift and he plunged once more into its cool and welcome veil. Ahead hovered the brooding mass of the pharaonic arch that formed the entrance to the Egyptian Avenue, a sloping tunnel, lined by mausoleums. With no lanterns lit, the avenue was an obsidian shaft. At its far end, luminous panes of silver fog swirled. He stepped inside the echoing space, a gloved hand brushing the bronze tomb doors as he trod the rising slope.

He froze as a figure appeared at the end of the stony

tunnel—the silhouette of a small woman in long skirts, her face hidden by a deep cowl. "Maisy?" Thraxton called out, echoingly. "Maisy, is that you?"

But even as he spoke the words, Thraxton realized that the young prostitute had been dressed much more gaily, and would likely have left in the opposite direction, heading straight for the cemetery's front gates. His mind vaulted back to the stone angel that crooked a finger and beckoned to him from the fog. The shadow-form seemed to regard him for a moment, then slid from sight.

Thraxton quivered with nervous excitement. He scurried up the tunnel and emerged into the Circle of Lebanon, twenty sunken tombs arranged around an ancient cedar of Lebanon. Darkness clung to the place: the towering cedar flung a wide shadow; the cold stone corralled a twisting torus of fog. The silvery tissues teased apart momentarily and he saw the vague shape again, thirty feet away.

"Hello?" he called out, lumbering after it. The shadow plunged into the fog and vanished and Thraxton pursued, the only sound his heavy breathing and the squeak of fine leather boots. A moment later he felt like a fool chasing his own shadow, for he had transited a complete circle and wound up back at the Egyptian Avenue. Whatever it was had eluded him. Just then the mists cleaved and a wan shaft of light broke through, illuminating a scattering of white blobs on the stony ground. He crouched and touched a finger to one. A white petal adhered to the tip of his gloved index finger. He rolled the petal between his fingertips.

It seemed fresh. Had the petals been there when he first entered the circle?

The back of Thraxton's neck prickled as he sensed eyes upon him. When he looked up, a figure stood at the top of the stone stairs that climbed out of the circle, watching. As he rose from the ground, it took a step backward, pulled the fog about its shoulders like a cloak... and merged into the seamless gray.

2

The Mummy's Curse

Skin the color of old papyrus flaking and peeling away from the skull. Leathery lips drawn back, showing yellow, twisted teeth.

A tittering laugh.

Hollow sockets with eyes that had shriveled into raisins thousands of years ago.

An answering guffaw.

A skull lonesome for its lower jaw.

A booming voice answered by a wail of laughter.

A Canopic jar with its contents: a dried and embalmed heart, liver and lungs, wrapped in linen, placed carefully alongside.

A crystal bowl of black sturgeon's eggs settled in a bed of crushed ice.

The redolence of perfume mixed with the pervasive reek of corruption.

Sunday evening and the upper crust of London society

were in attendance at a soirée in the unlikely environs of the Mummy Room in the British Museum.

Champagne corks popped. Servants scurried. In a corner of the room a quartet sawed away at violins and cellos. Here and there, elegantly dressed men and women stood in loose knots, speaking in loud voices, gesturing with excessive animation and laughing too long at the meagerest of witticisms.

Inside their glass cases, the desiccated corpses and mummies of ancient Egypt danced a frozen ballet of death, knees drawn up into fetal postures, spines twisted into sinuous contortions that counterfeited the final agonies of death. In their day they had been the aristocracy of ancient Egypt. Now they had been snatched from two thousand years of darkness and silence to be itemized, catalogued, and put on public display, a human life reduced to a curiosity to be gawked at over canapés and champagne.

The party had been in progress for almost an hour when Lord Thraxton appeared at the door, a light mist of rain beaded on the shoulders of his frock coat. A servant took his top hat, cloak and walking stick. As he strode into the hall he exchanged greetings and pleasantries with a gathering of cabinet ministers and their wives, then quickly excused himself and moved away. A balding banker with a voluminous beard accosted him and babbled something about investments in the Americas. Thraxton muttered back some vague incoherencies about annuities and yearly stipends and moved on. He accepted and returned more greetings from baronesses, viceroys, judges and heirs apparent. All the time he spoke his eyes searched the room until he found the person he'd been looking for.

Making conversation in a clutch of well-dressed gentlemen and ladies was a tall man with hazel eyes and blonde hair curling up on his collar. Thraxton strode deliberately over and slapped a hand on the man's shoulder. "Algy, old fellow," he boomed. "How is that scorching case of the clap of yours?" Thraxton bowed slightly to the group and then, seeing their horrified reactions, quickly added, "Please... do not recoil so. He is only slightly infectious."

Algernon tried to laugh it off. "You must forgive Lord Thraxton. He has the most obtuse sense of humor."

"Yes. Beg pardon, but I really must steal my friend for a moment." Thraxton grinned as he jostled Algernon loose and propelled him in the direction of the refreshments table.

"Thank you, Geoffrey," Algernon muttered as they walked away. "I had wished to be rescued, but perhaps not at the cost of my good name and standing in society."

Algernon Hyde-Davies had been Thraxton's friend and confidant since they met as schoolboys. They sauntered to a discreet corner of the gathering where Thraxton leaned close and whispered conspiratorially to his old chum.

"Do not take on so, Algy. It's not as if they were persons of any import. After all, they were talking to you."

An ancient serving person shuffled over and offered up a tray quivering with crystal flutes of champagne. They each took a glass and stood sipping.

"So, Algernon, how goes my little soirée?"

"Swimmingly, Geoffrey. As usual, you are fashionably late for your own affair."

"Of course."

"I must say, you seem quite ebullient tonight."

"I feel positively messianic, Algy. After all, I raised the dead this morning. Albeit only after she raised me."

A white-haired dowager in a sparkling tiara nodded and smiled toothily as she sailed past like an ancient shipwreck. Both men bowed slightly in return.

"I had an encounter, this morning, Algy. Something quite remarkable."

"Yes, you certainly did, and quite a sum it cost, too."

"You misunderstand. I saw something... a spirit..." he shook his head, trying to conjure the right word "...an angel."

"Yes, I agree. The young girl was quite an angel, I did request only the best for you."

"Don't be tiresome, Algy. I speak in earnest."

"What?"

"After I left the tomb, I saw something, a dark spirit or wraith. I pursued it, but it vanished before my eyes."

"Fascinating," Algernon drawled in a voice that suggested he found the subject anything but. "Tell me, was it still foggy?"

Thraxton acquiesced with a reluctant nod.

"Geoffrey, I have witnessed a fourteen-passenger London omnibus—not six feet away—vanish before my eyes in a pea-souper. I did not report it to London Transport as a supernatural disapparition of one of their vehicles."

"Damn your skepticism. I know what I saw. We must return to Highgate some dark night, when the spirits walk abroad."

"Sounds tiresome, damp and dismal."

"We may catch a ghost."

"More likely an upper-respiratory infection—wet fogs enflame the bronchioles."

Thraxton suppressed a look of profound irritation, forcing a nod and a smile to a passing judge. "I trust you took care of all the, ah, financial arrangements this morning?"

"Yes, Geoffrey. Four of Mayfair's best harlots as mourners and the services of Messrs. Alcock and Fitch, Undertakers. Total expenditure one hundred and fifty pounds. And now this soirée? Thirty-two magnums of champagne. Eighteen pounds of black Russian caviar. A string quartet and ten serving folk. Total expenditure two-hundred and twelve pounds, ten shillings and thruppence. Really, Lord Thraxton, even your purse must know some limits!"

The smile lurking at the corners of Thraxton's mouth betrayed the pleasure he took in such acts of decadence. "As always, Algy, you are ever the empiricist. But one cannot reduce one's life to a line of pounds, shillings and pence scribbled on a ledger sheet by some dusty clerk. I already told you, I intend to die a poor, lonely and destitute man, thereby leaving nothing for my detestable relatives to squabble over. For it has ever been my experience that in matters of money…"

Thraxton trailed off as his eye happened to fall upon a gentleman at the far end of the room: a short, middle-aged man with large, bushy side-whiskers and a shock of white at each temple—Augustus Skinner, a literary critic who wrote for *Blackwell's Gazette* amongst other periodicals. In his last review of a book of poetry published by Thraxton, Skinner had dryly observed: "This latest book of doggerel—I hesitate to elevate such scratchings with the appellation of 'verse'—is a decided improvement upon Lord Thraxton's previous efforts. At nearly thirty pages, the volume, though diminutive, burned for a full half hour in my fireplace, supplying at least some warmth and illumination that a reading of its sorry contents failed to provide."

At the sight of Skinner's countenance, ballooned with laughter as he held court with three other gentlemen, Thraxton's own face blackened like a thunder cloud. "Skinner!" Thraxton spat. "What is that man doing at *my* party, drinking *my* champagne?"

Algernon knew disaster was imminent. He had seen his friend in such a high dudgeon only a handful of times in their acquaintance. Each time the episode had ended in broken furniture, swollen knuckles, threats of law suits. "Really, Geoffrey, Augustus Skinner is on the museum's board of directors. One can hardly expect him not to attend a cultural event—"

"Culture? What does that worm know of culture? He is a critic, a destroyer of culture who should be thrashed like the loathsome cur he is!"

Before Algernon could stop him, Thraxton stalked across the room toward the unsuspecting critic. Algernon rushed after and grabbed him by the arm. "Geoffrey, they're unwrapping a mummy. Come see!"

"After I've made a mummy out of Mister Skinner!"

"There's the most attractive lady. I believe she is in mourning." It was a piece of news Algernon had been keeping to himself, but in order to avoid what was surely to be a horrendous scene, he now blurted it out.

At the mention of the word "mourning," Thraxton stopped abruptly. Algernon suddenly had his full attention. "A lady, you say? In mourning?"

Deep within the bowels of the museum, a lecture theater had been commandeered for the mummy unwrapping. When Thraxton and Algernon slipped inside, a small crowd of thirty or so were gathered around a table at which Sir Hector Chelmsford, noted antiquarian and fellow of the Royal Society, was conducting the proceedings, assisted by several colleagues. On the table in front of them the mummy of a young Egyptian commoner—a woman, scarcely in her nineteenth year—was being peeled of its tannin-stained wrappings.

The two friends jostled through the crowd, seeking a vantage point. A gentleman took a step to his left, and in the opening Thraxton suddenly had a clear view of the proceedings. More importantly, on the far side of the examination table, at the front of the gathering, stood a young woman in her late twenties. Her long, blonde ringlets and peaches and cream complexion stood out in great contrast to the black mourning dress and jet earrings and necklace glittering at her throat. Even from twenty feet away, Thraxton could see that her eyes were a shade of milky blue. The sparkle in those eyes and eager smile showed her delight and fascination in the proceedings.

Thraxton spoke close to Algernon's ear. "A handsome woman. Who is she?"

From his pained expression, it was clear that Algernon felt reluctant to share the information with Thraxton. "Constance Pennethorne. Widow of the late Charles Pennethorne, the banker."

"She seems a merry widow. I wonder how long it's been since she vaulted the old money-lender?"

The crowd gasped as Sir Hector peeled away another layer of wrappings to reveal a solid gold Ankh lying upon the mummy's chest.

"Ah-hah!" exclaimed Sir Hector. "We have discovered an Ankh, a talisman often found within the wrappings of mummies, traditionally placed over the heart."

Thraxton stepped from his place in the crowd, sauntered up to the examining table and calmly snatched the golden Ankh from the hand of the surprised Sir Hector, flourishing it aloft for all to see. "The Ankh, symbol of life everlasting," Thraxton announced to the crowd.

Sir Hector, mouth agape, looked on, speechless and dumbfounded.

"But as the poet Mister Keats has taught us, the only thing everlasting is truth and beauty. And so I give this Ankh to the most beautiful lady here." Thraxton strode over to Constance Pennethorne, dipped a slight bow, and presented the Ankh to her. Clearly surprised, she received the amulet with a delighted smile and a curtsey.

The crowd broke into spontaneous applause, while Sir Hector broke into spontaneous combustion. As Thraxton stepped away to return to his place, Sir Hector rushed over. "See here, Lord Thraxton," he sputtered. "I really must protest. That is an historical artifact. It belongs to the museum!"

Thraxton slapped Sir Hector on the shoulder good-naturedly and whispered in his ear. "There, there! Be a good sport, old fellow. Let's not forget the great beneficence I have shown the museum. In fact, I believe I'm just about to make my annual gift. Please don't put me in a parsimonious mood." He gave Sir Hector's shoulder a bruising squeeze, "Besides," he said reassuringly, "plenty more mummies where that one came from." And with that, Thraxton traipsed away, leaving Sir Hector to wheeze and vent like a small round kettle left on the boil.

Algernon was watching from the back of the crowd, and a jealous grimace flashed across his face.

A refreshments table had been laid out along one wall of the Mummy Room. Algernon was munching a watercress sandwich when he saw Constance Pennethorne approach the table and eye the punch bowl. This time he decided he would not let the opportunity slip by. He choked down the mouthful of sandwich he was chewing, and tossed the half-eaten remainder behind a nearby sarcophagus from the reign of Akhenaton. As he stepped over and bowed low to her, his tongue worked frantically to pry loose a piece of watercress stuck between his teeth.

"Mrs. Pennethorne? My name is Algernon... Algernon Hyde-Davies."

Constance looked up from the punch bowl straight into Algernon's eyes. Her gaze was disarmingly intense and seemed to look straight into his brain, almost as if she could see everything he was thinking. Algernon wondered if he had watercress wedged between his teeth and felt his cheeks warming, but Constance smiled and offered her hand.

"So nice to make your acquaintance, Mister Hyde-Davies. You are a friend of the impetuous Lord Thraxton, are you not?"

Algernon took her gloved hand and held it gently.

"I have that, ahem, honor, ma'am. I do hope that my friend's ostentation caused you no embarrassment. Geoffrey does have rather a flair for the dramatic—"

With his usual timing, Thraxton suddenly appeared at the table. "Not again, Algy!" he exclaimed. "My friend is always apologizing for my behavior!"

"Then you must find him a very useful friend to have, Lord Thraxton."

The quickness of her answer took them both by surprise. Thraxton smiled and laughed. "By that I take it you know of me, ma'am?"

Algernon scooped a dipper full of crimson punch into a glass and offered it to Mrs. Pennethorne.

"I know of your reputation." She accepted the punch, smiled graciously, and thanked Algernon before returning her attention to Thraxton. "Some of my confidants describe you as nothing less than the wickedest man in London."

Thraxton's smile buckled slightly. The woman was very blunt.

"Your confidants flatter me, Mrs. Pennethorne, but off-hand I can think of at least three men who are much wickeder than I. Pray tell, what else do these confidants say about me?"

"That you are given to a great many dalliances, including Lady Warrington, a married woman, and Eliza Perkins, an actress on the London stage, not to mention the never-ending parade of pretty young horsebreakers you are seen in the company of."

Algernon found it impossible to keep the smirk from his face as Thraxton cleared his throat and shifted his feet uneasily. Thraxton was used to being the one to shock and raise eyebrows. It appeared as though he had finally met his equal in the disarmingly beautiful Mrs. Pennethorne. While the Lord squirmed, Constance took a sip of her punch and turned her aqueous eyes once more to Algernon. "I confess I know nothing of you, Mister Hyde-Davies. Have you no reputation to besmirch? Or are you merely given to being discreet?"

Algernon found his tongue knotted like a badly tied cravat as his mind grappled for a witty retort. She suddenly raised her eyes to look at something over his shoulder. Algernon caught the direction of her gaze and turned to look.

An elderly couple hovered a few feet away.

"Ah," Mrs. Pennethorne said, "I see my friends the Wakefields are waiting for me." She turned back to Algernon and Thraxton. "Lovely party, Lord Thraxton. I did so enjoy myself and thank you again for my little memento of ancient Egypt." She offered him her hand.

"Perhaps you will think of me when you wear it," Thraxton said, kissing her gloved knuckles.

"Perhaps." Constance turned to Algernon and once again offered her hand. "So pleasant to meet you, Mister Hyde-Davies."

As he took her hand, Algernon could not tear his eyes from hers long enough to bow. "Yuh, yes," he stammered. "And pleasant meeting you. Was. For me. I mean... pleasant." He smiled. Her eyes truly were amazing. Such a shade of blue.

"Mister Hyde-Davies?"

"Er, yes?"

"My hand, sir. I shall require its return."

Algernon realized he was still gripping her hand. He released it and stammered an apology.

She bowed her head demurely and ended with, "Good day to you both, sirs."

Quite entranced, Algernon and Thraxton watched her walk away on the arms of Mr. and Mrs. Wakefield.

"What a singularly splendid lady," Algernon enthused. "Lovely, and yet so quick-witted and agile of mind."

"Yeeeesss," Thraxton drawled. "Nicely adequate bosom, too. Perhaps I shall send her my card. What do you say, Algy?"

"Oh, I hardly think Mrs. Pennethorne is for you, Geoffrey!"

"Why ever not?"

"Not really your type, old fellow. I mean, she is a lady. A woman of great refinement and sensibility. A true gentlewoman!"

Thraxton plunged a glass into the punch bowl and dredged it out, dripping. "But I consider myself a man of great sensitivity and refinement. Am I not?" As he said it he turned and threw his arms wide. In doing so he banged shoulders with another man, sloshing red punch down the front of the man's white shirt and black dinner jacket.

The owner of the dinner jacket was none other than Augustus Skinner.

"You clumsy oaf!" Skinner roared. He tore a handkerchief from his pocket and agitatedly blotted the front of his jacket. "You did that on purpose, you swine!"

Thraxton was anything but perturbed. "Either I am an oaf, or I am a swine. I can hardly be both."

"A gentleman would at least have the decency to apologize."

"A gentleman would not be staggering about like a drunken ape, crashing into people."

Skinner's face flushed crimson. He visibly bristled. "Of all the outrageous impudence! You shall apologize!"

"I apologize? You have caused me to spill my punch! It is you who should apologize."

"Evidently you are a drunkard, as well as a shoddy poet!" Skinner shouted the last line at the top of his lungs.

Conversation stopped. The cellos groaned themselves into silence. All eyes in the room fastened upon Lord Thraxton and Augustus Skinner.

A wistful smile appeared on Thraxton's lips. Algernon knew that smile. It meant Thraxton was about to do something very rash. Algernon took his friend by the arm and attempted to lead him away. "Geoffrey, perhaps we should—"

Thraxton pushed his friend's hand away, quite violently, while never taking his gaze from Skinner's face.

"Good God," Thraxton said. "Just when I had begun to embrace Mister Darwin's theories, here is proof positive that evolution works in both directions. How is it that someone found a suit to fit this monkey?"

"Geoffrey, please—" Algernon started to say.

"How dare you!"

"I'm sorry," Thraxton said. "I should not insult a monkey so, for I have seen monkeys in the London Zoo and they appear to be creatures capable of at least some level of reasoning. No, what we have here is much further down the tree of life, something more akin to a slug or a leech."

"You scoundrel!"

Resignedly, Algernon went over to the refreshment table and poured himself a glass of punch. Now Thraxton had started, there was no stopping him.

"Yes, a leech, for that's what all critics are—leeches sucking on the body of art. And only after they're fat and bloated with the blood of artists do they drop off and slither away."

Skinner shook with fury. "You will take that back, sir. Take it back or I will see you in the law courts!"

"I take nothing back from you! You... you leech!"

"Then... then... then... I must demand satisfaction!"

Skinner tore off one of his white cotton gloves and slapped Thraxton smartly across the face. In truth, the slap was barely perceptible, but in the tense silence of the room, it resounded like a gunshot.

Something dangerous came into Thraxton's face. His eyes shone lambent with anger. For a terrifying moment, it seemed likely that he would leap upon his antagonizer and box him senseless, but instead, a cruel smile formed on his lips. "Very well," he said, mildly. "I accept your challenge. Wimbledon Common. Dawn tomorrow. I shall bring my dueling pistols. Be sure to bring your seconds." Thraxton turned his back on Skinner and walked over to Algernon, throwing an arm around his shoulders. "Do you know, Algy," he said, good-naturedly, "I've just tossed off a full glass of punch and I'm still thirsty. Let's see if there's any of that wonderful champagne left."

3

◦◦◦∙❧◦∙◦◦◦

PISTOLS AT DAWN

Wimbledon Common slumbered beneath shifting panes of mist burnished silver by the rising sun. In the near distance, the windmill loomed, a four-armed giant poised to stride over the land, smashing all within reach. The trees were stark, skeletal beings the wind had twisted into tortured shapes. A flight of pigeons whirred overhead like a premonition, circling once, twice, three times before vanishing. In the fog-muffled air, fragments of human speech carried indistinctly, mixed incongruously with the clatter of silverware on china and, stranger still, the spit and hiss of meat sizzling in a pan.

Lord Geoffrey Thraxton, draped in a heavy wool blanket, lounged at a small folding table while Harold, his servant, clattered pans. At another table, the blue flames of alcohol burners lapped at two silver warming trays. Harold finished sautéing a pair of kidneys, spooned them onto a plate alongside a brace of poached quail's eggs, and set the steaming plateful down in front of his master.

"Ah, breakfast at last," Thraxton exclaimed as he cut into the deviled kidneys. He stabbed a steaming hot forkful and slid it cautiously past his lips. Juices filled his mouth as he chewed. He swallowed, then dabbed his lips with a linen napkin. "Kidneys are first-rate this morning, Harold."

"Thank you, milord."

Thraxton looked around at Algernon. He had deliberately chosen to stand some distance away in order to keep the smell of frying meat from turning a stomach already queasy with the earliness of the hour and the deadly gravity of the occasion.

"Certain you won't partake of some deviled kidneys, Algy?" Thraxton asked casually. "They really are quite sumptuous."

Algernon shook his head quickly. "Geoffrey, this is madness. Dueling is against the law. You could be charged with murder."

"Surely not if he kills me? That hardly seems just."

They both looked up at the sound of retching. Augustus Skinner leaned against a tree for support as he heaved again. Even from this distance, the sound of vomit splattering against a tree trunk was clearly discernible.

Thraxton knifed into one of the poached quail's eggs and runny yellow yolk squirted under his blade. As he forked a morsel into his mouth, yolk dribbled down his chin. He dabbed it away with the napkin, then swirled a mouthful of claret to wash the film of grease from his tongue. "Is this from my cellar, Harold?"

"Yes, milord."

"Let me see."

Harold interrupted his efforts with the sauté pan to pull a bottle from a straw hamper and present it, label-first, for his master's perusal. Thraxton snatched the bottle from him, yanked the cork and sniffed at the open neck. Finding the bouquet very much to his liking, he sloshed himself another glassful.

"This really is a wonderful claret!" He held up the bottle and waved it at Algernon. "Certain you won't indulge?"

Algernon did not answer, for he was looking at something to his left. Thraxton followed his gaze to three men in long frock coats and top hats who approached silently through the mist. The men were Skinner's seconds. Two of the men he recognized: Sir Alfred Beecham and his idiot son Nigel. Thraxton knew and detested both of them. The third man, a tall, thin, gangly-limbed individual, dressed in a white top hat, hung back so that his features were never clearly discernible in the haze. From the black Gladstone bag that dangled from one hand, Thraxton guessed that the man was a physician Beecham had brought with him.

Thraxton continued to graze on his breakfast until father and son stood before him.

"Are you ready to go forward with this action, sir?" Sir Beecham asked in a grave tone.

Thraxton looked up at the older man while he continued to chew. When he had swallowed his mouthful, he wiped his lips on the napkin and took another swig of claret before answering. "Yes." He threw a look in Skinner's direction. "Are you sure your man is? I expect to be shot at, not spewed upon."

The seconds turned and looked at Skinner, who was wiping vomit from his mouth with the back of his hand. "I believe Mister Skinner is ready, sir."

Thraxton tossed the napkin on the table and rose from his seat. "Very well, then. Let us get on. And just to be a good sport I insist your man have the first shot."

Algernon's face fell at the remark. "Not the first shot, Geoffrey. I implore you—!"

Thraxton clapped a reassuring hand on his friend's shoulder. "Be of good faith, Algy. Augustus Skinner has never hit his mark in print. I doubt he will do much better with a pistol."

Sir Beecham scowled, turned on his heel and stalked off. Skinner, still leaning against a tree for support, looked up as his seconds approached.

"Augustus," Sir Beecham said. "He has given you the first shot. All you must do is stand and face him, then discharge your pistol into the air. He will likewise be obliged to follow suit. You both will have shown courage... the honor of both men shall then be satisfied."

But Augustus Skinner was quaking with a mixture of fear and anger. "Thraxton has no honor! He is an impudent cur!"

Sir Beecham grimaced and hardened his words. "Look, sir, Parliament outlawed dueling twenty years ago. If you kill Lord Thraxton, you will be tried and found guilty of murder. If you wound him grievously and do not kill him, he will likely drag you through the courts until you expend your last penny. Remember, no matter how black his character or soiled his reputation, he is a Peer of the Realm. As challenger, you will be seen as the aggressor. The course of action I suggest will resolve this dispute here and now, on the field of honor."

Skinner did not look at Sir Beecham, but kept his gaze on Thraxton, who was warming up by doing some deep knee bends then springing upright.

"What say you, Augustus? Discharge your pistol into the air and an hour from now we will all be back in London, warming ourselves in front of the fire with a splendid yarn to tell over brandy and cigars."

Augustus Skinner turned eyes on Sir Beecham that were bloodshot and pouchy from lack of sleep. His lips compressed tightly as though his mouth held a hot stone he wished to spit out. His only answer was a resolute shake of his head.

Sir Beecham's shoulders slumped. He looked back at the coaches and the black hearse that had been ordered to transport the loser of the duel. He removed his top hat and waved at the driver to prepare the hearse.

One man would walk away from the duel. The other would be carried.

* * *

The pistols had been primed and loaded. The ground had been chosen. The distance had been measured off. Now Thraxton and Skinner faced each other across a scant twenty paces of open field. The pale white disk of the sun floated above the trees, a glaucous eye peering blindly through thickening fog.

The men's seconds stood together, well clear of the line of fire. Despite the chill of the morning both duelists had removed their coats and stood in shirt sleeves so as to be less encumbered. Algernon held Thraxton's coat draped across one arm, still warm from his body. He prayed that its owner would still be warm when it was slipped back upon his shoulders in just a few minutes. Thraxton and Skinner faced one another, their breath pluming in the air. It struck Algernon as odd to think that the breath of one of these men was about to be stopped forever. The birdsong, which had been clamorous since dawn, ceased abruptly. Even the scant breeze dropped. Ears strained for a sound and caught nothing as a preternatural silence fell over the proceedings.

"Are you gentlemen ready?" Sir Beecham's voice resounded in the silence.

"Yes!" Thraxton called out, nodding assent.

"Mister Skinner. Are you ready, sir?"

Skinner threw a terrified look at his seconds. His shoulders heaved as he sucked in and let out several deep breaths before he gave a quick nod.

Beecham looked at Algernon, who let out a sigh and nodded his assent.

"Lord Thraxton," Sir Beecham called out. "Prepare to receive Mister Skinner's fire."

It was an accepted practice in dueling for the party receiving fire to turn his body sideways, so as to present a smaller target. Thraxton, however, faced his opponent square on, the pistol held relaxed at his side.

"Damn you, Geoffrey," Algernon muttered under his breath. "Don't give him an easy target. Turn, man, turn!"

Thraxton remained as immovable as a statue.

"Old Skinner's trembling like a leaf," Harold whispered to Algernon. "Lord Thraxton's steady as a rock."

"Of course," Algernon replied. "He's in love with the idea of a romantic death."

Skinner needed both trembling hands to draw back the firing pin. He raised the quivering pistol, fighting to steady his shaking hand.

As Thraxton watched the slow elevation of Skinner's pistol, all senses seemed to expand beyond the constraints of his body. He heard the desolate cawing of a crow, the soughing of the breeze through the bare limbs of the birch trees. The white frost on the grass was beginning to melt, and beads of dew sparkled in the slanting rays of early sunlight. He felt the soft steady beating of his heart, the shifting weight of flesh and muscle on bone, the ponderous mass of the pistol in his hand. When he looked back at Skinner, the black bore of the pistol's muzzle was centered on his face. Thraxton took a deep breath, felt the cold air stretch his lungs, and let it out.

He knew it would be his last.

"Death," he whispered to himself. "Here I am, Death. Are you ready for me?"

The pistol muzzle tremored as Skinner's finger tightened on the trigger. There was the tiniest of clicks as the mechanism released and the hammer sprung down on the pan. The flint sparked. The powder lit with a flash of orange and a *pffffftttt* sound. A fraction of a second later the pistol fired with the solid percussive bang of a thunderclap.

Thraxton saw the flash and felt a hot finger trace the side of his scalp. For a moment he stood, not moving, looking at the white cloud of smoke behind which his opponent had vanished. He put a hand to his forehead, expecting to find a gaping wound. Nothing. His fingers traced along the side of his head. The top of his ear burned and when he brought his hand away, there was blood on it. The slightest of nicks. The pistol ball had passed within a gnat's wing of his skull, leaving only singed hair and a tiny cut on one ear.

Finally, the tendrils of smoke rose, curled, dissipated, and Skinner, who had not yet lowered his discharged pistol, reappeared. When he saw his opponent still standing, unscathed, Skinner's face contorted in a mask of terror and despair. The pistol, now just a spent and useless weight, dragged his arm down. He seemed to deflate. His knees wobbled, threatening to buckle.

Skinner's seconds exchanged worried glances. After a reluctant pause, Sir Beecham cleared his throat and called out again.

"Mister Skinner. Prepare to receive Lord Thraxton's fire."

Thraxton drew back the hammer of his dueling pistol and settled into a comfortable stance. He raised the pistol high in the air, and then lowered it slowly and with great deliberation until Skinner's face, the pistol's fore sight and aft sight, coincided.

By now Skinner was shaking uncontrollably and sagging at the knees.

Thraxton held his aim for an interminably long time. A flight of pigeons circled over the field, wings creaking. Thraxton dropped his aim and waited for them to disappear. Then he resumed his stance and once again raised the pistol. To Algernon, it was clear that Thraxton was drawing this out, deliberately, agonizingly.

Both men's seconds became aware of a sound. At first they threw puzzled glances at each other. But as it grew louder it became obvious that the sound was Skinner blubbering. Suddenly he cried out as his legs buckled and he dropped to his knees. Thraxton relaxed his aim and waited calmly as Skinner wobbled back to his feet. Then he licked a finger and rubbed at some imaginary lint on the pistol's foresight, before dropping back into his stance. He lowered the pistol slowly, slowly, slowly, until Skinner was once more dead in his sights.

Seconds passed. Skinner was almost dancing he was shaking so hard. A stain of urine appeared in the crotch of his trousers and ran steaming down the inseam of his left leg into his boot. Then Skinner broke down, and with a moan, he turned and ran away toward the trees.

His seconds were outraged.

"Mister Skinner!" Sir Beecham called out. "Mister Skinner, you must stand your ground!"

But Skinner was running as fast as his rubbery legs would allow.

Thraxton had not dropped his aim, and kept Skinner's fleeing back squarely in his sights. When he was almost at the trees, Thraxton lowered his aim slightly and squeezed the trigger. The pistol fired and kicked in his hand. Skinner grabbed his right buttock and went down screaming.

Harold let out a loud cackle and turned to Algernon. "In the arse! I knew he would. Lord Thraxton always shoots them in the arse!"

Skinner's seconds ran across the field to where their man lay writhing in agony. Algernon stood watching them, a look of disgust on his face. For a moment he felt his own gorge rise and feared he would be sick. He turned his face away, sucked in a lungful of cold morning air, and the feeling subsided.

Thraxton strode quickly toward his waiting seconds, a whimsical smile on his face. He tossed the pistol to Harold, who caught it deftly, then snatched his coat from his friend's arms and threw it about his shoulders. "Looks like you will have to put up with me for a while longer, Algy," Thraxton japed as he dropped into his seat at the folding table and rubbed his hands together famishedly. "Now let's see if I can finish my breakfast."

Harold hurried away to his warming pans. Thraxton flashed a triumphant grin at Algernon.

Despite the immense relief that his friend had survived the duel, Algernon found little to smile about. "You had bested him, Geoffrey. Clearly you had. The honorable thing to do would have been to discharge your pistol in the air."

"Oh come now," Thraxton replied. He seized the bottle of claret and glugged out a gobletful. "The man has been a pain in my arse for years; it's only fair I return the favor."

"Be lucky if you haven't crippled him."

"I held my shot. Surely you saw that?" Thraxton waved his goblet toward where the seconds were struggling to lift his fallen opponent. "At that range I doubt the ball would have penetrated much further than half an inch. Especially in Mister Skinner's fat arse."

Harold placed a fresh plate of kidneys in front of Thraxton, who tucked into them hungrily.

"Strewth, I'm ravenous. Funny what a brush with death will do for the old appetite." He noticed that Algernon was frowning down at him with obvious disapproval. "Stop scowling at me and grab a plate."

Algernon was about to reply but was interrupted by the continued screams of Skinner who was being loaded into his coach by his two seconds and the coachman.

Thraxton chewed while he watched with vague interest. "Do wish the fellow would stop yowling like that. It's rather spoiling my digestion." He quaffed a mouthful of claret, wiped his mouth with the linen napkin, then tossed it down upon his plate. "Harold, pack the things up. We're leaving."

Thraxton jumped up from the table and pulled his arms

into the sleeves of his coat. As he turned to walk back to the coaches he looked up and froze. The third of Augustus Skinner's seconds, the man in the white top hat with the black Gladstone bag was standing close by, staring at him. Even this close, the swirling fog made it difficult to discern his features, but he was a tall, thin, hirsute man, with large mustachios that flowed into extravagant mutton-chop whiskers. Perched on the bridge of the hawk-like nose was a pair of rose-tinted pince-nez spectacles, which the diffuse light polished into glowing red discs. The glaring look he threw at Thraxton seethed with recrimination.

"What the deuce do you want?" Thraxton spat. "I gave your man the first shot, did I not?"

The doctor took his time to respond. "You show an abhorrent disrespect for death, sir."

"If death requires me to fear it... then it shall be disappointed."

The doctor's lips compressed like the mouth of a purse whose strings have been cinched tight. "Death will not be mocked, nor sneered at. And there are many doors death can enter by... as you will learn to your cost."

And with that the figure in the white top hat strode toward the waiting carriages and abruptly vanished in the fog.

Thraxton shuddered from a sudden chill. It was damp and penetratingly cold on the common.

There was something about the man... something eerily disturbing. Thraxton personally abhorred white top hats and found them the most gauche of fashions—they were invariably the choice of effete dandies, arrogant oiks and the kind of drunken swells one saw swanning about the periphery of dance floors at places such as the Cremorne Pleasure Gardens. What kind of doctor wore a white top hat?

At that moment, the mists unscrolled, the sun brightened and the world returned like a hazy mirage. Algernon and Thraxton's servant stood waiting by the folding table.

"Harold!" Thraxton shouted, having made a sudden decision. "Pack everything up and take the brougham home. Mister Hyde-Davies and I will be traveling by different means." Thraxton flashed a mischievous grin as he rejoined his friend. "What say you, Algy? I've never actually ridden in a hearse."

As the hearse rattled onto the cobbled road that led back to London, Thraxton's spirits were still soaring. He lay in the open coffin, his hands folded on his chest. Algernon crouched in the space beside the coffin, gazing out the large glass windows.

"God, I've never felt more alive," Thraxton said. "I want to indulge all my senses. I want to squeeze the ripe fruit of life and suck the juices from it. We must celebrate, Algy!"

"Drinks at the Athenaeum?"

Thraxton raised his head and peered over the side of the coffin at his friend. "Oh dear me, I think we can do better than that. After all, I'm a man reborn, a full-grown child with every nerve jangling to be filled with sensation. We shall surrender the day to drunkenness, lechery and every form of wretched excess!"

Algernon looked out at a pastoral landscape the expanding sprawl of London had yet to devour: yellow barley fields, bushy hedgerows, cows grazing in lush stands of clover. For a moment he envied the beasts their lives of quiet rumination and sighed.

He knew it would be many hours before he saw his bed that night.

4

THE ARMS OF MORPHEUS

Madame Rachelle's enjoyed the reputation of being the very best brothel in Mayfair, with only the choicest, freshest girls.

Thraxton and Algernon lounged on a floral couch in an elaborately decorated parlor while a line of young prostitutes paraded before them dressed in lingerie and stockings. Thraxton, an old hand at this sort of thing, eyed each girl with obvious delight as she passed. But each time a girl looked upon Algernon and smiled coyly, he could not meet her gaze and dropped his eyes to the Persian rug at his feet.

In an effort to cater to the peccadilloes of the gentry, no matter how unorthodox, the brothel boasted women of every age and nationality. Some of the girls were as young as twelve or thirteen. These were typically dressed in sailor suits, or rustic smocks, their hair done up in pigtails and bows to make them look even younger. Often they clutched a doll to their flat chests to complete the effect. The older women, ranging from their teens to their early twenties, presented body types for every taste, from voluptuous maids with juddering bosoms that threatened to spill over the tops of their bustiers, to slender waifs laced into corsets so tight their waspish waists could be spanned by a man's hands.

"Come on, Algy," Thraxton griped as the girls made their third pass by the sofa. "Don't take all day about it. You're not marrying her, for God's sake. Choose!"

Algernon looked up shyly at a fair-skinned blonde girl. "Oh, wuh-well, I, I suppose this young lady has a-a k-kind face," he stammered. He indicated the woman with a slight nod. She smiled and dropped into his lap, draping a slender arm around his neck.

"About damned time, too!" Thraxton said with good-natured irritation. He returned his attention to the parade of female flesh. "Let's see. Spoiled for choice, really. Don't care for the little 'uns. Too thin. I like a wench with a nice, ripe arse. Something I can slam into from behind." Thraxton grabbed the hand of a buxom brunette. She let out a squeal as he pulled her down onto his lap. But then a redhead also caught his eye. "What the hell, I'm feeling my oats today!" He grabbed the redhead's hand and pulled her down next to him. Both women draped themselves around him and began to caress his neck and face, running their fingers through his thick mop of wavy black hair. The women giggled and cooed as he kissed first one, and then the other. *Ah*, he thought, *is there anything more sublime than the feel of satin warmed by a woman's body?*

* * *

It was early afternoon when the two friends clambered into a hansom cab and rattled away from the front door of Madame Rachelle's. Thraxton slumped against the worn leather cushion, his face slackened by a lazy look of satiety.

"Home now, Geoffrey?" Algernon said, his voice full of hope.

Thraxton glared disbelievingly at his friend, brows knotted in consternation. "Certainly not. We are only just beginning! Besides, I feel it, Algy. Don't you feel it?"

Algernon replied with a weary look, "I feel like a glove that's been turned inside out."

"I feel the pull," Thraxton said, his face dissolving dreamily. "The pull of the mystic east."

Half an hour later the cab dropped them in one of the very worst parts of London, a district where white faces and fine gentleman's clothes struck a discordant note. The buildings hereabouts were shabby and run down. The dank and fetid reek of the Thames meant the river was close—no more than a few streets away. As soon as Thraxton had paid the fare, the cabbie cracked his whip over the horse's head, anxious to be gone.

What they failed to see were three shabby figures lurking in a darkened doorway across the street. The middle figure was Mordecai Fowler, a short, stout man, barely five feet tall and nearly as wide, though much of this bulk was due to the two undervests, two shirts, one waistcoat, two jackets, and three holed and ragged overcoats he was wearing. Beneath the crumpled bowler jammed over his lank and greasy black hair was a gorilla-like face with bushy black sideburns and coarse black stubble prickling his chin. To his left was the cadaverous Walter Crynge, six-foot-six and skeletally thin with a complexion the color of pus. Smallpox and gonorrhea had left huge pockmarks and open sores in his skin, while the ravages of syphilis had gnawed the cartilage of his nose until it collapsed inward, leaving only two oval holes in the front of his face. Many years ago, Crynge had been honestly employed as an undertaker's assistant. The worn black frock coat and battered black top hat were all that remained of what he had stolen from his former employer. To Fowler's right loomed the huge and bestial Barnabus Snudge, a bone-crushing Minotaur of a man. Snudge's wiry red hair was combed forward over his low forehead and covered his eyes like an Old English sheepdog. Snudge boasted the strength of an ox, but fell far short of matching its intelligence. Mordecai and his cronies were mobsmen, denizens of London's huge underworld, a vast criminal society that lived and thrived in the shadows of the wealthiest city on earth. That night the three were out "wilding," prowling the streets for mugs and toffs with purses crammed with coins.

Fowler's black eyes glittered as he studied the two figures across the way. From their clothes he could clearly see they were men of means—gentlemen. "Wot 'ave we got 'ere, eh, lads?" Fowler spat contemptuously. "A coupla toffs, out slummin'!"

"Yeth," Crynge lisped, his ulcerous tongue waggling around the rotted stumps of the few teeth left in his mouth. "Bloody toffs!"

"Wot they doin' on our patch, Mister Fowler?" Snudge muttered dimly.

"Come to rub shoulders with the less fortunate," Fowler said. "Have themselves a bloody good old larf at how us rats live in the gutter. That's wot the likes of them is here for, Snudgy." Fowler slipped a hand inside his outermost coat. His stubby fingers closed around a gnarled, wormwood handle. "I fink it's time my friend Mister Pierce made some new acquaint-tin-sees," Fowler said. "Come along, lads."

The three men stepped out of the shadowed doorway and tromped toward the unsuspecting friends.

Just then the sound of horses' hooves grew louder as a pair of brewer's carts, laden with barrels, turned the corner and clopped toward Algernon and Thraxton.

The carts stopped the mobsmen in their tracks. Unknowingly shielded by the passing carts, the two gents stepped to a battered green door, which opened at the first knock and drew them inside. Just a few feet away, Fowler and his mobsmen could only watch as their prey made good an unwitting escape.

"The toffs have gone into the Chinee's place," Fowler rumbled. "Gone to chase the dragon."

"That's a bloomin' shame," said Snudge. "Coulda had ourselves a bit o' fun wiv them toffs."

"We could wait here for them," Crynge suggested.

Fowler grunted, scratching a stubbly throat with his filthy nails. "Naw. We got a job. Our friend the doctor has ordered a fresh 'un and he'll pay a lot more than wot them toffs has in their pockets." Fowler shook himself like a crow fluffing its feathers, yanked his coat shut and cinched the rope belt tight. "We'll need shovels and the 'orse and cart." He nodded to his men. "Come on, lads. Plenty more mischief to be done tonight."

With that, the three mobsmen crossed the street and stepped into a narrow alleyway where the shadows swallowed them up once more.

"Opium," Thraxton blurted as he pulled the pipe from his lips and exhaled a stream of smoke, "is the truest of all vices."

"Whysh that?" Algernon said, struggling not to slur his words and slurring all the more for it.

Each lay on a low palette covered by a thin mattress. The palettes were scarcely six inches apart, but in the gloom of the opium den it was impossible to make out each other's features in the sputtering light of a solitary greasy candle.

"Because... because..." Thraxton paused. "I'm sorry, I can't remember. What were you saying?"

"Me? I wasn't saying anything. It was you." They both

fell silent. For a while the only sound was the faint crackle of opium burning in the bowls of their pipes.

"Oh God, Algy," Thraxton moaned from inside a cloud of smoke. He narrowed his eyes and tried to locate his friend's face in the gloom. "What am I doing with my life?"

As Algernon slipped beneath the surface of an opium dream the pipe fell from his lips and clattered to the floor. He slumped on the mattress and began to snore.

Thraxton put the pipe to his lips and drew deeply, filling his lungs, holding it in. In his mind's eye he could see the smoke billowing inside, a violet nimbus roiling in a body as hollow and empty as a porcelain doll's. He pulled the pipe from his lips and released the breath. The plume he exhaled drifted sluggishly across the narrow room and burst against the wall, where it coalesced into the shape of a wizened old Chinese man sitting in a broken and lopsided chair. The old man, who must have been in his nineties, had a long gray braid of hair draped over one shoulder and was dressed in the traditional silks of old China. His lips were clamped around the mouthpiece of an opium pipe, which he never removed as he puffed, but rather drew in air through the side of his mouth and jetted out smoke through both tiny nostrils. The old man's glittering black eyes remained fixed upon Thraxton all along.

"I know who you are," Thraxton said.

With those words the old man's wrinkled face blurred, dissolved, and rose up to the ceiling as smoke, revealing the grinning skull beneath. Death's bony fingers continued to hold the pipe to the lipless mouth. But as it drew in again, smoke leaked from the eye sockets and the fleshless nostrils.

"I see through your disguises," Thraxton continued, "all of them. If you want me, take me now. But I tell you this. I shall not love again. So there is nothing you can take from me."

Thraxton's eyes began to droop.

"Nothing."

The pipe dragged from his lips and began to burn a hole in the mattress.

"Nothing."

A trap door opened beneath him and he fell for a thousand years.

5

THE HIGHGATE SPECTER

The horse and cart clopped slowly up Swain's Lane, the road that ascended in a steepening grade from Highgate Village to the cemetery. Seated three abreast on the seat were Mordecai Fowler, Walter Crynge, and Barnabus Snudge, who held the reins of a sagging-backed gray mare so mangy and skeletal that every rib showed clearly, and whose rheumy eyes seemed wistful for the glue pot. It was fully dark by now. At this hour no one would be traveling this road, for the only place it led to was the cemetery at the top of the hill. And although the dead of Highgate were not used to receiving visitors at such an hour, on this particular night they would have plenty of company.

Fowler's eyes scanned the cemetery railings moving slowly past. They reached the point where the cemetery beyond the railings lay in an obsidian pool of shadow cast by a stand of mature oak trees. "This'll do us," Fowler spoke in a low mutter. "Roit here." He nodded to Snudge, who gave a tug on the reins and the cart lurched to a stop. All three jumped down and walked around to the back of the cart where they unloaded a pick, a shovel, three Bullseye lanterns and armfuls of heavy sacking. Without a word and with practiced moves, they crept stealthily to the railings and threw several layers of sack cloth over the spikes. Next they tossed over the pick and shovels. Snudge heaved his shovel a little too far and the metal blade struck a gravestone with a ringing *clang*.

Fowler balled his fist and gave Snudge a solid punch in the ear.

"Stupid arse!" Fowler cursed in a low voice. "Want the whole bleedin' world to know we're here? You'll have the sexton on us!"

"Ow!" Snudge whined, rubbing his throbbing ear. "That hurt, that did!"

"Shattup and give us a leg-up!"

Snudge bent down while Fowler stepped into his cupped hands and then clambered onto the wall. Uttering low grunts and breathy curses, his short legs kicking, Fowler struggled to heave his rotund bulk over the railings. He finally dropped heavily to the other side and stood there panting. "You two," he hissed. "Get yer arses over here and hurry up about it!"

A few minutes later all three had cleared the railings and were creeping stealthily through the graves, the metal shields of their Bullseye lanterns narrowed to a slit to conceal their glow. Despite the darkness and the confusion of pathways, the three made their way unerringly through the cemetery until they reached a grave mounded with loose soil that had yet to be topped by a stone slab.

"Right," said Fowler tossing the spade to Snudge. "You start diggin' while I keeps an eye out for the sexton."

Snudge had to quickly drop the pick he was carrying to catch the shovel Fowler tossed to him. In the dark he missed the catch and the spade handle whacked him in the nose, springing tears to his eyes.

"Mister Crynge," Fowler said. "You hold the lantern while Snudgy digs, but keep the light low. The sexton's sure to be prowlin' around 'ere somewhere."

"Yeath, Mither Fowler!" lisped Crynge.

Snudge drove the spade into the grave. The soil was loose and easy to dig. He tossed a heaped spadeful to one side, nervously looking about. Snudge had always been afraid of the dark. Of churchyards and creepy places. Cemeteries, especially at night, held a unique terror for him.

"I doesn't much like this sort o' work, Mister Fowler," Snudge said. "It don't half give me the willies."

"I'll give ya somethin' worse than the willies if you don't hurry up with that diggin'! The doctor pays good money for a nice fresh corpse. It might just as well be yours."

Snudge grudgingly resumed his spadework. As he tossed another shovelful of dirt onto the pile he looked up and saw the stone angel on the monument next to the grave he was digging in. The angel's eyes were cast downwards. She seemed to be looking straight at him. Snudge had only a confused, childlike knowledge of religion, but he knew that what he was doing was a sin, and that God was watching him. "I'm going to hell," Snudge muttered. "And I'm digging my own way there."

"You go now!"

Rough hands shook him. Thraxton's eyes flickered open. A young Chinese face hovered over him.

"You go now!" the young Chinese man was saying.

Many hands seized Thraxton and dragged him to his feet; someone rammed his top hat upon his head and thrust the walking stick into his hand. Then he was hustled through the warren of tiny rooms and cubicles that made up the opium den. Along the way he passed by other smokers sprawled on low couches, each one drowning in an opiate fog. A door opened upon the night and Thraxton was propelled through it.

Sudden darkness. Cold air washed over him. He was out on the street. A second later the door opened again as Algernon stumbled through it and bowled into him. Thraxton caught his friend before he could fall.

The two looked around, dazed and disoriented. It was late afternoon when they entered the opium den. Now it was dark. At some point rain had fallen. The cobblestones gleamed wet under the gas light.

"I could have asked to have been prized from the arms of Morpheus a bit more gently," Thraxton remarked.

"Where are we?"

"I was rather hoping you'd remember."

Both men looked up at the clop-clop of approaching hooves. Miraculously, it was a hackney, moving fast toward them.

"I say," said Algernon. "There's a bit of luck." He stepped forward and waved at the driver. They were in a part of town avoided by most cabmen, but it was late and this one was taking an unusual shortcut, eager to be home and in the warmth of his bed. He saw the two friends and veered to go around them, unwilling to stop. However, Thraxton stepped into the middle of the narrow road, blocking the way and daring the cabbie to run over him, who barely managed to pull up the horse in time.

"You must be mad," the exasperated cabbie breathed. "I'd like to run you over."

"Your last fare of the night, my good man," Thraxton shouted up to the driver. "Belgravia, my man, but take the long way round, via Highgate Cemetery."

"Highgate? At this hour?" repeated the nonplussed driver. "But that's miles outta me way, guvnor!"

"I'll make it worth your loss of sleep." Thraxton fished a sovereign from his pocket and tossed it up. "There's another for you when we get home."

"Right! Right you are, sir!" said the driver, who quickly pocketed the coin. The two companions had barely clambered aboard when he cracked his whip over the horse's head and the hackney lurched away.

* * *

The road from Highgate Village wound in a ponderous uphill climb to where the cemetery had been built. By the time the Hackney cab reached the top, the horse was steaming with sweat, the bit between its teeth dripping white foam.

In the cab, the friends sprawled in their seats, heads lolling. Algernon was out to the world, mouth open and snoring. Thraxton rested his head on the window frame and gazed out as the cab jogged along, his eyes opening and closing as he fought sleep. From this elevation it was possible to see over the cemetery's low wall with its spiked railings. Between the twisted silhouettes of tree limbs, the tops of gravestones showed sepulchral white in a moon that darted through ghostly gray clouds.

Suddenly, Thraxton stiffened, his eyes opening wide as he was jolted wide awake by something he saw. He struggled to sit upright in his seat and began furiously banging on the ceiling with his walking stick. "Driver! Stop! Stop, I say!"

The cab jerked to a halt, shaking Algernon awake. "What? Are we home?" he asked, dopily.

"Did you see it?" Thraxton said.

"See it? See what?"

"A wraith! A spirit. Moving through the gravestones."

Algernon groaned. An incipient migraine throbbed behind his eyes and he massaged both temples with his fingertips. "Geoffrey, it's the opium. You're still dreaming, man."

Thraxton scanned the cemetery, peering intently. "No, I

saw it. A dark wraith. At first I thought it was a shadow. But then it broke free of the earth and floated over the ground without touching." He fixed his friend with a manic gaze. "It was a ghost, Algy. A spirit!"

Without another word, Thraxton flung open the door and jumped down. The astonished driver watched open-mouthed as one of his passengers sprinted across the road, coat tails flapping, leaped up onto the cemetery wall, and vaulted athletically over the railings in a single bound.

Algernon stumbled out of the cab a moment later. "Geoffrey!" he shouted after. "What the devil!" But Thraxton had vanished. Algernon started after him, but paused a moment to yell back to the driver. "Wait here!"

"Sir?" asked the puzzled driver.

"Wait! Just... wait!"

Algernon ran to the cemetery wall. He easily clambered up onto the lower half of the wall, but paused as he puzzled how best to climb over the railings. They were cruelly spiked and wicked sharp. Visions of imminent impalement and serious trauma to the masculine parts of his anatomy flashed through his mind as he threw a leg over the railings and cautiously, gingerly, and with leg muscles trembling, eased himself over.

When he hit the ground on the far side and looked about he was faced with nothing but darkness and the ominous shadows of tilting gravestones. Just then the moon sailed out from beneath a dense black cloud, flooding the roiling fog with a diffuse light that illuminated the cemetery grounds. In its supernal glow, he glimpsed a madman in the far distance, running pell-mell through the gravestones.

Thraxton.

"Geoffrey!" Algernon yelled, taking to his heels in pursuit. "Geoffrey!"

"Wot's that?" Fowler said, rising from a crouch. He snapped the shields shut on his Bullseye lantern and looked about frantically, his dark eyes wide and pooled with night. Oblivious, Snudge drove his shovel into the dirt and heaved another spadeful onto the growing heap.

"Snudge!" Fowler hissed. "Shut up! Crynge, douse that light!"

All three mobsmen froze, listening.

Minutes passed. Nothing but the thin hiss of wind in the treetops.

Finally, Fowler let out his breath. "Right. It's nuffink. Get on with it, Snudge."

The moon plunged into a dense wall of cloud, snuffing out its light. The few visible stars were the only illumination. By now Thraxton's eyes were beginning to adjust. He could make out the sepulchral white shapes of gravestones, the irregular, crouching masses of trees. He heard a twig snap and watched as a swatch of darkness tore loose from the fabric of night and floated across the cemetery.

The dark wraith.

The sight of it set Thraxton's scalp prickling. Torn between fear and fascination, he followed silently, heart pounding. The wraith left the pathway and glided on a diagonal course through the gravestones. In the darkness it was difficult to follow and Thraxton had to stop several times as he lost sight of the specter. Then suddenly he found himself almost on top of it as the wraith stopped before a solitary grave. As he watched, it seemed to get smaller—a spirit descending into its grave? Thraxton took another step and a dry twig snapped under his foot with the crack of a pistol shot. At the sound, the wraith sprang up full-sized again and glided away. Thraxton gave chase, stumbling blindly over stone curbs and tussocks of grass.

The wraith reached the main path and glided toward the massive pharaonic arch that formed the entrance to the Egyptian Avenue, a dark and umbrous tunnel. Thraxton knew that if the wraith passed inside he could no longer follow it. Surprisingly, the wraith stopped just outside and seemed to wait for him. Thraxton approached slowly, fearful of making the spirit bolt away again and a little fearful for himself.

Up close the wraith took the shape of a small woman wearing a black lace dress with a cape and deeply cowled bonnet which seemed to contain a black nothingness. It seemed aware of his presence, for the cowl followed his every movement as he cautiously approached. He decided to address it directly. "Dark spirit, stay," Thraxton urged. "I mean you no harm. I wish only to speak with you. You hold the secrets of death, which I would learn. Speak… if you can."

The spectral form remained silent, although its attention remained fixed upon him. Thraxton took a half step forward and it darted away. Thraxton gave chase, without really understanding what he meant to do if he actually caught it, or if it were possible to lay hands on something as immaterial as a spirit. The wraith weaved a zigzag path through the gravestones, seeming to waft effortlessly along as he blundered behind. When he was within an arm span Thraxton reached out and almost touched it, but then the toe of his boot slammed into a low grave marker, sprawling him full length. When he scrambled to his feet and looked about, it was nowhere to be seen. Once again, the dark wraith had vanished.

By now Algernon was thoroughly lost. He climbed atop a grave topped by a carved slab of stone and peered about. A roiling white lake of fog submerged the graves. A stone angel, its arms thrown up to heaven, rose from the milky surface like the figurehead of a ship. Algernon heard a soft footfall from behind and spun around. At first he saw nothing, but then noticed a shadowy form standing close by. This was no angel, but a distinctly man-shaped shadow that loomed. "Geoffrey?" Algernon hissed. "Is that you, Geoffrey?"

Suddenly a blinding star flared in the darkness and he found himself squinting into a dazzling yellow beam.

"HALT!" a voice yelled from behind the glare of a lantern. "Don't move, Sonny Jim. I got an elephant gun pointed right at ya. So much as twitch and I'll blow yer bleedin' head off!"

The light from the lantern Crynge held showed that Snudge was knee deep down in the grave. He tossed another spadeful onto the slumping pile of earth and paused to wipe the sweat from his brow. "Why is it I has to do all the diggin', Mistah Fowler?" Snudge whined. "Why can't you and Walter dig for a spell?"

Fowler scowled at the idiot's features below him. "Why? I'll tell ya why, Snudgy: 'cause I'm here to think. Mister Crynge is here to hold the lantern, and you're here 'cause you've got a broad back and a thick skull, that's why."

Crynge hissed with laughter at the remark.

Snudge surlily turned back to his digging. As he slammed his spade into the earth, the blade scraped along a stone with a screech that raised gooseflesh. He hefted another mounded shovelful and flung it aside. "Well it don't seem right to me—" he moaned.

"Shattup!" Fowler snapped, raising his hand for silence. They all stood, listening. Faint footfalls approached. "Someone's comin'!" Fowler said. "Hide!" He flung a furious look at Crynge. "Douse that bleedin' light!"

Crynge slammed the shields down over the Bullseye lantern, quenching the light. Snudge crouched down in the grave, while Fowler and Crynge ducked behind nearby gravestones.

A dark shape glided toward where the mobsmen were hiding and the crunch of fallen leaves being crushed underfoot was plain to hear. As the form passed his hiding spot, Fowler sprang from behind the gravestone and threw his arms around it.

The dark wraith let out a piercing shriek that carried throughout the cemetery.

"What have we got here, eh?" Fowler chortled. "What have we here?"

The small form kicked and struggled in Fowler's embrace. "Mister Crynge, fetch the lantern over here!"

Crynge hurried over with the lantern and shone its light on the struggling figure. Fowler snatched back the deep cowl, revealing the terrified face of a young woman. As Crynge shone the beam full in her face, she squirmed in Fowler's grip, twisting her face away from the light as though in pain.

"Hallo, hallo," said Fowler. "Looks like we done all right, lads. No more diggin' fer us."

"Wotcha mean, Mistah Fowler?" said Snudge dimly. "I thought you said—"

"Don't think, Snudgy boy, you'll strain somefink. We come for a body and we got one right here."

"But she ain't dead, Mordecai," ventured Crynge.

Fowler glared at Crynge as if he were an idiot. "Well we can fix that, can't we?" He turned his attention back to the woman. "Let's have a look at you, darlin'." He grabbed the woman's face and twisted it toward the light. "Not a bad looker, either. Pale as a bleedin' pillowcase, but not bad at all. Seems a shame, don't it, a good waste of flesh? I don't see why we can't have ourselves a bit o' fun. Do some pokin' around inside before the doctors do their pokin' around. Snudgy, hang onto her."

He shoved the woman to Snudge who pinioned her in his huge arms.

"Now then, my little moxie," Mordecai said with relish. "Let's see what yer hidin' under that dress." Fowler grabbed the hem of the black lace dress and started to lift. Suddenly a walking stick smashed down on his wrist with bruising force. Fowler bellowed in pain. The three mobsmen looked around in alarm. Shadowed behind the glare of the lantern, a male silhouette faced them.

"Let her go!"

Fowler rubbed at his throbbing wrist and glared at the dark shape. "You'd like to broke my wrist," he growled through gritted teeth. "Mister Crynge, shine the light on him."

Crynge swung the lantern around to focus its beam upon Thraxton. He stood squinting into the glare, feet slightly apart, the walking stick clutched in both hands, ready to wield it again.

"It's a bleedin' toff!" Fowler exclaimed, surprised and relieved it was not a night watchman or the sexton he had expected.

"Let the girl go and leave," Thraxton said coolly, "or I'll give you louts the thrashing of your lives."

For a long moment, the three stood and gawked. Crynge and Snudge, always fearful of authority, were terrified.

But after his initial shock and fright, Fowler had regained himself. He let out a dark chuckle. "How you gonna do that, Mister Toff, seein' how there's three of us and only one of you?"

"Release the woman and I'll let you walk out of here. Or, if you prefer, you can be carried out." To reinforce his point, Thraxton slapped the walking stick against the gloved palm of his hand.

Fowler spoke without taking his eyes off Thraxton. "Snudgy, you got your cosh wiv ya?"

"Yeah, but I got hold of the girl."

"Let 'er go," Fowler said. "We only need one body. Plus I'll bet this toff's pockets are crammed full of shiny sovs."

Snudge let go of the girl. She looked at Thraxton and then back at the three mobsmen, as if uncertain what to do.

"Run!" Thraxton urged.

She hesitated.

"Run!"

The girl ran off into the darkness.

"Right, lads!" Fowler yelled. "Scrag him!" The three mobsmen fell upon Thraxton and a confused melee ensued. Thraxton swung the walking stick left and right. One blow connected with Crynge's angular cheekbone and sent him down wailing. Another slammed into Fowler's pug nose, bloodying it. But then Snudge lunged forward and slammed the cosh into Thraxton's head with a sickening *thwack*.

A burst of light exploded behind Thraxton's eyes and his legs went rubbery. Then someone grabbed the world and stood it on its side. He glimpsed Fowler's demon face, contorted with hatred, the lantern lying drunkenly askew upon the ground, the stone angel on its plinth. As the world began a slow, sickening revolution, he staggered down a steepening slope and tumbled into the dark maw of the open grave. He landed on his back in the soft earth and lay there, stunned and helpless.

Mordecai Fowler jumped down into the shallow grave and stood astride him.

"Mister Crynge," Fowler said. "Bring the light over here. I wanna see his face when he starts screamin'."

Crynge collected the fallen lantern and shone the light down into the grave. Thraxton's eyes were glassy and barely open as he fought to remain conscious.

"Now then, Mister Toff," Fowler crowed. "Gonna gives us all a good thrashin' was ya?" He chuckled. "Handy you bein' in a grave and all, ain't it? 'Cause when I'm done with ya, I just gotta kick a bit o'dirt over ya and let the worms do the rest."

"I thought we was gonna need a body, Mistah Fowler?" Snudge interrupted.

"Shut yer pie hole!"

Fowler dug into his coats and drew his metal spike from its scabbard, holding the sharp tip close to Thraxton's face so he could see it. "I got someone I wants ya to meet. Say 'allo to my friend Mister Pierce. Mister Pierce likes toffs. Oh, but you ain't gonna like Mister Pierce—not after he's had some fun wiv your pretty toff's face." Fowler moved the tip of the spike to the underside of Thraxton's chin. "I shoves Mister Pierce in 'ere..." Fowler lightly pressed the tip into the soft flesh on the underside of Thraxton's chin. Under the needlepoint, blood began to bead and drip. "...he goes right up through your tongue, and out yer nose." Fowler moved the spike to Thraxton's right cheek and pressed in lightly. Blood welled up under the tip and ran in a trickle down Thraxton's cheek and into his ear. "Or I shoves him in here, and he comes out yer earhole." Fowler moved the tip of the spike so that it hovered over Thraxton's right eye. "Maybe I'll put both yer eyes out, just fer a larf. You can spend the rest of yer natural tappin' yer way around London, hawking penny boxes of Lucifers."

Fowler's eyes glittered with excitement. "No, I ain't gonna kill you, but I am gonna make you suffer somethin' awful. When I'm done wiv ya no woman's ever gonna want you—not even the most pox-rotten whore in London. I'm gonna make your pretty toff's face a horror to look at. You'll have to wear a mask to go outdoors, because you'll look so 'orrible you'll frighten the ladies and kiddies." Fowler dropped a knee on Thraxton's chest, grabbed him by the hair, and brought his arm back, ready to plunge the spike into Thraxton's face.

A whistle blast froze him. Fowler looked up in alarm.

The glow of a lantern jogged up and down as the sexton hurried toward them, blasting on his whistle. Trailing in his wake, another figure stumbled in the darkness, struggling to keep up—Algernon Hyde-Davies.

"The sexton!" exclaimed Snudge. "We're rumbled!"

"He'll have the Peelers down on us!" Crynge said.

Fowler hesitated. He had the spike an inch away from the toff's face. He could mutilate him with one quick thrust. He looked up again. The lantern was closer. Fowler pressed the tip of the spike against Thraxton's cheek.

KABOOOOOOM!

The cacophonous report of the elephant gun shook the world into jelly. Fowler sprang to his feet, stepping on Thraxton's chest as he leapt up from the grave.

"Scarper!" he bellowed.

Ears still ringing from the gun blast, the three mobsmen dropped everything and took to their heels. A few seconds later the sexton and Algernon ran past, oblivious to the fact that Thraxton lay in the open grave, barely conscious.

As the sexton's whistle blasts receded into the distance, the young woman in her black lace dress crept back into the circle of light. She looked down into the grave and let out a pitying gasp when she saw Thraxton lying there. Believing him dead, she was afraid to come any closer, but then his eyelids trembled.

Still alive.

The woman tugged off one of her black lace gloves. In her haste she dropped the glove as she fell to her knees at the side of the open grave and reached down to touch his face.

The lantern Crynge abandoned in his haste had fallen off-kilter and threw a slanting light across the scene. When Thraxton cracked his eyes, the only thing in his field of vision was the brightly illuminated angel against the backdrop of night sky. His eyes closed drowsily and the next time he opened them he saw the angel step down from her pediment. As she hovered over him the night fell back from her face, revealing startling violet eyes that gleamed wetly, high cheekbones and skin pale as white marble framed by long strands of dark auburn hair. The angel reached down and laid a soft, cool hand against his cheek. "Am I dead?" he whispered. "Surely you are an angel."

The angel's only answer was a solitary tear that trickled down her cheek. Thraxton's eyelids flickered. Darkness was sweeping over him in waves. He flailed against it like a swimmer striking out for a distant shore he would never reach. The image of the angel was the only light in the darkness and he knew that if he lost his grip upon it he would die. But then another wave broke and Thraxton realized he was caught in an ineluctable undertow.

His eyes closed a final time, and in the darkness of the grave he drowned.

6

The Man Who Crawled in Through the Wallpaper

The laudanum was nearly gone.

Augustus Skinner fumbled the slender, smoke-brown bottle from the bedside table, pressed it to his lips, and gulped the final mouthful. He reached to set the bottle back, but it slipped through his clumsy fingers and toppled to the rug somewhere. He fell back in the bed, his body undulating liquidly in oceanic waves of warmth, his face flushed and perspiring. The wound still throbbed, but the pain was a voice calling his name from a long way away—insistent, but easily ignored.

The physician who presided at the duel, Doctor Silas Garrette, dug the lead ball out a week ago, but infection had set in. He explained to Skinner that—as with wounds the doctor had treated while an army surgeon serving in Crimea—the ball had not been clean and had undoubtedly pushed foreign matter (fibers of clothing, dirt, gun oil) into the wound, which had painfully abscessed and swollen into a red mass the size of an orange, suppurating pus and a sticky red ooze. Now the critic had run out of laudanum, and had dispatched a servant with an urgent summons for the doctor to return. That was an hour ago, but laudanum had the effect of dissolving time as well as pain, and Skinner fell into a chaotic tangle of disturbing dreams.

The knocking forced his eyes open. Part of the dream? No, the knock came again.

"Come," Skinner called out, eyes squeezed shut in an attempt to retard the giddy, counter-clock revolution of the room.

The knocking continued: a woodpecker hammering on a tree.

Skinner opened his eyes to find the door to his room had mysteriously vanished, leaving six or seven or eight blank walls. The rapping resumed, and this time his eyes followed the sound to its source: a bulge in the hideous yellow wallpaper next to the dresser. But then a hand appeared, pushing through the floral pattern as if moving a branch aside, and then an arm squeezed through, followed by a shoulder and a white top hat as a man clambered out of the wallpaper. He stood for a moment brushing away the detritus of the wallpaper's floral design from his sleeves, calmly looking down at Skinner.

It was the doctor, Silas Garrette.

Skinner's mind was whirling from the effects of the laudanum, and he knew he was witnessing a particularly vivid hallucination. He had once visited a carnival—a bit of whimsy where various woodland creatures (rabbits, moles, dormice) had been dressed in the tiny clothes of men and women and posed as if attending a tea party. The doctor bore a striking similarity to one of those figures, as if someone had dressed up a stuffed stoat in a gentleman's suit, complete with a white top hat and a pair of rose-tinted pince-nez over the beady brown eyes. Skinner's gaze traced downward, expecting to see a bushy tail protruding from the back of the man's suit trousers and finding its absence somehow jarring.

"Are you real, sir, or some phantasm conjured by laudanum?"

The doctor touched the brim of his white top hat, but never removed it, despite the fact they were indoors, which struck Skinner as the very height of poor manners.

"It is I, sir, Doctor Garrette. You summoned me." The physician's face was like a cemetery statue disappearing beneath a tangle of overgrown foliage: a voluminous pair of bushy mustachios entwined enormous sideburns sculpted like elaborate topiary. The top hat seemed to float atop a hedgerow of frizzy, tightly curled hair, which matched the mustachios in its ersatz, shoe polish shade of brown—a cheap dye job.

"Thank God you have come. The pain…" he sucked in a deep breath and shudderingly released it, "…is worse."

The white top hat nodded. "I need to drain the pus."

"Again?"

"It will relieve the pressure. That is why it throbs so. Please turn over."

The doctor brought the candle closer. Laying face down, prostrate across his bed, Skinner could not see what was happening behind him, but watched as the candle flame stretched the doctor's gangly shadow across the bedroom wall. Skinner's face burned with the ignominy of the situation as he lay sprawled in the posture of a naughty boy awaiting a good spanking, the chill of the room raising goose bumps as the doctor lifted his night gown and icy digits palpated his hind quarters.

"The wound needs to be lanced," Doctor Garrette intoned in a gravely professional voice.

"Laudanum," Skinner said. "Give me laudanum first."

The doctor moved to the bedside table where his black Gladstone bag yawned. He reached a hand down its throat and drew out a smoky-brown bottle stoppered with a cork. "This is a very strong tincture of laudanum dissolved in gin," he said. "I must caution you. It is stronger than the laudanum you buy in the shops. I mix it myself. You are not to take more than a thimbleful."

Skinner snatched the bottle from the doctor, yanked the cork with his teeth and gulped a mouthful. The inside of his cheeks puckered as what felt like cold mercury trickled down his throat.

The doctor unrolled a leather holster of medical instruments across the bed and drew something out—from the glitter of steel, a scalpel. "Do you require something to bite on?"

"Just cut me, and be done!"

Skinner fixed his gaze upon the yellow wallpaper and watched the doctor's shadow loom over him, the arm raised, the scalpel flourished. The shadow arm came down and Skinner let out a howl as the wicked keen blade sliced a burning path.

Skinner fumbled the laudanum bottle to his lips and glugged a second mouthful.

"Again, I warn you," the doctor chided. "An overdose would be fatal!"

"Yes, I heard you!"

The doctor applied a fresh dressing to the wound, which throbbed, throbbed, throbbed with the pounding of Skinner's heart. Finally the physician finished his ministrations and the critic slumped back into the bed pillows.

"And now my bill, sir," Garrette said.

"Can't it wait?"

"I have children. I must think of them."

"Top drawer," Skinner waved vaguely. "Take what is owed you."

Augustus Skinner did not remember the doctor leaving. In truth, he did not remember much else, for the laudanum had taken effect and he felt his body dissolving into a buoyant gas until all that remained of him was a head floating like a cork on a puddle of ether.

7

RISEN FROM THE GRAVE

The Night Hawk is one of the largest species of moth, with a wingspan measuring as much as 6 inches.

Algernon pondered the illustration. The moth was dark brown in color. Fuzzy antler-like antenna protruded from its forehead. The eyes were gleaming black domes set on either side of the head that seemed to stare out of the page, fixing the viewer with its uncanny gaze.

A loud metallic clang. He looked up from his book. Two young nurses were passing out bedpans and one had just tumbled from the wheeled cart as they pushed it along the ward. He was in the Whittington hospital. When Thraxton had been brought in, no one had known for certain who he was, and so he had been placed in a general ward, along with the common folk and their mundane ailments.

Algernon sat in a straight-backed chair next to the head of the bed, reading a book on moths and butterflies as he kept vigil over his friend. It had been three days by this time, but to the concern of all, Thraxton showed no signs of awakening. He looked down at his friend. Thraxton's face was almost as white as the bed sheet tucked under his chin—apart from the mark that Snudge's cosh had left, a livid red welt that ran from cheekbone to temple, and around which spilled waves of glossy black hair.

It was not the first time Algernon had kept vigil at his friend's bedside. They met as first-year boys at public school. In keeping with a proud school tradition, the younger boys were relentlessly bullied by the older boys, as they themselves had been bullied in their time.

This was just such an occasion.

Algernon had been standing with his classmates in the quadrangle awaiting the school bell when the most notorious bully in school, Tom Bagby, or "Baggers" as he was known, sauntered over dragging behind his usual pack of toadies. Bagby had flashed a cruel smile at Algernon and then, without warning or provocation, drove a vicious punch straight into his face. The blow floored Algernon, and then Bagby leapt on top, pinning the younger boy's arms as he rained punches on his face and chest. Algernon's first-year friends, intent only on self-preservation, instantly bolted for cover. As the bully-boy pummeled his helpless victim, Bagby's cronies cheered and shouted, "Go on! Bash him, Baggers!"

Suddenly a blur of fury and flying fists crashed into Bagby and knocked him tumbling. To the shock of everyone, the figure that scrambled to his feet, small hands balled into trembling fists, was the new first-year boy, who was shorter even than Algernon. Bagby snarled and lunged at the new boy and the fight began. The younger boy fought like a maelstrom, but it was a vastly unfair competition. Bagby was a fifth-year boy, head and shoulders taller, and he was the school boxing champion. He knocked the younger boy down once and then again and then a third time. Still, the new boy dragged himself to his feet each time. A fourth. A fifth. A sixth. A seventh. But despite the fact that his nose dripped blood and both lips were split, the younger boy refused to stay down. As the beating continued, even Bagby's thuggish friends grew frightened and called for him to stop. Throughout, the younger boy never cried, although Bagby himself was on the verge of tears, for an opponent who refused to give up terrified him. And so the beating continued until a final uppercut knocked the smaller boy to the ground and sprawled him senseless. Then a school master, black robes flapping like the wings of an agitated crow, burst through the melee to stop the fight—as always, too late. The milling mob of boys instantly dilated around the small prone form as the bullies scattered and fled.

The unconscious boy was carried to the school infirmary where Algernon was permitted to keep watch at his rescuer's bedside. After several hours, the new boy finally cracked open his bruised and swollen eyes, squinted up at Algernon and spoke in a croaky voice: "My name's Geoffrey."

"Mine's Algernon."

"Did I thrash him?"

Algernon told him that he had indeed triumphed and that he was the talk of the school.

It was the beginning of a life-long friendship.

Algernon smiled, thinking about that time, then drew his gaze back to the book he was reading.

The Hawk Moth is a native of England and Europe, although varieties of the species may be found...

"I saw her, Algy. She was an angel with wings."

Algernon startled at the sound of Thraxton's voice.

"Geoffrey! You're awake!"

Thraxton's eyes slitted open.

"How long..." His mouth was dry as sand and he could barely speak. "How long...?"

Algernon leapt to his feet and leaned over his old friend. "Three days."

"Three days?" Thraxton put a hand to the side of his head and moaned.

"You are fortunate to be alive! You've got a lump the size of a goose egg on your head. Do you remember anything?"

Thraxton opened his eyes a little wider, straining to focus on his friend's face.

"I remember the angel: the violet eyes... alabaster skin... long, dark hair. The touch of her hand, cool, like marble made flesh."

"Angel?" Algernon sighed. "You're rambling, Geoffrey. The sexton and I found you lying in a grave. You'd been coshed by Resurrection Men out body-snatching. No doubt to satisfy the insatiable demand of our respected medical colleges. It's a wonder you are not being dissected by a class of student surgeons right now!"

Thraxton struggled to raise himself in the bed.

"What are you doing? Lie still!"

"Doing? I'm trying to sit up. Help me!"

Against his better judgment, Algernon dragged his friend upright. "Perhaps I should call for the nurse," he said, looking around for the matron.

Thraxton grabbed his friend's sleeve to prevent him from leaving. "I was dead, Algy. An angel's touch brought me back from the abyss of death."

"There was no angel, Geoffrey. It's just part of your delirium. You've been unconscious for three days."

"No! I saw her," Thraxton insisted. "She was an angel. A dark angel in the night."

"You're rambling. I'll fetch the nurse."

"Never mind the nurse," Thraxton said, throwing back the bedclothes and tottering out of bed. "Call us a carriage." As he gained his feet, he staggered and would have fallen had he not grabbed the brass bedstead for support.

"Geoffrey, this time I will not allow you to have your way. Get back in that bed. There is no way you are leaving this hospital. Do you understand? I absolutely forbid it!"

"This is madness! Sheer madness!" Algernon complained. "If anything happens, I suppose I shall be to blame."

He and Thraxton were seated in a hansom cab that

plodded up Swain's Lane toward the front gates of the London cemetery at Highgate.

"Do stop wittering, Algy," Thraxton said, a hand held over his eyes to shield them from the light. "I've got a beastly headache and your constant blathering is only making it worse."

Ten minutes later they passed through the iron gates of Highgate Cemetery and proceeded on foot. By now it was late afternoon, dense black cloud shrouded the sky, and the two men shambled through the disintegrating twilight. Thraxton was still unsteady on his feet, and had to lean on Algernon's shoulder for support. They made their way along the winding paths until they arrived at the grave that Thraxton had fallen into. In the days that had passed since the incident with Fowler's men, the London Cemetery Company had hastily filled in the grave and placed an iron mortgate atop it to deter any further attempts by Resurrection Men.

"This is it," Thraxton said, "the spot where I had my tussle with the three ruffians." He removed his hand from Algernon's shoulder and shuffled to the neighboring grave, gazing up at the stone angel perched atop its pedestal. "This is her. The angel," Thraxton said, his voice falling into a reverent whisper.

The stone angel stared down at them, head slightly tilted, the blind stone eyes stunned with loss.

"She came alive, Algy. I saw her step down and kneel over me. She was a spirit made real."

Algernon looked away, trying to conceal his open skepticism. His eyes were drawn to a crumpled black shape in the grass and he stooped to pick it up. It was wet with dew, but as he unfolded the wadded ball, he instantly recognized what it was. He cleared his throat to snatch his friend's attention.

"What?" Thraxton asked.

"A glove. A woman's glove. Proof, I would say, that your angel was no visitor from the spirit world." He found a label inside the glove and examined it. "Unless those who have passed over to the other side are now having their gloves made by T. Sayers of Oxford Street, London."

At the news, doubt clouded Thraxton's face. Then a faint gray wisp of smoke swirled about them. Sniffing a familiar scent, Thraxton looked up.

A white-haired gentleman in a battered cap stood close by, observing them. A lit lantern dangled loosely from his fingertips. Cradled in the crook of his other arm was a firearm with the heft and girth of a small naval cannon. The elderly man drew the lit pipe from between his lips and nodded to them with a good-natured grin.

"Ah," Algernon said, recognizing the man. "Now, Geoffrey, here is the true angel you owe your life to."

8

THE SEXTON OF HIGHGATE

Silver smoke swirled, curling into graceful arabesques that formed, shivered, and collapsed as they floated up and crashed against the rough wooden beams and cracked plaster ceiling of the tiny cottage. The monstrous elephant gun rested on two hooks above the fireplace. Now the owner of the firearm, the sexton of Highgate Cemetery, rammed a poker into the seething red coals, agitating them until the fire flared and a crackle of sparks swooped up the chimney flue. Satisfied, the sexton settled the iron poker in its stand and dropped heavily into a creaky, much-repaired cane chair. Algernon and Thraxton sat in the tiny parlor's only other furniture: two battered and threadbare armchairs. All three men puffed at cigars Thraxton had produced from the humidor he kept tucked in his overcoat pocket.

"That's quite a weapon," Thraxton acknowledged, drawing on his cigar.

"I calls her Old Bessie," the sexton said. "After me late wife. I keeps her handy in case the Resurrection Men come nosin' around. The din of Old Bessie goin' off is enough to shake your bowels loose. Loud as a bleedin' cannon!"

The sexton functioned as both a caretaker responsible for the upkeep of the cemetery and as night watchman. Algernon and Thraxton had tarried too long at the cemetery, and so when it was discovered their cab driver had given up on his passengers and driven off, the sexton invited the pair to wait in his tiny cottage until a carriage might be summoned from Highgate Village.

"Yes, I can quite agree with that assertion," Thraxton said. "And a damned good thing, too."

All three men chuckled and puffed, but then Thraxton burst out: "Ah! But I am quite forgetting!" He reached for the walking stick next to his chair. "What is a cigar unless it's accompanied by brandy?"

Thraxton possessed a large collection of walking sticks of which this was his favorite: the stick with the gold phoenix handle. He gave the phoenix a twist and it unscrewed in his hands. Then he tipped up the cane until out slid a slender glass tube filled with amber liquid—brandy. A cork stoppered one end of the tube, a narrow silver sipping cup screwed to the other. Thraxton yanked the cork from the tube while the sexton rummaged in the tiny room for a motley collection of drinking vessels: a battered pewter tankard, a dusty Toby jug and a filthy cracked tea cup. (Which, fortunately, the sexton kept for his own use.) Thraxton splashed a jigger of brandy into each and the men chinked drinking vessels and toasted the Queen's and then each other's health. Thraxton's tankard had a dead, metallic taste to it, but the first sip of brandy washed it away and sent a glowing rush through him more warming than the fire.

For a moment, silence prevailed as the three men sipped their liquor and puffed like chimneys. Thraxton was far from recovered from his ordeal, and as lethargy overtook him, he slipped into a philosophic frame of mind. "What say you, sexton? You live among the dead." Thraxton's fascination was evident in his voice. "The other night I saw a spirit, a dark wraith gliding between the graves. Have you seen it, too?"

The sexton was an elderly gentleman with bushy gray sideburns whose volume compensated for the sparse wisp of gray hair frizzling his balding head. He was seventy, but spry for his age and now, at Thraxton's question, mischief sparkled in his eye. "Oh, I seen things, gents. All manner of things. These pathways are walked during the nights, sometimes more than in the day."

"Ghosts moaning and rattling chains?" Algernon quipped, not entirely able to conceal his condescension.

The sexton met his gaze with surprising resolve. "It's not the dead I'm afraid of, sir, it's the livin'. That's why I carry Old Bess on me rounds. No, there's nothing to fear from ghosts."

"Why do they walk?" Thraxton asked. "Are they unhappy spirits banished to the earthly plane?"

The sexton removed the cigar from his lips and spat

something into the fire that sizzled. "I reckon they walk 'cause they miss what they had when they was alive."

Thraxton leaned forward slightly in his chair, hanging upon every word. "And what is that?"

"Love," the sexton said calmly. "It's the only thing we ever really have to call our own. And no one and nuffink can ever take it away from you, not even death."

Surprise flashed across Thraxton's face. He puffed at his cigar for several minutes, mulling over the sexton's words before speaking again.

"What do you think happens when we die, Algy?" Thraxton asked. "Is there an afterlife? A soul that survives physical death?"

"As a scientist, I'm afraid I would need some form of empirical evidence."

"Such as what? Place the body upon a scale and weigh it before and after death to determine the weight of the soul?"

Algernon chuckled. "That has been tried already, but yes, I would require some form of tangible proof."

"Have you ever been in love, sir?" the sexton asked.

"Yes," Algernon said, pride swelling in his voice. "Yes, I have."

"Was it real?"

"Oh, it was real all right. Positively. No question."

"Could you have measured it? Weighed it on a scale?"

"No... well... obviously... no," Algernon stammered.

"I guess love don't exist, then, eh?"

Algernon choked on his own words, obviously stymied.

Thraxton laughed. "He's got you there, Algy."

As Algernon wrestled for a scientifically reasoned comeback, Thraxton leaned from his chair, knocked the slug of ash from his cigar into the fire, then fell back in his seat.

"Very well then, Geoffrey," Algernon said, "have you ever witnessed evidence of the supernatural?"

Thraxton thought for a moment, drawing deeply on his cigar and blowing a perfect smoke ring. All three watched it rise, dilating until it burst against the ceiling and dispersed. At first, he spoke slowly, haltingly, as if he were pulling the words from a dark, secret place where they had been long-hidden. "I was still a child when my mother died. For weeks, as I lay in my little bed at night, I would talk to her. And it would seem that I could hear her voice in my head, talking back to me."

Algernon pursed his lips skeptically and countered, "Grief makes us imagine strange things, Geoffrey."

"That's what my father said. When I told him of hearing my mother's voice, I was strapped. To make me stronger. To make me a man. After a number of these strappings, I no longer heard her voice. Although, even after all these years, I have never stopped listening for it."

As he spoke of his mother, Thraxton's lips quivered, as if from the pain of an old and deep wound being probed. Algernon noticed the change, as the cynical, often callous man he knew melted away. His face seemed suddenly young—the face of a child who had become lost in a forest and who never found his way home.

"I've known you all these years," Algernon said. "Yet I have never heard you speak of your mother."

For a moment Thraxton's eyes betrayed his reluctance to go on such a journey, but he began to speak again, and once started, it was impossible to stop him. "My mother was an angel," he said, then laughed scornfully at his own pronouncement. "I know every man thinks that. But for my mother it was true, for she never seemed a part of the real world. She was a sickly woman—frail and fragile. In most of my memories she is in her sick bed. She had never been strong. As a child she nearly died from rheumatic fever. It weakened her heart. Giving birth to me overstrained her already delicate disposition. Mother never fully recovered her strength. I suppose that means I am responsible for her death. At least, my father always felt that way, and never failed to remind me of it. Mostly, though, he simply ignored me, which, perhaps, was worse."

The fire popped and shot a fiery ember that landed on the hearth rug, scorching yet another burn mark. Thraxton sipped his brandy and continued. "When I was not at my studies, I would be permitted to visit my mother in her rooms. She was a very beautiful lady. I remember combing the long auburn hair that reached almost to her waist. She had a pale complexion, translucent as alabaster; no doubt because she rarely went outside and so her skin never suffered the harsh rays of the sun…"

He paused and puffed at his cigar.

"We would play games or she would read to me. But my

favorite thing was when she wound me in her arms and we lay together, my back pressed to her chest, her arms wrapped tight as she rocked me. I remember the warmth of her body, her breath on my neck. I remember feeling her heart beating close to mine, the resonance of her chest as she sang to me. I think I shall never know moments of happiness as great as those. Since then I have learned the terrible truth—all love leads to the cemetery. And the greater the love the deeper the loss. That is why I shall never love again."

His eyes were focused on the images playing out in his head; he did not see the throbbing coals of the fire, the sexton lolling in the lopsided chair, or even the room before him.

"How old were you, sir," the sexton asked, "when your mother passed?"

Thraxton's eyes refocused as his mind journeyed back across many years. He looked at the sexton's face, half-lit from one side, like a phase of the moon.

"I was nine years old when her heart finally failed. I remember the weeks before her death, when she was too ill to see me for more than a few minutes before I was shooed out of the room by the physician. One day, I found Mary, one of our domestics, sobbing outside my mother's rooms. When she saw me, Mary pulled me to her and hugged me. My face was buried in her apron and she hugged me so tight I could hardly breathe. And I knew then—I knew…"

Thraxton's voice broke on the last word. His eyes shone as he raised the pewter mug, gulped the last swallow of brandy, and set the tankard at his feet.

"I was taken in to see her. She had been laid out in the bed. My father lifted me so that I might kiss her. I remember the feel of her lips. Stiff. Waxen. Cold.

"From that moment on, I was forgotten. It was as if I too died that day, for even the tiny amount of affection I occasionally received from my father was withdrawn. I became a ghost, a very small ghost that haunted the hallways of that vast house. My father remarried two years later and things became very much worse. For now I was a reminder. All the portraits of my mother were taken down, but every time my father or his new wife saw my face, they saw my mother's face. I became a recrimination. The greatest crime one can commit against a child is to withhold love. How can one thrive, grow, without it?

"Then there was the day—four years after my mother's death—when I was playing in the grounds of our house near the family mausoleum. The place was always kept locked, but on this particular day I saw that the door had been left open.

"I was a young boy and naturally curious. I entered and found lanterns burning. The crypt contained the coffins of our family, going back generations. I found my mother's coffin. I remember reading her name on it. The coffin screws were silver doves. They had been removed and set upon the bier. Even as a young boy I knew what happened to bodies left exposed after death. I had seen dead animals in the woods of our estates. I wondered if she would look the same. I had no fear when I lifted the lid and finally looked inside."

Thraxton tapped the ash from his cigar and drew deeply

on it, then exhaled a lungful of silver smoke.

"Perhaps it was the coldness of the crypt, or the dry air within, but her body was in a perfect state of preservation. In truth, she looked little different than the day she died. She was still beautiful. Still young. Although her hair was longer, for it had continued to grow, as had her fingernails. I remember touching the back of her hand. The skin felt like cold, stiff leather. When I lifted her arm, it was light as a bird's wing.

"She looked to be sleeping, not dead. I recalled all the happy hours I had spent in her arms. And so I climbed into the coffin, and lay with my back to her chest. I wrapped her arms around me, and pulled the coffin lid down upon us. It was dark, but the darkness did not frighten me, for I was once again in my mother's arms, in a place where nothing could hurt me. The coffin smelled of the rose petals scattered inside. After some time I must have fallen asleep. I was awakened by a flash of light—the coffin lid being thrown open—and found myself looking up into the face of our groundskeeper, a rough, foul-tempered man. He was very angry, though not nearly as angry as my father proved to be. I received the strapping of a lifetime. At first I thought it was because of what I had done, but now, as an adult, I realize why he was so angry.

"My mother always wore an amulet around her neck. It contained a piece of amber with a small insect trapped inside. As a child I was always fascinated with it, and my mother let me look at it whenever I asked. The amulet had been a present from my father on the first anniversary of their wedding. My mother had been buried with the amulet. But a day after I received my strapping, my stepmother appeared at the dinner table wearing my mother's amulet. My father had presented it to her as a gift on their third wedding anniversary."

As he remembered it, Thraxton's face contorted with hatred and disgust.

"My father had robbed my mother's grave for a trinket to present to his... his whore! I ask you, what kind of monster does that?"

Thraxton looked away into the shadows, a muscle twitching in his lower jaw.

"From the way I stared at the amulet all through dinner it became very obvious to my father that I knew exactly where it came from. I'm sure it became apparent to him that I was becoming more than just an inconvenient reminder of my mother. Needless to say I was packed off to public school soon after. Which, of course, is where I first met you, old stick."

For the first time since he had begun his reverie, Thraxton looked over at Algernon. But with the exertions of the night, coupled with the brandy and Thraxton's droning, his friend had nodded off long ago. The Toby jug dangled loosely from his fingers, ready to spill. A small pile of ash from his cigar was burning a hole in the threadbare upholstery of the chair arm. Thraxton reached over, pulled the jug from Algernon's fingers and set it on the floor, then gently retrieved the cigar and tossed it in the fire.

"That's quite a story, milord."

Thraxton looked up to find the sexton's kind eyes fixed upon him. He was about to say something when he was interrupted by a faint but eerie screech. When Thraxton turned to look, an icy chill ran through him. At the window a pair of luminous yellow eyes peered in at them from the blackness.

The sexton got up, ambled to the window and opened it. In sprang an enormous black tomcat with huge golden eyes. "It's only me moggy, Pluto," the sexton said.

Pluto jumped down from the windowsill, swayed over to Thraxton and dropped something small and black at his feet.

A dead mouse.

9

The Widow's Weeds

Although Algernon had only enjoyed perhaps twenty minutes of sleep in the last forty-eight hours, it was a Monday morning and those who were not of the leisure class had jobs to go to. After a hastily eaten breakfast, he hailed a cab in order to catch the steamer for Kew Gardens where he held the position of head botanist. (A position he owed thanks in large part to Thraxton's influence and patronage of the Royal Botanical Gardens.)

Lord Thraxton's day, meanwhile, assumed its usual leisurely pace. After breakfast, he retired to his rooms and slept until early afternoon. Upon awakening, he called for his blue brougham to be brought around. An hour later the carriage deposited him, once again, at the London Cemetery at Highgate.

During his late breakfast, Thraxton had decided to revisit the cemetery during the hours of daylight while the events of the previous night were still fresh in his mind. Compared with last night's miasmic fog, the day turned out to be dry and crisp under bright sunshine and brilliant blue skies, and the winding paths were strewn ankle-deep with the scarlet and gold of autumn's glory. But after strolling for the better part of an hour, he found the cemetery so different in daylight that it conjured none of the associations he had been seeking. Weary, and still feeling the effects of his nocturnal misadventure, he abandoned his search, but determined to make some productive use of the visit by composing a new poem.

He had brought his book of blank pages and pen, and now he sought out the place in the cemetery where he usually wrote. The gravestone slab was elevated a foot and a half from the ground on stout stone legs, so as to form a kind of table or low bench. The epitaph showed that the grave belonged to one Emily Fitzsimmons, who had shuffled from this mortal coil at age sixty-three, much to the eternal grief of her adoring husband Walter and their two children Amelia and Francis. Thraxton sat upon the grave, facing toward the massive stone gateway flanked by a pair of faux obelisks that formed the entrance to the Egyptian Avenue. With the book resting upon his thighs, he took out his favorite pen and jotted the title of today's poem at the top of the blank page: "The Highgate Spirit."

Thraxton's eyes danced along the whorls and curlicues of his handwriting set in blue ink upon a blank white page. He had his title, his theme. As a form of meditation, he gazed skyward, watching puffy white clouds tumbling and reforming while he awaited inspiration. After ten minutes he came to himself and realized that the muse was uncharacteristically silent that day. Clearly her throat was in need of a little lubrication.

Thraxton set down his pen and picked up his phoenix handle walking stick. Before leaving home he had refilled the glass tube with an aged and oakey brandy. He unscrewed the sipping cup, and yanked the cork loose with his teeth. Careful not to waste a drop, he filled the cup then quickly drained it and poured himself another. Despite the brilliant sunshine it was a chilly, brisk day and the brandy warmed his innards. He was reassembling the walking stick when he caught a movement out of the corner of his eye and turned to look.

In the shadows sprawled beneath a canopy of elm trees, a slender black shape glided silently through the distant gravestones.

He stood up and looked, but it had vanished.

Thraxton dropped the walking stick and took off running.

As he reached the path he glimpsed it again, fleetingly. It seemed to be moving in a direction slanting diagonally away from him. Thraxton abandoned the path and crashed through the underbrush. It was darker beneath the canopy of trees. Although the cemetery had only been open a few years, many of the graves here were already overgrown. Thraxton leaped over graves in his haste, eyes scanning ahead for another sight of the black wraith. He spotted it, barely fifty feet away, gliding away from him. He lost sight momentarily as he dodged around a stand of elm trees, but kept running. He leapt over another grave and almost crashed into a dark crouching form.

A woman in a veil and black mourning dress knelt at a handsome marble grave while she placed flowers upon it. She looked up with a startled expression, eyes wide, mouth open as Thraxton stood over her, panting and flushed.

It took a moment for them to recognize one another.

"Mrs. Pennethorne!" Thraxton blurted. He suddenly noticed the fresh flowers laid upon the grave and the name *Charles Pennethorne* engraved on the handsome marble headstone. In her widow's black lace dress and black bonnet, Thraxton had mistaken Constance for the specter he had seen the evening before.

"I... I... please, forgive me," Thraxton stammered. "I did not mean to intrude. I thought you... I mean, I most humbly beg your pardon."

Mortified by his own bumbling stupidity, Thraxton bowed slightly and was about to take his leave when Constance rose and graciously offered her hand.

"Not at all," she said, smiling to show she had recovered from her initial surprise. "Once again, Lord Thraxton, your entrance displays great dramatic flair."

Thraxton felt himself blushing and thought, *Congratulations, Geoffrey. You've made a complete arse of yourself.*

She laughed at his obvious embarrassment. "No, it is good to see you again. I have not forgotten your generosity at the British Museum."

Thraxton gently shook her hand and nodded politely at the grave. "Your beloved late husband, I take it?"

She nodded.

"Forgive me. I shall intrude upon your grief no further."

He turned to leave, but she put a hand on his arm. "No, please. I was just about to leave. My friends are waiting at the gate. Perhaps you would be gallant enough to walk with me?"

And so the pair strolled together along the leaf-strewn paths. It was considerably warmer in the sunshine. Were it not for the bare trees and the dense carpet of fallen leaves, it could almost have been taken for a spring day.

"You are here to visit a loved one, Lord Thraxton?"

"No, I come here to write," Thraxton replied. "I find the melancholy atmosphere of Highgate, all this sorrow and brooding loss turned to stone, conjures my poetic muse."

Constance smiled. "Ah, you are a poet?"

"There are those who would argue the point, but yes, I title myself as such. It is so much more agreeable than admitting that I basically do nothing at all."

Constance could not hold back a wry smile, which Thraxton took as a sign of encouragement. "Forgive my boldness, Mrs. Pennethorne, but I must confess that upon seeing you at your husband's grave, I was struck by how your great natural beauty was rendered quite transcendent by a widow's grief."

"You are terrible flatterer, Lord Thraxton."

"It would seem a sin to keep such pulchritude wrapped

in a widow's weeds forever. I believe there are seasons in all things—life and death. Perhaps when your season of grief has passed, you will be free to open your heart again to another love among the living?"

Constance stopped and looked up into his face. "I may, in time, love another. But I will never stop loving my husband. I do not believe that love ends at the tomb door."

"Why, yes," he hurried to add. "Of course. Remembrance for the dead is a noble thing."

"Not merely remembrance," she corrected. "My husband is still very much a part of my life. I spoke with him just last Wednesday."

Thraxton smiled, and then quickly dropped the expression lest she think he was mocking her. Still, he did not know quite what to make of her statement, so he assumed an expression of serious attentiveness. "You are speaking poetically, I imagine?"

"Not at all."

Thraxton's expression betrayed his puzzlement. Constance resumed walking and he kept pace with her. She flashed him a wistful little smile and asked, "Do you believe in the survival of the soul after death?"

The words triggered a jolt of electricity through Thraxton.

"I very much want to." For some reason Thraxton felt compelled to tell Constance about the dark wraith and his near brush with death, leaving out all details of how he and Algernon wound up at Highgate. Constance listened attentively throughout, her expression thoughtful but never revealing whether she thought he was deluded or not. By the time he finished his story they had reached the cemetery's gated entrance. An elderly couple sat on one of the wooden benches, and now they arose as Thraxton and Constance approached. It occurred to him that he had seen them someplace before, and then he remembered the evening at the British Museum.

"Ah," he said. "The inevitable Wakefields."

"Yes, I do hope I haven't kept them waiting too long." She turned to Thraxton and offered her hand. It was obvious their tête-à-têtes had concluded. "It was so good to see you again, Lord Thraxton."

Thraxton doffed his top hat and bowed as he kissed her hand.

"I came here seeking only silence and contemplation," Thraxton said. "Who would have guessed I would find serene beauty as well."

Constance blushed a little at the compliment. She turned and walked toward the waiting Wakefields. Thraxton watched as she shared a few words with the elderly couple that he could not catch from where he stood. Constance finished and walked back to speak with him.

"Lord Thraxton," she said. "Do you know anything of the spiritualist movement?"

The question surprised him. "I... a little. What I read in the newspapers."

"We are having a séance this Saturday evening. If you are free to attend, you may find it enlightening."

She pressed a card into his hand that bore an address in Mayfair not far from his own home.

"Yes, thank you. I believe I am free."

"Wonderful."

Constance started to walk away again when she remembered something and turned back.

"Oh, and do be sure to bring your friend with you—Mister Hyde-Davies."

10

An Ill-favored Augury

The carriage was black, worn and shabby—like hundreds of its ilk that juddered along the bumpy cobblestone streets of London. Its anonymity had been chosen for precisely that reason. Likewise, the rumpled sack of rags slouched in the driver's seat was a gin-addled consumptive whose memory could be relied upon to be unreliable.

Another deliberate choice.

The carriage was drawn to the curb to allow traffic to squeeze past. Inside, Doctor Silas Garrette lounged on the scuffed leather seat. He palmed a pack of Tarot cards in one hand and now he laid out the cards on the seat beside him: a Five of Pentacles, a Hanged Man, the Death card, a Six of Wands... he turned the final card and his jaw clenched.

The Tower, struck by lightning, collapsing masonry tumbling down on several terrified figures below.

Garrette ground his molars, then swept up the cards with a deft movement.

Overhead, the driver coughed liquidly, hawked and spat. A gleaming wad of phlegm flew past the carriage window and splattered in the gutter.

The doctor sat plunged in thought, the deck of Tarot cards flexing in his hand. What he had seen in the reading disturbed him greatly. He began to shuffle them for a second reading, but was interrupted by the bruising drum of knuckles on the carriage door. He looked up at the face of a filthy gorilla framed in the window. The door opened and the carriage listed on its saggy springs as Mordecai Fowler squeezed aboard, his rank stink crowding in with him. The mobsman oofed as he sank onto the worn seat opposite.

"Well?" Garrette said. "I trust you have it?"

Fowler lifted his bowler hat and resettled it, offering a slack grin. "Ah, that," Fowler began. "We had a bit of bother—"

"Bother?" Silas Garrette's face stiffened like hardening cement. "What do you mean, bother?"

"We had company."

"Company? At Highgate? In the middle of the night?"

"We almost 'ad her out the ground when this moxie shows up… and then this toff wiv a walking stick. He starts a barney, but Snudge gives him the cosh. I'm ready to finish 'im off when the sexton comes running wiv a bloody great gun. Nearly took me 'ead off."

"What on earth are you talking about?" the doctor barked, hurling a look of pure death.

"A toff it were. Wiv a fancy walkin' stick. He gimme this. Fowler tilted his head to show off a livid purple welt along his jawline. Fowler growled, "Ever I see that barsterd again…"

The doctor's brows arched skeptically. "He's not dead?"

Fowler squirmed. "No. Yeah. I dunno. Most like he is."

"Most like?" The doctor's lip curled.

Fowler gave a noncommittal shrug. "Good as, I reckon. Good as dead."

"But you failed in your primary mission."

Fowler forced a cheery laugh. "Not to worry, guvnor. No shortage of stiffs in this manor. The peelers dredge a fresh moxie out the Thames every other day—"

"Fool!" Garrette spat. "This was no ordinary corpse. I can procure the stinking carcass of a diseased whore from any dozen of you flesh-peddlers. This was a unique specimen!"

"Oh, you mean the stillborn? The mooncalf that done her in?"

"Do not ever speak that word in my presence!"

Fowler failed to see the rising anger in the doctor's face and blundered on: "Hundreds of them sort flushed down the sewers every day."

The doctor lunged across the carriage with a demon's ferocious speed and Fowler could only squawk to find the wicked keen edge of a scalpel pressed against his Adam's apple. With his free hand the mobsman stealthily groped for the gnarled handle of Mister Pierce, only to feel the leather scabbard part in two and slide away as the spike hit the carriage floor with a *thunk*. Fowler's eyes bugged. He had seen men who were fast with a blade before, but the doctor moved quick as a nightmare.

"Listen to me, Fowler," Garrette hissed. "I need these... children... for my studies. They are especially precious to me." In the dim carriage, the twin rose disks of his pince-nez glowed luminous. The doctor's posture finally relaxed. He drew back into the shadows on his side of the carriage, a venomous eel withdrawing into its sea cave. Fowler caught a brief flash of silver as the blade slipped back into the doctor's coat pocket in one fluid motion.

The mobsman shuddered and rubbed stubby fingers along his prickling windpipe, expecting them to come away red, but finding no blood. When he at last found his voice again, Fowler muttered: "I'll keep me ears and eyes peeled."

He rummaged the floorboards until he snatched up Mister Pierce and the flapping ends of the leather scabbard the scalpel had cleanly cut in two—without so much as nicking his belly. Fowler heaved his bulk out of the carriage door and was about to bang it shut when the doctor froze him with a word.

"Mordecai—"

Fowler hurled a guarded scowl back at the shadowy figure. Coins chinked and then a flung purse smacked him in the chest. Fowler grunted and caught it by reflex. A fat coin purse filled his hand.

"You know what I am seeking," the doctor said. "Find it and I can be even more generous."

Fowler touched the brim of his battered bowler in badly feigned respect and slouched away, face fixed in a mocking leer.

Silas Garrette leaned back against the worn seat cushions, his eyes slitted in thought. The nostrils of his hawkish nose flared as he snorted, partly from disgust and partly to flush the stink of Fowler's ripeness from his lungs. The lumpen buffoon had encountered some kind of gentleman in the cemetery. The details somersaulted in Garrette's head. A gentleman? A walking stick? He thought of the duel and the encounter with the brash Lord Thraxton loomed in his mind, but he shook it off. Too bizarre a coincidence. But when he touched a hand to the Tarot deck in his pocket, the cards seemed to pulse under his fingertips.

There was no such thing as coincidence. This could prove a bad augury indeed.

Garrette reached up and knuckled the ceiling of the carriage. The driver shook himself awake and stung the horses' ears with the tip of his lash. The carriage lunged forward and the heavy London traffic soon swallowed them up.

II

A ROMP IN EDEN

The gardens at Kew spread over hundreds of acres of land. But its crowning glory was the greenhouses: glittering edifices of curved glass and ironwork that scintillated in the sun. The largest of these was the Palm House, the design of which presaged that most famous architectural triumph of the time, the Crystal Palace.

While the wan September sun was scarcely able to warm the chill from the day, inside the Palm House the climate was turgidly Amazonian. It needed to be to sustain the towering palm trees, breadfruit, elephant grasses, and the thousands of exotic plant species that grew in a burst of equatorial greenery quite dazzling to the senses. The effect of entering the Palm House was always remarkable, but especially so on a chilly day, for in a single stride one passed from the dull browns and muted earth tones of autumnal England into the humid fecundity of a tropical rainforest.

The Palm House was the bailiwick of Algernon Hyde-Davies, who was employed there as head botanist. It was his job to oversee the cataloguing and cultivation of all the thousands of new and hitherto unknown species of flora that arrived each day, shipped in from every corner of Victoria's sprawling empire.

On this particular morning Algernon was in one of the smaller greenhouses overseeing the transplantation of seedlings ready to be moved into the Palm House. His staff of gardeners stood at a long table while they presented wooden flats filled with hundreds of seedlings for Algernon's perusal. He moved along the line like a drill officer inspecting his troops.

"Too much light," Algernon said, eyeing a flat filled with green seedlings whose leaves all had brown tips. "Try moving them to a more shaded area."

"Yes, Mister Hyde-Davies," replied the gardener.

Algernon moved onto the next flat. These were stunted and leaning every which way.

"Oh, dear," Algernon exclaimed. He tugged one of the seedlings free from the soil and inspected it. The stem of the plant was long and thin, the tiny leaves half the size they should have been. The roots had black fungus growing on them.

"See that, Baines?" Algernon said holding up the seedling to the gardener, a young man of eighteen with a red spotty complexion and fiery ginger hair. "Stunted growth, small leaves, black on the root system. We all know what that means, do we not?"

He looked at Baines, awaiting an answer. The young man's face reddened further.

"Er, I suppose." Several emotions swept across Baines' face: embarrassment, frustration, and finally gloomy resignation. "I, I dunno, sir."

"You planted them too deep," Algernon gently chided. "The poor plant took all its energy trying to dig itself out of the ground. You're not burying a corpse, remember. No need to plant them six feet deep. They're just little seedlings. Delicate babies. They need to see the sun just as much as you and I. Understand?"

The young man dropped his eyes to the pathetic display of withered seedlings he stood behind.

Algernon clapped a hand on the younger man's shoulder and reassured in an avuncular tone, "Don't worry, Baines. You'll get it soon enough. Before we're finished I'll make a first rate gardener out of you." He moved on to the next box of seedlings. "Now," he said brightly. "How are these coming along?"

Before the gardener could answer, Parkinson, one of Algernon's junior botanists came rushing into the greenhouse in a state of agitation, his face flushed.

"Mister Hyde-Davies, sir!"

"What ever's the matter, Parkinson?"

Parkinson was out of breath and so excited he could barely talk. "There's a man, sir. In the Palm House. A naked man!"

Algernon's expression showed his total bewilderment. "A naked man, you say? In the Palm House?"

Parkinson nodded his head rapidly. "Naked, sir. Totally starkers."

Algernon couldn't quite believe his ears. "A naked man—" He suddenly stopped as an awful premonition came over him. *No. He wouldn't! Would he? Not even he would do such a thing. But then again, who else?*

Algernon and Parkinson sprinted along the winding pathways of the Palm House.

"Mister Greenley's chasing him, sir," Parkinson yelled, "but he's a slippery fellow. Look, there's some of his togs!"

They found a gray silk top hat crowning a ficus tree. Ten feet on a pair of boots and socks lay where the owner had kicked them off. Farther still a pair of men's trousers dangled from the lowest limb of a palm tree. They continued on, finding various items of hastily tossed-aside clothing. Finally Algernon spotted something thrust into the soft soil of a planter—a walking stick topped with a golden phoenix rising from the flames. Now there could be no doubt as to who the naked man was.

Algernon snatched the walking stick from the soil. He looked around the Palm House agitatedly. Seeing nothing he looked up at the glass domed ceiling and yelled at the top of his lungs.

"GEOFFREY!"

A naked man burst from the nearby bushes.

"Hello, Algy," Thraxton shouted, chortling gleefully as he ran past.

"Geoffrey, what the deuce—" Algernon began to say, when a second later Mister Greenley, a gray-haired man in his late fifties, burst from the same bushes in hot pursuit, wielding a gardening rake with an obvious intent to do Thraxton some serious mischief.

"I'll get ya, you swine!" Greenley yelled after the fleeing Thraxton.

Algernon and Parkinson joined the pursuit and now the four of them crashed pell-mell through the dense vegetation. Even as he ran, Algernon could see his position as head botanist evaporating before his eyes. His best friend was engaging in a demonstration of public lewdness that could very well land them both in the law courts if not at least the newspapers. Meanwhile his head gardener was trying his damndest to emasculate a peer of the realm with a gardening implement. If word of this got out, Kew's head botanist would be lucky to find a position as a gardener in a municipal vegetable allotment.

A respectable middle-class family—a husband and wife, and their fifteen-year-old daughter—were strolling along one of the paths when Thraxton leapt from the undergrowth directly in front of them. All three stood in open-mouthed astonishment at the unwarranted appearance of a naked virile man. Then the wife screamed and swooned into her husband's arms. The schoolgirl's eyes widened in delight at her first glimpse of male genitalia. She held a pigtail to her mouth and giggled.

A moment later Mister Greenley burst from the bushes. He

swung the rake at Thraxton's head, narrowly missing. Thraxton ducked under the whizzing rake and took off running again just as Algernon and Parkinson reached the pathway.

"Geoffrey!" Algernon cried helplessly. "For God's sake, man, put your clothes back on!"

Mister Greenley trembled with rage as he stopped to catch his breath. "Filthy swine. Wait till I lay my hands on him."

Greenley made as if to run after Thraxton again, but Algernon grabbed his arm to restrain him.

"No! Please, Mister Greenley, Parkinson, leave this to me. I will endeavor to make him see reason."

But Mister Greenley's blood was up. He had no intention of allowing such a lecher to escape without a good hiding. "I don't care if he is a lord," he spat. "Prancing around naked in front of God and the world. The man ought to be horsewhipped."

"Yes, thank you, Mister Greenley," Algernon repeated, attempting to assert his authority. "That will be all. I shall deal with this matter myself."

"Horsewhipped, I say!"

"Please."

Mister Greenley cast a furious scowl in the direction he had seen Thraxton disappear. With great reluctance he shouldered his rake and walked slowly toward the door. Algernon gave Parkinson a nod to indicate that he should follow Greenley's lead. When both men had gone, he stepped off the path and pushed his way into the lush vegetation.

"Geoffrey," he called. "Put your clothes back on. You'll cause a scandal. You'll get me the sack!"

Thraxton's disembodied voice came from somewhere in front of him. "They won't sack you, Algy. Not while I give so generously to the Royal Botanical Society."

Thraxton stepped from behind a spectacular breadfruit tree, his naked torso glistening. "Come on," Thraxton urged. "Get your clothes off, Algy. You have recreated Eden. This is our natural world. Let us be natural, too." He struck a dramatic pose, one armed raised. "I am the new Adam, and I have found my Eve."

With that Thraxton turned and ran off into the undergrowth, chortling inanely.

"Geoffrey!" Algernon watched his friend's bare bottom vanish and hurried to follow. After several minutes' searching he came upon Thraxton again. He was standing on tiptoe, straining to reach up and touch the huge orange and purple bloom of an exotic tropical flower.

"Geoffrey, no!" Algernon cried in alarm. "Do not touch it!"

"Why ever not?" Thraxton asked. "It is exquisite!"

"It is a bloom that cannot abide the touch of man. If you lay hands upon it, the flower will die. Please... please... let it be."

Thraxton relaxed his stretching fingers. He drew back and turned to look at Algernon.

"A mere touch will kill it?"

Algernon nodded in affirmation.

Thraxton was quite struck by the thought.

"Why is it those things of the greatest beauty are always just beyond our grasp?"

"I believe I have found my Eve," Thraxton said.

He was fully clothed once again, to the great relief of Algernon, and the two were strolling around the pond that lay immediately in front of the Palm House. Compared to the dripping humidity of the greenhouses, the day was dry and bracing.

"Who is this demi-goddess?" Algernon asked. "Another actress? Surely not the wife of that fellow you told me about—Sir whatshisname?"

"Algy, you disappoint me. You know me better than that. Do I wax eloquent about every single one of my conquests?"

"Yes, Geoffrey, now that you mention it, you do tend to rattle on about them—every single one."

"Mmmn, quite," Thraxton said, looking hurt. "This is different. I have truly met my inamorata."

Algernon was unable to conceal a look of deep skepticism. Thraxton noticed and cleared his throat, but continued. "Actually she is the woman you pointed out to me that day at the British Museum—Constance Pennethorne."

Algernon's face dropped at the news, but Thraxton was oblivious.

"We met the other day in Highgate Cemetery. We had some time to talk and, I may dare say, to open our very souls to one another. I found out that not only is she a woman of great beauty, she is also a creature of rare intelligence and spirit."

Algernon looked away so that Thraxton could not read what was written on his face. In the center of the pond stood a Laocoön-like statue of a naked athlete struggling with a serpent. Algernon suddenly felt a deep empathy for the fellow—he could practically feel the serpent's coils tightening around his own neck.

"And she feels the same about you?" Algernon probed.

"I have little doubt of it. She's invited me to a very exciting evening this Saturday. A séance of all things. I'm looking forward to it profoundly."

Algernon turned back to look at Thraxton. He had forgotten to recompose his face and Thraxton noticed his dour expression.

"Oh, there's no need to look so glum, old stick," Thraxton said good-naturedly. "Of course, you're invited, too. She went out of her way to mention it, in fact."

Thraxton punched his old friend in the shoulder. "Should be quite an adventure, eh? Conversing with spirits of the departed!"

12

Séance in the Dark

Five figures sat around a circular table covered in a white tablecloth embroidered with floral patterns. At the center of the table, a softly hissing lantern, turned down low, provided the only source of light apart from the ruddy glow of coals in the fireplace. From their gilded frames, the portraits of the Wakefield family—a grandfather with white hair and a long white beard, a matronly woman wrapped in a fox stole, a young girl of three in pigtails—looked down upon the séance with luminous eyes that seemed to move in the flickering light.

Thraxton was seated between Mister Wakefield, a thin, ascetic man with white hair; to his left, and Constance Pennethorne to his right. Algernon sat to the right of Constance, while to his right sat Mrs. Wakefield, whose emaciation did not bode well for her cooking abilities. As is often the case with couples married so long, the two more closely resembled brother and sister than husband and wife.

"Now, if the sitters would kindly take hold of each other's hands," said Mister Wakefield in his broad Yorkshire accent. Grateful of the excuse for the intimacy of touch, Thraxton reached for Constance's hand. She flashed him a polite smile, but then turned her attention to Algernon. As she took his hand in hers she gave it a slight squeeze that immediately brought Algernon's surprised eyes up to meet hers. Thraxton noticed the brief exchange and felt a twinge of jealousy. Mister Wakefield took hold of Thraxton's left hand.

"My good lady wife's hands must remain free," Mister Wakefield announced, "so she may write upon the pad."

"We are to hear no rappings, then?" Thraxton asked. "Witness no ghostly manifestations?"

Mister Wakefield shifted a little in his chair and cleared his throat, clearly agitated by the question. "No, Lord Thraxton. My wife and I leave such theatrics to the frauds and music hall conjurers. We of the Spiritualist Church are interested only in sober communication with the spirits of the departed. What we practice is called automatic writing. My wife, who acts as medium, enters a trance, whereupon we may put any questions we like—so long as they are serious—to the spiritual presences hovering around us. They will guide my wife's hand as it moves across the paper."

"Ah, quite," Thraxton said, frowning. He, of course, had been hoping for knocks and table rapping, for disembodied voices and levitating trumpets, even to see milky white ectoplasm streaming from the mouth, nostrils and sundry other orifices of Mrs. Wakefield. In short, all the sensational manifestations of the séances he had read about in the *London Standard*. Instead he would have to be content with an old woman scrawling on a notepad with a pencil. And if he wasn't very much mistaken, the affections of Constance Pennethorne seemed to be taking a turn toward Algernon instead of himself. The evening was proving to be a crashing disappointment.

Mister Wakefield begged for silence while his wife steeled her mind for contact with the Other Side. All attention remained fixed upon Mrs. Wakefield as she sat with her eyes closed, lids trembling, then suddenly slumped in the chair, head lolling forward so that her chin rested upon her chest. For a while the only sound in the room was her slow, steady breathing.

Wonderful, Thraxton thought to himself. *The old crone's fallen asleep*.

Everyone jumped as Mrs. Wakefield gasped and stiffened. A sudden chill descended upon the room. Thraxton sensed it and the hair at the back of his neck bristled. Algernon, ever the skeptical scientist, wrote it off as nothing more than a draft from the fireplace.

In a trembling voice, Mrs. Wakefield asked the spirit presences hovering near if they bore a message for one of her sitters. Her right hand began to shake with uncontrollable tremors, and then suddenly shot across the paper, scribbling down words at an unbelievable rate. Interspersed with the words, written in a free-flowing cursive script of excellent penmanship, were strange icons and hieratic symbols, the meaning of which Thraxton could not even guess at. The scribbling went on for seven or eight lines and then stopped. Mrs. Wakefield's hand flew back to the corner of the pad and sat there quivering, as if waiting for another message to come through.

Mister Wakefield leant over from his seat and read aloud what was written on the pad. "My dearest Constance—"

Constance drew in a shuddering breath at the mention of her name, her eyes filling with tears. Mister Wakefield continued reading.

"How I miss you, my darling. How I miss our quiet evenings together, the sound of your voice, and your sweet singing. But despair not, for time on this side passes quickly. Soon we will be reunited in eternal bliss."

"But what if Constance were to remarry?" Algernon blurted the question aloud before he could check himself. All eyes, save Mrs. Wakefield's, immediately turned upon him. He cleared his throat and squirmed in his chair. But to his surprise, Constance squeezed his hand in reassurance and turned to Mrs. Wakefield. "Yes," she said. "I should like to ask my husband that very question. What if I were to remarry?"

Mrs. Wakefield drew in a deep breath. Her hand quivered, then shot across the page. Words flowed for several lines and then stopped. Like an automaton, her arm flew back to its resting place.

"We are all one in the spirit world," Mister Wakefield read aloud. "There is no jealousy here. Only love. Endless compassion. If you wish to remarry, do so. With my blessing."

Constance breathed an audible sigh of relief. She turned at once to Algernon and smiled broadly.

Watching how much attention Constance was paying to Algernon, Thraxton sulked.

"Lord Thraxton?" Mister Wakefield addressed him. "Do you have a question to put to the spirits? A loved one you wish to speak with?"

Thraxton thought immediately of his mother. But what would he say? What could he ask? And after all these years? For some reason the idea terrified him. There was too much to say. Too much to be answered in a few scribbled lines. "No," he fought for the right words. "I mean yes, there is a loved one I wish to speak with, but... but not now. I should need to prepare myself first."

"I understand," Mister Wakefield said. "It is no trivial thing to open one's heart to a love long thought to have been lost." He turned his eyes to Algernon. "What about you, Mister Hyde-Davies? Do you have a question for the spirits? A deceased loved one you wish to converse with?"

During the exchange with Constance, Algernon had toyed with exposing the fraud by asking to speak with his father, who was still very much alive. But having just witnessed how much comfort Constance took from these exchanges, he decided against causing her any pain. He shook his head.

"Wait," Thraxton interjected. "Did you say I might ask any question of the spirits?"

"Yes, Lord Thraxton. The spirits see everything in our

world, past, present, and future."

"Very well, then. I wonder if the spirits could tell me the name of my inamorata, the woman I might marry."

All eyes returned to Mrs. Wakefield. She sat slumped in her chair, trance-bound, her mind presumably floating somewhere above the séance table as it communed with the ghostly presences hovering there. As they watched, a tremor rippled across the features of her face that was quite disturbing to see. Her right hand resumed its quaking, then shot across the page, this time not writing but sketching geometrical shapes: a triangle mounted atop a rectangle, and then a curving shape coming out of the triangle, and several ovate circles attached to it. Her hand flew back to the center of the rectangle and wrote something, a single word in large block letters. Having finished, Mrs. Wakefield's hand jerked back to its resting point.

"I, I've never seen anything quite like this," said Mister Wakefield upon examining the pad of paper. "In all our séances, I've never..." He trailed off, stymied. "I, I'm afraid I simply don't know what to make of this."

He turned the pad around and pushed it across the table toward Thraxton. On the pad was a simple, almost child-like drawing of a rectangular building topped by a triangular pitched roof. At the front of the building were two double doors. Above the doors written in Roman script, as if chiseled there, was the word ELYSIUM. Strangest of all, growing out of a hole in the roof was a huge flower with a slender stem and curving, orchid-like petals.

When Thraxton looked at the drawing, an involuntary shudder passed through the core of his being.

"Elysium," Constance said, reading the word aloud. "What does that mean?"

Thraxton was familiar with the term. "In Greek mythology, Elysium is the abode assigned to the blessed after death," he explained. "It is the place where the dead live in a state of ideal happiness."

"But what is this building supposed to be?" Constance asked.

Thraxton lifted the pad and turned it so that both Constance and Algernon could see the rough sketch of a small rectangular building topped by a pitched roof.

"Is it not obvious?" he asked. "It is a tomb."

13

AN ENCOUNTER AT THE NECROPOLIS

The whole of the next day Thraxton was in a peevish and irritable mood. The previous evening's séance had been filled with revelations, all of which left him baffled and perplexed. Constance Pennethorne's invitation to the event had seemed to be an open encouragement to his affection. But, once there, her rather familiar behavior with Algernon had sent a very contrary message.

So, too, the message delivered by the medium had both intrigued and unnerved him. The possible proof of life after death stirred a host of vague hopes and longings in the depths of Thraxton's being. But then there was the ominous image of the tomb. What was he to make of that? Over breakfast and then lunch, his mind spawned one interpretation after another, each darker than the one before it.

By mid-afternoon the tumult of thoughts racing through his brain had given him a headache. To relieve the pain he took a little laudanum, and then a little more. But as always, laudanum brought out in Thraxton the intense melancholia that always lurked just beneath the surface. During these attacks, Thraxton knew of only one way to abate them, which was to surrender and immerse himself in the feeling. To this end he instructed Harold to ready his brougham. An hour later Thraxton found himself once more in Highgate Cemetery sitting in his favorite spot, atop the ever stoic and uncomplaining Emily Fitzsimmons.

He wracked his throbbing brain for a way of turning Constance Pennethorne's affections back in his direction. Obviously, his reputation was a black mark against him. Even his wealth and title seemed to leave her unimpressed. What quality did he possess that Algernon lacked? He sat tapping his pen against the blank notepad until the answer sprang into his mind. He was a poet. All women found poets irresistible. He would write a poem about Constance. Ergo, she would melt. He would conquer.

Thraxton quickly scribbled a title at the top of the page: "Sweet Constancy." Now he had his theme, he had but to conjure inspiration. He stared into lengthening afternoon shadows while words and phrases tumbled in his mind. Suddenly he became aware of sobbing. He turned his head slightly, listening. Yes, it was sobbing, and a man's sobbing at that.

Thraxton left his notepad in the care of Mrs. Fitzsimmons and followed the elegiac sound to its source. Up ahead, a small funeral party had gathered around an open grave into which a coffin was being lowered. The sexton lingered in the shade of an ancient oak, observing from a discreet distance as he puffed at a long-stemmed clay pipe. Partly to share the moment with someone, and partly to share the aroma of tobacco smoke, Thraxton walked over to join him and the two watched the service in silence.

The source of the sobbing was indeed a man. He was of the same approximate age as Thraxton. His dress distinguished him also as a gentleman, though the grave he wept over was in an area of plots affordable to those of the middle classes. The man was being supported by a male friend and a woman. The unrestrained show of emotion on the man's face, and his obvious heartbreak was enough to touch the soul of any man or woman, profound as it was.

"Bloomin' shame, that is," remarked the sexton, turning his head slightly to acknowledge Thraxton's presence.

"His mother?"

"His wife. Not even thirty years of age. And quite the beauty, I understand."

Seeing a man so close in age, status, and even appearance to himself, it was impossible not to feel pangs of sympathy.

"How terribly, terribly sad."

"Aye," the sexton agreed. "We're all mortal flesh, but when they goes so young it's hard to fathom why. I suppose only Gawd hisself knows."

In a show of sadness, the sexton tugged the handkerchief that dangled from the breast pocket of his wool overcoat and blew his nose with a loud, honking sound. He opened the handkerchief to examine its contents, then folded it and vigorously wiped his large nose before tucking the handkerchief back into his breast pocket. With that the sexton shrugged and wandered off to complete his rounds.

The mourners filed past as each tossed a handful of earth into the grave, and then the grief-stricken man was led away by his friends. The mourners hadn't got farther than twenty feet away before the gravediggers, who had been leaning on their shovels through the service, rushed forward and began hurling spadefuls of loose dirt into the grave with an urgency that spoke more of men impatient to get to their dinners than the kind of respect that should be shown to the deceased. Thraxton lingered a moment longer and then turned away. As he walked back toward Emily Fitzsimmons and the interrupted poem, he could hear the drumming of dirt clods bouncing off the coffin lid.

Another hour passed with Thraxton still penning his ode to Constance Pennethorne. Dusk was falling with the surreal haste only autumn can manifest, and in the failing light Thraxton could barely make out his own writing as his pen skipped across the page. He heard approaching footsteps and looked up. A figure in a halo of yellow light moved toward him like an apparition. It was the sexton, carrying a lantern.

"I'm sorry, Lord Thraxton, but we close the gates in five minutes."

"Another half hour? The muse is particularly loquacious today. I should hate to silence her just now."

The sexton scratched his stubbly chin, a doubting look

on his face. "I'm sorry, milord, but rules is rules."

Thraxton reached into his pocket, pulled out a gold half-sovereign, and tossed it to the sexton who caught it deftly. From the heft of the coin alone, the sexton could guess at its denomination and became suddenly tractable.

"But seein' as you are a gentleman," he continued, "and a lord, I don't see as how any harm can come of it."

"Thank you, my man," Thraxton said.

"I'll fetch you a lantern, shall I, sir?"

"That would be most commodious."

The sexton touched the brim of his cap and silently dragged the halo of light away with him, leaving the deepening gloom to descend upon Thraxton. He looked down at his notebook, but it was so dark now he could barely make out its shape on the gravestone beneath him. Thraxton recapped his fountain pen and set it alongside the notebook then folded his arms to wait for the return of the sexton. After a few moments it suddenly struck him just how far away the sexton's little hut was. He would have a long wait in the darkness.

Thraxton lay on the gravestone, hands folded on his chest in a mock posture of repose. He closed his eyes and listened to the sounds of the cemetery: the keening call of a nighthawk, the thrum of bat wings flitting overhead, the fallen leaves rustled by the wind. His eyes snapped open. There was no wind. It was a deathly calm night. Thraxton got up from the gravestone, fumbling in the darkness for his walking stick. His fingers closed upon it and he crept slowly toward the crackle of leaves being trodden underfoot.

On such a moonless night the pathways were like currents of lighter shadow flowing through a greater river of darkness. Breath held, ears pricked, eyes wide, Thraxton seemed to sense movement ahead and followed, moving as stealthily as possible. His mind pitched back to that fateful night of his tussle with the thugs and the angel with the violet eyes who had caressed his cheek. Was this the wraith he had pursued?

But there was barely light to see the way. After five minutes of aimless stumbling, he gave up, turned around, and sauntered back toward the waiting Emily Fitzsimmons and the book and pen he had abandoned. But when he reached the massive pharaonic arch that led to the Egyptian Avenue, his scalp prickled with recognition.

It was here that I first saw the specter, he thought. *It seemed to sink into the ground, as if trying to re-enter its grave.*

Highgate Cemetery reflected the rigorous stratification latent in every aspect of English society. The mausoleums of the Lebanon Circle were occupied by the deceased wealthy. But the plots on either side of the path were amongst the cheapest plots in the cemetery. Not coincidentally the gardeners rarely visited the place, so that many of the graves were strangled in ivy.

Thraxton stepped from the path, eyes scanning the graves. A flash of brightness caught his eye. One headstone had a carved stone vase at its base. Placed in the vase was a long-stemmed flower with an elaborate white bloom. At first he threw it a cursory glance, but something about it drew his eyes back. He looked again, this time with a more discriminating gaze.

"This is the grave," Thraxton said aloud, stooping to pluck the flower from its vase. He turned the bloom over in his hand. It was fresh, and perfumed the air with a hot house scent quite foreign to an English fall.

A remarkable flower, he thought. *I have never seen its like.* He tapped the bloom against his lips and smiled. *But I know just the chap who can identify it.*

14

THE WHITE BLOOM

All that day Algernon rehearsed exactly what he would say to Thraxton. They had been friends for far too many years, and their friendship was far too valuable to attempt to conceal something of this magnitude. He would simply have to tell Thraxton, and let the consequences play out as they may.

But now as the hansom cab clopped along the avenue towards Thraxton's home on Belgrave Square, he began to have second thoughts. What if Geoffrey flew into a rage? What if he simply took umbrage and turned his back, never to speak to him again? Algernon owed him so much—too much. He regretted putting himself into such a state of indebtedness to another man, and yet it had never seemed that way at the time.

The spiked railings that marked the fronts of the row of houses of which Thraxton's was one hove into view and his mouth was suddenly dry, his pulse thudding.

Damn it, he thought. *I will tell Geoffrey, no matter what the consequences. I will open my heart and inform him that Constance Pennethorne has given me certain signs of encouragement and that I mean to press my suit with her. Yea, that I will marry her, if she would have me.*

The cab jerked to a halt outside Thraxton's residence. But as he paid the driver and stepped down, his resolve began to crumble and dissolve. *What if I am mistaken? What if I have misread her signs? Women are wont to flirt, to tease. Many delight in making fools of men.*

As he lifted the heavy brass ring clamped in the lion's jaws and brought it down upon the striker plate several times, his misgivings grew. *What if Constance is such a woman? What if I destroy a lifelong friendship for naught?*

He heard movement from within, the thunder of footsteps approaching at a run. He was surprised when the door was opened not by Harold, the manservant, but Thraxton himself, his face flushed with excitement. "Good heavens, Geoffrey! Whatever's the matter?"

Thraxton ignored the question, his eyes falling instead upon the cab which he restrained from moving away with a violent wave. "Proof, Algy!" Thraxton cried. "That's what the matter is."

"Whatever are you babbling about?"

"This!" Thraxton said, holding up the white bloom.

Algernon cast the flower a cursory glance, but then looked again, closer.

"What kind of flower is it, Algy?" Thraxton asked.

"Good Lord." Algernon's brows knotted in puzzlement. "I don't know. It may not be from the spirit world, but it is quite unearthly."

The specimen room at Kew was lined floor to ceiling with cabinets containing wide, shallow drawers filled with plant specimens harvested from the four corners of the earth. Algernon had the white bloom set on top of a cabinet. Next to the bloom he paged through a huge volume filled with exquisite watercolor paintings of different genera of flowers. Thraxton looked over his shoulder as Algernon leafed through the heavy pages.

"I have never seen the like of it. Certain species of cactus have flowers somewhat like this. On the other hand, it does also resemble a genus of tropical orchid." As he flipped another page, a sudden thought struck him. Without another word he abandoned the book and the white flower and walked over to one of the cabinets and began opening and closing drawers as he quickly surveyed their contents. Solidly in Algernon's world, Thraxton followed him around in silence.

"Then again," he said, opening another drawer, quickly scanning the contents then banging it shut and moving to the drawer above, "it is so exotic and exquisite it could be from some far-flung place, such as from the Galapagos Islands. I believe we have a rather spectacular collection… somewhere."

Not finding what he was looking for, Algernon slammed

the last drawer shut and quickly set off, moving deeper into the specimen room, ducking in between rows of tall cabinets, and crossing to the very back of the room where the cabinets reached to the ceiling a good thirty feet and had to be scaled by a ladder that leaned up against them. "Stay there, Geoffrey."

Thraxton waited passively while Algernon scampered to the top of the creaking ladder and began rummaging through some high drawers near the ceiling. He lifted out one of the blooms and inspected it. "No, these are clearly not the same," he called down. "The leaves are quite different in structure."

"What if it really was a spirit, Algy? An angel made flesh?"

Algernon slammed the drawer shut and descended. He threw Thraxton a withering look as he stepped from the ladder. "The only spirit present that night was the spirit you keep in that walking stick of yours."

"I was not drunk, Algy. I swear I wasn't. Not one drop passed my—well, all right, perhaps a drop or two—but I was not drunk."

Algernon stood with his arms crossed on his chest, a hand to his chin as he thought for several long minutes without speaking. "A hybrid!" he announced at last.

"What?" asked Thraxton.

"A hybrid. The flower. It could well be a hybrid. The creation of some clever horticulturist. Perhaps that's why I cannot find its analogue anywhere in our collection."

Algernon strode quickly in the direction of where he had left the bloom next to the open catalogue. Thraxton hurried to keep up with him. "If so," he continued, "it really is a remarkable piece of work. I certainly have never seen the like—" He suddenly stopped. The catalogue lay open on the desk where he had left it, but the white bloom had mysteriously vanished. "It's gone!"

He and Thraxton exchanged stunned looks.

"I left it right here and now it's gone!"

"Someone must have taken it," Thraxton said.

Algernon looked around as if not quite believing what was transpiring. "But you and I are the only ones in this room, Geoffrey."

Thraxton thought for a second, and then looked up at Algernon. "Perhaps… the spirit?"

Algernon sighed. "Geoffrey, I assure you it was no spirit you saw that night at Highgate, and no spirit who just now took the bloom. Most likely Parkinson or one of the other botanists came in while we were in the back, saw it lying out and put it away in a drawer somewhere."

Both men looked about. The specimen room was huge and was filled with thousands of drawers. The door from the specimen room led into one of the smaller greenhouses. Through the glass window set into the door, Algernon spotted someone working. He went over to the door and opened it. Mister Greenley, the man who had chased Thraxton with a rake the day of his au naturel romp, was repotting some ferns and looked up when he heard his name called.

"Mister Greenley!"

"Yessir?"

"Mister Greenley, we were just examining a specimen, a flower with a white bloom. It... it seems to have gone missing. Did you see anyone come in here?"

Mister Greenley rubbed at his chin, leaving a smudge of dirt. "No, sir. I've been the only one here."

Algernon's face registered his disappointment. "Ah, I see. Thank you."

Mister Greenley continued to stare expectantly.

"Do carry on, Mister Greenley."

Algernon closed the door to the greenhouse and turned back to Thraxton, a baffled look on his face.

"We will find it, Geoffrey," Algernon said as he loaded Thraxton into his waiting brougham outside the Palm House at Kew. "The flower will turn up somewhere, I promise you."

Thraxton settled himself into the seat. Algernon was about to slam the carriage door when Thraxton was struck by a sudden thought.

"Hold on a moment! That chap you spoke to. His name is Greenley?"

"Yes. He is my head gardener."

"The grave where we found the flower, did you happen to notice the name on the headstone?"

As a scientist, Algernon was rather embarrassed to admit that his powers of observation had been lax. He shook his head.

"Greenley," Thraxton said slowly. "Florence Greenley."

Algernon's eyes widened in surprise. "Really? I understand that Mister Greenley is a widower..." He shook his head. The idea was patently absurd. "But I know the man. He is gruff and plain-speaking, but scrupulously honest and a strict teetotaler. Why on earth would he steal the flower?"

"Why indeed?" Thraxton asked, suddenly very suspicious. "Tell me. Do you perchance know where our Mister Greenley lives?"

15

DOCTOR GARRETTE'S CHILDREN

He was ambushed from behind as his key turned in the lock of his office door.

"Ah, Doctor Garrette, you are returned."

Garrette stiffened. He had the door half open and now he pulled it shut and turned to face his ambusher. By the wheedling voice and asthmatic breathing, he could guess who it was. "Mrs. Parker... I believe I paid this month's rent already."

Rose Parker was his landlady, a jovial widow of extra-generous proportions who took a great interest in all her tenants—too much interest for Silas Garrette's tastes. "On time as always," Mrs. Parker said, and chuckled, setting her multiple chins into oceanic motion. "I don't know how you manage it, I never see any patients come to your office."

As soon as his key scratched in the lock, the children must have heard, for they began calling to him from the other side of the door: *Father, father!* Garrette blanched inwardly. Surely she must hear them, too.

"As I have already explained, Mrs. Parker, I make a great many house calls."

"You must be exhausted then, tramping all over the city."

"Yes. I am very tired."

Father... Father are you there? the thin, reedy voices called as one.

"I would love to see how you have fixed up the premises—"

He was frantic to get away, before his prying landlady could ask about the childish voices emanating from inside the office. "Some other time, Mrs. Parker. As I just said, I am extremely tired." And with that he slid in through the door and snatched it shut behind him before she had a chance to detain him any longer.

Dr. Garrette's hands shook as he locked the door from the inside.

Father... welcome home, Father. The children waited behind another locked door, yet Silas Garrette could hear them plainly. He strode across the office to a second door, produced a heavy iron key and unlocked it. The door opened on a dark, windowless room, little more than a deep, narrow closet.

Papa, we have missed you, the children droned as one.

As he swung wide the door, the astringent smell of ethyl alcohol, chloroform, and other noxious chemicals bowled over him in an invisible cloud. He paused for a moment, allowing fresh air to swoosh in and intermingle before he stepped into the closed space.

Papa... Papa... the voices called from the darkness.

"Patience, my lovely children," Dr. Garrette muttered. His hand groped across a work bench until his fingers closed upon a box of matches. He struck one and lit the gas mantle. The flame blossomed, illuminating the darkness.

The room was long and narrow with the work bench on one side. Atop the bench sat a gleaming row of glass vessels. Inside each one, a fetus floated in a clear preserving liquid.

His children.

They were all freaks; examples of gross deformities that nature would not allow to reach full-term: conjoined twins, fetuses with heads like baby pigs, one with four arms next to a worm with no arms or legs, a Cyclops... Each one a mother's nightmare. A father's despair.

"My beautiful children," he breathed, stroking each jar in turn. He reached the final jar and lifted it to the light, gazing at the fetus floating within: his favorite, called Janus, a conjoined twin with two faces on one head. He did not consider them freaks, but believed them to be nature's attempt at the next leap in human evolution. The god-like spawn of a future race.

Garrette held the jar close to his ear, listening. "What is that you said, Janus? Ah, yes, when will your new sibling be joining our little family? Soon, Janus, very soon."

He kissed the fetus' jar, which was covered with a sticky residue that left a bitter chemical taste in his mouth. The preserving liquid was his own experimental formulation—

mostly ethyl alcohol mixed with chloroform and several other compounds. It worked reasonably well, although now, after many years, the liquid was becoming cloudy and increasingly turbid as the specimens within slowly decayed and disintegrated. He set the jar down carefully and stepped to the back of the room.

A mirror hung on the far wall and Silas Garrette studied a reflection split in two by a fine crack running diagonally across its wavy surface. He removed the rose-colored pince-nez spectacles and tucked them into a breast pocket. Then he doffed the white top hat. Two white phrenology busts sat on a table beneath the mirror. Dr. Garrette set the white top hat atop one. Next, he drew off the brown wig and draped it over the other bust. Following a long-established ritual, he peeled off false eyebrows, moustaches and then the elaborate side-whiskers which had been glued on with spirit gum. When he had finished, the visage that looked back from the mirror was unrecognizable. The head was completely bald and hairless—down to the lack of eyelashes. A tracery of fine red scars veined the skin of his scalp and crept down one side of his face: a souvenir from the Crimean War of an incendiary shell that had exploded over the hospital tent he had been working in. The tent had burned to the ground killing all inside, both wounded and medical staff. By a twisted miracle, he had survived. They found him a mile away, catatonic, staring into a dark wood, clothes smoldering, hair singed off.

Garrette moved closer to his crazed reflection, palpating

the puckered skin of his scalp with his long, spatulate fingers, staring at a face that eerily mocked the unformed faces of his children, buoyant in their glassy wombs.

He reached down a bottle of chloroform from its shelf, then drew a clean linen handkerchief from his waistcoat pocket and flicked it open. Then he uncorked the bottle with his teeth and dribbled chloroform onto the handkerchief. That done, he carefully recorked the bottle and dropped into a battered leather armchair pushed into a corner. He draped the handkerchief loosely over his nose and mouth, the material sucking in and out as he began a series of slow, deep breaths. The gaslight flared in the fume-laden air of the room, making the shadows squirm, the light refracting weirdly through the glass jars in which his children hung suspended. In a matter of moments, the doctor's breathing deepened and became sonorant; his eyelids began to droop as with every breath his body relaxed more and more, until by the tenth inhalation, his eyes flickered shut as an echoing mine shaft of sound opened up beneath him and he and the armchair submerged through the floorboards, gliding down into a soft-edged darkness.

16

A Damned Good Thrashing

For a brief, blink-and-you-missed-it moment, Soho Square had been one of the most fashionable addresses in London. But times and fashion had moved on. Now, as the middle and upper classes migrated to the west end of town, it lapsed from swank to gauche to geographically undesirable while the surrounding slums expanded until they nibbled at its edges with sharp, ratty teeth. These days, instead of the clatter of brougham carriages, the streets resounded with the cries of costermongers and the iron wheels of delivery carts. Yet it endured as a lone enclave of middle-class respectability, although within staggering distance of a number of cheap drinking establishments that sprouted overnight like gin blossoms on a drunkard's nose. The square's geographical disadvantages were further exacerbated by its proximity to a narrow alleyway of slime-slippery cobblestones that zigged and zagged until it ended at a narrow footbridge spanning a rivulet of vileness known as Filthy Ditch, the noxious threshold that marked the entrance to the Seven Dials Rookery.

The pride of Soho Square was its rows of Georgian houses, still handsome, but now resembling the face of an aging dowager whose beauty had faded and which now bore the odd smudge of soot. Still, the place kept up a defiant stance of respectability, although the spiked black iron railings guarding every front door seemed an inadequate defense against the forces of entropy.

At this hour, one-thirty on a Sunday afternoon, a gleaming blue brougham was parked across the street from the square's finest row of houses. Seated at the reins was a young man of around twenty years with a bowler hat pulled down to his rather large ears. The door of the carriage opened and Lord Geoffrey Thraxton stepped down. He dashed across the street, dodging the constant stream of London traffic—omnibuses, hansom cabs, commercial wagons—to number forty-two and skipped up the steps. Here he banged the door's heavy brass knocker several times and waited. Finally, a frumpy young woman opened the door. Judging by her dress she was a domestic servant—most likely (given the diminished social standing of the street) a maid-of-all-work.

"Good day," he smiled. "Is Mister Greenley at home?"

From the way the young woman looked at Thraxton, it was clear she was unused to answering the door to anyone loftier than a delivery man.

"Mister Greenley?" she asked in a tremulous voice. "Yes,

sir. He is, sir. Who shall I say is calling?"

"I am Lord Thraxton." He produced a card from his jacket pocket and presented it to her.

The woman took the card and stared at it, her eyes stumbling over the elaborate typeface.

"And what is your name, my dear?"

The girl looked momentarily vacant. "Clara," she suddenly remembered. "Me name is Clara."

"A lovely name. If you would present your master with my card I would be ever so grateful."

Cradling the card in both hands as if it were made of porcelain, Clara stepped back into the house and pushed the door to, leaving a gap. Thraxton could hear the swish of her skirts as she rushed away. From deep within the house he caught the murmur of voices—a woman's, evidently Clara's, that was barely audible and the booming resonance of a male voice in response. Then he heard footsteps on floorboards—the forceful, unhurried tread of a large man.

Thraxton took a step backward as the door swung inward and Robert Greenley stepped out. It was the first time he had seen the gardener up close—during their first encounter Thraxton had been running away. Greenley was a big man, an inch taller than Thraxton, and broad with it. In his late fifties, he was mostly bald on top. The hair at the sides of his head was silver and seemed to flow evenly into the sideburns that ran down either side of his face and stopped level with his square jaw. The glittering violet eyes were narrowed suspiciously, the small mouth pursed in a sucked-in expression. The long nose had an off-center tilt and was as crooked as a country lane: testament that it had been broken more than once. The expression on the severe face was of mistrustful alertness. Greenley's eyes moved swiftly over Thraxton's face and frame, taking the measure of him.

"Good day, Mister Greenley," Thraxton said pleasantly, lifting his top hat respectfully before settling it back upon his head.

"What is your business, sir?" Mister Greenley demanded in blunt tones.

"I happened to chance upon an item of apparel which I believe belongs to your... ahem... *daughter?*" The last word Thraxton phrased as a question.

At the mention of the word "daughter," Greenley's eyes widened, his lips parting slightly.

Thraxton reached into the top pocket of his frock coat and drew out the black lace glove Algernon had discovered at Highgate. He handed the glove to Mister Greenley. From the flash of his eyes it was obvious the gardener recognized it.

"Where did you get this?" Greenley's tone was both suspicious and hostile.

He had been ready to tell Mister Greenley the full story of how he came to find the glove, but the man's combative tone made Thraxton change his mind. Regrettably, he decided to lie. "I found it... in the park."

"Park? Which park?"

"Which park?" Thraxton repeated. He furrowed his brow as if struggling to remember. "I believe... I believe it was Hyde Park—"

"You are a liar! My daughter has never been in Hyde Park! Or any other park! How is it that you claim to know my daughter?"

Thraxton was caught off-guard by the vehemence of Greenley's demeanor.

"I... well, I don't know her... exactly—"

"And yet you have her glove?" Greenley roared. He had merely glanced at the calling card without reading it, but now his eyes narrowed as he recognized Thraxton from the imbroglio in the Palm House at Kew. "Wait! I know you now. You are Lord Thraxton, the infamous blackguard and seducer. And I think you know me, sir. How dare you come to my house claiming to know my daughter!"

Thraxton was just opening his mouth to try and explain further when Greenley lunged forward and drove his fist into Thraxton's stomach, doubling him over and sending him tumbling down the front steps. Thraxton didn't have time to count them, but they were marble and sharp-edged and left bruises from his shoulder blade to his hip. He landed sprawled on the pavement at the bottom of the steps. His top hat flew off and rolled into the street, where it was crushed beneath the wheels of a passing omnibus.

Mister Greenley stood at the top of the steps, glaring down at the prostrate figure of Thraxton, his face flushed purple, hands balled into trembling fists. "If you ever darken my door again, Lord or no Lord, I will thrash you within an inch of your life!"

And with that Mister Greenley stormed back into the house and slammed the door with a boom like cannon fire.

Harold had watched the whole episode from the driver's seat of the brougham, and now he jumped down and rushed to help his master who was slowly and painfully picking himself up from the pavement.

"Lord Thraxton, sir!"

"Yes, I'm quite all right. Don't fuss, Harold." Thraxton straightened up, wincing as he rubbed his stomach.

"He's a fighter, that one," Harold said. "Former pro, I'd say. Didja see the way he threw that punch?"

"I more than saw, Harold... I felt."

Harold dodged into the road to snatch up Thraxton's top hat before it could be run over a second time. He handed the hat to his master, who looked at it askance. The wheel of the bus had flattened the hat and very nearly cut it in two. Ruined. Thraxton looked up at the front of the Georgian house as a movement in one of the top windows caught his eye. A dark crack appeared in the curtain as someone on the third floor looked down at him. Thraxton returned the stare. The window was so dark he could not see a face, but the small pale hand holding the curtain aside was clearly a woman's. The observer must have realized that she, in turn, was being observed, for suddenly the hand jerked away and the curtain fell shut again.

Thraxton took in the top rooms of Greenley's house. All

the windows of the uppermost floor were tightly curtained against the light. It must be dark as night inside, he reasoned. His attention was drawn to the house next door, separated from Greenley's by a narrow ginnel. His eyes trailed along the side of the building to the roof. A mere ten feet separated the two buildings.

A lesser man might have decided to go home and nurse his bruises, but Thraxton had been thrown from horses a hundred times before. He knew the quickest way to recover was to ignore the pain, climb back into the saddle, grit one's teeth—and take another thrashing.

Thraxton handed his crushed hat to Harold.

"Is we goin' home, sir?"

"You are. Take the brougham. I shall be returning by cab."

"Shall I tell Aggie to lay on the supper?"

"No, I have matters to attend to. I may be home quite late."

As Harold drove away in the brougham, Thraxton stepped up to the front door of the neighboring house and knocked several times. There was a brief delay and then the door was opened by a stout man in his forties with curly black hair and waxed mustachios. The man had evidently been eating his dinner when Thraxton knocked, for he had a bib tucked into the neck of his shirt and his tongue was chasing an errant chunk of potato around his lips as he opened the door.

"Good day," Thraxton said pleasantly.

"What might I do for you, sir?"

"I'd like to rent your room, my good man," Thraxton said.

The man frowned in confusion. "I'm sorry, sir, but we have no room to let."

Thraxton was quite undeterred by the news. He pointed to the upper right-hand room with his walking stick.

"That room there. The top one."

The eyes of the baffled homeowner followed the point of Thraxton's walking stick almost against his will. He looked back at Thraxton. From the cut of his clothes, he appeared to be a gentleman, yet he was acting like a madman.

"I assure you, sir," the man continued to protest, "you are mistaken. We have no room to let."

Thraxton produced his purse and began counting out shillings and sixpences.

"Just for the one night," Thraxton continued cheerfully. "That's all."

"But, sir," the man continued, then stopped. There were an awful lot of coins in the gentleman's hand and he continued to count out more. Still, he was not running a lodging house.

"It's like I keep telling you. We have no…" The man's eyes were drawn back down to the coins that continued to spill from the purse into Thraxton's open palm. "…rooms to—" The man stopped. There must have been a pound's worth of coins in the stranger's hand. He cleared his throat.

"The, uh… the room at the top was it, sir?"

The homeowner opened the door and Thraxton strode into the top bedroom. Clothing hung in an open armoire.

Hairbrushes, tonics, and other personal effects of a male persuasion lay scattered upon a cheap dresser.

"I'll have the belongings moved out for you, sir." The homeowner beamed. He had ten shillings and sixpence in his hip pocket. And all for a single night's occupancy of his worthless brother-in-law's room.

"That won't be necessary," Thraxton said. "I shan't actually be requiring the use of the inside of the room." He walked across the small bedroom to the window, threw up the casement, and clambered out onto the roof.

"But... but that's the roof, sir!"

Thraxton stuck his head back inside the window. "Yes," he agreed. "And this will do quite nicely. Close the door on the way out, will you? There's a good chap."

Thoroughly bemused, the homeowner let himself out, carefully closing the door behind him. Suddenly the seven pounds, two shillings and sixpence in his hip pocket seemed unimportant, as he began to fear he had let a lunatic into his house. He stood on the landing uncertain of what to do. What if the man intended to kill himself by throwing himself from the roof? Worse still, what if the man refused to come down?

17

The Night Garden

Thraxton crouched on the rooftop smoking a cigar—his last. Three hours had passed and the sun was beginning to sink low over the church spires and rooftops of London. From his lofty perch, the entire city lay spread out before him. Steam ships churned up the Thames, black smoke pluming from their funnels. Meanwhile the chimneys atop thousands of rooftops fumed as people arrived home from work and lit their evening fires. Lamp lighters moved slowly up the streets, trailing behind them a glowing necklace of amber light. For ten minutes the wind picked up, swirling. Hot ash and cinders stung his eyes. And then the wind gusted and died as the day breathed out its last gasp and fell into a sudden slumber with the onset of twilight.

Through all the hours of Thraxton's vigil, the black curtains of the third floor windows had not stirred. Now the ruddy glow of a coal fire throbbed in the front parlor windows. Thraxton could smell dinners cooking on stovetops—bacon frying, cabbages boiling—and his stomach growled. His knees were beginning to cramp. He stood up and tossed the butt of his cigar away, watching it meteor to the street below in a sputtering of sparks. The day had been remarkably balmy for England in mid-September, but as the enflamed lids of cloud closed upon the sun's fiery eye, the temperature plummeted and a chill crept through his clothes.

Just five minutes, Thraxton told himself. *Five more minutes and I shall quit this vigil.*

He sat down again to wait. The five minutes dragged, the minute hand of his pocket watch slumping forward leadenly. Then, breaking his promise to himself, he waited another five minutes. Nothing. It was time to go. He stood up, legs throbbing as the blood rushed back in.

And then, on the rooftop opposite, a stairwell door opened and a diminutive figure stepped out. It was a woman, dressed in a black lace dress that reached to her feet. Her hands were hidden under black lace gloves, the face concealed behind a black veil set within a deeply cowled bonnet. Even so, the figure was clearly feminine and instantly recognizable as that which he had mistaken for a spirit in the gloom of Highgate Cemetery.

"My dark angel!"

At his shout, the figure spun around.

"You are real then. I had feared you were but a phantasm of my cracked skull. Will you not speak?"

The figure in black dithered, clearly torn between retreating to the stairwell or escaping to the nearby greenhouse.

"Please! To hear your voice is all I ask."

The cowl turned toward him, but in its shadowed depths, Thraxton could not discern any human feature. Yet it was clear the figure was looking straight at him. He knew the hesitation might last only seconds. If the figure retreated behind the stairwell door, he might never see her again. He walked down the slippery slope of the tiles to the edge of the roof. Ten feet of empty air separated the two buildings. He glanced down. The alleyway between the two buildings formed a gloomy chasm: a spine-shattering plunge of maybe sixty feet to the cobbles below.

I can jump it, Thraxton thought.

When he looked up again the figure had turned and had one hand on the doorknob of the stairwell door. He must act quickly.

Thraxton backed up several paces, then took three running steps and leapt into space. He was an athletic man and the gap was one he could normally have jumped easily, but the roof slates were slick with moss and years of accumulated soot, and so his foot slipped as he drove off. Instantly, he knew he was not going to make the distance. Feet and arms windmilling, he barely made the edge of the adjacent roof, slamming down hard on the tiles, then slid off the steep pitch, and just managed to save himself by grabbing the rain guttering, which left him dangling, legs kicking sixty feet from the cobblestones below.

The female figure screamed, "Dear God, sir! You will fall to your death!"

"Ah," Thraxton said. "Now she speaks!"

Arms trembling, Thraxton threw one leg up onto the tiles and strained to pull himself up. But under his weight, the rusted iron brackets holding the guttering began to bend. *Now would not be an opportune moment to die, Geoffrey,* he thought as he grappled for a handhold on the slippery tiles. His fingertips caught a tiny ridge, and as he heaved himself up onto the roof, the brackets snapped and a long section of guttering tore loose and fell, tumbling end over end and crashed down into the alleyway below.

Thraxton lay on his back, breathing hard. The cowled woman stood over him, a hand held to her unseen mouth. *Not the most heroic entrance, Geoffrey, but at least you are alive.* "My dark angel," Thraxton said, tottering to his feet. Up close, she was very petite. He was a good head and shoulders taller than her. "Once again, I have crossed the abyss of death to reach you—"

"Shhh!" the woman said. She grabbed Thraxton's hand, led him to the greenhouse door and pulled him inside. In one stride they stepped from the chill and smoke of London into tropical air perfumed by flowers. He watched as she moved unerringly through darkness he could barely see in, lighting candle lanterns. As their glow spread, he found himself inside a miniature of the Palm House at Kew. Large palms spread their fronds against the glass ceiling. Blooms of every hue drooped atop their stems. Around them, the air thrummed with flitting shapes: huge moths that swooped about their heads. A few landed on their shoulders, skittered here and there, antennae quivering, then fluttered away again.

"How remarkable!" Thraxton said.

"This is my Night Garden. My father made it for me." She took his hand and led him deeper. "We must be very quiet. My father does not allow gentlemen callers. He would be vexed if he discovered you were here. But then I fear you already know something of my father's anger."

"Yes." Thraxton placed a hand on his sore abdomen and grimaced. "Your father is a man of very few words but very hard fists."

At the back of the greenhouse was a small sitting area with two chairs arranged face to face on either side of a wrought-iron table. Nearby was a day bed, the sheets rumpled, making it clear that someone slept there.

The woman indicated that Thraxton should sit and then dropped into the other chair. For once, the normally voluble Thraxton found himself at a loss for words. It was difficult to think of how to commence a conversation with an enigmatic stranger whose cowled face he could not see. She seemed to sense his unease and broke the silence. "I... am grateful to you, sir... for saving me from those ruffians. I feel I must repay you somehow."

"To see your face is the only reward I would wish for."

The cowl dipped demurely. "Perhaps I am ugly. Perhaps it would prove a scant reward."

Thraxton leaned toward her in his chair. "No, I have seen your face, if only briefly. Since then it is the last thing I see before falling asleep. The first thing upon awakening. Might not I share that vision once again?"

A slight shake of the cowl indicated *no*.

Disappointed, Thraxton settled back in his seat. *Patience, Geoffrey. This bird is easily startled.*

"Might I at least know your name?"

"My name is Aurelia."

The string of airy vowels struck his ear like music. He rose from his chair, bowed slightly and reached for her hand.

"Aurelia, I am Geoffrey."

She hesitated, and then offered her hand. Thraxton took it lightly and kissed the black lace fingers of her glove. As his lips came away, he felt a slight tremor run through her. The cowl dipped again, bashfully, and he could tell that she was delighted to be treated so decorously. He released her hand and took his seat again.

"Tell me, Aurelia, have you always had the power to capture men's hearts?"

At his words, she leapt to her feet in agitation and moved quickly to the glass, looking out over London.

Too much, Geoffrey, he thought. *Slowly. Slowly.*

By now, the sun was the orangey tip of a hot poker dipping in the Thames with an almost perceptible sizzle. Instantly, twilight surrendered to night as the smoky skies of London sponged up the last of the light. An unlit candle lantern sat atop the iron table between the two chairs and now Aurelia produced a box of matches and he heard the rasp of a match being struck. She lifted the glass of the candle lantern, lit the wick, and then carefully lowered the glass shade.

"The moths in my Night Garden are my butterflies. They pollinate the flowers but I must be careful with the lanterns. Moths are drawn to the flame but they are consumed by its slightest touch."

"Are we any different?" Thraxton asked. "For we are drawn to the light of one another. And is love not a form of burning?"

Aurelia set the matches down atop the table and sank back into her seat. "People die. Love endures… immortal."

"I mean love as a death of the self. For in love, both man and woman die and are born again into each other." When he spoke of such things, Thraxton genuinely meant them, even though he had seldom in his life ever practiced such lofty ideals. Yet his words seemed to touch Aurelia, and for a moment she became very still.

"Please, sir, turn away."

Although puzzled, Thraxton complied with her request. He fixed his gaze on one of the tightly furled blooms growing in the flower bed next to where they sat. From behind he heard the rustle of veil and hood being removed.

After a moment's delay, she said, "You may look now."

Thraxton turned back his gaze. Aurelia was just settling her long auburn hair upon her shoulders. Even in the warm yellow glow of the candle lanterns she was ethereally pale, but strikingly beautiful. His eyes moved raptly over her face, taking in the fine features: the high cheekbones, the full lips, the startling violet eyes. Her skin seemed as translucent as parchment; a blue vein pulsed in her temple as if her skin were a thin envelope straining to hold the life pulsing inside. But what might have been an imperfection in another woman merely added to her exotic appeal. Even Thraxton, who had gorged himself on beauty over the years, was astonished.

"You say nothing, sir. Am I that ugly?"

Thraxton cleared his throat. "Now I know why the moth throws himself willingly upon the flame."

Her eyes darted away, suddenly shy again, but the smile betrayed her pleasure at the compliment. "Look!" she whispered and nodded at something.

With difficulty, Thraxton tore his eyes away to follow her gaze. Beyond the glass, a full moon rose dripping from the Thames, setting the river alight with silver fire. A quiver of movement pulled his attention lower, and Thraxton saw what Aurelia was really referring to.

In their flowerbeds, Thraxton recognized the white blooms of an exotic flower that he and Algernon had discovered at Highgate. Even as he watched, the flower was unfurling, opening. Thraxton had never witnessed such a phenomenon, and when he turned his astonished gaze back to Aurelia, he saw her eyes wide with delight.

"My father created them for my Night Garden. He wanted to name them after me, but I call them my Night Angels, for they bloom by moonstroke."

Her eyes flickered up to meet his and Thraxton could not

stop himself from falling into the depths of the violet pools. But the hunger of his gaze made Aurelia look away. "You are staring, sir. It is impolite."

"Forgive me, but I want to hold this moment in my mind forever."

"Your words… they are like a poem."

"Indeed, I have some pretensions in that direction." *God, destroy me now with a bolt of lightning and sweep away my ashes with her hair.*

She searched for something on the floor beside her chair and offered it to him: a small, leather-bound volume. Thraxton opened the book to where a silk tassel split the pages. As his eyes scanned the first line, he recognized the poem.

"Browning?"

"'Porphyria's Lover,'" Aurelia said, suddenly a breathless young girl. "Do you know it?"

Thraxton could not hide the stab of jealousy at her gushing over another poet's work.

"Yes. One of Browning's less tedious efforts."

The black silk dress rustled as she shifted excitedly in her seat. Her eyes flashed with an excitement that made him catch his breath. "I think it is wonderful!"

"A strange choice for one of your sex. A woman visits her lover and he strangles her with a rope of her own hair."

"Oh, but it is soooooooooooo romantic!"

Thraxton laughed. Her girlish delight was infectious. At the same moment he tingled with an electric shock of surprise. He felt more than attraction to her beauty. More than lust for her body. He wanted to know her. To become part of her mysterious world.

"Why do you think he kills her?" she asked.

The question caught him off guard and he realized with chagrin that he had read the poem without ever really trying to analyze it, but sitting in this fantastical greenhouse, with this fantastical young lady, the reason seemed suddenly obvious. When he answered, he was surprised to find his voice quavering with emotion.

"I think… I think he kills her because at that moment he is certain with every atom of his being of his absolute love for her…" Thraxton's voice trailed off to a whisper and she was leaning forward in her chair to catch his words. "…and her absolute love for him." His voice broke on the last word and he had to swallow before he could continue. "By killing her, he seeks to freeze that moment—the happiest moment of his life—forever."

A knot of silence tightened, drawing their faces closer together. He became aware of everything: the moths perched in her hair like living brooches. The imperceptible respiration of the flowers. The pulse of his heart and of hers, smaller, quicker. The moment ripened around them.

I must kiss her. I must kiss her now!

Had she been any other woman, he would have seized her, ravished her, but something held him back. The moment was fragile as spun glass. A breath could shatter it.

"Aurelia!" A man's voice called from someplace far away, far below. "Aurelia, are you up there?"

Her eyes widened with fear. "My father! He must not find you!"

Moths scattered in a burst of wingbeats as she seized his hand and hurried him to the door. As they stepped out of the conservatory, the chill night air was like a slap of reproach.

"It seems I must leap again."

"No! You must not!"

"Aurelia, are you up there?" Robert Greenley's voice ascended before him up the throat of the stairwell. He was close—nearly at the top of the stairs. She pulled him behind a chimney stack that marked the common wall shared between the Greenley house and its neighbor.

"Stay here!" she said. "My father brings tea up to me at this hour. You must wait until he enters the conservatory, then go straight down the stairs. The front door is directly opposite. Clara, our maid is about. You must not let her see you or she'll be sure to tell my father."

With that, Aurelia rushed back inside the conservatory. The door had barely closed before the stairwell door barged open and Greenley backed through it, carrying a tray clattering with a pot of tea and two china cups. Thraxton ducked into the shadows of the chimney stack and listened until he heard the conservatory door bump shut. Without looking he slipped into the stairwell and was halfway down the staircase when he almost collided with a young and rather harried-looking young woman trudging up the stairs—Clara, the maid. For a moment the two stood gawping at each other. Clara, frightened to see a strange man coming down the stairs, dropped the basket of washing she was carrying and put her hands to her mouth.

Thraxton had been caught in flagrante before and quickly hit upon a course of action. His fingers dipped into the pockets of his waistcoat and he drew out a gold sovereign. Clara's eyes saucered as he pressed the heavy coin into her hand. Putting a finger to his lips he whispered, "Shuussssssh," gave her a conspiratorial wink, then pushed past and trotted down the stairs as if nothing were amiss.

Clara watched him go and then looked again at the gold coin in her hand. It winked golden in the light as she turned it over. A sovereign! As a maid-of-all-work in a less-than-illustrious household, she commanded an income of only seven pounds a year. To be a given a golden sovereign, a seventh of her yearly income, in one fell swoop was dizzying. Clara gaped at the coin in her hand and looked up the stairs her master had just climbed a moment before. Then she slipped the coin into the pocket of her pinny, hefted her basket of clean laundry, and plodded on up the stairs.

Thraxton let himself out of the front door of Greenley's house, skipped down the steps he had been knocked down just a few hours earlier, and ran out into the street, oblivious to the shouts of the cab driver that nearly ran him over. He threw one last laughing look up at the rooftop, and then swaggered away up the street.

18

LOST IN THE MIASMA

On the first week of October, a trough of stagnant air clamped a bowl of cold air over London so that the smoke belching from thousands of chimney stacks rose into the skies until it hit the tops of the clouds and could rise no further. In the days that followed the bowl filled with more and more smoke, until the fog and smoke coalesced into a choking gray shroud that smothered London from east to west, north to south. So thick was the fog that gas lights in the shops and streets had to be lit three hours earlier than usual. In the weird world of eternal twilight, the people of London carried on as best they could, although at times the fog thickened until it congealed into a sulfurous, gritty murk sometimes brown, sometimes reddish-yellow, at other times a sickly shade of green that dimmed the beams of coach lights and gas lamps and slowed traffic first to a walking pace, and then to a crawl as coaches and omnibuses had to be led by men carrying torches. Finally, everything stuttered to a halt as the fog tightened around the city's throat like a silk scarf in a strangler's hands.

Theaters closed. Railways stopped. Law courts recessed. Commerce ceased.

Shops remained dark because shop assistants could not get to work. The blind now led the sighted, for the only way to navigate the streets was by the tapping of a white cane, a hand fumbling along a cinderous brick wall.

On the worst day of the fog, Doctor Garrette left his office on Hogarth Road to walk to the home of Augustus Skinner on Holland Park Avenue. It was not an hour past noon and already it was dark. Fog seethed and boiled along the empty streets. A rain of soot sifted down from clouds too bloated to hold any more. Even indoors, with windows and doors shut tight, people wheezed and gagged. To filter the air, Doctor Garrette breathed through a white handkerchief folded over his mouth, held in place by a long silk scarf wound three times around his head. Along the route he tramped past horseless, abandoned omnibuses and carriages, through streets illuminated only vaguely by the feeble yellow flicker of streetlamps straining to push back the darkness.

Only seldom did he encounter other living beings. Crossing Cromwell Road, he passed a gang of Irish navvies: grubby-faced laborers in filthy work clothes. They shambled past in single file, each with a hand on the shoulder of the man in front, a pick or shovel thrown over the other. The fog here was so dense that neither the front of the line nor the end was visible. In the murk the men appeared like lost souls damned to the underworld, on their way to dig down to an even deeper level of hell.

On Wrights Lane, he collided with a tubercular street urchin, shoeless, feet bare to the ankles; the boy, scarcely nine years old, walked hunched over with pain, puffing on the dog-end of a cigarette filched from the gutter, the small body wracked now and then by a cough like broken glass shaken in a sack. "Spare a farthing, guvnor?"

Dr. Garrette eyed the boy critically: the bony cheeks, the haunted eyes staring from the dark caverns of his eye sockets. The street-Arab's disease was far advanced; he would be dead within a few days. Money, succor, pity were all futile. With an unsentimentality learned in the hospital tents of Crimea, the doctor turned his face away and kept walking.

On he strode in a silence so uncanny it was hard to believe that an invisible metropolis sprawled for miles around him. As he turned onto Holland Park Avenue his foot skidded in a pile of something wet and soft and he nearly fell. He stopped, removed a soot-speckled white glove, wiped a finger along the side of his shoe and brought it up to his nose, sniffing: excrement, not horse manure, but human. He flicked the ordure from his finger and slipped the glove back on.

"Come!"

The bedroom door opened and Silas Garrette entered, a whiff of brimstone fog creeping in with him.

"Doctor... thank the Lord!"

He stepped to the bedside and stood looking down at Augustus Skinner through his rose-tinted pince-nez. The Blackwell's critic lay in an untidy heap, the tangle of bedclothes flung aside, his face flushed and sweaty. On the bedside table an uncorked bottle of laudanum lay on its side like an expression of utter emptiness. "You are no better?"

"No. I am burning with fever and the pain... it throbs so. I have not slept in two days."

"The laudanum did not help?"

"Yes, but it's gone. I need more. I must have more laudanum. Quickly!"

Dr. Garrette settled his Gladstone bag on the bedside table and opened it. He reached in and took out a slender bottle of smoky glass stoppered with a cork, set it down on the table and then rummaged some more and produced its twin. "I have but two bottles left—"

"I'll take them both!"

The doctor pondered deeply on this as he stroked the bottle with slender fingers that seemed long enough to sport a fourth joint. "A tincture of laudanum of this strength is difficult to procure, especially now with the fog. The trains do not run. Even horse-drawn carts make no deliveries to the apothecaries."

"It's about the money, is it? How much do you want?"

The doctor quickly muttered the price.

Augustus Skinner spluttered, choking on his indignation. "That's triple what I paid you before!"

The doctor's lips pursed as if he had just licked a rusty

nail. He replaced the bottles in his bag and snapped it shut. "I have walked a quarter mile in the worst London fog," he said. "If my professional services are no longer needed…"

And with that he turned to leave.

"NO! Wait. Please, please. I am not myself. The pain. My mind is clouded." Skinner nodded at the chest of drawers. "There's money in the top drawer."

"Very good," the doctor murmured. He opened the bag and set two bottles of laudanum atop the table then took out a leather holster of instruments. "If you would turn over."

Augustus Skinner groaned then howled as Doctor Garrette drew the scalpel through the infection once again to lance it, only this time he removed his glove and probed the finger with which he had wiped the filth from his shoe into the wound, pushing it deep until it touched the pistol ball he claimed to have removed a week before. By the time he had finished redressing the wound, Skinner was shivering with agony. Garrette handed him the bottle of laudanum and Skinner gulped down several large draughts. Within minutes he was woozy and delirious as the laudanum took effect.

Dr. Garrette opened the drawer of the dresser. Inside he counted out forty pounds, a considerable sum.

As he stepped back out the front door, Silas Garrette found the fog's clammy embrace cozy and soothing. He had taken but half the money in the top drawer—twenty pounds—folded the large notes in half and placed them in his Gladstone bag. Best not to be greedy. He had his children to consider, but he would have the rest and more in time.

There would be more visits, many more. As a medical man it was his professional opinion that Mr. Skinner's recovery would take a long time.

A very long time, indeed.

19

THE SURPRISE GUEST

It was just eleven o'clock the next morning when Thraxton's blue brougham drew up outside the row of Georgian houses on Warwick Square where his friend Mister Algernon Hyde-Davies resided. In particularly lively spirits, Thraxton sprang from the carriage before it had come to a complete halt, dashed up the front steps and gave the brass knocker an over-ebullient thrashing. After an inexcusably long pause, the door was opened by Horace Claypole, a callow youth who served as Algernon's butler, footman, and valet. Horace had been en route between the kitchen and parlor when Thraxton began knocking and he still balanced a large tray of petit fours in one hand.

"Hello, Horace," Thraxton chirped good-naturedly and barged past the surprised and rather slow-witted Horace, stealing a petit four and cramming the entire confection into his mouth. He breezed toward the parlor doors before the servant had a chance to detain him.

"But, Lord Thraxton," Horace blubbered, stumbling after. "Should I not announce, you?"

"Mmmn, no need," Thraxton mumbled around a vanilla crème and flaky pastry. "I shall announshh myshelf."

"B-but, s-sir!"

It was too late; Thraxton flung wide the double parlor doors and swept inside. "Algy," he mumbled, spitting crumbs. "I have the besht newsh—" Thraxton froze in mid-chew, stunned to find that his friend was entertaining company and even more stunned to discover who that company was: Constance Pennethorne and her limpet-like escorts, Mister and Mrs. Wakefield. As Thraxton burst in upon them, the conversation shriveled and died mid-sentence and now all eyes turned upon the stunned lord and the flummoxed Horace, who cringed in the hallway behind him.

Tongue working frantically, Thraxton choked down the rest of the petit four. "Ah… you are entertaining. I didn't realize. I beg your indulgence…" Thraxton's eyes roved around the room. The Wakefields looked mildly surprised. But Constance Pennethorne and Algernon both wore the guilty expressions of conspirators caught plotting treason. For his part, Thraxton's face reddened as he realized he had just committed yet another social blunder. "I, puh-please, I," he stammered. "Forgive my intrusion. I… I should come back another time." He bowed dramatically to all present and took a step backward, closing the doors after him, an act that made him look and feel like the mechanical bird in a cuckoo clock.

No one in the parlor spoke of Thraxton's dramatic appearance and even more dramatic disappearance. Algernon had a cup of tea balanced on his knee, a marzipan in his hand that he was just about to take a bite out of when his friend had burst into the room. Forgetting the tea, he leaped to his feet dumping a full cup of Darjeeling onto the Persian rug. He looked down distractedly at the broken china and steaming puddle, then ran after Thraxton, the cake still clutched in his hand.

Algernon rushed down the hall to the front door, dodging around the slow-witted Horace, who was still lurking. But by the time he snatched the door open, Thraxton's brougham was pulling away.

Blast, Algernon thought. *Now I've done it!*

When Doctor Garrette snatched open the office door in response to the indefatigable knocking, Death hovered on the threshold. Or, at least, Death's ambassador: an undertaker in full regalia—black top hat and frock coat—a slender figure wrapped in black crepe and slathered with the lugubrious air that is a requisite of the trade.

The doctor had been *relaxing* in his closet and his mind had not yet fully surfaced from its chloroform stupor. He recognized the figure instantly, but his tongue lolled clumsily in his mouth.

"Doctor Garrette," the undertaker said.

"Dear, dear me!" Suddenly, a round, fat face squeezed in beneath the undertaker's arm: Mrs. Parker, the landlady. "An undertaker at your door, Doctor Garrette! I do hope nothing is amiss with your family?"

"Um, no, nothing of the kind," Garrette said, dragging his voice from its hiding place in the shadows. *Damn the woman!*

"A patient, then?" Mrs. Parker wheedled. "An unfortunate outcome to one of your treatments? I understand, even the best of doctors can only do so much when it comes to matters of mortality—"

"It is nothing," Garrette began, his voice choked with exasperation to be rid of the over-inquisitive nuisance. "A private matter. Good day, Mrs. Parker." And with that he gripped the undertaker's shoulder, yanked him inside, and slammed the door in his landlady's face.

As soon as he had the undertaker to himself, Garrette rounded upon him. "I told you to never come here in person!"

The undertaker's grim-faced countenance never wavered. "I sent a boy three times to your door. He knocks but receives no reply. Perhaps, on future occasions, I should send him round with a note—"

"No! No notes. Nothing written. I have expressly told you so!"

"Then how, pray tell, am I to communicate with you?"

As he struggled for an answer, Garrette threw a quick glance back at the door to the inner room. To his relief, it was shut. He had remembered to close the door behind him. But what if the children began to call? He must be rid of the undertaker as quickly as possible. When he looked back, Garrette was alarmed to see that the undertaker's eyes had followed his gaze to the door of his cupboard and lingered upon it, clearly speculating as to what lay inside. His heart kicked in his chest. "What is it?" he snarled. "What have you come for?"

The undertaker dragged his gaze from the door and met Garrette's beady eyes. "My fee. The duel for which I recommended your services as attending physician. We had an agreement."

"Yes."

"The gentleman was wounded but survived."

"Yes."

"Therefore, he is still your patient."

"He is."

"Three pounds was the sum we settled upon."

It was a lie: two pounds was the actual sum, but Garrette was frantic to be rid of the man. He snatched his Gladstone bag from the desk and opened it. As he did so the bank notes he had taken from Augustus Skinner's top drawer spilled onto the floor. Garrette swooped down and snatched them up, but the undertaker clearly saw the notes and could likely guess their denomination by their size.

"It appears your practice is very profitable at the moment," the undertaker said. "Clearly the gentleman requires a great deal of doctoring. Yet it looked as if he received but a simple flesh wound."

Silas Garrette's hands trembled with rage as he jammed

the bills back inside his black bag. He peeled off a single bill—five pounds, he had nothing smaller—and dangled the note for the undertaker.

"Take it and go."

The undertaker plucked the bill from Garrette's hand, folded it carefully, and slipped it into a pocket. The ghost of a smirk rippled across his features for an instant before his face resettled into the placid lake of mournful sobriety. "I shall trouble you no more, then." And with that he turned to go. But as he palmed the doorknob, he paused and turned back to the doctor.

"Ah, there is some other business."

"What?" Garrette snapped.

"A duel. Tomorrow morning at dawn. The usual place, Wimbledon Common. Once again the seconds have asked me to provide an attending doctor. Are you free... or shall I find another physician?"

Garrette's hatred for the man was temporarily eclipsed by the greed that flared in his chest.

"No. Yes. That is, I shall be there."

"Good. Then we must hope for a happy outcome. Perhaps one duelist will die and the other be grievously wounded, so that we may both profit equally."

Silas Garrette said nothing as the office door opened and he watched the back of Death's ambassador step through it. He banged the door shut after him and turned the key in the lock, securing the door. He detested the fact that he was reliant upon the undertaker. Involving another in his affairs always posed a risk, and yet he needed another source of income—and soon.

Augustus Skinner was clearly about to take a turn for the worse.

20

LORD OF THE UNDERWORLD

" If your nightmare had a nightmare, it would look like Mordecai Fowler," that was how the saying went in the Seven Dials Rookery.

The "rookeries" were underworld strongholds, slum-land enclaves inhabited by entire communities of criminals and their women and children. Rookeries existed in virtually every large city, including Manchester, Liverpool, Birmingham, and especially London, which was home to several. The most notorious of these was the Seven Dials, a squalid huddle of smoking chimneys and grime-blackened buildings that seemed to have been formed of filth and soot. Snaking through the Seven Dials was a labyrinth of narrow alleyways that wound through a dismal clutter of shabby forecourts, decrepit tenements, dilapidated warehouses, and abandoned factories.

The eastern boundary of the Seven Dials was marked

by a narrow canal the locals called "Filthy Ditch." It had originally been a tidal stream, but now was little more than an open sewer, for it was used by the inhabitants of the rookery as a place to dump all their unwanteds: old rags, rubbish, rotting food, dead animals, human excrement, and the occasional abortion. In summer, the reek from Filthy Ditch often drifted as far as the Houses of Parliament where ministers, confronted by a symptom of urban blight too noisome even for them to ignore, would resolve to forward a motion to appoint a committee to conduct a study to look into cleaning up the ditch. But then the summer recess would begin, the members would return home to their constituencies in the countryside, and the matter would be quietly forgotten.

Guarded by ferocious guard dogs and gangs of club-wielding thugs, rookeries such as the Seven Dials were too dangerous even for London's Metropolitan Police force to enter, except in large numbers and heavily armed. Even then, the prospect of actually catching a criminal once hidden in the warren of buildings was slim, for the denizens of the rookery had cut hidden escape hatches and doors through walls and ceilings, into cellars and out of roofs. At the first blast of a Peeler's whistle, a fugitive could flee through a maze of secret passageways, skylights, manholes, trap doors, tunnels, cellars and hidden entrances and exits. Because of the danger, and the meager chance of actually making an arrest, the police shunned entering such places except under the most exceptional circumstances.

If it was dangerous for the police, then it was doubly so for the honest citizenry. Anyone foolish enough to enter the rookeries would be lucky to escape with his life. Once a Protestant missionary, newly returned from spreading The Word amongst the savages in Africa, entered the Seven Dials for the purposes of ministering to the poor. The hapless missionary soon found the natives of the Seven Dials far more savage than any he encountered in the Dark Continent. The women attacked him first, beating him insensible and stripping him naked. When their menfolk arrived, they completed the job by shaving the missionary's head, ramming his mouth full of hot mustard, and hurling him into the reeking canal.

Unlike most of the denizens of the rookeries, Mordecai Fowler was the product of a respectable middle-class family. Few of his childhood memories of that time remained, and those that did were bleak. Fowler's father, a bank officer, suffered from a weakness for the drink. After his drunkenness led to a discrepancy in the books of some thirty shillings (which was never found), he was sacked from the bank and subsequently plunged even more precipitously into the ravages of alcohol. Over the weeks that followed the family's meager savings were exchanged for small glasses of gin which Fowler's father tossed down his throat. Soon little Mordecai, scarcely six at the time, grew accustomed to hiding in the closet under the stairs with his mother while angry creditors pounded their fists upon the door. Mordecai saw his father only infrequently during that period, which was just as well, for on the occasions when he staggered home, drunk and railing, it would end with a beating for Mordecai and his mother, whose loud wailing would go on for hours.

With no money to pay for school, Mordecai was left to his own devices, and spent most of his days running wild on the streets around his home. Mordecai had no friends, and being unnaturally small for his age, soon became the target of local bullies. Soon he began to shun human company and spent most of his time by himself, playing in the alleyways behind his house. Here Mordecai found new friends that he, in turn, could bully—rats. The junior Fowler whiled away many happy hours crucifying them against walls, amputating their arms and legs with an old pair of scissors, or dousing them with paraffin and setting them alight so he could watch them run in wild circles. How their agonized squeals made little Mordecai laugh. His experiments soon diminished the local rat population enough to make them scarce, and then he became the terror of the neighborhood cats and dogs.

But it wasn't just the power of life and death he wielded over the lesser creatures that fascinated little Mordecai. More intoxicating still was his ability to induce suffering. He applied himself to the pursuit of this knowledge with a diligence he had never shown at school. He knew exactly the right size of rock to tie to a cat before he threw it in the canal, so it would frantically paddle for long, agonizing minutes before exhausting itself and being pulled under.

After physics came self-taught lessons in anatomy, as Mordecai knew which tendons to sever so that when he set fire to the dog, its hind legs dragged uselessly as it frantically sought to get away.

By the time he was nine years old, an age at which most middle-class boys were playing with tops, or cantering a broomstick horse up and down the hallways, little Mordecai could have taught the agents of the Inquisition a trick or two.

Then one day the police came to inform Mordecai's mother that her husband's body had been dredged from the canal where he had fallen in a drunken stupor. At the news, Fowler's mother began a keening that continued for days. Once the news of his father's death reached the family's creditors, they descended upon the house like buzzards on carrion, for they knew there was little chance of being paid with the family breadwinner dead.

For Mordecai's mother, the breaking point came when the court-appointed bailiffs entered the house with a warrant to take away the family silver, the only items of value the family still possessed. Shrieking and wailing, she had to be restrained by police officers as bailiffs stuffed the plates, tureens, cutlery, and serving trays into canvas sacks and lugged them out. By this time the house was bare to the floorboards, and Mordecai and his mother were sleeping on bundles of rags. After the episode of the silver, Mordecai's mother fell into a distraction, and wandered the house, moaning and sighing as she wrung an old polishing rag in her hands, her long gray hair hanging down in dishevelment.

Not long after, Mordecai's mother was committed to Bethlem Royal Hospital, after which he never saw her again. With his father dead and his mother asylumed, the house was sold to pay off the voracious creditors and Mordecai was sent to live with a distant uncle. The man was a much-respected and deeply pious church alderman who crept into Mordecai's room by night and sodomized him, then attempted to beat the carnal devil out of the young boy with birch twigs until his buttocks were striped and bleeding.

After six months of this treatment, Mordecai ran away, and became one of the many thousands of urchins living rough on the streets of London. In time, he wandered into the Seven Dials Rookery where he fell in with a gang of pickpockets and became their apprentice. Mordecai proved an adept thief, and as he grew older, progressed in the criminal hierarchy from dip to cracksman, to bully boy and so on up the ladder. Over the years, his innate Machiavellianism showed in a willingness to be more ruthless, despicable, and crueler than all others. By age forty, he had bludgeoned his way to the position of high mobsman, lord of the Seven Dials Underworld. Feared by all, Fowler's word was the closest thing that passed for law in the rookery.

It was still early morning when Mordecai Fowler, Barnabus Snudge, and Walter Crynge materialized from the swirling yellow fog and tromped across the loose planks of a narrow footbridge spanning the reeking ditch that marked entry into the Seven Dials. The mobsmen's luck had not been good that night, and they were returning home with just a handful of shillings bullied from the purses of terrorized Whitechapel whores.

It was dark in the rookery, as all the gas lights had long since been smashed by children whose mothers and fathers took a parental pride in their offspring's wanton vandalism. But despite the gloom and blinding fog, Fowler and his cronies navigated the echoing alleyways with unerring familiarity, and soon arrived at the abandoned three-story factory building that served as Fowler's lair.

This part of the building had once been a match factory. The large, high-ceilinged ground-floor rooms which had been the factory floor were now strewn with abandoned clutter. Narrow, creaking wooden stairways ran up to second and third floors where a warren of small rooms had once functioned as offices for clerks and accountants.

Fowler and his two cronies thundered up the swaying wooden stairs, passed through a darkened empty space, and then climbed another flight of stairs to the third floor loft. The loft had once been the storeroom for the match factory. A few half-empty barrels of tar, sulfur and other materials were scattered here and there, but most anything of value had been hauled out and sold long ago.

It was dark in the loft, except for one corner where stubs of candles guttered on a table around which fifteen or more black silhouettes huddled—more of Fowler's mobsmen betting on a game of dice. Lit by the flickering candlelight, the motley assortment of grizzled, grimy, soot-streaked faces could have belonged to a coven of devils roasting a soul in hell. The men cursed and brayed at each other over the rattle of dice in a cup and the banging down of coins as bets were laid.

"Wot the bleedin' hell are you lot up to?" Fowler bellowed. The men fell silent and cast guilty looks at one another.

"Go to, you lazy layabouts! Get yer arses out o' here. There's pockets to be picked, purses to be cut, mugs to be coshed, mischief to be done."

The game broke up as the men evaporated into the shadows.

Fowler snatched a candle from the table and crossed the floor to a wooden door, which he unlocked with a large iron key. Inside he fired a match with a dirty thumbnail and lit a lantern hanging from the ceiling.

The room had once been the factory manager's office. The hideous oak desk was still there, but in one corner sat a broken-backed bed, an iron-banded trunk fastened with an enormous, rusty padlock, and a sideboard that was the desk's equal in hideousness. Piled atop the sideboard in a careless heap was Fowler's swag: a collection of silverware taken from the many middle-class residences he and his "cracksmen" had burglarized over the years.

Fowler's feet were hot and burning from hours of walking. His throat was parched. Atop the sideboard was a heavy stone jug of water. Fowler hoisted the jug and poured water into a tarnished silver goblet. For all his many vices, because of the ruin that drink had brought upon his family, he had been a strict teetotaler all his life. Despite the metallic taste of the goblet, the water was cool and refreshing in Fowler's mouth and he drained the goblet and filled it again. As he quaffed the second goblet his eyes trailed along the silver strewn across the sideboard: tureens, tankards, serving trays, butter dishes, all of it of the very best quality. He had no love or appreciation of beauty of any kind, but he knew all the hallmarks and could differentiate the good stuff from worthless "tat." This was all the "good stuff."

The cutlery was kept in a cherry and walnut box lined with blue damask, against which the highly polished silverware gleamed brightly. His eyes trailed avariciously across the neat rows of knives, forks, and spoons until they came to an empty space.

Fowler yanked the goblet from his lips. Water ran down his chin and dribbled onto the front of his waistcoat.

An empty space.

In the room outside, the dice players had dispersed, and now five of Fowler's highest ranking mobsmen, his leftenants, sat around the table playing cards. They all looked up, startled, when the office door banged open and Fowler's ominous silhouette choked the open doorway. "Come in here, you lot!" he bellowed. "Crynge and Snudge, too. All of ya."

The leftenants exchanged worried looks as they filed into the room. The High Mobsman stood behind the hideous desk. Crynge and Snudge took up their usual positions to his left and right. "Close the door," Fowler said to the last man in the room. "And lock it up tight."

The mobsman did as he'd been told and joined the others.

For several minutes Fowler said nothing as he stood glaring at the five men assembled on the other side of the table, his protruding lower lip jutting out even further than normal. His bushy mutton-chop whiskers bristled as the muscles in his jowls clenched and unclenched. Fowler was in a black mood—they saw that instantly. And when Mordecai Fowler was in a black mood, someone usually suffered, horribly and painfully.

"Someone's taken somefink wot belongs to me," he said slowly, black eyes moving from one man to the next. "A piece of me silver."

The men exchanged stunned glances. Everyone knew that stealing from Fowler was suicide. Stealing his precious silver went beyond suicide. It was begging for a slow, painful, lingering death.

"Naw," began Tommy Tailor cheerfully, "ain't been stole, Mordecai. You probably just mislaid—"

"AIN'T MISLAID!" Fowler bellowed. "Ain't mislaid," he repeated, his voice lowered to a rumbling threat. "It was took. And by one of you barsterds."

"But wu-wu-wu-we wouldn't take nuffink o' yours," Whitey Smith stammered. "You nu-nu-nu-know that, Mordecai. It's gu-gotta be someone else—"

"Ain't nobody but you five allowed in here!" Fowler yelled. "So it had to be one of you."

"Wot about Crynge and Snudge?" Tailor protested.

"They was wiv me the whole day. So I knows it ain't them. That leaves you five."

Each man blanched as Fowler reached into his coats and drew out a steel spike about eighteen inches long and less than the thickness of a man's little finger with a point sharpened to infinity. Only the tip was a polished silver color. The remainder of the shaft was a dark mottled red that could have been rust or just as easily dried blood. The spike was set in a tortured lump of wormwood that served as a handle and around which Fowler's thick fingers clenched. In the closest he had ever come to humor, Fowler had christened the spike "Mister Pierce." He kept it in a leather scabbard inside one of his coats, and it was his favorite weapon, for it killed not by shock and trauma like a bullet, nor with the artery-severing quickness of a knife blade. Instead the thin, needle-like spike could be thrust through soft tissue and cartilage again and again, causing terrible suffering, but leaving the victim alive and screaming.

"Put your right hands on the table. All of ya."

The men hesitated. No one wanted to be the first.

"NOW!" Fowler bellowed.

The five men leapt forward and placed their right hands, palm down, on the surface of the oak desk.

"Now, you're all gonna swear an oath that it wasn't you wot took my silver." He took a step toward the table. All five men flinched and snatched their hands away.

"I didn't tell ya to move!" Fowler screamed.

The five slowly placed their hands back on the tabletop.

Fowler reached inside his coats again, yanked out a pistol that had been tucked into his pants, and tossed it to Crynge.

"Mister Crynge, the first man wot takes his hand off that table... shoot him dead."

"Right you are, Mister Fowler," Crynge cackled.

The five men watched in growing terror as the cadaverous Crynge drew back the hammer and leveled the pistol at them. Only then did the awful gravity of the situation become apparent.

One of them would not leave the room alive.

"Now, I want you all to repeat after me—" he began, but was interrupted by Tommy Tailor.

"Mister Fowler, you know you can trust us lads." Tailor flashed his gap-toothed grin. "It ain't worth all this bother, now is it? All over a tiny little spoon—"

"Shut yer trap!" he barked. Tommy Tailor dropped his gaze to the table and licked his lips nervously.

"Now," Fowler continued, "repeat after me: I swear—"

"I swear," the men intoned as one.

"On my worthless life—"

"On my worthless life," they echoed.

"That I ain't never stole nuffink from Mordecai Fowler, and I never, ever would."

The men repeated the line, stumbling over the words.

"So 'elp me Gawd."

"So help me God."

"There," Fowler said, lips peeling back from his yellow

tombstone teeth in an approximation of a smile. "That weren't so bad, now wuz it?"

He turned as if to walk away but then pivoted sharply, raised Mister Pierce high over his head, and swung with all his might, driving the spike through the back of Tommy Tailor's hand, pinning it to the tabletop.

Tailor let out an ear-splitting shriek and stared in wide-eyed horror at his impaled hand.

"Spoon?" Fowler bellowed in Tailor's agonized face. "I didn't never say it was a spoon wot was took! I just said it was me silver! Only the thieving rat-barsterd wot took it woulda known that!"

Tommy Tailor crumpled to his knees. Shivering with pain and shock, he tore his gaze from the spike and looked up at Fowler.

"I'm sorry, Mordecai. It was a mistake. Honest. I was just lookin' at it. I wasn't never gonna steal it. Honest I wasn't. Hope to die—"

"Hope to die?" Fowler interrupted. "Oh, you're gonna hope to die, all right. You're gonna hope as hard as you can, Tommy me laddo." He threw a glance at the other four, who had stepped away, cowering, from the table. "Hold 'im!" he barked.

Eager to distance themselves from Tailor's guilt, the four mobsmen rushed forward, seized their former comrade, and dragged him to his feet.

Fowler's huge hands rummaged through Tailor's clothing with bruising thoroughness. They found something in his

inside jacket pocket and yanked it out, holding it up for all
to see. Almost lost in Fowler's swollen fist was a tiny silver
spoon of the kind used for teething babies.

"Wot's this, eh?" Fowler yelled in Tailor's face. "Wot the
bleedin' hell's this?"

"I, I'm sorry, Mordecai!" Tailor stammered. "I'm sorry—"

"You greedy little barsterd!" Fowler spat. "You piece of
filth! You think you can steal from me?"

Fowler looked at the spoon clenched in his massive hand
and a thought occurred to him.

"You want this, eh?" He shook the spoon under Tailor's
nose. "You want it?"

"No! No, I don't want it—" Tailor stammered.

"Well, you can bleedin' well have it!" He yelled at the
four men restraining Tailor, "Hold his head! Hold it tight!"

Fowler grabbed Tailor by the throat and began to squeeze.
When Tailor opened his mouth to breathe, Fowler rammed
the spoon in. As it twisted back and forth, the spoon
broke off Tailor's front teeth. The room filled with horrible
choking as Fowler forced the spoon down his throat. When
the spoon was halfway down his gullet, Fowler grabbed
Tailor's mouth and held it shut with both hands.

"Now swallow it, you vermin! Swallow it!"

Tears of pain and terror poured down Tailor's face as
he somehow managed to swallow the spoon, choking and
gagging the whole time. Fowler let go of his jaws and stepped
away, smiling. Tailor, convulsing and shuddering with pain
and terror, had to be held up or he would have collapsed.

"I'm sorry," Tailor rasped, his voice in ruins as his lacerated throat began to swell.

"Oh, you're sorry now, are ya, Tommy?"

"I'll, I'll make it up to ya. Honest... I... I..." He tried to say more but couldn't get the words out.

"You'll make it up to me, will ya? All right, then." He held out his empty hand to Tailor. "Give us the spoon back and I'll let you off."

Tailor, a broken man, choked out a sob. "I, I, I can't give it back. It's in me belly, ain't it?"

Fowler became suddenly thoughtful. "Oh, I see. You can't give it back because it's in yer belly."

He casually reached down, slid open one of the drawers in the table, and pulled out a large butcher's knife with a ten-inch blade.

"Well, we'll just have to go lookin' for it then, won't we? Only it might take a while, 'cause I ain't no doctor."

As Fowler stumped around the table, he stropped the knife blade up and down the leg of his trousers. At the sight of the butcher's knife, Tailor broke down and started to sob and beg for his life. The other four mobsmen let go and began to ease themselves toward the door.

"Where d'you lot think you're slopin' off to?" Fowler screamed. "Get back here and hold him!"

The gang of stray mobsmen lurking outside the room, eavesdropping, exchanged horrified looks as the first bloodcurdling screams began. After ten minutes, none could stand it any longer and hurried outside. But even in the street, Tommy Tailor's screams could be plainly heard, echoing down the dark, dank alleyways of the rookery. After half an hour the screams subsided into the groans of a damned soul being tortured in the lowest circle of hell. After forty-five minutes they were the convulsive gasps of a soul eager to quit a body that had become a prison of suffering. Then even that stopped and in its place there was an ominous silence.

After an hour, the door burst open and the four survivors of Fowler's inquisition spilled out, eager to distance themselves from the blood-soaked atrocity of torn and mortified flesh splashed across the floorboards. Though they were hard, violent men themselves, many of them accomplished murderers and thugs, all were ashen-faced and trembling at the horrors they had been forced to witness.

Mordecai Fowler sauntered out of the room a few moments later, the front of his clothes spattered in blood and gore. He carefully wiped the sticky slime adhering to the small silver spoon on a rag that had once been a piece of Tommy Tailor's shirt. Then Fowler blew on the spoon until it fogged with his breath and gave it a final polish on his sleeve, smiling at his own upside down reflection in the spoon's tiny bowl.

As Fowler left the room, the four surviving mobsmen exchanged cowed glances. All knew that there was one less devil in hell that night, for he was walking the earth wrapped in the skin of Mordecai Fowler.

21

THE HIGHGATE ANGEL

Once again, Thraxton sat atop the uncomplaining Emily Fitzsimmons. A lantern borrowed from the sexton hissed quietly on the grave slab next to him. Its shifting glow threw Thraxton's eerily stretched shadow thirty feet across the ground, where it broke its back over a row of nearby gravestones. Thraxton looked up into the face of a nearby angel. As the lantern light ebbed and shifted, it gave a mock animation to the statue, which seemed to stir restlessly on its pedestal. Although he was wrapped in a heavy woolen cloak, the stone slab radiated cold through his buttocks and the backs of his legs, and he shivered and pulled the cloak tighter about his shoulders.

In the nearby trees, skeletal and bare, a horned owl dropped from its perch and flapped silent and ghostly through the branch tops until it disappeared. Then a moth flitted from the darkness and swooped in spin-dizzy circles about the lantern. Thraxton reached out and snatched it from the air. Although he tried to hold it fast, the moth wriggled between his fingers, skittered across the back of his hand and fluttered straight up into the night. When Thraxton dropped his gaze from the dark sky, a small figure stood in front of him.

He exclaimed, startled. The figure laughed and pushed back a deep cowl revealing features that by now were etched into Thraxton's being.

Aurelia.

"Strewth! You are as quiet as dust!"

Aurelia smiled, but her eyes were guarded. "I did not know if you would come."

He leaned forward, an elbow resting on his knee as he looked up into her face, which glowed luminous in the lantern light.

"Dear God. Could you have doubted it?"

Again she smiled, but something about the intensity of his gaze unnerved her and she lowered her eyes. She wore a white flower pinned to her dress—a Night Angel—and now she touched a hand to it. "My mother is waiting for her flower."

With the softly hissing lantern swinging at his side, Thraxton allowed Aurelia to take his hand and lead him through the jumble of headstones to the darkly wooded spot where the grave of Florence Greenley lay. During the day the spot was deeply shaded. Now, hidden from the wan glow of an orange crescent moon, the grave was pooled in impenetrable darkness. Even with the lantern light, Thraxton stumbled on the uneven ground and wondered at Aurelia's ability to see in the dark.

"Hello, Mother," Aurelia said upon reaching the simple headstone. "I have come as I promised and brought this kind gentleman to meet you."

She looked up at Thraxton and smiled. "My mother says hello."

Thraxton's mouth dropped open. He was at a loss. "Ah, er, hello… Mrs. Greenley."

Aurelia unpinned the flower and her silk dress rustled as she knelt to place the single bloom in the stone urn. Still kneeling, she pressed a hand against the headstone and bowed her head. When she rose a moment later and turned to Thraxton, her eyes held a liquid gleam.

"My mother says you are a kind man. That you have a compassionate soul, but you must first learn to listen to your heart."

They walked back to the pathway without speaking. Finally it was Aurelia who broke the silence.

"My mother died giving birth to me."

"How tragic. You never knew her."

She stopped and turned to face him. "Oh, but I do know her. As I came into this world she left it. But our souls touched in passing. I speak to her every time I come."

Thraxton looked down at her face, his pulse suddenly racing, his breathing quickened. He slipped his free hand around her waist and slowly drew her toward him. He brought his face close to hers, until all he could see was her eyes. Their mouths moved closer, until they passed the same breath back and forth between them. And then Aurelia slid from his grasp, slippery as the moth. She ran giggling up the path and plunged into the blackness of the huge pharaonic arch that formed the entrance to the Egyptian Avenue.

Thraxton pursued, the lantern held high, footsteps echoing as he ran up the sloping tunnel. The avenue opened out onto the Circle of Lebanon, the ring of catacombs that surrounded an ancient cedar tree.

Thraxton called out Aurelia's name, but received no answer. He trod around the circular pathway until he returned once more to the Egyptian Avenue where she stood, waiting. "You should be more careful," he said. "Running in the dark. You will hurt yourself."

"You sound like my father."

"Does he know of your nocturnal wanderings?"

She laughed. "If he did he would forbid them. I do not wish you to think I feel ill of my father. In truth, he has devoted his life to me, but I am not one of his flowers to be kept in a hot house. I must feel the night air. And so I steal out, when he is asleep."

"What you do is very dangerous, Aurelia."

A look of irritation swept her face, like a naughty child receiving a scolding.

"I have done so for years and suffered no harm."

"But you are just a young girl and London is such a wicked place."

Aurelia took a step toward him, her face earnest. "I believe that if you look for wickedness you will find wickedness. But if you look for goodness, you shall find goodness."

"And the other night? Those Resurrection Men?"

"And you were there to save me." She smiled. "The world is full of good people." She reached out and took his hand. Feeling the touch of that small gloved hand with its thin, child-like fingers, a thrill tremored through Thraxton he would not have thought himself capable of feeling.

"Come," she said. "I will show you."

22

THE STREETS OF LONDON

While at the cemetery, high atop Highgate Hill, they had been above the fog. Now, as they alighted from the hansom cab, they stepped into the murk of what locals called "a London particular."

"Whitechapel," Thraxton noted with growing unease and he looked around at the narrow streets with their dingy, darkened houses. "No place for a lady at any time of day, but especially after dark." But, before he could change his mind, the cab driver cracked the whip over the horse's ears, and the hansom clattered away.

It unnerved Thraxton, who muttered, "A bad omen. Even the cab drivers shun such places after dark."

In answer, Aurelia took Thraxton's hand. "But there are good people here. Poor people but still good, still kind. You shall see."

They set off along a narrow street that snaked past

crumbling tenements, dilapidated and shoddily built premises in various states of collapse, many spilling their bricks onto the road. Here and there, light glimmered from cracked-pane windows, showing that these ruins were still inhabited. But despite the ramshackle nature of the area, on nearly every corner stood a brightly illuminated pub or gin house bursting with light and raucous laughter. Outside, booze-sozzled men slumped in the street where they had passed out, and wives paced anxiously, hoping their husbands would leave before bingeing away the week's money. As they passed the nearest gin palace a stout woman stood propping up the wall next to the door, a red feather boa thrown around her neck in an attempt at gaiety. When Aurelia and Thraxton approached she stepped forward into the light. A prostitute. Under the garish make-up, her face— prematurely old in her forties—showed a life of hardship. "Allo, Aurelia, love," she said in a friendly squawk.

"Hello, Maggie."

Thraxton felt the woman's eyes crawl up and down him. Then she turned to Aurelia. "Here, you're not on the game, are you?"

Aurelia laughed. "No, this is just a gentlemen friend."

She flashed a gap-toothed grin winking with gold. "I could do with gentlemen friends like him, with them pretty blue eyes and wavy black hair."

For once, Thraxton was glad of the poor light, for he could feel his face flushing.

"How is your little girl, Maggie? Is her cough better?"

The woman sighed dramatically and grasped both of Aurelia's hands. "Yes, yes she is, my pet. And Gawd bless you for the money. I was able to take my little darlin' to a proper doctor. Bless your heart!"

"I am happy to hear she is well," Aurelia said, smiling. "Take care, Maggie." She pulled her hands free and strode on with Thraxton.

"You, too, my dear," the prostitute called after them. "And make sure he pays you up front. It's the posh gents what are the most apt to do a runner after they've got what they're after!"

They walked on, arm in arm, and Thraxton could not resist shooting a last look back before the fog swallowed the gin shop. "Dear God! You know that woman? She is a common whore!"

"She has four children to feed. Her husband took to drink. He used to beat her and her children. Now she has to survive the best she can."

Thraxton, who had taken so much pleasure in outraging the sensibilities of the society he moved in, for once had to admit that he was shocked—shocked that such a gentle creature as Aurelia knew and conversed with common street people; shocked that such a vulnerable young woman could walk some of the most dangerous streets in London without fear.

But more surprises were in store for both of them.

* * *

Even though he had lost all sense of direction, Thraxton could tell they were approaching the river, for the temperature dropped and the fog grew so dense that at times they could see no farther than a few feet. Aurelia and Thraxton clung tight together, afraid that if they lost their grip they would lose each other forever. Though their eyes smarted and burned from the fog, there was a sense of the magical about its intimacy, for it seemed at times as though they were the only people in London. Aurelia led them through a Gordian knot of tumble-down alleyways and narrow ginnels that helter-skeltered up and down. Here and there a faint glimmer of light showed at a window. As they passed one, Aurelia drew Thraxton over and they peered in through the grimy glass.

Inside, a young woman sat at a rickety table in a squalid room, her head slumped onto her arms in a state of exhaustion. Atop the table sat a glue pot and a stack of paper matchboxes the woman had been laboriously gluing together by hand. Protruding from beneath the table were the grubby legs of a child, asleep on a pillow, covered by a thin blanket.

"This woman glues matchboxes together," Aurelia said. "She works fourteen hours a day and earns only a few shillings a week."

Thraxton bit his lip as he looked in at the pitiful scene. The coal scuttle beside the fireplace was empty. No fire burned in the grate. The room must be as cold inside as out.

On the next street, they stopped at another window. At

least here a fire burned in the grate and two smoky candles spilled a dim light. A husband and wife sat at either side of a table sewing gloves. The woman had a young girl, perhaps five years old, pinned to her skirts who was sewing the fingers of the gloves. The little girl yawned, eyes drooping, but every time she started to nod off, her mother gave her a little slap to wake her up.

"Dear God," Thraxton exclaimed. "That poor child!"

"The lady does not mean to be cruel, but they must eat and they have so little money. My father gives me a small weekly allowance. When I am able I push a few pennies under the door for these poor people. It makes so little difference in my life, yet it can make such a big difference in theirs."

Aurelia's words squeezed Thraxton's throat like a giant hand. His chin quivered and his eyes pooled so that he had to turn his face away.

"What is wrong?"

"Dear lady, you make me ashamed. You have so little for yourself, and yet your first thought is always for the happiness of others."

She touched his shoulder. "Please, do not take on so. I know you are a good and kind person."

A mirthless laugh ripped from Thraxton's lips. "Truth is I am not. I have spent my entire life in idleness, indulging every base appetite without restraint or thought as to whom I may injure. I am a wretch, and it is only in this moment that I have come to realize the full depth of my wretchedness."

Aurelia put a lace-gloved hand to Thraxton's cheek and

turned his face to hers. "No. I know you are not a bad man. I see goodness in you. You are brave and fearless. You risked your life to save mine."

Thraxton pulled her hands from his face and kissed them.

"Surely you are an angel. Perhaps you have come to redeem me."

Maggie banged down a sixpence on the bar and knocked back the glass of gin the barman set before her to wash away the taste of her last customer. Then she pushed her way through a throng of drunken men who casually groped her and took up her place outside the gin shop, hoping for another customer. From up the street she heard footsteps approaching, and then a man shambled out of the fog, head down, hands in pockets, and Maggie stepped out to block the pavement.

"Cold out, ain't it, dearie?" she called. "But it's warm inside!"

However, the man tossed her only the slightest of glances and weaved around her. She watched him disappear into the fog and sighed, but as she turned to look back, a hand clamped over her mouth and shoved her back into the wall so hard her head smacked hard against the bricks. When she saw who was holding a hand over her mouth, her eyes widened more from fear than pain: Mordecai Fowler, flanked on either side by his two main cronies, Barnabus Snudge and Walter Crynge.

"Hallo, Maggie me old gal," Fowler said. "How's business?" Fowler's free hand rummaged through Maggie's clothing until he found a single coin and snatched it out.

"I'll be blowed," he said, looking at the coin. "A gold sov! Who give you this?" He pried his grimy hand loose from her mouth, allowing her to speak.

"A toff give it me. Hour ago. He's still in there." She indicated the gin shop with a jerk of her head.

Fowler's lips peeled back from a twisted snaggle of yellow teeth. He tossed the gold sovereign and caught it again. "You was gonna tip this up to me, wasn't ya, Maggie?"

"Yeah, Mordecai... straight up I was."

Just then the toff, a well-dressed man in top hat and frock coat, reeled out of the gin palace.

"There he is now, Mordecai," Crynge said. "In his cups from the look of it."

Staggering drunk, the man collided with the lamp post and hung from it while he regained his equilibrium, then weaved away up the street. Although Fowler didn't yet know it, the gent was in fact Tristram Lloyd-Babbage, a venerated judge and pillar of the law. It was not uncommon to see such high-borns jostling shoulders with the poor, for many affluent gents had a penchant for "slumming," where, far from society's prying eyes and protected by anonymity, they could indulge their appetites for underage prostitutes and lethally strong liquor.

"A bleedin' toff!" Fowler spat. "I hate bleedin' toffs."

Fowler gave a nod and he and his two compatriots hurried

after the man and fell in lockstep. Fowler stepped forward and threw an arm around the man's shoulders like they were old friends. "Allow me to help you, sir. Bit dodgy around here at night… especially for a gent such as yourself."

"Damned decent of you, old man," the magistrate slurred. "Perhaps you could hail me a hansom cab?"

"Oh, yes, sir," Fowler said. "As luck would have it, we are right close to where one parks. It's down here, sir."

Fowler steered the drunkard into the obsidian mouth of an alleyway. Snudge threw a look both ways as he pulled out his cosh, and then followed them in. The cadaverous Crynge took up a position at the entrance to the alleyway, keeping lookout.

"It's black as a coal pit!" the judge slurred. "Are you certain this is right?"

"Oh, yes, sir," Fowler said. "In fact, I got your ride home right here!" And with that Fowler scruffed Lloyd-Babbage by the back of his coat and hurled him forward, sprawling him on the cobblestones. Fowler then leapt on, knees slamming into his chest, pinning him to the ground.

Lloyd-Babbage wheezed as Fowler's bulk squeezed the breath from his lungs. "See here, you scoundrel, I am a magistrate! Unhand me or you'll know the law's displeasure."

"Oh you is a magistrate is ya?" A sick leer twisted the mobsman's features. "You shouldn't oughta told me that. My friend Mister Pierce, he hates magistrates." Fowler fumbled in his coats, drew the thin metal skewer from its leather scabbard and pressed its needle tip against the judge's cheek. "Magistrates is liars what talk out both sides of their mouths. But Mister Pierce, he knows how to shut their lying gobs forever!"

Fowler's pupils dilated wildly as a bestial roar ripped out of him and he plunged the spike into the judge's face again and again and again and again...

When Lloyd-Babbage's bloodcurdling screams shattered the stillness of the night, Maggie was still lurking by the gin shop door, afraid to stay, but too afraid to run away. She listened in horror, a hand clamped over her mouth, as the screaming continued, seeming never to end. Finally, she could stand the shrieks no longer and ran sobbing into the night.

Thraxton and Aurelia had finally reached the City of London proper, and in their travels had crossed the invisible border that separated some of the very poorest in London from the some of the very wealthiest. Now, as they turned to walk up a wide, generous boulevard, lined by trees and fine houses, Thraxton suddenly stopped. "Listen!" he said.

"What?"

"That sound."

Suddenly Aurelia heard it, too. "Music?"

"Mozart... no, Strauss. They're playing a waltz."

This time, Thraxton led Aurelia along the pavement until they found the music's source: a huge house, candelabras blazing in every window; outside, parked on both sides of the street, a fleet of carriages awaited their owners.

The wealthy homeowners were throwing a ball. Through the windows, Thraxton and Aurelia could see crystal chandeliers, walls lined with enormous paintings with gilt-edged frames, elegant couples gliding across a ballroom. The front doors and windows of the house were thrown open to allow the heat to escape.

"How wonderful!" Aurelia said.

"Shall we join them?"

She looked at him wonderingly. "You know these people?"

"No, but then I only ever attend parties to which I am not invited." He grinned and pulled her by the hand. "Come. Let's go."

But Aurelia drew back, resisting. "No! No, I couldn't possibly!"

Thraxton would normally have bullied until he got his way, but he caught the flash of fear in her eyes and assumed she declined because she was embarrassed by the simplicity of her dress. "Very well, then. We have music. We can still dance." And with that, Thraxton slipped one hand around her waist and stretched out the other, ready to dance. Aurelia looked at him uncertainly, and then slipped her hand in his. Together they began to waltz in the middle of the street, ignoring the stares of the carriage drivers huddled beneath their cloaks and stepping carefully to dodge the piles of horse manure.

Standing in the shadows at the side of the front doors was a dour and serious-looking man with graying hair dressed in the formal velvet uniform of a servant. He watched the couple waltzing in the street as he calmly drew on a cigarette. After a moment, he flicked the cigarette away, straightened his attire, and slipped back inside the house.

Thraxton and Aurelia spun and whirled up and down the street until she dissolved in fits of giggles. "Oh! You are making me dizzy!"

Thraxton laughed and waltzed her about even faster. But in mid-spin they almost collided with someone standing in the road—the servant, who coughed into his glove to gain their attention. They stopped. Thraxton instantly assumed the man was there to see them off and grew belligerent. "Now see here, my man. We were simply—"

The doorman said nothing and held out a tray upon which sat two glasses of champagne.

"Oh, I see," Thraxton laughed. He handed a glass to Aurelia and took one for himself. "Thank you, my man. Damned decent of you!"

The servant bowed from the waist then sauntered back to his post beside the front door. Aurelia and Thraxton looked at each other and clinked glasses, giggling like children as they sipped their champagne.

"My feet are sore."

"Mine, too."

"How far have we walked?"

"Miles... over half the city."

Thraxton and Aurelia trudged the last few steps to the

front steps of her house. To the east, the rising sun stained the fog a ruddy crimson.

"I don't want to go," Aurelia said.

"Then don't."

"But I must. It's dawn."

He took her head in his hands.

"You are my dawn, bright and glorious."

He brought his face close to hers. His lips barely brushed hers. More a promissory note than a real kiss—he did not want to frighten her. But to his surprise she leaned in and kissed him back—her lips closed, but the kiss both soft and warm. When she pulled away, Aurelia's violet eyes were sparkling.

When he spoke, Thraxton's heart was overflowing. "Aurelia, you've shown me your world, now I want to share my world with you. I can take you to the finest balls. I can take you rowing on the Serpentine. We could tour Europe. The Americas. Anywhere. I can take you to Italy… to Tuscany, away from the damp and fogs of England. The sunlight there is the most wonderful thing you can imagine—"

He stopped as Aurelia's smile collapsed and she pulled away.

"Nuh, no," she stammered breathlessly. "I was wrong. This was wrong. It is impossible. You do not know me. I cannot do these things. I simply cannot!"

He reached for her but she tore from his grasp, ran up the steps, unlocked the front door and vanished inside without ever looking back. For some time Thraxton stood there, staring up at the door, dumbfounded. Finally, his shoulders slumped, his head dropped, and then he turned and walked away up the street.

23

A Mind at War

From outside the tent came the concussive boom of artillery and the steely clash of armies colliding. Inside, the muddy tent floor was strewn with hundreds of dead, dying and grievously wounded soldiers packed so tight it was difficult to step between them. Doctor Jonas Hooke bent over a rickety operating table, the front of his gown sprayed with blood, sawing off limbs, probing pliers into gaping wounds, ripping loose jagged chunks of shrapnel, sewing slippery coils of intestine back into place. The smell was atrocious, the ground the tent was pitched on little more than churned-up muck weltered with gore and the filthy boots tracked from the latrine pits. Through it all, he floated at the center of a sickly sweet cloud of chloroform that numbed and blurred everything and reduced life to a ghastly dream glimpsed only in snatches of fitful sleep.

After each surgery, the body on the litter before him

would be hauled off and a fresh one slapped down. Soon the faces merged in an anonymous blur of flesh tone. All he saw were wounds to suture and mangled limbs to amputate. He grew adept at holding the scalpel in either hand, so as cramp set in he would transfer it from one to the other. In truth he was more butcher than surgeon, and quickly learned the slaughterhouse tricks for removing a hand with a few quick scalpel cuts, a leg or an arm with the frenzied violining of a bone saw, a mangled hand with a dextrous whack of the cleaver. Orderlies dragged away arms and legs to be stacked in piles. Carts laden with torsos missing heads and limbs were dragged from the mud in carts pulled by whinnying horses, eyes rolling and crazed from the incessant gun and cannon fire.

The earth ceased to exist. He stood with one foot astride heaven and hell, severing the silky fibers that bound human souls to the earthly plane.

One day he was sewing up a soldier after pushing the man's guts back into his body, when he looked up to see a strange and uncanny apparition—a tall, thin man in a black frock coat with a bone-white top hat. Unseen and ignored by the orderlies and doctors rushing back and forth, he stood among the dying wounded littering the tent floor.. His face was elaborately mustachioed with bushy sideburns. The man wore rose-tinted pince-nez and was staring directly at him. He seemed uncannily familiar and now he smiled and raised his hand, covering one eye with something square: a Tarot card, the Hanged Man.

Suddenly, all sound drained away, as if his ears had been stoppered with wax. For a moment stretched to breaking, he no longer heard the shouts of the doctors and nurses, the moans of the dying or the skull-numbing concussion of heavy artillery.

Then the sound returned in a rush. He heard a *plooooooomph* sound and looked up to see a bright star shining through the surgical tent's canvas roof as an incendiary shell exploded directly overhead. Instantly, the canvas roof dissolved into flames and a cataract of fire swept through the canvas structure, burning alive wounded soldiers, nurses and surgical officers alike.

Somehow, miraculously, he survived. When they found him, standing stock-still, staring into the woods a half-mile from the scorched remains of the medical tent, his clothes were still smoldering and all his hair had been burned off, down to the eyelashes. The blast had temporarily deafened him and cut the cords connecting his words to his tongue, his mind to his limbs. When the doctors moved an arm or a leg, it froze in that position, like a broken marionette, although the glint of intelligence in his eyes showed a still-functioning mind entombed in a body.

"Catatonia, brought on by an attack of the nerves," they wrote on his medical discharge papers. He was shipped back to England to convalesce in a sanatorium in the countryside, one entire wing of which was populated with cases like his: soldiers whose bodies were intact, but whose minds had been broken in Crimea.

Like many other patients, he was wheeled about the grounds in a bath chair, and on days of pleasant weather, parked facing a formal garden with a reflecting pond; beyond that, a pleasant stretch of lawn gently descended into an ancient wood bordering the property. Here he would lay slumped in the chair, limbs twisted, gazing blindly at the view before him.

Then one day a shape emerged from the woods, the figure of a man who strode up the sloping green lawn. As he approached, it was evident that the man was dressed in the high fashion of a gentleman with luxurious side-whiskers, a mop of curly brown hair. He wore rose-colored pince-nez spectacles perched upon the bridge of his nose. Atop his head was a white top hat, tilted ever so slightly to one side. It was the same figure he had glimpsed the moment before the incendiary shell exploded. The mustachioed man with the Tarot card. The hirsute figure reached the reflecting pond and strode straight across, his feet not leaving so much as a ripple in its mirror surface. The Tarot reader reached the bath chair and stood looking down at him.

He somehow knew the top-hatted gentleman had come for him. The bath chair crashed to its side as he lurched out of it. Without ever speaking, the gent in the white top hat turned and walked away and he followed, splashing clumsily through the reflecting pool as the figure he followed floated over it, descended the greensward, and plunged into the dense woods.

Although two entered the woods, only one emerged from

217

the other side, for Doctor Jonas Hooke vanished and the creature named Silas Garrette assumed his place.

24

Idylls in the Sunshine

Although exhausted from his noctivagations, Thraxton found himself unable to sleep when he returned home. His mind teemed with images of Aurelia and a thousand conflicting emotions. After an hour spent wrestling with his pillows, he abandoned his bed, dressed, summoned a cab, and made his way to Hyde Park.

A warm easterly wind from the Continent had blown in overnight and swept away the fog that had suffocated London. Now it seemed that, after a week's sequestration from the daylight, the entire citizenry of the metropolis had poured from their houses and into London's parks to enjoy a late gift of autumn sunshine. It was a sunny and crisp, almost balmy day. Nannies pushed babies in perambulators. Young children skipped through piles of leaves or threw armfuls at each other, shrieking with gaiety. Couples of all ages strolled along the leaf-strewn paths, arm in arm.

Thraxton walked alone through their midst, head down, deep in thought, when suddenly he looked up at the sound of familiar laughter.

A couple stood in a shaft of sunlight at the edge of the Serpentine watching the row boats. Behind them the water sparkled. The woman was wearing a bright yellow dress that seemed to burn in the sun. The gentleman had removed his top hat and his fair hair shone. The young people were shadowed by an elderly couple who stood close by: obvious chaperones. It took a moment before Thraxton realized who the young couple was: his friend Algernon and Constance Pennethorne, no longer dressed in mourning black.

At about the same instant, the couple looked up and recognized Thraxton. For a moment all stood silent, forming a frozen tableaux, but then Thraxton dropped his gaze and strolled on as if he hadn't seen them.

"Geoffrey!" his friend cried after him.

Thraxton stopped and turned. Algernon whispered something to Constance and then ran to join him.

"Oh, hello, Algy. I thought that might be you. I did not wish to intrude."

"Geoffrey, I, I must explain…"

"Explain? What is there to explain?"

"I had meant to tell you, but events seem to have overtaken me. I know that you entertained some feelings for Constance, and as you are my best friend I had not wanted you to feel betrayed—"

"Algy, old fellow," Thraxton interrupted. "I am not

a complete dullard. I could see from the beginning that Constance only had eyes for you. Which merely confirms my opinion that she is a woman of good sense as well as great beauty and breeding."

"Then... we are still friends?"

Thraxton laughed and playfully punched Algernon's shoulder. "Forever, you clot!"

Relief flooded across Algernon's features. "Well, then. That's splendid. Absolutely splendid!"

"When will you marry?"

"Marry? Geoffrey, it is a scant year since her husband died. She has only just taken off the mourning dress. What would people say?"

Thraxton looked back at Constance. She was watching the two of them with obvious trepidation. Her blonde hair was done in large ringlets. She carried a fetching parasol, which she balanced upon her shoulder.

"What do you care what the world will say?"

"Geoffrey, I am not you. I have to think of my position—of our position—in society!"

"Listen to me, Algy. Society cares nothing for you or your happiness. In these last few days I have seen things that have knocked the scales from my eyes. There are so many in this world who live in poverty and desperation. We are lucky to have so much. Why delay happiness for one day, one minute, one second? I say to hell with society and its worthless conventions. Marry her, Algy, as soon as possible and let society go hang!"

Algernon cast a look back at his intended. It was clear that Thraxton's words had fired him with boldness. "I... do you really think? I... yes, damn it all, we shall! Let them all go to blazes, I will speak to Constance right now!"

Algernon started to walk away but then turned back.

"I am sorry, Geoffrey, was there something you wished to tell me?"

"I have met her, Algy."

"Met who?"

"My inamorata. I am in love."

Algernon smirked. "Another beauty with a slender waist and an ample bosom?"

Thraxton flinched at the stab of irritation. "No. No, this time it is different. She is beautiful, that is true, but it is more than that. We have a spiritual kinship. With her I feel what voyagers must feel when they first glimpse the shore of an undiscovered country that will forever be their home."

But Algernon was barely paying attention as he stared back at Constance with love in his eyes. It was obvious that his mind was already tumbling over the idea of immediately marrying her. "Yes, wonderful. Excuse me, but I really must get back."

And with that he strode away. For a moment, resentment flared in Thraxton's chest as he watched Algernon rejoin Constance. Although Thraxton could not hear from this distance, Algernon said something that made Constance put both hands to her face. Then she laughed, threw her arms around his shoulders and hugged him. Watching them,

Thraxton felt jealous. But it only lasted a moment and then he was full of understanding for it was obvious that his friend was as besotted with Constance Pennethorne as he was with Aurelia, and he could not begrudge his oldest friend a chance at happiness.

Thraxton realized with a stab of shock that he was changing—that he had changed. He felt that his turn was coming shortly and that he and Aurelia would also enjoy many happy days strolling in the sunshine.

Unfortunately, as he was soon to find out, this idyllic vision was something that could never possibly happen.

25

DINNER AT MIDNIGHT

When her husband was still alive, Constance Pennethorne had frequently dined in the late evening, usually around eight o'clock, but she had never dined as late as midnight. Now she and Algernon were the only customers in a small but fashionable restaurant in London's West End. The restaurant normally closed at eleven, but Thraxton had paid the owners generously to keep the kitchen open and supply a single waiter. Even so, the restaurant seemed empty and desolate as the waiter drew a chair out for Constance and then seated Algernon next to her.

"Who is this young woman of Lord Thraxton's," Constance asked, "that we must dine in the middle of the night?"

"It does seem odd, even for Geoffrey."

"Does she sleep during the day only to emerge from her rooms after dark like one of the 'gay' ladies who frequent pleasure gardens such as the Cremorne?"

Algernon's eyes widened with alarm at Constance's uncharacteristically spiteful tone, but he paused until the waiter had placed the napkin on his knee and stepped away before responding.

"Knowing Geoffrey there will be a reason. Probably a strange one."

They heard the clatter of an arriving coach and moments later Geoffrey and Aurelia entered the restaurant. They were met by the owner, who greeted Lord Thraxton solicitously and took their coats and wraps.

"So that's the mystery woman," Constance whispered. "She seems a rather pale and sickly creature. I imagined Lord Thraxton's tastes would run to a more robust woman."

"Please, dearest," Algernon chided, "do not be unchari-table."

As Thraxton and Aurelia reached the table, Algernon rose to greet them.

"Constance, Algy." Thraxton bowed and kissed Constance's hand, then shook his friend's hand.

"I want you to meet Miss Aurelia Greenley. Aurelia, these are my friends, Mrs. Constance Pennethorne and Mister Algernon Hyde-Davies."

At the mention of the name "Greenley," Algernon's eyes widened and his mouth dropped open. Thraxton's mystery woman was wearing one of the mysterious blooms they had discovered at Highgate Cemetery. Suddenly all the dots connected: this was the daughter of his head gardener, the irascible Robert Greenley.

Aurelia, her head bowed, looked up at them and smiled shyly.

When they were all seated, Constance directed her gaze at the nervous Aurelia and began her interrogation.

"Tell me, Aurelia," Constance purred. "Do you eat here often?"

"Oh... no."

Just then the waiter arrived bearing a magnum of champagne, popped the cork, and soon champagne flutes hissed with foamy effervescence.

"London has so many wonderful restaurants," Constance persisted. "Where then do you dine?"

"I... have never dined in a restaurant before."

"Really? You must be very hungry, then." Constance hid her smile by sipping her champagne.

Thraxton and Algernon squirmed in their chairs. For some reason Constance was enjoying being cruel.

"That is a very pretty necklace you have," Aurelia said.

All eyes focused on the necklace dangling around Constance's neck. Thraxton recognized it immediately: the gold Ankh he had snatched from Sir Hector Chelmsford at the British Museum and presented to her.

"Thank you," Constance said, touching a hand to the Ankh. "It was given to me by Lord Thraxton. He is very impetuous when it comes to giving lavish gifts to ladies... but you must already know that."

Thraxton's face colored as Aurelia looked at him questioningly.

Aurelia wore no jewelry because she owned none, but Constance noticed the white bloom pinned to her dress. "That is a very lovely flower you are wearing." Constance's eyes danced across the bloom. "Although I don't think I've ever seen a flower quite like it."

Aurelia unpinned the flower (a Night Angel from her garden) and handed it across the table to Constance. "Please, Constance. I should like you to have it. You are so beautiful with your lovely hair and pretty dress, it would look much better on you than on me."

The gesture, by its graciousness and generosity, took Constance by surprise.

"Oh, why... thank you. But you are very lovely yourself."

"I am sure I must seem quite plain. Your dress is so very pretty. You have such roses in your cheeks, and your gentleman, Mister Algernon, is so fine and handsome. Together you are like a painting on a box of chocolates."

Everyone laughed, except for Aurelia, whose hurt look revealed she believed they were laughing at her. But then Constance took Aurelia's hand and squeezed it and it was obvious by the liquid glitter of her eyes that Aurelia's simple honesty had touched her. Relieved that she was not the source of their amusement, Aurelia's face brightened, and the laughter resumed.

Dinner was consumed with gusto by all, but from the confusion over which silverware to use and the way Aurelia waxed on rapturously about every course, it was obvious she had never enjoyed fine dining before. When the last of the plates had been cleared away, the owner of the restaurant hovered close by and it was obvious that he wanted to send his people home and head for his own bed.

Algernon went outside to awaken the slumbering carriage drivers, while Thraxton settled the reckoning. The two women conversed as they waited for their coats.

"Thank you so much for the flower," Constance said. "It is exquisite. But I must give you something in return." And with that she pulled the Ankh necklace over her head and then placed it over Aurelia's head.

"Oh, no!" exclaimed Aurelia. "No, I couldn't possibly."

But when Aurelia tried to remove the necklace, Constance held her hands to prevent it.

"Please, accept this as a token of our new friendship. It has brought me luck, for I met Algernon because of it. I am sure it will bring you luck, too."

Aurelia's eyes filled with tears as the two women hugged each other.

It was raining when they left the restaurant. The dark mares pulling Thraxton's blue brougham clopped along wet cobblestones gleaming under the gas lamps. Inside Thraxton talked animatedly. "I thought that went swimmingly. They were very taken with you."

Aurelia had a hand to her face, covering her eyes.

"What, what is it?"

"Dizzy... please... take me home."

"But I thought we would drive around Hyde Park. We can watch the sun come up—"

"I want to go home—now!"

"It's just the champagne, my darling. It will pass. You just need some air—"

Aurelia dropped her hand and glared at Thraxton. "There is so much you do not know about me!"

Stung by the venom in her voice, Thraxton lost his words.

"I cannot watch the sunrise," Aurelia said. "I cannot go rowing on the Serpentine. This is my world—the darkness. It is the only world I can ever know."

"I don't understand."

"I have… a malady. One which forbids me from that which all other humans enjoy. The sun, the daylight, is my enemy."

Thraxton was finally beginning to grasp what she was saying. "So… the black curtains of your room… the paleness of your skin…"

"Yes. Light is a drop of slow poison oozing through my veins. The same malady killed my mother. In time, it will kill me, too." Her voice softened. She gripped Thraxton's hands. "I am like my flowers. During the day I remain tightly folded within myself. It is only at night that I may bloom. Geoffrey, you are a kind and good man. You have fine friends with fine manners and fine clothes. But you should forget me. I can never be a part of your world."

"Yes you can. You must. I have money. A title. We can make a life together."

She pulled her hands from his, shook her head and drew in a long, shuddering breath.

"There is a gulf between us more vast than you can know.

229

I have lived most of my life alone in a darkened room. I never went to school. I have never strolled in a London park. Until tonight I'd never dined in a restaurant. The only friends I have are whores and beggars and the wretched poor. I know almost nothing of your world and can never know it. You and I may long for one another as day longs for night, but in the same way, we can never be together."

A large tear streamed down her cheek.

"Never!"

Suddenly she snatched the door handle and flung herself out of the moving carriage. Thraxton reached out to grab her, but caught only a blast of cold night air. He yelled for Harold to stop, banging the ceiling with his walking stick. The carriage had barely slowed when his feet hit the wet cobblestones and he ran back to look for Aurelia.

But she had vanished into the night.

26

The Unanswered Letter

Thraxton sat in the gloom of his brougham, watching the clatter and bustle of traffic moving along the darkening street: shire horses hauling wagons laden with large wooden barrels, costermongers pushing carts stacked with shiny apples, pickled herrings, wilting petunias, as well as the teeming clamor of hansom cabs and omnibuses carrying Londoners home after a day of labor.

Finally an overloaded omnibus slowed long enough for a single passenger to alight from its top deck. Although the figure was hidden beneath a black umbrella, Thraxton could tell by the way the man moved who it was: Robert Greenley. He watched as Greenley crossed the road, dodging traffic and then trudged wearily up the front steps of his house. Clara, the maid, must have been waiting by the door for now it cracked open, spilling warm light, and Greenley entered. Thraxton snipped the end from a fresh cigar and lit it. Half an hour later he finished puffing his third cigar and tossed the butt out the window of his carriage. By now, the downstairs windows had gone dark and gas light shone behind the curtains of the second-story windows Thraxton knew to be Greenley's bedroom. After only ten minutes that, too, was extinguished. Fortunately for Thraxton, Robert Greenley was very much a creature of habit. He worked a twelve-hour day at the Royal Botanical Gardens at Kew and usually arrived home around seven in the evening. After a light supper, he would retire to bed where he read his Bible for maybe ten minutes and then he would turn out the light.

The bedroom light extinguished, Thraxton waited another ten minutes and then stepped down from his carriage.

At the front door, he eschewed the use of the heavy brass knocker, and instead rapped with his gloved knuckles using his special knock: three slow knocks, and then two quick knocks. After a short delay, the door opened and Clara's moon face appeared in the crack.

"I am sorry, sir, but she will not see you."

"But it's been nearly two weeks. Tell her I will come every day for a year if need be."

"I can't do nuffink, sir," Clara said and began to shut the door.

"Wait!" Thraxton reached into his breast pocket and drew out an envelope. "Will you give her this letter… please?"

Clara hesitated, then cracked the door wider and reluctantly took the letter from his hand.

He pulled a coin from his pocket and placed it in her

hand. Greed flashed in her eyes when she saw it was a half sovereign. She slipped the heavy coin into her pinny and quietly closed the door.

A single candle burned atop the dresser in Aurelia's room. She sat on the low stool before it, encircled in its trembling halo of light. Thraxton's letter sat in her lap, the envelope still damp from the rain. Her hands shook as she tore it open, unfolded the letter, and held the paper close to the flame. Her eyes skipped frantically over the elegant whorls and loops of Thraxton's handwriting before she could calm herself enough to read what they said.

My Dearest Aurelia,

If I have offended you through any word or deed, I do humbly beg your forgiveness. I know you are a delicate and rare creature, much like the flowers in your Night Garden. You have said that we are from two different worlds that can never meet. Any world that does not include you is one I do not wish to live in. You are my dark angel of the night, the very nourishment for my soul. I would renounce the world in order to be with you. I will wait every night for you at our special place at Highgate. If you do not appear after one week, I will have my final answer.

Yours forever, Geoffrey

Aurelia looked up at her reflection in the mirror. Half of her face was hidden by the frame, but as she leaned forward the right side of her face appeared, marked with ugly blisters. The turmoil of her emotions, her fatal susceptibility to light, had triggered an attack of her illness. For days she lay in bed, wracked with abdominal pains, her flesh burning with an angry red rash that erupted across her skin.

She looked down at the letter and the words prismed and shattered. A swollen teardrop fell and plopped onto the letter, bleeding ink as it ran down the page.

For the first time in weeks Augustus Skinner had descended from his rooms. He sat cushioned on a pile of feather pillows stacked on his favorite armchair. He was wrapped in a richly embroidered dressing gown, a burgundy smoking cap atop his head. The only sound in the parlor was the ticking of the carriage clock on the mantelpiece and the sputter of coals burning in the grate. Skinner sat staring into the fire's seething redness, shivering despite the warmth of the room. The sweaty pallor of his face and the dark circles beneath his eyes showed that, despite the regular visits of Doctor Garrette, his health had suffered a precipitous decline.

His eyes swiveled up to the clock as it chimed the quarter hour. He had promised himself he would not take another dose of laudanum until the hour struck, but the sweats had started and his stomach cramped from a monstrous, insatiable craving. He looked at the smoky bottle on the table next to him, then back at the clock. The hands had barely moved. He still had three quarters of an hour to go. He looked down at his lap to find his hands restlessly wringing.

Three quarters of an hour to go.

A knock at the door. "Come," he shouted.

His servant, Bradwell, entered.

"The doctor, sir."

Silas Garrette followed him in, clutching his black leather bag. Bradwell took his coat, but left when Garrette refused to surrender the top hat.

"I am in hell, sir," Skinner said. "In hell."

Silas Garrette stood looking down at the older man, who shuddered violently. Normally, Garrette would have been comforted by such obvious suffering, but on this day he was in a vile mood. The duel he had attended that morning had gone badly. When the fatal moment came, both men had raised their pistols and discharged them harmlessly into the air. No death. No wounds. To add insult to lack of injury, both duelists, once old friends who had become the bitterest of enemies, were reconciled by the ordeal and quit the field with their arms thrown about each others' shoulders, jabbering cheerfully about a celebratory meal.

A detestable outcome.

On the carriage ride to Augustus Skinner's home, Garrette had become increasingly desperate—his revenue source could literally curl up and die at any moment. He clearly needed to up the ante.

"No better?"

Skinner shook his head.

The doctor set his Gladstone bag on the table and opened it. He removed three bottles of laudanum and set them down in plain view. "You are still taking the laudanum?"

"Yes. Too much!"

"It will help with healing."

"I suffer, sir. I suffer, and all because of the damned duel—"

"And Lord Thraxton, the man who shot you?"

"Yes, damn Thraxton. Damn him to bloody hell!"

Skinner bellowed the last few words, lurching up in the chair, which caused a jolt of agony to ripple across his face.

"It seems wholly unjust," Garrette agreed. "While you are forced to lie up in your rooms, wracked by excruciating pain, Lord Thraxton parades around London society with his usual impudent bravado."

"He boasts of this affair?"

Silas Garrette's smirk insinuated it was so. "I understand it is a favorite topic of discussion at the best soirées."

"Yes, I have no doubt of it. Well, let them wag their tongues until they wear them out. Lord Thraxton is a fool. A womanizer. A philanderer who lives for excess in drunkenness and carousing. He makes new enemies daily. I am a patient man. I can sit back in the shadows and watch. I have no doubt some day he will receive his come-uppance."

"There is always the law."

"Pshaw! I am not interested in pursuing this matter in the courts. I was the one who challenged Lord Thraxton. I was the one who had the advantage of the first shot! And even though dueling is against the law, it is still considered a matter of honor amongst gentlemen of our class. It is improbable a jury would find in my favor. No, I would be more of a laughing stock than I already am."

"There are ways of striking back, besides the courts," Silas Garrette said, peering over the top of his rose-colored pince-nez. "Other means not so... public." For the first time Skinner noticed that the doctor's beady brown eyes never blinked.

"What are you insinuating? Revenge? I shall have no part in anything illegal."

"That is the very meat of my argument. You need have no part in this at all. I could be your proxy."

Skinner's eyes asked the question he was afraid to utter aloud.

"In my profession," Garrette continued, "I have occasion to render my services—as an act of charity—to those of the lowest strata of society. There are many men amongst the underclass who can fall no farther and thus have nothing to lose. These men can be persuaded to undertake any action, no matter the potential consequence, for a sum of money."

By now Skinner's heart was pounding, his mouth dry.

Garrette smiled. "If some tragic misfortune were to befall Lord Thraxton, in the eyes of the law and of society you will be completely innocent. And yet... yet he will know exactly who exacted this heavy price."

Skinner looked terrified. But then he deliberately leaned

his weight back onto his right buttock, so that the pain flared like a lighthouse beam cutting through the laudanum fog swirling in his mind, sharpening and illumining everything. He was shut up in his rooms, probably crippled for life, suffering miserably all because of this impudent upstart. Revenge was a pool of sweet, cool water and he wanted to slake a burning thirst, to ladle it into himself until it dripped from his chin.

"And how much will your services cost me?" Skinner asked, already sensing that the hirsute Doctor Garrette was stretching wide the jaws of a sprung steel trap and goading him to step into it.

The beady eyes glittered. The upper lip foliage twitched into a smile. He had still not blinked. "Twenty guineas. A payment of half to secure my services. The remainder payable upon completion of the task."

Silas Garrette's words echoed in Skinner's mind. He knew that this could end badly. He knew that a wise man would abandon this imbroglio to the past and move on with his life. But such arguments held little weight against suffering in the here and now.

"If I were interested. What exactly would I get for my twenty guineas?"

Behind the rose-tinted lenses, Silas Garrette's lashless eyelids closed slowly, almost dreamily, and then opened again. He raised his head slightly and the rose-colored pince-nez caught the flare of naked gas light and glowed crimson.

"Every man, even the foulest, even the most brutish, has

something he loves. Something he would protect. Something the loss of which would wound him to the quick. I will find that thing. And when I do, Lord Thraxton will suffer a wound so deep, so terrible... it will never heal."

The night was dry and still, but cold. Thraxton stood in the flare of a bull-nose lantern, shifting from foot to foot, swinging his arms and stamping his feet in an attempt to stay warm. He spun around at the sound of leaves rustling, but saw nothing. He had waited a full week in Highgate Cemetery, but Aurelia had not shown. Tonight was the final night. If she did not appear, he would have his answer.

Again the sound of leaves rustling. *It's just the wind*, he thought, but then realized that the night was still. From the darkness came a lilting laugh. Thraxton sprang to his feet and looked around. "Aurelia?"

Again the laughter, this time from the right. He moved cautiously toward the sound, feeling for curbstones with his feet, blinded by the glare thrown from his own lantern. More laughter, behind him now. He spun. A feminine silhouette beckoned from atop a grave, arms reaching up to the sky. A stone angel. But then Thraxton realized that this angel had no wings. He vaulted up onto the stone table and seized the angel by the waist, finding it warm and soft—Aurelia. She shrieked as he grabbed her and they both overbalanced and toppled, crashing into a pile of leaves. The fall was harder than he anticipated. Aurelia lay with her eyes closed, unmoving, and Thraxton feared she had been knocked unconscious.

"Aurelia!" He massaged her wrists, trying to revive her. "Aurelia, are you injured?"

But she was unresponsive. Thraxton stroked her face with his hand. Her eyes remained shut, but then she began to giggle.

"Dear God, you frightened me!"

Aurelia opened her eyes and flashed a devilish smile. Their faces were very close. Thraxton moved in and kissed her softly, tentatively. When she did not resist, the kiss deepened as his passion soared and she returned it with the same intensity.

An hour later they stood at the front steps of Aurelia's house.

"I suppose I must bid you goodnight," Thraxton said.

But Aurelia took him by the hand and led him up the steps. All the windows were dark. The household was asleep. She quietly turned her key in the lock and they crept inside.

In the perfumed warmth of the Night Garden, Aurelia moved between rows of flowers, lighting candle lanterns and carefully lowering their glass shields. Thraxton watched as she lit the last lantern, then he slipped his hands around her slim waist, spun her around and kissed her deeply. Together they sank onto the day bed. They kissed until they lost themselves, chewing drowsily on each other's mouths. Thraxton's fingers moved down the buttons of her dress from the neck down. As he unfastened each one, the skin of her chest showed stark white against the black lace. He began a series of light kisses from her navel up her chest, pausing at the hollow of her throat and then up her neck, nibbling at her chin before his lips returned to hers. Aurelia gasped with pleasure and hugged him closer, her lips grazing his ear as she whispered, "Yes... yes... oh, yes."

As they made love in the narrow bed, a moth landed on Thraxton's shoulder, skittered across his naked back, and onto the bare thigh Aurelia had cinched tight around his waist. The moon burst from a pall of black cloud, its white beam surging through the glass roof. At its touch, the Night Angels stirred atop their stalks, petals spreading wide, sobbing their perfume into the air until the moths spun in circles, drunk with their scent. As their lovemaking rushed to its climax, a moth flittered up to the candle lantern. Drawn by its light, the moth crawled beneath the open glass as if to kiss the flame, igniting instantly. It flared bright and tumbled away. When it hit the floor, nothing remained but embers.

Dawn was breaking over London as Thraxton strolled away from Robert Greenley's house. He turned and looked back to see Aurelia, standing at the window of the Night Garden. He smiled and raised a hand and she waved back.

His mind racing with hopeful thoughts, Thraxton did not notice the black carriage parked across the street. Couched in the shadows within, Silas Garrette reclined upon the worn leather cushion, a blanket thrown over his lap, his white top hat on the seat beside him. He had been following Thraxton's shiny blue brougham for days and his patience had been rewarded. He had promised Skinner he would wound Lord Thraxton. Now he had found the entry point for that wound—all he had to do was apply the point of the scalpel and draw the blade through the meat until every last tendon and sinew was severed.

When the omnibus reached Mister Greenley's stop, a half dozen passengers arose from their seats, and he was forced to wait his turn to clomp down the curving metal stairs from the top deck. It was past seven p.m., long past dark, and the pavement milled with people making their way home. A river of black top hats trudged before him, until the river parted and flowed around either side of a solitary white top hat that blocked the flow. When he reached the spot, Mister Greenley almost collided with an elaborately whiskered gentleman in tinted pince-nez. From the black Gladstone bag gripped in one hand, Greenley guessed his profession. When their eyes met, the man touched the brim of the white top hat in greeting and spoke.

"Good day, sir."

Greenley stopped, surprised to be addressed in the street by a complete stranger.

"What is your business, sir?"

"My name is Doctor Garrette. I am currently treating a patient, a man of letters."

"And of what concern is that to me?"

"You and he share a mutual foe. I speak of Lord Thraxton."

Greenley's eyes flared at the name, but he said nothing.

Silas Garrette looked around at the people brushing past.

"Might we not continue this discussion in private? The matter touches upon a most delicate matter... concerning your daughter."

27

THE GATHERING STORM

Clara opened the front door and stepped inside. It was her day off, and instead of wearing her maid's uniform, she was dressed in the height of fashion: a yellow skirt over a crinoline, a blouse with mutton leg sleeves, and a new hat with brilliant feathers and lace pinned to her hair. She stopped for a second to admire herself in the hallway mirror, lifting her skirts and extending a toe coquettishly to admire her new lace-up boots while she twirled the parasol she had purchased to complete her outfit.

Unbeknownst to her, Mister Greenley had just stepped from the parlor and stood silently watching. She jumped when he cleared his throat to let her know she was not alone.

"Oh, Mister Greenley. You gave me such a start!"

Mister Greenley stood silently appraising his maid's new clothes, his gaze overbrimming with recrimination.

"It's my day off, sir," she hastily pointed out.

Greenley sniffed at the comment. "Is that a new outfit?"

"Yes," Clara said uncertainly.

"It looks very expensive. Where did you get the money from?"

"The money? I, I saved it, sir."

"You've been stealing, haven't you?"

"No!" Clara gasped. "I ain't never stole nuthin', sir—"

"Don't lie to me, girl!" Greenley bellowed. "I pay your wages. I know full well how much money you have and it's certainly not enough to dress like a harlot."

"But, Mister Greenley, this is what the fashionable ladies of London are wearing—"

"Not on the wage of a maid-of-all-work they aren't!"

"I didn't steal it!" Clara shouted defiantly. "I never stole nothing!"

Mister Greenley's brows contracted in a fearsome glower.

"Don't back-talk me, girl! I will not brook lying, thieving, dishonesty or secrecy in my home!" Mister Greenley lunged toward her and Clara flinched away, expecting a blow across the face. When it didn't come she ventured a trembling look at her tormentor. Mister Greenley's face was a clenched fist hovering close.

"Now," he said, his voice trembling with violence straining to be unleashed, "tell me what is happening in my house... after I am in my bed."

* * *

Once again, Thraxton idled in his carriage until the light in Greenley's bedroom went out. Then he trotted across the road, swinging his walking stick, and danced up the marble steps. Things were going to change. He was already planning strategies of how he would reintroduce himself to Robert Greenley in a more advantageous way, so that he would come to look upon Thraxton as a future son-in-law.

But Thraxton's knuckles met only thin air as the door snatched open before he had a chance to knock. Clara greeted him with an inscrutable expression as he entered, and then, instead of leading him up the stairs as usual, she held open the door to the front parlor.

"Miss Aurelia's waiting for you in here, sir," she said, her voice stretched to a brittle whisper.

Thraxton threw a puzzled look at her. Clara kept her eyes downcast, lips trembling.

Even before he entered the room, Thraxton knew it was a trap.

Through the open door he could see a white top hat sitting atop the sideboard. The likes of Mister Greenley would never wear a top hat—especially a white top hat. Thraxton knew there was someone waiting for him in the room, a stranger to the household. He stepped inside the parlor and the sharp bark of a cough pulled his eyes right.

Robert Greenley sat in a tall wingback chair, his meaty forearms stretched out along the chair arms, huge, knobby-knuckled hands gripping the leather so hard they left indentations. The violet eyes glowed incandescent in a face chiseled from granite.

Thraxton swallowed hard. The trap was sprung and he was caught.

"Sit down, sir!" Greenley commanded.

The words were like a scalpel slicing the tendons at the back of his knees. Thraxton collapsed onto the only seat: a low, floral-patterned ottoman that forced him to look up at Greenley.

Two smaller chairs flanked Greenley's. Aurelia sat in one. She never once looked up at him, but kept her eyes fixed upon the carpet. In the other chair lounged the owner of the white top hat: a tall, weaselly man with a head covered by a mop of brown curls and the most preposterous side-whiskers. As Thraxton's gaze fell upon him, the man tipped his head slightly, peering over the top of the rose-colored pince-nez perched on the bridge of the hawkish nose. His dark brown eyes held the voracious stare of a ferret that has cornered a rabbit in its burrow. The face was chillingly familiar. Thraxton was certain that he knew the man from somewhere, and then he remembered the tall, thin doctor who had spoken to him after the duel with Augustus Skinner. The realization thrust a knife blade of anxiety between his shoulder blades.

"So," Robert Greenley said, his voice quaking with rage. "You have been found out, sir!"

"Found out? What are you insinuating—"

"I have discovered the truth, sir, of how you have been routinely bribing a domestic servant in my household to gain access to my daughter for immoral purposes."

"That's a damned lie!"

Greenley's voice rumbled like an earthquake. "I'm afraid your denials are wasted on me. Clara has made a full confession."

"And what does Aurelia say?"

Greenley seemed to blow up with rage, coming half out of his chair. "That is none of your damned business! For her part in this sordid affair, I fully intended to sack Clara and throw her out on the street. However, my daughter has begged me to show mercy. I grudgingly acceded to her wishes, but only after she swore a solemn oath never to see you or have congress with you again. Is that not so, Aurelia?"

Thraxton looked at Aurelia, who looked straight ahead and acknowledged only with the slightest nod of her head.

"This is monstrous! Sir, if you truly love your daughter—"

"I do love my daughter!" Greenley interrupted. "And that is why I must protect her from men such as you—blackguards and seducers who prey on the naïveté of young women."

Thraxton could sit still no longer and sprang to his feet.

"I do not believe for one second that Aurelia feels this way."

Greenley rose from his chair. "Then perhaps you will believe it from her own lips. Aurelia, what do you have to say?"

All eyes fixed on Aurelia, who never looked up as she answered in a small voice, "I… I wish never to see you again…"

Thraxton unleashed a look of utter hatred at Greenley. "Those are your words, not hers."

"Believe what you will. This gentleman is Silas Garrette, a medical doctor. He has examined my daughter and finds that she is no longer a virgin."

Thraxton's mouth filled with a metallic bitterness.

"Have you had carnal knowledge of my daughter, sir?"

Thraxton's knees trembled. It angered him having to lie, but he had to think of Aurelia. He took a breath, tried to quell the rising surge of dread in his chest and turned his gaze back to Robert Greenley. "What is it you wish, sir? I will do anything—"

"I wish never to see your despicable face again. If I do, I will pursue this matter further—in the courts. I will bring legal action against you so that you may never see my daughter again. Given the evidence I can mount of your bribery of my domestic and your infamy as a seducer and womanizer, I have no doubt that any judge in England would take my word over yours—Lord or no Lord."

Thraxton felt all hope slipping away. Anger would not serve him. He had to be diplomatic. "Perhaps... perhaps there were some... minor... improprieties in the way I pursued my courtship of your daughter. But my intentions toward Aurelia have never been anything but honorable."

"Honorable? You?" Greenley snorted. "Get out! Get out before I beat you like the filthy cur you are!"

For a moment violence seemed imminent. Thraxton stood, jaw tensing as he wrestled with his emotions, but then his shoulders slumped. He cast a final despairing look at Aurelia, who never once raised her eyes to meet his, and then turned on his heel. He paused at the threshold of the door and looked back. "Believe me when I say this. Neither you, nor the courts, nor the law, nor God, nor Death itself will prevent me from being with Aurelia if that is what she wishes."

Thraxton stepped outside and the front door slammed behind him with a thunderous crash that threatened to collapse the entire row of houses.

A fine mist of rain was falling as he stepped into the street. Hansom cabs passed in either direction. Pairs of horses clopped by pulling ponderously laden omnibuses. He looked at his waiting brougham.

But Thraxton had nowhere to go.

Mordecai Fowler and his two cohorts stepped from the alley to find a black carriage waiting at the curbside. The side glass had been let down and now a hand extended from the open window clutching a white top hat, which it rocked from side to side as a signal.

"Wait here, you two."

"What is it?" Crynge asked.

"Business," Fowler answered, then trooped over to the carriage and clambered in. He settled himself on the leather seat and nodded at the tall man sitting opposite.

"Doctor Garrette."

"Mordecai," Silas Garrette said, nodding in response.

"Job for me?"

"Yeeeesssssss."

"The usual? Another knocked-up dolly-mop?"

Garrette shook his head, light flashing from the rose-colored pince-nez. "Not this time. There is a girl I want taken."

"A girl someone would be lookin' for if she went missin'?"

"Oh, I very much think so."

Fowler lifted the bowler hat from his greasy mop of hair and resettled it. "Risky. Nobody cares if a whore goes missin'—the Grips dredge 'em out the river every other day. But a girl from a good family gets snatched, people notice. The Grips notice."

"I will pay double the usual rate."

Fowler ruminated, sensing there was a lot more he wasn't being told. "How do we get hold of this girl?"

"She steals out of the house at night to meet her lover."

Fowler grinned. "A toff, I'll wager."

Garrette nodded.

Fowler's filthy fingernails scratched his stubbly chin with a *rasp-rasp* sound.

"Five times the usual."

Garrette didn't need to think about it. "Done."

"What do you have in mind for her?"

The man behind the rose-colored lenses flashed a guillotine smile. "Something special. Something quite extraordinary."

28

LORD THRAXTON'S CARD

Clara was dusting on the third floor. From further up the hallway came the sound of sobbing. She stopped dusting and listened, twisting the feather duster in her hands with agitation. Finally, she could stand it no more. She set the duster down and knocked on Aurelia's door. The only reply was more sobbing. She hesitated for a moment, then opened the door and slipped inside.

A single candle provided the only meager light in the tightly curtained room. Aurelia lay prostrate upon her bed, weeping. Clara watched for a moment, shifting uneasily.

"Here now, Miss Aurelia. You shouldn't still be crying. It's been two weeks!"

But Aurelia's sobbing continued. Clara wrung her hands as she listened to the pitiful wailing.

"Please don't take on so. It tears me apart to hear you. I suppose you must hate me for what I done. But I didn't have no choice, honest I didn't. You know what a temper your father has."

Aurelia looked up at her maid, eyes puffy and swollen, tears running down both cheeks. "I must speak to him, Clara."

"You best never speak to Lord Thraxton again, Miss Aurelia. Especially after what Mister Greenley said. You'll get us all in trouble. Your father could take him to court. Ruin him."

Aurelia threw her face into the pillow. "You do not understand. I must speak to Geoffrey. I must let him know!"

Clara's eyes widened in sudden realization. "Here... you ain't... is ya?"

Aurelia lifted her head and shot Clara a look that whispered more than words could.

Clara put her hands to her face. "Oh my Gawd! Oh my Gawd! What is to become of us? What is to become of us all?"

Aurelia pulled herself into a sitting position, wiping away tears with the back of her hands. "If Geoffrey only knew. He could speak with my father, make him see reason. Otherwise... otherwise... I am ruined! But, I don't even know where he lives."

Aurelia wailed and threw herself back on the bed flailing at the sheets in her despair. After several moments of silence Clara lifted her head and spoke. "I... I knows."

Aurelia pulled her head up from the pillows and pushed a wild strand of auburn hair from her eyes. "What?"

"Your gentleman. Lord Thraxton. I knows where he lives."

"But... how?"

"The first day he come here he give Mister Greenley his calling card. Your father got angry and threw it on the floor. I picked it up. I shoulda chucked it out, but I kept it. I dunno why."

Half an hour later Aurelia stood by the front door, dressed in her black lace dress and deep cowl, her face screened by a black lace veil. A nervous and agitated Clara hovered around her.

"You won't tell Mister Greenley it was me what give you the card, Miss Aurelia, will ya? I don't know what I'd do if your father gave me the sack. I got no family to live with. I'd wind up on the street."

Aurelia took hold of Clara's hands and squeezed. "I won't, Clara. No matter what, I shall protect you."

The grandfather clock in the hallway chimed quarter to the hour.

"Oh, Gawd," Clara said. "It's nearly seven o'clock. Mister Greenley will be home any minute."

Aurelia snatched the front door open, stepped out, looked both ways up the street, then scurried down the steps.

"You be careful, dear!" Clara called after her, and quickly closed the door.

Sitting on the curbstone across the street was a small boy, barefoot despite the cold. A crudely fashioned broom of sorts lay across his thin legs, the kind used by crossing sweepers who earned a tossed coin by sweeping the streets clear of horse manure and filth so that the better class of people might cross without soiling their clothes. The young boy was Titch, a tiny, undernourished street urchin Mordecai Fowler had placed there as lookout. He had swept the crossings for a full two weeks. Now at the sight of a lady in a black lace dress, Titch tossed away the broom, sprang to his feet and ran up the street, bare feet slapping the cobblestones, until he reached the narrow alleyway that wound a tortuous path to the Seven Dials Rookery.

It was already dark; coach lanterns gleamed on the carriages and wagons that trundled by. Aurelia hurried along to the corner of the street. She needed to catch an omnibus that could take her to Piccadilly Circus, from where she would have to walk to Thraxton's house. Just as she turned the corner, Aurelia saw the lumbering omnibus approaching. She raised her hand and the driver saw her and steered toward the curb. But as it drew up, Mister Greenley was sitting on the lower deck of the very same omnibus. They saw each other through the glass at the same instant. Greenley realized who it was and leaped to his feet, shouting and pushing as he fought to get off.

Aurelia turned and ran away. When she darted a look back, Greenley was stepping down and shouted after her. But Aurelia, terrified of her father, ran blindly on, with nothing more on her mind than flight. She should have realized that she was running directly toward the Seven Dials, an area where even she, with all her skills, would not be safe after dark.

"Aurelia!" her father yelled. "Stop! Stop at once!"

She hitched up her lace dress higher, but he was still gaining. She spotted a narrow alley up ahead and darted into it. The alleyway was treacherous with missing cobbles and deep potholes filled with icy water. She threaded a path around the hazards as the alley steeply descended past shuttered, glassless windows and derelict tenements. As she rounded a blind bend she collided with a short, stout, but well-padded figure.

Mordecai Fowler.

He clamped a hand around her thin wrist and with the other hand ripped off her bonnet and veil. "Hallo, hallo! I knows you. You're the little moxie what nearly got my wrist broke!"

The High Mobsman was not alone. Walter Crynge and the hulking Barnabus Snudge stood close behind.

Pounding footfalls echoed in the alleyway, and a moment later Robert Greenley rounded the bend. He slid to a halt when he saw that his daughter had been seized by ruffians. "Unhand my daughter, you filthy swine!"

"Swine am I? A swine?" Fowler's lips curled back from his higgledy teeth. "I fink you need a lesson in manners, mister!"

Greenley sprang forward and dropped into a bare-knuckle fighter's stance, fists up and ready, weight balanced on the balls of his feet.

Fowler roughly shoved Aurelia at Crynge. "Hold her," he muttered. He reached into his coats and drew out his favorite weapon, Mister Pierce, then lunged at Greenley, swinging wildly with the spike. Greenley dodged to one side and slammed a deadening punch to the shoulder that knocked the spike from Fowler's hand. He followed with a wicked uppercut that snapped the mobsman's head back and sat him down hard on the cobblestones. The force of the punch made him bite down hard on his tongue and now he spat out a mouthful of blood.

Greenley windmilled his fists, threatening. "Release my daughter or I'll give you louts the beating of a lifetime."

But then Barnabus Snudge stepped from the doorway wielding his cosh and slammed it across the back of Greenley's head with a sickening *thwack*. Greenley sagged to the ground and lay there, moaning.

Fowler sprang to his feet, took a running start and kicked the prostrate Greenley in the kidney. "Give us that here," he said, snatching the cosh from Snudge, then proceeded to rain blows down upon Greenley's head and shoulders.

"Noooooooooo!" Aurelia screamed. "Stop! You will kill him!"

Fowler continued his flailing assault, dealing Greenley blow after blow until his arm was too tired to swing. He tossed the cosh back to Snudge, then retrieved Mister Pierce and his hat. As he settled the bowler back atop his unkempt mop of black hair, Fowler leered at Aurelia, taking in the wide violet eyes and the beautiful face. "Come along, my little dolly-mop. We'll have a bit o' fun you and me. Your old dad won't know you when we've done wiv ya!"

Aurelia shrieked as Fowler and his mobsmen dragged her away.

Minutes passed. Greenley moaned, blinked his eyes open and stirred. He put a hand to the cobbles and tried to rise, but then collapsed and did not move again.

29

BLOOD SPORTS

It was the kind of dream one is relieved to awaken from. As Augustus Skinner surfaced from the silken veils of a laudanum dream, the images still clung to his mind like a pernicious mist—ghastly images of a surgeon, his gown splashed with gore, standing over him, scalpel in hand, operating on him. In the dream he had still been conscious, and could feel pain but was gripped with paralysis. And although he wanted to scream, he could not. He felt the knife cutting through his chest, the hand reaching in and ripping out his still beating heart, then thrusting it in his face for him to see.

He awoke shouting.

Doctor Garrette sat in the chair facing his bed, his hands folded atop the black Gladstone bag in his lap. "You were asleep when I came in."

Augustus struggled to gather himself. He had sweated

through his nightgown and the bedclothes were soaked. The drawn curtains prevented him from telling whether it was day or night. "You. At times I feel as though you are only here to prolong my suffering."

Garrette said nothing, but opened the Gladstone bag, took out a fresh bottle of laudanum and set it on the bedside table. Skinner's eyes lingered on the bottle. He licked his lips. He had drained the last one a few hours ago and tumbled into the warm, foaming surf of sleep.

"It is done," the doctor gravely announced.

"What is done?"

"Your revenge. You wanted to destroy Lord Thraxton. How does one destroy a man who fears nothing, including his own death?" Garrette smiled. "One destroys the thing that man loves."

Skinner was afraid to hear more, but terrified not to.

"Thraxton was conducting a secret liaison with a young woman from a respectable family. I arranged for that woman to be abducted by one of the foulest degenerates in London." He stroked his side-whiskers and grinned. "As I promised—a wound that never heals."

Skinner pushed himself up in bed, a throb of pain from his inflamed wound driving hot tears into his eyes. "What have you done? I wanted Thraxton broken, ruined financially. I never wanted this! An innocent girl? Are you mad?"

Garrette bristled at the words. "Now to the matter of money. I have my children to think of."

Augustus Skinner spluttered with rage. "You have twisted

my mind with your laudanum! You have schemed to strip my will!"

"A hundred guineas was the sum we agreed upon."

Skinner shook his head violently. "Not a penny. Not a ha'penny. Not a farthing will you get from me! I shall summon the police and have you arrested."

"You forget to whom you are speaking. You hired me. That makes you complicit."

"You monster. Get out. Get out of my rooms!"

Silas Garrette snatched the laudanum from the bedside table, yanked the cork and tipped the bottle up, pouring out the liquid on the rug. Skinner groaned to watch the bottle gurgle itself empty.

The doctor hurled the bottle aside, grabbed his black bag and stalked to the door. Before he left he spun and threw a murderous look back. "I have yet to present you with my final bill, sir. Prepare yourself for the reckoning."

Thraxton was already drunk when he reeled in through the doors of the Turnspit public house, a smoky, low-ceilinged dive in Quaker's Alley. He bought a whiskey and paid far too much to the barkeep who could tell when gentlemen "in their cups" were not up to the mathematics of change making.

A great noise and hubbub emanated from the back of the pub.

"What's all the din about?" Thraxton asked.

"Bit o' sport in the back room, sir. You're in time. They just started."

Thraxton slid his whiskey off the bar and tottered through an arched opening into the back room. A pall of silver cigar smoke swirled about the gas lights flickering overhead. The reek of tobacco smoke, beer slops and wet fur was overpowering. A throng of men crowded around a rat pit, a rectangular ring enclosed by short wooden walls. Despite the low nature of the pub, the crowd consisted almost entirely of top-hatted gentleman with a scattering of red-tunicked army officers here and there. In the pit a hundred rats squealed in terror as a single Bull Terrier moved through them like a whirlwind, pouncing upon rat after rat. Wagers had been laid upon how many rats the dog could kill and the time taken. Beneath bellowed curses and shouts of encouragement such as "Come on, Billy!" came the terrified squealing of rats. In an attempt to get away, the rats formed heaps of bodies, scrabbling to climb the corners of the pit, but there was no escape. Billy lunged, dipped his nose into the squirming pile, bit down, shook, then tossed. Dying rats flew through the air, spraying blood that spattered the faces of the men who howled like devils ravenous for suffering.

Thraxton dropped his glass of whiskey, gorge rising. He had seen rat baiting. Indeed, he once had been a member of the cheering rabble crouched around the rat pit; but now he saw death, even the death of a rat, as an abomination. He pushed through the squeeze of bodies, vaulted into the rat pit and began seizing rats and tossing them out of the pit.

"Life is precious!" he cried. "All life! Even a rat's!"

But his words were drowned in the resulting furor of shouts and curses. Money had been wagered on the outcome of this match and the braying mob, furious at the interference, now vented its rage on Thraxton.

A burly man, the dog's owner, jumped into the pit, wrapped his arms around Thraxton, and slammed him against the low wall. Many hands seized and held him, and a rain of drunken fists pummeled him about the face and shoulders. He was hoisted semi-conscious from the pit and dragged through the pub, crashing into tables and knocking down chairs. The door was flung open and he was hurled into the gutter, his top hat tossed into the street, then someone flung his walking stick after. It smacked him across the bridge of the nose, flushing his eyes with tears.

Across the street, two shabbily dressed men looked at each other and grinned. One was Bobby Sharples, the other was Ned Utley. Both were members of Fowler's mob who ran out of the Seven Dials. Sharples and Utley were known in the criminal vernacular as bug hunters: thieves who specialized in robbing drunks. Places such as the Turnspit, which attracted a crowd of gentlemen with pockets full of coins to be pilfered and gold watches to snatch, were favored hunting grounds of theirs. The two men slouched across the street and confronted Thraxton just as he was wobbling to his feet.

"What do you scoundrels want?" Thraxton asked.

"We come to collect the toll, guvnor."

"Toll?" Thraxton asked, adjusting his dress and resettling his top hat.

"That's right," Ned agreed. "There's a toll for walkin' down this street. You tip up everything ya got…" Ned's eyes ran up and down Thraxton's clothes and noticed a gold watch chain. "…including that watch, and nuthin' bad'll happen to ya."

Bobby Sharples slapped a cudgel against his palm. "Show him the knife, Ned." His accomplice reached into his coat and drew out a crudely fashioned "knife" which was little more than a seven-inch piece of flat iron sharpened to a point at one end with some heavy cloth sacking wrapped around the other end to form a handle.

"I made this special," Ned said. "For guttin' a gennulman like a fish."

"So that's a knife is it?" Thraxton said. Tonight he was carrying the walking stick with a handle in the shape of a snarling silver tiger. He thumbed a catch then drew out a concealed sword with a metallic *schuuulllliiiing*. "This is a sword," Thraxton said calmly, leveling the tip at Ned Utley's throat. "I purchased it for skewering miscreants."

The men's eyes bugged as the sword blade flashed in the lamp light. Then, without as much as a word or look between them, both men turned and bolted, running as fast as their legs would carry them.

The pummeling he had received in the pit, followed by the tussle with the bug hunters adrenalized Thraxton, burning the alcohol from his blood. Although his head throbbed, he felt brutally sober. Now there was nothing left to hold back his constant thoughts of Aurelia.

He struck off up the road, searching for a cab, but after a few minutes walking came across a figure standing beneath a gas lamp.

A whore, plying her trade.

Why not? he thought. *Anything to take my mind off Aurelia.*

The woman looked young enough. Normally at the thought of such sport, he would feel a surge of lust. But now he searched himself and found nothing. Perhaps that would come once they set to the business.

"G'devenin', sir. Care for a bit of sport?" the woman slurred. Even from several feet away she reeked of gin. "A shilling's all I ask. Ya can do whatever ya like to me. I don't care nuffink."

The face, which had seemed to carry the natural bloom of youth from afar, was painted like a porcelain doll, gaudy with heavy pancake and large spots of rouge dotting the cheeks. The eyes, which would not meet his, were dulled and dead. "Yer a gent, I can tell. I know what gents like. I can lift up me skirts. And I does it all ways."

It was the voice that sent an electric shock of recognition through Thraxton.

"Maisy... is it you?"

For the first time, the woman's blurred eyes focused on his.

"Geoffrey?"

It was indeed Maisy, the young prostitute he had had sex with in the tomb.

"My God, Maisy! What happened? Why are you on the street?"

The girl's face collapsed, her lower lip quivered. "Madame Rachelle chucked me out." Maisy began to cry, tears leaving trails through the thick pancake on her face.

"But why?"

"I'm rotten with the pox, sir. I know who give it me. And him a Member of Parliament and all. I'm no good to no one no more. I'm all used up. I'd drown meself in the Thames if I wasn't scared of goin' to hell."

She began to sob and Thraxton folded her into his arms and held her. "My poor child! I cannot bear to think of you suffering." Thraxton put a hand under her chin and gently lifted her face to the light. The face beneath the thick pancake was covered with open sores.

"Come," he said, putting an arm around her and leading her away. "I will not rest until we find you a new home."

Thraxton pounded on the door with the ferrule of his walking stick until at last a grate slid open and a pair of piggy eyes—female—glared out at him. "We're all full," a woman squawked. "Come back in the morning!"

The slit banged shut. Thraxton pounded again. The slit flew open. Before the shrill voice could speak again, Thraxton held up a change purse and shook it so the coins chinked.

The clash of silver spoke more eloquently than words.

On the other side of the door, a bolt shot back with a clunk and the door squealed open to reveal a stout, matronly woman.

"We've nothin' but a spot on the floor…"

"Then give her your bed… and some hot food."

"Kitchen's closed—"

"Then open it!" Thraxton grabbed the woman's hand and poured coins from his purse into it. "You are a charity are you not?"

The flash of silver sweetened the woman's churlish temperament. "Well, yes, sir. Right away, sir. We don't get many visits from gennulmen."

"You are to treat this girl with kindness. Do you understand?"

"Oh yes, sir. All our girls are well taken care of, like they was me own children."

Thraxton sniffed at the comment. It was impossible to envisage a man drunk enough to impregnate the bestial woman, let alone her being a mother to any resulting offspring. He laid a gentle hand on Maisy's arm. "Here at least is a bed for you and something to eat."

Maisy threw herself at Thraxton and hugged him. "Gawd bless you, sir. Gawd bless you."

He kissed Maisy's forehead and allowed the matron to lead her away.

"I shall return," Thraxton warned. "Be kind to her."

But as the hansom cab took him away, they passed

another prostitute shivering in the halo of light beneath a gas lamp.

She looked no older than ten.

When Thraxton stumbled into his front hallway, drooping with weariness, he found a single lantern burning on the hallway table. His manservant, Harold, sat in the circle of light, and from his state of half-dress it was apparent he had been roughly awakened from sleep.

"Harold? What are you doing up?"

"You got a visitor, Lord Thraxton."

"A visitor? At this hour?"

Harold nodded at the darkness beside the front door. A shadowy figure rose stiffly from a chair and limped forward until the light fell across his face. Thraxton gasped aloud when he saw who it was.

"Mister Greenley?"

He was almost unrecognizable. One side of his face was massively bruised—his left eye swollen shut. It was obvious he had received a horrendous beating. Although Thraxton counted the man his worst enemy, it was pitiful to see him in such a state.

"Dear God, what has happened, sir?"

"It is Aurelia," Greenley said, his normally booming voice dried to a brittle husk. "She has been taken."

* * *

"If we do not act now, this young lady may be dead... or worse!"

Sergeant Dawkins looked across the counter of the police station at Thraxton and Algernon and his soft brown eyes shone with sympathy. "Bushy sideburns you say? A short, stout fella built like an ape?"

"Yes," Greenley piped in. Although badly injured, he had insisted on accompanying Thraxton and Algernon to the Mayfair Police Station. Too weak to stand, he sat propped on a bench, a white bandage wrapped around his head.

"Him and two others: a walking skeleton with a hideous face and a third I glimpsed only briefly, the one who coshed me, a huge shambling brute."

The officer nodded knowingly. "The men you describe are known to us, sir. The first would be Mordecai Fowler, the leader of a gang of criminals and ne'er-do-wells. The other two miscreants are Walter Crynge and Barnabus Snudge, known associates of Fowler's."

"You say you know these men?" Algernon asked.

The police officer stroked one of his waxed and twirled mustachios as he spoke. "Everyone in the Metropolitan Police Force knows them. Fowler and his men run out of the Seven Dials, the worst rookery in London."

Hope surged in Thraxton at the news. "Then if you know where they are, you must take your men and go after them. There is not a moment to lose!"

The officer cleared his throat and frowned. "You have no idea about the rookeries, do you, sir? Last week we tried to arrest a man in Seven Dials. I had one officer shot dead and there's three more still in 'orspital. One who's never expected to walk again."

"But this is England, for God's sake!" Thraxton said. "You cannot tell me these ruffians are beyond the reach of the law!"

"There is no law in the rookeries, sir. Right now, I'm down so many men, I couldn't entertain goin' into the Seven Dials—especially at night. You'd need an army to go after Fowler on his own patch and come out alive. In the morning, once it comes light, I can have a dozen more men drafted in from other London boroughs—"

"In the morning?" Thraxton interrupted. "We can't wait until morning! Who knows what unspeakable atrocities could have been committed upon Aurelia by then? We are talking about the life of a young woman!"

Sergeant Dawkins leaned his hands on the counter and stared down at them as he spoke. "I'm sorry, sir, but that's how it has to be. My hands are tied."

After a fast ride home in the brougham, the three men stood in Thraxton's rooms. Thraxton finished loading one of his dueling pistols, passed it to Algernon and warned, "Handle it with great care, Algy." Thraxton moved to a desk, slid open a drawer and produced two leather purses that chinked with coins. He tossed one to Algernon.

"Strewth!" Algernon said. "How much is in here?"

"Fifty sovereigns." Thraxton tucked the second purse into a coat pocket. "I'm hoping we can buy Aurelia's freedom. If not, the pistols will have to do the bargaining for us." He threw a quick look at Robert Greenley who sat on the edge of Thraxton's bed, his face buried in his hands. Thraxton said nothing and crossed the room to an elephant's foot umbrella stand which held more than a dozen walking sticks of all descriptions. Thraxton found the silver tiger walking stick and held it out to Algernon.

"Take this."

"A walking stick? I hardly think I'll need to strike a dapper air where we're going!"

"Not just a walking stick. Watch."

Thraxton released the catch and drew the blade in one fluid motion. Algernon's eyes saucered as he found himself staring at a sword tip hovering inches from his face.

"Good Lord! I feel as if we're going to war."

"We are, Algy. We are." Thraxton sorted through walking sticks until he found a stick with a handle in the shape of a roaring boar and drew it out.

"What fiendishly clever trick does that one do?" Algernon asked.

Thraxton thumbed a catch and the stick broke in two like a shotgun. Sure enough, he loaded a single shotgun shell into the breech. "Unleash hell, if need be," he replied.

30

DESCENT INTO THE UNDERWORLD

Thraxton's brougham clopped down foggy streets that grew darker, narrower, bumpier and meaner the closer they approached to the Seven Dials. Thraxton, Algernon and Mister Greenley peered out the carriage windows at the shabby, darkened houses around. No one had spoken since they left Thraxton's house. Each knew the danger and difficulty of the enterprise they were about to undertake. Most of all, each tried to avoid thinking about the fate of Aurelia.

None too soon, the carriage shook to a halt and Algernon and Thraxton clambered out.

Harold, reigns and whip in hand, peered down from the driver's seat at his master. "Are you sure about this, sir? It looks very dodgy about here."

Thraxton threw a quick look around. The gas lamps were all dark as every glass pane had been shattered—vandalized by the wild children of the rookery. "It is very dodgy,

Harold. Keep your whip handy. If anyone challenges you—man, woman, or child—use the whip on them and then on the horses."

Thraxton turned to Aurelia's father. "Sir, I'd prefer it if you stayed in the carriage."

"What?" Greenley roared. "This is my daughter who has been kidnapped!" He barged out of the carriage, shouldering aside the two friends.

"Begging your pardon, sir," Algernon said. "You're hardly in any condition—"

"Condition? Condition?" Greenley blustered. "In my day I've knocked down some of the hardest men in London." He raised a scarred and calloused fist the size of a sledgehammer head and shook it angrily. "I'll show these bastards what my condition is!" But then his knees buckled and he had to hang on to the carriage for support.

Thraxton put a hand on the older man's shoulder. "Mister Greenley, we appreciate your bravery and your skill at fisticuffs. That is precisely why we need you to stay with Harold. He is just a young lad. We need your powers to help protect the brougham. When Algy and I return with Aurelia, we must have the carriage ready to make good our escape."

Greenley's fists fell to his sides, his head drooped. "Yes, very well..." he muttered in an exhausted voice.

Thraxton patted his shoulder. "Stout fellow."

He looked at his friend. "Come on, Algy, we've not a moment to spare."

The two men left the safety of the brougham and entered

a narrow alley plunged in a darkness so unfathomable they had to feel their way by dragging one hand along a cinderous, loose-bricked wall. Finally they emerged at a junction of alleyways lit by the diffuse light of the moon, orange and swollen as a rotten pumpkin. As they walked along the narrow lane, they passed huddled forms slumped in doorways which proved to be the homeless poor sleeping rough on the streets.

"How will we ever find our way?" Algernon asked.

"The police sergeant mentioned a wooden bridge that marks the entrance to the rookery proper."

Sure enough, they soon came upon a small arched wooden bridge. Someone had dumped a bundle of rags in front of it. When they approached, the bundle of rags sat up—a beggar. A small chalkboard dangled from a string around the man's neck and was scrawled with a single word: BLIND.

"Who approaches?" the man shouted, hearing their footsteps.

"We're looking for Mordecai Fowler," Thraxton said.

"To cross the bridge you must pay a toll." The man held out a hand to beg. When he lifted his head they could see only empty black sockets where eyes should have been. Algernon handed the man two shillings. He took the coins, pressed them into his empty eye sockets and looked up at them, giggling inanely. "Ah, now I see you. Oh, and there is a third who walks with you... Death!"

"Come, Algy." They brushed past the gibbering blind man and clomped across the bridge, which shivered and swayed beneath their feet.

"God, the stench!"

"An open sewer!'"

Both Thraxton and Algernon quickly produced handkerchiefs and clamped them over their faces.

On the far side of the bridge they entered an intractable maze of blind alleyways and narrow ginnels—everywhere a study in entropy. Buildings leaned as if wearied by the weight of their own masonry, spilling their guts, brick by brick onto the roadway. Some had bulging walls propped up by huge beams; others were missing walls and had roofs that had collapsed, opening rooms to the elements.

Someone threw open an upstairs window, shouted "gardyloo" and emptied a full chamber pot out the window. Thraxton and Algernon dodged as filth splattered across the cobbles at their feet and trickled into the gutter that ran down the middle of the narrow street. Suddenly a door banged open and a gang of boys charged out: ten, fifteen, twenty, they seemed to keep coming forever, all shrieking and whooping at the top of their lungs. The boys surged in a mob around Thraxton and Algernon, tugging at their coat sleeves, slapping them on the back, pinching their legs, so that in the confused melee, neither man noticed small, quick hands dipping into their pockets. The mob of boys dispersed as rapidly as it appeared, laughing and cat-calling as they dashed away and were swallowed by the darkness. Only one remained visible: a diminutive tyke who lagged behind his compatriots.

"You there, boy!" Thraxton called. "What's your name?"

"They calls me Titch, 'cause I'm small for me age."

"How'd you like to earn a nice, shiny sixpence, Titch?"

The boy turned to look back, a silhouette at the far end of the alley. "Wot I need a poxy sixpence for when I got me a purseful of sovs?" Titch tossed a purse in his hand.

Thraxton's hands reflexively went to his pockets, only to find that his money had been lifted. "He's got my sovereigns!"

Algernon batted at his pockets and found that he had also been robbed.

"And mine!"

"Quickly, after him!"

Thraxton and Algernon sprinted after the boy who seemed always to remain just beyond their reach and then suddenly vanished. The two men stopped to catch their breath.

"It's useless," Algernon said, panting hard. "We'll never catch him."

"I have a feeling they were merely sent to delay us. No doubt Mister Fowler already knows we are about."

With no illumination save for the moonlight oozing through bilious clouds of fog, they stumbled down blind alleyways that forced them to turn back time and again, until their minds had become as knotted as the streets and they lost all sense of direction.

"You were right, Algy. Truly we have entered a labyrinth."

But in their slow, stumbling progress, the two friends were being watched. Shadowy figures looked down from rooftops whistling to alert one another of the invaders' progress. Titch, the boy who had lifted the purse of sovereigns, had also scaled to the rooftops. He tossed the bag he held and caught it just to hear the pile of sovs chink, and laughed as he watched the two gentlemen's bumbling progress. He put two fingers to his mouth and let out a long and low whistle.

Thraxton heard it, looked up and saw the glitter of eyes among the tiles.

"We're being watched."

They passed another courtyard, overgrown with waist-high weeds and strewn with rubbish. Suddenly a pack of ferocious dogs burst from the shadows, barking madly as they galloped straight toward them.

Thraxton and Algernon took to their heels, but the snarling pack quickly overtook them as they ran, the fastest dogs leaping up and snapping at their legs, trying to bring them down. They saw a partly collapsed house up ahead with the front door cracked slightly. Without a word they threw themselves at the door, barging it open then kicking it shut after them. The door resounded to the thud of dogs throwing themselves against it. Thankfully, the door still retained its bolt and Algernon quickly threw it, locking the dogs out. "It appears we are trapped," he said, looking around. They were in a small, bare, windowless room.

The dogs continued to growl and hurl themselves at the door with such ferocity that the screws holding the bolt to the door frame began to tear loose. Thraxton rushed to the far wall and rapped it with his knuckles. As he suspected, the building lacked even the illusion of solidity: the wall was little more than a skimming of plaster over thin wooden laths. His foot burst through with the first kick. He and Algernon took turns and soon kicked a hole large enough to crawl through.

The hovel they emerged into on the other side of the wall was inhabited by a family of sorts—five children of varied ages, dressed in rags, the youngest, a boy of two, playing naked on the dirt floor. The other children huddled together, shivering under old sacking. On a tattered mattress stained with every kind of filth a skeletally thin woman with a huge mop of frizzy gray hair held the top of her dress down as she nursed a baby.

The woman looked up at the men distractedly, not in the least perturbed by their crashing entry through the wall.

"Have you a ha'penny for a pound of praties, sir?" the woman asked in a thick Irish accent. "Only we ain't eaten this week. Me paps have dried and the babby will na take suck."

It was the most abject scene of hopelessness either man had ever witnessed. The woman's enormous, vacant eyes rolled over them as she rocked back and forth clutching the child.

"We must help the poor creature. I have nothing left, Algy. Do you?"

Algernon rummaged in his pockets and found a single coin: a silver sixpence.

"It's only a sixpence, I'm afraid." The woman took the coin from him and stared at it blankly. She stopped her rocking and held the baby up for Algernon to see. He leant forward to look only to recoil in horror at the stench of corruption. The baby was dead and had swollen obscenely, its skin a bruised purple color.

"Dear God!" Algernon gasped. "The baby has been dead for a week!"

"The poor woman is quite deranged," Thraxton said. "I never would have believed such things could happen in England."

Something crashed in the room they had just left. Dogs howled and whined. The door had finally burst open.

"We can't help these poor souls, Algy. The dogs have our scent. We must away, before we bring them in here."

Thraxton and Algernon slipped out the front door only to find themselves in another blind alley. But framed at the end of the alley was a large building of many stories.

"It looks like an old factory or warehouse," Algernon said.

"Yes," Thraxton agreed. "The largest and tallest building in the rookery with the highest vantage point. I'll wager that's where we'll find Mordecai Fowler."

Aurelia lay on the bare floorboards of the snug, a tiny windowless room high in the rafters of the old factory. Her arms were lashed to the legs of a table. She looked up in fear at the rattle of a key turning in a lock. The door opened and Mordecai Fowler squeezed inside followed by Fanny, a disheveled slattern. The two tromped across the bare floorboards to where Aurelia lay and stood eyeing her critically.

"Well, well," Fanny said. "You 'ave found a proper little darlin' ain't ya, Mordecai?"

Mordecai grinned as he scratched the matted beard under his chin. "'Ow much do ya reckon, then?"

The woman crouched over Aurelia, groping her thighs and buttocks like she was appraising a sheep at auction. Aurelia squeezed her eyes shut and turned her head away, but Fanny grabbed her chin and twisted her face toward the light of the greasy candle. "She's no girl, but she's fresh, this one is. If she's not been diddled, I hear tell of private clubs where rich gents will tip up as much as two to three hundred pounds for a nice, tight quim."

"Well, we best find out if she's still a virgin then, ain't we?"

"Hold her legs," Fanny said.

Fowler grabbed one booted foot while his slattern grabbed the other. Aurelia screamed as they lifted her skirts and began to spread her legs. "No, please, I beg you!"

"Shaddup!" Fanny shouted, back-handing Aurelia across the face. Aurelia continued to kick and squirm, but Fanny finally caught hold of her foot and pushed her legs wide.

They were interrupted when a trap door opened in the ceiling, a pair of legs dangled, then Titch dropped onto the table beneath and sprang to the floor.

"What do you bleedin' well want?" Fowler yelled.

"Mister Fowler, look wot I got!" Titch handed Fowler the bag of coins he'd lifted. Fowler opened the purse and spilled golden sovereigns into his hand.

"Bleedin' hell! There must be fifty sovs in here. Wheredja gettit?"

"Coupla toffs. We lifted it from 'em easy as you like."

"Pair of toffs? Here in Seven Dials?"

Fowler's eyes flickered over Aurelia, putting it all together. "They come for you, ain't they, my little dolly-mop?"

Aurelia trembled, her face flushed with hope. Fowler shot a penetrating look at Titch.

"Two toffs, you said?"

"That's right, Mister Fowler."

"And they had fifty sovereigns between 'em?"

"Yeah."

"Then how come there's only one purse?"

Titch's mouth opened, but no words came out.

"Seems more likely they had two purses, each with fifty sovs in it. I know you got sticky fingers, Titch. You sure there wasn't no more?"

"No, straight up there wasn't, Mordecai!"

Fowler's face twisted in a sick parody of a smile. He patted Titch on the head with a filthy hand. "There's a good, honest lad." But then the hand tightened, gripping a handful of Titch's hair and Fowler dragged him closer. He thrust his free hand down the front of the boy's trousers and pulled out the second leather purse. "What's this, eh?" Fowler bellowed in Titch's face. "What the bleedin' hell is this?"

"I was gonna tip that up to you, Mistah Fowler, honest I was!"

Fowler tossed the bag of sovereigns to Fanny, then

clamped a huge hand around the boy's throat and squeezed until his mouth gaped and his eyes bulged.

"Nobody steals from me! Nobody!"

"Mordecai, he's just a nipper. Let him go!" Fanny rushed forward and tried to pull Mordecai's hand free, but received a punch in the side of the head that knocked her to the floor howling in pain.

Fowler slammed Titch against the wall and drew Mister Pierce from its leather scabbard.

"Dear God!" Aurelia cried. "Please no. He is just a child!"

But the bloodlust was surging through Fowler's brain and now there was no preventing what was about to happen. "Mister Pierce don't like you, Titch. He says you been a very bad boy. A very, very bad boy!"

Fowler drove the spike into Titch's stomach and wrenched upward. Titch's eyes widened, his mouth gaped in shock. He coughed once, spraying droplets of blood. His face spasmed and then relaxed. Fowler let go and Titch slid down the wall until he sat slumped in a widening pool of blood, his eyes dead and staring.

Aurelia turned her face away and squeezed her eyes shut. Surely she had been captured by devils and dragged down to the lowest level of hell.

31

An Audience with the Devil

Thraxton and Algernon stood looking up at a giant red devil, ten feet tall. Next to the painted devil faded white lettering spelled out "Lucifer Matches." The building had once been a match factory, but times had changed and the foul-smelling Lucifers were beginning to fall from favor. Congreve matches, which used white phosphorus and had no smell, were now the choice of many.

Running alongside the factory was the foul Lethe known as Filthy Ditch. In their peripatetic wandering, Thraxton and Algernon had scribed a ragged circle and now found themselves back at the same narrow canal they had crossed over to enter the rookery.

The two friends studied the façade of the hulking brick building. "How do we get in?" Algernon whispered.

Thraxton nodded. Up ahead an open doorway gaped blackly. The two men ducked inside. No sooner had they entered than a long, low whistle sounded. At the signal, men stepped from shadowed doorways and quietly dropped over walls until a small army of around thirty stealthily converged outside the door the two gents had just entered.

Inside the match factory, most everything of value had long since been pilfered, stripped and hauled away. They found themselves in the echoing first floor, a large space empty apart from a stout ladder that passed vertically through a hatch in the ceiling. They both stared up at the ominous black opening.

"Should we go up?" Algernon whispered. "Someone could be waiting for us."

Before Thraxton could answer both men heard a sharp whistle and suddenly the door banged open as a horde of mobsmen armed with cudgels and clubs poured in.

"Yes!" Thraxton shouted. "We should go up!"

Algernon scrambled up the ladder as fast as he could. His friend followed close behind and was almost through the hatch when a mobsman seized his leg. Thraxton back-heeled him in the face, sending him tumbling back down the ladder, knocking other mobsmen with him. The second floor was also empty but had a second ladder nearby that ascended through another hatch in the ceiling. The two friends sprinted to it and began to climb just as the first mobsmen reached the second floor.

"They're goin up!" one of the mobsmen yelled. "Stop 'em, Charlie!"

But both men had already reached the third floor. Holes

gaped in the roof through which moonlight streamed, dimly illumining the room. A few wooden barrels stood here and there, labeled "tar" and "sulfur."

"Algy," Thraxton shouted. "Keep them at bay!"

As the mobsmen surged up the ladder, Algernon held them off, flailing wildly with his walking stick, beating the heads and shoulders of mobsmen who tried to surge out of the open hatchway and stamping on the hands that gripped the ladder rungs. Thraxton spun the barrel over to the opening, pried the wooden top loose with the tusks of his snarling boar's head walking stick, and then tipped it over. Thick black pitch poured out, deluging the mobsmen clinging to the ladder. Angry curses and shouts came from below. Blinded and coated with slippery tar, men toppled from the ladder onto those below.

"Algy. Let's tip it up!"

Both men grabbed the bottom of the barrel and upended it so that it dropped into the open hatchway like a cork in a bottle, sealing the opening. Thraxton heaved his weight onto the barrel to firmly wedge it into place.

"They won't be coming up that way, soon," Thraxton said.

"Yes, but there's probably other ways up here."

Thraxton drew the dueling pistol from his belt. "We'll need these, now."

The two men ran through a succession of empty rooms. The match factory seemed empty and deserted and Thraxton began to wonder if it really was Fowler's lair. They reached a final darkened doorway and exchanged glances.

"I wish we'd brought lanterns," Algernon whispered.

"Could be a trap. Keep your pistol ready." Thraxton cocked his pistol and Algernon followed suit. Cautiously, they eased through the doorway into darkness, eyes wide, straining to make anything out.

"Nothing... I don't think—" Thraxton started to say, but then a vertical panel slammed down behind them, sealing off the doorway they had just come through and blocking their retreat. Blinding light flared as the two men found themselves caught in the convergence of several lantern beams.

"Well, if it ain't the toffs!" a voice boomed.

Thraxton and Algernon pointed their pistols this way and that. They knew immediately who the voice belonged to and now he stepped forward from behind the glare, a surprisingly short, fat, bestial man: Mordecai Fowler. Both men trained their pistols on him, but he showed no concern, taking another step forward.

"Thought I'd have a little party for you, so I rounded up all the lads."

"You know what I've come for," Thraxton said.

"Yeah," Fowler hissed, the simian face smirking. "Your little dolly-mop. Tells me you're a lord and how you're gonna come and get her. That you ain't feared of nuthin'. She don't half moan when you're giving her the old in-and-out," Fowler preened, thrusting his hips obscenely. "Especially wiv this." He drew out Mister Pierce and showed it to Thraxton. The polished tip shone silver in the lantern glare.

Thraxton's jaw clenched. A horrible sickness roiled in the pit of his stomach. "If you have so much as touched her, Fowler…" Thraxton said in a trembling voice.

"That's Mistah Fowler, Esquire, to you, Your Lordship. You is a lord, isn't ya? Well, Lord Toff, you're on my patch now. And here I'm more than a lord—I'm the king. I decide who lives… and who don't live."

"We have money," Algernon said. "We are willing to pay—"

"*Had* money," Fowler corrected. He drew one of the sacks of sovereigns from his coat and shook it before their eyes. "Mine now." Fowler nodded and one of his men stepped forward from behind the Bullseye lantern beams, dragging something which he dumped at Fowler's feet. A body. Fowler rolled it over with a kick. Titch's dead face stared up at the ceiling. "Poor little Titch. He tried to steal from me. He won't do that no more, will he?"

Fowler nodded to one of his men. "Get rid of him, before he starts to stink up the place."

The darkness resounded with the twin *thwacks* of deadbolts being shot and then two wooden doors swung open onto the night, spilling in a swirl of smoky air. Beyond the doors, a short loading balcony jutted out onto a precipitous drop. Dangling above, the jib of a crane used to winch goods up to this third-floor room from the ground below. In the hazy distance glimmered the gas lights of London.

Two burly men stepped forward and dragged away Titch's corpse. When they reached the open loading doors, they hefted the small corpse between them, gave a one-two-heave-ho and launched the body into the darkness. Seconds later, a splash resounded as the tiny corpse cleared the cobblestone loading dock below and plunged into Filthy Ditch.

Fowler laughed darkly. "We comes from the filth and we goes back to the filth. That's how things are in the Seven Dials." The High Mobsman tossed the purse and caught it, reveling in the chink of sovereigns. "I consider this a payment for me allowin' you to make it this far alive. But now I'll be askin' for them fine pistols you and your mate have been wavin' about."

Thraxton answered by leveling the pistol directly at Fowler's nightmarish face. "The only thing you'll get from me is a pistol ball in the brain."

Fowler grinned in response. "Oh, I think you'll be well happy to give us them pistols, Lord Toff. And in return I'll give ya this here rope what Snudge is holdin'." He nodded to his men and the lanterns swiveled around, illuminating the room they stood in. Standing beside the open loading doors was Barnabus Snudge, who held tight to Aurelia, a gag in her mouth, wrists bound together. At the sight of his beloved, still alive, Thraxton's heart soared then sank. But then Fowler gave a nod and Aurelia was swung out onto the jib and left dangling by her wrists, high above the cobblestones.

"You see, if Snudgy here lets go of this rope, your little dolly-mop is gonna drop fifty feet straight down. Be nothing left but a bag of broken bones for you to snuggle up with. Won't look too pretty then, either, wiv a cobblestone smashed through her face."

Aurelia moaned beneath the gag.

"Now then," Fowler said. "Hand over them pistols."

Torn, Thraxton hesitated.

"If we surrender the pistols," Algernon muttered, "they're likely to shoot us anyway."

Thraxton gasped in exasperation. He glared at Fowler. "If we give you the pistols, you will release Aurelia. You give us your word as a gentleman?"

"As a gennulman?" Fowler cackled. "Oh yeah. My word as a gent all right."

Thraxton nodded to Algernon. Reluctantly, they uncocked the pistols and handed them, grip-first, to Fowler. He hefted them in his thick-fingered hands, ogling the pistols appreciatively.

"A matched set of dueling pistols. Very fine. Very fine, indeed," he said, then tucked them into the rope hawser tied around his waist that served as a belt.

"And now, as I am a gennulman of my word... Snudge, toss 'em the rope. Snudge threw the loose end of the rope to Thraxton. As he let go, Aurelia plummeted toward the ground, screaming. Thraxton dropped his walking stick and dove for the rope whiplashing across the floorboards. He managed to grab it, but Fowler kicked him in the side of the face, tumbling him over. His grip loosened and the rope sizzled through his fingers. Just before the end flew through his hands, he gripped the rope, burning his hands as he fought to slow it, arresting Aurelia's plummet just ten feet from the ground. She swooned.

Thraxton stiffened as a pistol was pressed into the side of his head. "Let go," Fowler said.

"You will have to shoot me."

Fowler sniggered. "We ain't gonna drop her again. That was just a bit of a larf. Naw, she's worth more to me alive."

Snudge grabbed the rope from Thraxton and started hauling the unconscious Aurelia back up until the other mobsmen were able to pull her back inside.

Thraxton found himself staring into the muzzle of one of his own pistols. "Now that you know I ain't playin', let's talk about dosh. I fink an 'undred pounds is a very tidy figure."

"A hundred pounds! You must be mad!"

"One 'undred or me and the lads will have ourselves a right gay old time wiv your little dolly-mop until her fanny's as loose as an old whore's."

"But it would take a month to liquidate my holdings and come up with such a sum!"

"Well, well. You have gotta problem then, ain't ya?"

"Ten guineas. I have it in my rooms. I can put the money in your hands in just a few hours. Ten guineas."

A shifty smile smeared across Fowler's face.

"Right then. Ten guineas. But you best be quick about it. If you're not back in four hours my friend Mister Pierce is gonna poke his nose into her business—if you know what I mean."

Thraxton choked on his anger, but said nothing. He picked up his walking stick. "Come on, Algy."

"Oh, he ain't goin' wiv ya."

"But you already have Aurelia. Surely you have no need of a second hostage."

"I don't want him for no hostage. I just wanna show you I mean what I say."

Fowler snatched loose one of the dueling pistols and tossed it to Walter Crynge. "Mister Crynge. Shoot blondie in the head."

Crynge cackled as he pressed the pistol to Algernon's temple. Thraxton's fingers fumbled along the length of his walking stick until they found and folded out a hidden trigger mechanism.

"Go on!" Fowler urged. "Top him!"

Crynge pulled back the hammer with his thumb.

Algernon realized he was about to die and threw a terrified look at his friend. Thraxton slowly raised the walking stick until it was pointed at Crynge's face. The boar's head stick contained a single-shot shotgun. Thraxton slipped his thumb into the boar's mouth and pressed the jaw down until it locked, cocking the weapon. He squeezed the trigger and the stick fired with a tremendous *boom*! The blast caught Crynge square in the face, splashing his brains across the wall and killing him instantly. Another of Fowler's men sprang forward and leveled a pistol at Thraxton, but his angry scowl turned to a look of horror as Algernon drew the sword cane and plunged it through his heart. The pistol tumbled from the mobsman's hands and discharged as it hit the floor. The bullet hit Tommy Ebbs in the leg and dropped him screaming to the floorboards. *Bang.* A confused melee followed. Shouts. Curses. More gunshots. Blinding gunpowder smoke billowed. But in the mayhem, no bullets hit their mark. The mobsmen panicked and bolted from the room. Thraxton snatched the dueling pistol from Crynge's cold fingers and raised it, but Fowler had thrown his arms around Aurelia and now he dragged her backward from the room using her as a shield. The door slammed after them and locked, leaving Algernon and Thraxton sealed in.

On the other side of the door, Fowler tried to regroup his men as Aurelia kicked and struggled in his arms.

"They ku-ku-killed Bob and Crynge," Whitey Smith stammered. "And Tu-Tu-Tommy's still in there!"

Fowler shoved Aurelia into Snudge's arms. "Lock her up in the snug."

Snudge wrapped his huge arms around Aurelia, but glared at Mordecai Fowler, his lower lip jutting. "Why'd you kill little Titch?" he demanded. "He was my friend."

"Why? 'Cause the little bleeder tried to steal from me. That's why I killed him!"

Snudge's face purpled with rage, but Fowler ignored him, turning to his men. "There's only the two of 'em. Follow me, you lot. We'll go downstairs and shoot up through the floorboards. That oughta make 'em dance!"

* * *

Tommy Ebbs moaned and writhed in agony. The bullet had shattered his femur and severed an artery. Blood gushed in a widening pool.

Algernon looked with amazement at the still-smoking walking stick clutched in Thraxton's hands. "Any more shells for that thing?"

"None, unfortunately."

"Now what? We're trapped."

Thraxton's eyes scoured the empty room until they found the rope still dangling from the crane jib.

"The rope. We can swing across to the next room."

"Fowler's in there."

They turned at the sound of a thump. Tommy had staggered upright on his one good leg and hopped toward the door; *thump, thump, thump*. Suddenly, the floorboards beneath him exploded with a cacophonous volley of shots. Hit twice more, Tommy screamed and toppled. A moment later, another volley erupted, blowing the floorboards to splinters and killing him outright.

Algernon looked at Thraxton. "We're dead if we remain in here."

"There's only one way out." Thraxton nodded at the open loading doors and the rope dangling from the jib. Thraxton seized the rope, lashed the loose end around a cleat screwed to the wall, stepped back a few paces, then threw himself into space, swung in an arc, and landed neatly in the open doorway next door. He leaned out the window and called out, "Algy, I'll swing the rope back. Get ready to catch it."

Unbeknownst to Thraxton, Fanny was creeping up behind him. Algernon caught the rope, then swung toward the open doorway. Fanny ran up behind Thraxton and shoved him just as Algernon swung in. The two collided and Thraxton grabbed his friend and hung on as they swung back out into empty space. But Fanny's own momentum carried her forward and she tumbled out and fell screaming all the way to the cobblestones below.

Algernon and Thraxton swung back together and fell in through the open doorway. Thraxton scrambled to his feet.

"Aurelia!" he shouted.

They heard pounding from somewhere, small fists beating against a door, then Aurelia's muted cries for help.

"Up there!" Algy said, pointing toward a door at the top of a narrow staircase.

The two friends pounded up the squealing steps. Fortunately, the dim-witted Snudge had left the key in the lock. Thraxton turned the key as Fowler and his mobsmen came thundering up the second-floor stairs and burst into the room.

"Look lively!" Algernon shouted. They snatched the key, ducked into the snug, and locked the door from the inside.

"Geoffrey!" Aurelia cried and leapt into Thraxton's arms.

"I had feared I would never see you alive."

"I am so sorry," Aurelia sobbed. "This is all because of my foolishness."

"We may not be alive much longer," Algernon said. "There's no way out of this room."

"No, there is!" Aurelia said, and pointed up at the hidden roof hatch young Titch had dropped through.

Outside the snug, the mobsmen hastily reloaded their pistols.

"We got you now!" Fowler shouted. "Come out. If I has to come in there it will be the worse for ya. And don't try nuffink with them fancy walkin' sticks!"

Fowler banged on the door of the snug with the meat of his fist and jumped back. No response. He looked around at his men.

"Right lads, give 'em a volley!"

The mobsmen leveled their pistols and fired a deafening fusillade, splintering the door into matchwood. When the gunpowder smoke cleared, he gave the nod and Snudge crashed through the ruined door. Fowler followed, rushing in with pistol drawn.

But the room was empty.

"Where the bleedin' hell?" Fowler muttered, bewildered. But then he looked up and saw the roof hatch open to the night sky. "They're up on the tiles. Get the lads out. All of them. I ain't done with Lord Toff yet, not by bleedin' half. When I get me mawleys on him, he'll beg for death!"

* * *

The rooftop pitched down precipitously on either side. The three crept along the apex, one foot on either side, but the slates were loose, missing or slick with decades of green slime and greasy soot. One slip and the hapless person would toboggan down the slippery tiles and be launched into thin air. Algernon led the way, with Aurelia in the middle and Thraxton following behind. Their only hope of escape was to slip back inside the building far enough away from Fowler and his mobsmen to make good their escape. But the dilapidated roof was treacherous: in places it sagged perilously or gaped with jagged holes.

To complicate matters, the air was choking. Dense fog crackled with fiery cinders. Chimney smoke roiled with the pestilential vapors rising from the canal below. They reached their first obstacle, a large chimney stack. Suddenly two of Fowler's men leaped out from behind. One was armed with a sickle that he swung wildly at Algernon's head. He missed and swung again, and this time Algernon dropped, thrust his walking stick between the man's legs, and twisted. The man's feet splayed beneath him and he fell. The man dropped the sickle, scrabbling for grip with both hands as he slid down the steeply pitched roof then flew out over the edge, screaming all the way to the ground. Meanwhile Thraxton faced off against a big man wielding a cudgel which whished through the air each time he swung at Thraxton's face, forcing him to back away—the walking stick too light to catch any of the blows. Behind him a hole gaped in the roof and he was being driven steadily toward it. Thraxton caught his heel on an upraised tile and fell at the edge of the yawning hole. His attacker laughed and raised the cudgel high over his head, but then Aurelia ran from behind and shoved him. The cudgel-wielder staggered forward, tripped over Thraxton's body and toppled through the hole, crashing to the floor of the room below with a bone-splintering thump followed by a low and agonized moaning.

"Look," Algernon said, pointing farther ahead. "The roof steps down and there's a walkway. If we can just reach—"

He was interrupted by the boom of gunfire and the slate tiles around them shattered and exploded as bullets whizzed past their heads. He looked back to see Mordecai Fowler clambering out of the trap door in the ceiling of the snug. He was shortly followed by twenty of his mobsmen. The pursuers saw the three and filed along the apex of the roof toward them.

"We must reach that walkway!" Thraxton said.

They hurried onward and unexpectedly came to the end of the roof. What had seemed to be an easy escape route proved to be a deadly trick of perspective. An unjumpable gap separated the roof of the building they were on from the building with the walkway. The drop to the cobblestones below was easily sixty feet.

Trapped.

"Well, well. No place to run to, eh, Lord Muck?" Fowler cackled as he duck-walked along the tiles toward them, dueling pistol in hand, his mobsmen marching behind. "After me and the lads have taken turns with your little dolly-mop she should be nicely broken in for the paying public. She'll make a nice two-shilling whore down in Whitechapel."

Fowler brayed a coarse laugh and his men joined in. "As for you, Mister Toff, you and my friend Mister Pierce are gonna spend some long, long hours gettin' to know each other."

"You think you're the equal of any gentleman, Fowler," Thraxton shouted back. "You think you are just as good as I am... prove it!"

"I don't gotta prove nuffink to the likes of you."

"You are the lowest form of filth. Lower than the lowest mud lark or sewer scavenger, for at least theirs is an honest trade. You could never be a gentleman. Not in this life nor any other."

Fowler flourished the dueling pistol as he shuffled closer. "Like I told ya, in the Seven Dials, I'm the king, and I decide who lives or dies."

Thraxton laughed scornfully. "A king? You? You are the king of nothing. Look around. You live in a cesspool of filth and decay. But even if you had been born into the highest house in the land, this is where you would end up. Because you are filth and could never be a gentleman, never."

"Oh, you are gonna wish you had a spare set of lungs, 'cause you're gonna need 'em for all the screamin' you're gonna do!"

"Prove me wrong, Fowler. If you really think you're a gent, then fight me like a gentleman."

Fowler's face concertinaed in puzzlement. "Wot?"

"A duel. That is how gentlemen settle their differences. Or have you not the spine for it?"

"Duel you? Why the bleedin' hell should I?"

"To prove yourself. To prove to your men that you've got the guts to fight me man-to-man."

"Rubbish!" Fowler laughed, but this time the men did not join in.

"Go on, Mordecai," Snudge goaded. "Fight 'im! Show 'im you ain't scared... unless you is scared. Scared like a little weasel."

Fowler threw a hateful glare at Snudge. "I ain't scared. I ain't scared of no bleedin' toff. I ain't scared of nuffink!"

"Go on, Mordecai," piped in another mobsmen. "Let's see you take him." Suddenly all the mobsmen joined in, calling for Fowler to accept the challenge.

"All right, all right!" Fowler bellowed. "A duel it is. I'll even give you the first shot, Lord Toff."

Thraxton walked up to Fowler and held out his hand. "I must reload the pistols."

"This one ain't been fired," Fowler said, patting the pistol in his hand.

Thraxton nodded and pulled out a slender powder horn, removed the cap, and began to pour gunpowder into the barrel of his dueling pistol. Algernon threw him a concerned look. Thraxton gave his friend the slightest nod to indicate that he knew full well his pistol had not been fired. Despite that, he poured enough powder for one shot but then kept pouring and pouring until he emptied the powder horn. Next, he drew a ball from his pocket, showed it to Fowler, dropped it in the barrel, then shoved a piece of wadding in and drove in the tamping rod, ramming everything home.

"Very good," Thraxton said. "I am ready."

"You challenged me," Fowler said. "That means I have first choice of weapons."

Thraxton nodded uneasily.

"Surprised a gutter-snipe like me knows the rules of dueling, aren't ya, Mister Toff?" He nodded at the pistol in Thraxton's hand. "I'll take that pistol." He snatched it from Thraxton. "And you can have this one."

Thraxton hesitated, looking suspiciously at the pistol in Fowler's pudgy hand, and then reluctantly took it.

"Sorry, Mister Toff, but we play my rules in Seven Dials." Fowler turned his head and called out: "Mister Crynge."

"He's dead," Snudge reminded.

"Oh, yeah. Well then, Mister Snudge, do us the honors."

Thraxton stepped over to Algernon and leaned in close.

"Algy, I have no right to ask you this, but if I should fall—"

"I will defend Aurelia to the death," Algernon replied, squeezing his friend's arm.

Thraxton hugged Aurelia, looking down into her tearful face. "Death, if it comes, shall not separate us."

"Geoffrey," she whispered breathlessly. "I must tell you… I carry your child."

Astonishment washed across Thraxton's face. He had not been fearful until that moment, but now he trembled as he paced off the distance and turned to face Fowler.

"Mistah Fowler!" Snudge called. "Prepare to receive Lord Toff's fire!"

Fowler stood face on, relaxed and unafraid, a smirk on his

face. Thraxton's breath plumed as he exhaled nervously. He raised the pistol slowly until the fore and aft sight coincided with Fowler's broad chest.

The mobsmen fell silent.

Thraxton's hand shook a little, and he fought to steady it. His finger tightened slowly on the trigger, squeezing until it released.

The hammer fell with an empty click.

Thraxton's eyes widened in shock. His jaw dropped.

Fowler cackled. "Oh dearie me. Seems I did forget to reload after all."

He nodded at Snudge who chuckled dimly, then shouted: "Mister Toff, prepare to receive Mister Fowler's fire."

Thraxton turned sideways, crouching slightly, his pistol hand drawn across his chest in an attempt to protect his heart and vital organs. He threw a last despairing look at Aurelia who watched with tears streaming down her face.

"You were right," Fowler brayed. "I ain't no gennulman, and I don't fight like one. Ain't that right, lads?" The mobsmen burst into laughter which drained away as Mordecai Fowler raised the dueling pistol and aimed.

"Death," Thraxton whispered under his breath. "Death, I need you. Where are you now?"

"Goodbye, Lord Toff!" Fowler bawled. His face clenched, lips pursed, as he squinted along the pistol barrel centering Thraxton's chest in his sights. His finger squeezed. The hammer fell. A flash of orange. A drawn out *pfffffffffffffffffftt* and then...

…nothing.

White smoke pearled from the gun. A stunned look spread across Fowler's grizzled features and then… KABOOOM! The pistol exploded in his face. For long seconds, everything vanished in a white cloud. When the smoke dispersed, Fowler was still standing, though his hat was gone and his hair and clothes were charred and smoldering. The ruined pistol, its barrel peeled back by the explosion, dropped from the burned stumps of his fingers. He staggered backwards, hands clamped to his face. When he pulled the hands away, nothing remained of his left eye but a gory socket. His face gaped with fish-mouthed wounds, ripped open by shrapnel from the exploding gun. By overcharging with too much powder, and then loading two balls into the muzzle and tamping everything down tight, Thraxton ensured that the resulting overpressure would destroy the pistol.

Maimed and partially blinded, Fowler took a staggering step, lost his footing and fell, sliding down the steep pitch of the roof. As he flew out over the edge, he flailed out and managed to catch hold of the guttering. But under Fowler's bulk, the guttering started to buckle and pull loose of the rusted brackets holding it to the brickwork.

"Lads!" Fowler called out. "Help me, lads!"

None of the mobsmen stirred.

"I'll fall! C'mon, lads. Snudge… Snudge, get your arse over here!"

But Snudge didn't move. "You killed little Titch. You shouldn't not a done that, Mordecai. And I ain't your horse to be doin' wot you say no more."

The guttering creaked as it tore away from the brickwork. Fowler let go with one hand, fumbled in his coats, drew out Mister Pierce and rammed the spike into the roof. He let go of the guttering and wrapped both hands around the handle of the spike, trying to heave himself back onto the roof, but the handle was slippery with blood—for once, his own blood.

"I ain't done wiv you, Lord Toff! You're gonna suffer, you and your pox-rotten dolly-mop! Soon as I get up this roof, I'll show you all about pain and sufferin'!" But then Fowler's hands lost their grip on the slippery handle. He grabbed at the guttering and as his weight hit it, the final rusted bolts sheared off. Fowler rode the downspout as it pivoted away from the building then buckled and collapsed. He fell fifty feet and splashed down in Filthy Ditch, sending up a huge spray of putrescence. Bubbles erupted for several seconds and then Fowler burst to the surface, gagging, spitting filth, gossamer wings drooping from his arms. He sank a second time, going down with a slurping sound. More bubbles, a huge stream at first that gradually slowed to a trickle and finally one huge bubble that formed on the surface, shimmering in obscene colors, then burst.

Silence.

All eyes turned to Snudge. As the second of Fowler's leftenants, he inherited command. Thraxton and Algernon shared fearful looks. They had but one weapon, the sword cane, against an armed mob of thirty men. Snudge carefully stepped down the roof's dizzy pitch, one hand resting against the tiles until he reached the spike Fowler had left impaled in the roof. He snatched it out and rose to his feet. For a moment he stood examining it. But then he seemed to lose interest and calmly flicked Mister Pierce away. The spike made a *whicker-whick* sound as it tumbled end over end, hit the surface of the ditch with a faint plash and vanished instantly. Snudge watched the fading ripples for a moment, then trudged back up the slope of the roof and walked away, back toward the trap door. Silently, the other men fell in behind him.

Thraxton, Aurelia and Algernon shared looks of disbelief as they watched the mobsmen meekly walk away.

By a miracle, they had all survived.

Footsore, battered and weary, Thraxton, Aurelia and Algernon crossed the rickety footbridge and finally emerged from the dark alleyway to find Aurelia's father and Harold still waiting by the brougham. On sight of him, Aurelia ran and threw her arms about her father, although she wept to see the beating he had suffered.

Mordecai Fowler was dead.

Of that much, Silas Garrette was certain. He sat in the gloom of a black carriage parked directly across from Robert Greenley's house, watching in disbelief as Thraxton's blue brougham discharged its passengers.

There he was, the Mocker of Death himself, the detestable Lord Thraxton, helping Greenley hobble up the front steps of his house. Behind followed the slender figure of Aurelia Greenley and a fair-haired man Garrette recognized as one of Thraxton's seconds from the duel.

The doctor did not linger to observe the happy homecoming. He rapped on the ceiling of the hansom with his knuckles, shouted, "Drive on!" and the carriage lurched away into the night.

He had seen all he needed to see. Thraxton either had the luck of all the angels on his side or he was a more formidable opponent than Garrette had estimated. Perhaps Mordecai Fowler had been a poor choice: ruthless and totally evil, but lacking in intelligence—a blunt cudgel where a keen scalpel was required.

No. There was no other choice. He would just have to do the job himself. Besides, he had seen Aurelia Greenley up close. Since then, he had been able to think of little other than the tiny life growing inside her.

He was impatient to greet his new child.

32

The World Disintegrates

Doctor James Fuller knew full well Thraxton was standing there, but did not look up from his desk or the open journal in which he was scribbling notes—in fact, he had not looked up from his writing since Thraxton entered the room more than ten minutes ago. He finished a sentence, dipped his quill in the inkpot and continued to write. At last, the doctor appeared to have finished his entry. He picked up a shaker and sprinkled the page with sand to blot the ink dry. Thraxton's wait seemed over; but no, the doctor then turned the page and began to write more.

It was a test of wills.

Even though Thraxton had been announced, Doctor Fuller's office was the one place where professional qualifications outranked inherited titles—lord or no lord.

Thraxton cleared his throat quietly at first and then a second time, thunderously.

"Do you have an appointment, sir?" the doctor asked without ever looking up as the pen continued to scratch across the page.

"I am here on a matter of great import."

"I am a doctor, sir." The physician pried his eyes up from the journal for the first time. His face was warty, gray-bearded, a lank straggle of hairs smeared sideways across his bald scalp. The eyes, round and heavy-lidded as a turtle's, peered at Thraxton over a pair of half-moon spectacles. "All of my business involves matters of great import."

"You have a patient, one Aurelia Greenley."

"Are you a relative?" The tone was accusative.

"No... yes... that is, I am her fiancé."

The doctor stabbed the quill into the inkpot and left it quivering there. "I know the Greenleys. They have been patients of mine for years. I recollect no mention of a suitor."

"Sir, you know that Mister Greenley was severely beaten and Aurelia kidnapped. I understand you treated both of them."

The doctor's shrug did nothing to either affirm or deny he knew of the event.

"I was the one who rescued Aurelia from the hands of the criminals who abducted her."

"That's as may be. As a physician, I am bound not to share privileged information with anyone outside the immediate family." And with that he yanked the quill from the inkpot, shook the excess ink onto a blotter sheet and began to scribble again. "The door you entered by is still there," he said without looking up. "Please close it from the other side."

BANG! The golden phoenix head of Thraxton's walking stick smashed down onto the open book, crushing the quill, narrowly avoiding smashing the doctor's fingers, and splattering a huge blot of black ink across the page.

The doctor recoiled in shock. "Are you mad?"

Thraxton leaned over the desk, his face looming. "Yes, I am mad—mad as a hatter. Perhaps you have heard of me. My name is Lord Thraxton. I am told I have something of a reputation: dueling, gambling, whoring. There are many who consider me the wickedest man in London. The fellow who snatched Aurelia is dead. I killed the bastard! What say you now?"

The doctor studied Thraxton's rage-contorted face for a moment and then, unexpectedly, burst into laughter. "Yes," he chuckled. "I think you are mad. Full of piss and vinegar as we used to say where I grew up." The doctor leaned back in his chair and regarded Thraxton over his steepled fingers. He clearly was not a man to be bullied or cowed by threats. "I see you are quite earnest." He shuffled his chair back to the desk, ripped the ink-sodden page from his journal and dropped it and the ruined quill into a waste paper bin near his feet. "Very well, I will tell you what I know." He nodded toward the chair on the far side of his desk. "I suggest you sit down."

Thraxton ignored the advice, which proved to be a mistake.

The doctor mused for a moment and then began. "Aurelia suffers from a malady of the blood. It is an inherited trait, passed down the generations on the maternal side. Exposure to sunlight produces rashes and blistering of the skin. But there are more serious symptoms: abdominal pain, cramps, even periods of delirium."

Thraxton's knees began to tremble. "What is this malady called?"

"Medicine has no name for it. It is very rare, although there are rumors that this disease affects some of the highest people in society. As high even as to touch the royal family—I expect you to be completely discreet about this, of course."

"Of course, but what—?"

"Is the prognosis?" The doctor removed his half-moon spectacles and set them on the desktop. "I am sorry to say it is not good. Aurelia has suffered these attacks since puberty. I do not believe she will have a long life…"

For Thraxton, the doctor's words were being drowned by the surf-like crash of his own heartbeat.

"… but with care and attention she may live a good few years. Of course, children are out of the question."

"Children?"

"Yes, the strain of childbirth would be entirely too much for her delicate condition. After all, her mother died giving birth to her…"

Thraxton could see the doctor's lips moving but could no longer hear his words for the percussive pounding in his head. Steely needles tattooed numbness across his face. The room suddenly upended and he staggered into something that crashed to the floor as purply darkness exploded behind both eyes.

The world constricted to a trembling point of light and then extinguished. For a time, nothing.

Then two sharp blades drove up through his sinuses and into his brain. His eyes fluttered. The knives plunged a second time, driving so deep they pierced the top of his skull.

Smelling salts.

His eyes snapped open and the world surged back around him. The doctor was kneeling beside him, an arm about his shoulders pulling him into a sitting position on the rug. The doctor brought the smelling salts up a third time, but Thraxton pushed his arm away.

"She carries your child?"

He looked dumbly at the doctor and nodded.

"Dear God," Doctor Fuller said. "Then she is in the hands of the angels."

Someone coughed in his ear, but his mind was in freefall.

"We're here, sir."

He could not move. Could not speak.

"Sir, we're here…"

Thraxton blinked—his mind was a servant scurrying from the far back reaches of a mansion in reply to the bell pull. His head swiveled to the right and he looked, vacantly. Harold's face was framed in the open window of his brougham and now he opened the door, spilling in light and damp, chill air. "Sir, we've arrived at Mister Hyde-Davies' home."

Thraxton dragged himself from the carriage seat, settling the black top hat on his head as he stepped down. The words the doctor had spoken kept playing over and over in his mind so loud they deafened him to all exterior sound or sensation as he stumbled numbly up the short path to the front door. At any other time he might have found it strange that the door stood wide open on a chill October day, but upon stepping inside he blundered into a scene so chaotic it jolted him from his reverie.

The front hallway was piled with luggage: chests, hampers, baskets of clothes, crates of books and even now the servant, Horace Claypole, clomped down the staircase, his arms being stretched from their joints by the weight of the huge portmanteau he lugged.

Thraxton looked around at the scene, bewildered.

"Geoffrey!" Algernon said as he sailed from the parlor. He was stripped to the shirt sleeves and carried armfuls of books which he thumped down atop a teetering stack.

"I... I have some news..." Thraxton started to say.

"And I, too! The most wonderful news—well, two pieces of news, really. But come, I am absolutely bursting to tell you."

Algernon's attention was snatched away briefly as he noticed Horace sagging beneath the weight of his burden, patiently waiting for instruction. "Put that down over there, Horace. Oh, and fetch the other portmanteau downstairs—the heavy one."

A frisson of despair rippled across Horace's face, who turned and trudged back up the stairs, grumbling to himself as he massaged his forearms.

Inside the parlor, Algernon pushed Thraxton into an armchair then threw himself down on the ottoman.

"I've done it!" Algernon said.

"Done what?"

"Taken your advice. And bloody good advice it was! You were right, Geoffrey. To hell with society. To hell with decorum. I have asked Constance to be my wife and she has consented."

"Oh... that's wonderful. When are you?"

"Next week. Tuesday. Yes, I'm not fibbing. Tuesday! Can you believe it? It's madness, I know." He chortled with wicked glee. "Of course, I expect you to be my best man. And I hope Aurelia is well enough to attend."

"Next Tuesday?"

"I see from your expression that even you think it insanely hasty, but I have my reasons, which brings me to my second piece of news."

His friend seemed ready to burst apart with excitement, so Thraxton prompted him with a nod.

"I can scarcely believe this myself, but I am about to undertake a voyage on behalf of the Royal Botanical Society. I am to journey to the Galapagos Islands to collect new plant specimens." Algernon laughed. "Can you believe it? Two of my profoundest dreams are coming true at once!"

Thraxton's face visibly paled.

"You... you look disappointed."

"The Galapagos? Where Mister Darwin went?"

"The same."

"The other side of the world?"

"Yes, marvelous, isn't it?"

"How long will you be gone?"

Algernon smiled skeptically. "You're not getting sentimental on me, are you? Surely not you, Geoffrey, of all people! You have Aurelia now. You shan't miss me a tick."

Thraxton cleared his throat. "Um, no... not at all. It is wonderful news. How... how long?"

"As you rightly said, it *is* the other side of the world, so it's a hell of a long voyage. Plus I will be conducting many months of exploration. I expect to be gone two years at the very least. Perhaps three."

"Three years?"

"Which is why I had to rush forward my nuptials. Constance and I shall be traveling as man and wife. Our new life together will be an adventure in every sense of the word."

To Thraxton, the happy news was poison surging through his veins. "That's... wonderful."

Algernon finally remembered himself. "Oh, but you had your own news? Is it about Aurelia? She is quite recovered, I expect?"

Thraxton started to say something, but the words caught in his throat. He swallowed their bitterness and forced a smile. "Yes, that was my news. Aurelia is... very well."

"Excellent. Then we shall expect you both at the wedding?"

"Yes," Thraxton smiled, rising from his chair. "Yes, of course."

Thraxton made his excuses and left shortly after. The open trunks, the bustle, it all made sense now: Algernon was packing up his household for the long sea voyage. As Thraxton stepped through the open front door, he almost collided with Constance.

"Lord Thraxton," she smiled. "You have heard our news, then?"

"Yes... wonderful... congratulations."

"And how is Aurelia?"

Thraxton was unprepared to see her and so had not had time to recompose his face. Although he did not utter a word, Constance instantly saw the terrible truth in his eyes. She seized his hand.

"Oh, God! Have you told—?"

"No!" Thraxton shook his head. "Please... you must not tell Algy."

"But we cannot go now—"

Thraxton squeezed her hand. "You must. You shall."

"No. This changes everything. You and he are best friends. We must be here for you."

Thraxton took her hand in both of his and squeezed it. A few moments passed before his power of speech returned and when it did his voice shook with emotion. "Constance, I have had little love in my life. In Algy, I have had more than a friend. More even than a brother. He has been the anchor that kept me tied to the earth, else I would have floated away into the clouds. I never deserved Algy, but you two deserve each other. He and I have shared a journey for most of our lives. Now you have come into his life as Aurelia has come into mine. Our paths have diverged. We each must make the journey separately."

"The years will fly," Constance said, although her lips trembled as she said it. "We shall all be back together soon enough."

Thraxton's face sketched a forlorn smile. "I think not. The woman I love lives in the darkness and I must follow her wheresoever that leads. I think it likely we shall never see each other again... on this side of the Great Divide."

Thraxton gave her hand a final squeeze. "Be happy," he said, although his voice broke on the last word.

And with that he walked away.

At the waiting brougham, Harold saw his master approaching and shook himself lively beneath a waxed leather cloak beaded with rain. His hands gripped the whip and reigns, but Thraxton shambled past the carriage as if he didn't see it and continued walking up Warwick Square under a fine, slanting rain.

"Guvnor!" Harold called, thinking his master had forgotten he had brought his own carriage.

"Lord Thraxton!" he called again. But when he still received no response, it became clear that his master's black mood had darkened ever further and that he wished to walk. Harold flicked the reigns lightly. The horses stirred and began to plod forward, so that the carriage followed twenty feet behind as Thraxton walked, stiff-backed into the damp fog, his cheeks running with more than just the misting drops of rain.

Silas Garrette leaned back in the armchair, closed his eyes, and breathed in deeply through the chloroform-soaked handkerchief draped across his face.

As always, just as he was going under, the voices began.

One at first, and then another, more and more joining in until a clamorous babble resonated inside his skull. Some spoke in English, some in foreign languages, some in an alien tongue decipherable only in dreams. He inhaled faster and faster, pumping chloroform into his lungs until the voices slipped away into silence. Then the images began. Mostly these were chaotic—a clutter of nightmares accumulated during his past life: Crimea, the hospital tent, when he went by a different name. But tonight, the images were orderly, comprehensible, and he soon realized that this was a dream of a very different quality. Soon he understood that his mind had tapped into a current flowing through the ether from the future going back in time to the present.

He was seated at a card table in a darkened space, the surrounding walls no more than the suggestion of a red smudge. Seated across from him was a woman, her face hidden by a white veil. A sudden wind blew and snatched the veil away and yet the woman's face remained a blur of indistinct features. From her gray-streaked auburn hair he guessed that she was nearly forty.

The woman reached down to a deck of cards on the red velvet table, drew one card from the deck, and set it down in front of him. It was a Tarot card.

The Hanged Man.

He looked up from the card. The woman's face blurred and then zoomed into focus. She was younger now, maybe thirty. A handsome woman, but her most striking feature was her eyes, which were a startling shade of violet.

The woman peeled another card from the Tarot deck and set it down next to the first.

The Nine of Wands.

A voice said: *I must wake up.*

He looked up. The face blurred, then sharpened. This time the woman was younger still, barely twenty. She took another card and set it down in front of him.

The new card was of a tower blasted by a bolt of lightning, shattered masonry tumbling to the earth.

This time the woman had become a girl of sixteen. She placed the next card.

The Hierophant Chiron, the wounded healer.

A dagger pierced his heart. He saw himself in the card and realized his fortune was being laid out in front of him.

Wake up. I must wake up!

This time when he raised his gaze, the woman was a girl still in pigtails. Maybe eight or nine. She played the last card.

The Death card.

Of course. An intense cold surged through him. His lungs cramped and he could no longer draw a breath.

I must wake up! Open your eyes! Wake up!

When he looked up again, the room, the table was gone. In front of him was a fetus, hanging suspended in darkness. The fetus was pale, the skin almost translucent. It sucked its thumb and watched him, revolving slowly.

WAKE UP!

His eyes tore open.

Darkness.

He was lying on the floor. At some point he had fallen from the chair. He groped blindly, felt the edge of a work bench, the legs of his toppled chair. Then he heard the hiss of escaping gas and realized where he was and what had happened: in the fume-laden workshop, the gas light had gone out.

He was asphyxiating.

He scrabbled to the door and pulled it open, spilling light from the outer office. He dragged himself to the window, but was too weak to open it. A hat stand stood close by. He pushed until it toppled, smashing through the window. Cold air blew in. He pulled his face close, sucking in chestfuls of oxygen, flushing his lungs.

He rolled onto his back and lay gasping as a headache hammered at the back of his eyes. Parts of the dream were already evaporating like ether in a dish, but he knew who the fetus was and the woman it would grow into. The unborn child was what he had been looking for all along—the next leap in human evolution.

She would bridge the void between life and death and open a dialogue between this world and the next that would confound all religions and bring an end to the reign of terror that death had held for aeons.

He realized now that nothing had been an accident—not the incendiary shell that exploded above his tent. Not the appearance of the man named Silas Garrette he had become. Not the encounter with Thraxton that led him to Aurelia Greenley, for the fetus he had glimpsed grew inside her. He knew that the future he had seen had to be prevented.

Aurelia Greenley and her unborn child must die.

For a moment, Thraxton thought he was too late.

The shadowy gates of the cemetery were closed. But the glow of a lantern showed between the bars. As he stepped down from his brougham, he saw a figure at the gates in a battered bowler hat and a heavy wool coat: Charlie, the sexton. He had slipped the chain around the bars and was just about to padlock them shut.

"I'm just closin' her up for the night," Charlie said. "Bit late if yer lookin' for a stroll about the grounds."

"Actually, it's you I've come to see."

"Me, sir?"

"Yes, I need some advice."

Charlie chuckled at the thought. "Don't rightly know what advice you'd been wantin' from the likes of me, sir. I ain't exactly had much heducation."

"No, I think you've had exactly the education I need," Thraxton said.

Charlie slipped the chain loose and swung the gate open.

"I'm just about to start me rounds, if you don't mind taggin' along."

"No, that would be perfect."

Encompassed in a halo of light from the lantern, the two men meandered together around the two main paths that looped the cemetery.

"Is there something you're wantin' to ask me about, sir?"

"Yes, but it seems ridiculous now."

"Might not seem that daft to me."

"You said your wife is buried here?"

"Yessir." The sexton raised his lantern higher to throw a wider circle of light around them. He nodded toward a stand of modest gravestones tilting this way and that.

"Right over there, by the oak trees. She was a lover of trees, my old gal was."

They strode on in silence. Thraxton grappled with how to phrase the next question as they passed beneath the pharaonic arch and entered the Egyptian Avenue, an echoing tunnel lined with tombs. Their shadows shuddered eerily along the tomb doors as the lantern jogged against the sexton's leg.

"The first time we met, you said that these paths were sometimes walked more at night than during the day."

"Did I say that?"

"I have never forgotten it."

They stopped outside one of the tomb doors.

"I talk a lot of rubbish sometimes, sir. Livin' on yer own does things to yer head."

The sexton pushed the tomb door open and entered. Thraxton followed. Inside, a lead coffin sat atop a bier. The sexton set his lantern down atop it and began to rummage in his coat pockets.

"No. I don't think it was rubbish. You spoke about walking the paths and losing yourself in conversation with your late wife."

The sexton fished a number of items from his pockets and arranged them on the leaden lid: a long hat pin, the broken stem of a clay pipe, and a box of Lucifer matches.

"It's not talkin' to the dead that's the difficult part," the sexton said. "It's the listenin'. Most people don't know how to listen. You listen wiv yer head, you don't hear nuffink. You listen with the heart." The sexton put a hand to his chest, his eyes lambent. "Then you'll hear."

Thraxton watched as the older man took the long hat pin and started to drill into the top of the lead coffin, twisting the pin back and forth.

"What exactly are you doing?"

The sexton paused.

"Oh this, sir? Regulations call for all above ground burials in the city of London to enclose the casket inside a lead coffin."

"I see."

"Only problem with that is, after the body gets a bit ripe, the unhealthy vapors given off start to build up inside. Sometimes they'll balloon the lead out until the coffin explodes."

Disgust rolled across Thraxton's face.

"Yeah, nasty," the sexton agreed. "Very nasty indeed. I should know… it's me what's had to clean it up a time or two."

He continued twisting the hat pin until it penetrated the lead and then worked it around in ever-widening circles to enlarge the hole. As he drew the pin out, Thraxton could hear the faint hiss of escaping gas. The sexton quickly pushed the narrow end of the broken pipe stem into the hole, and then struck a match. The invisible gas lit with a *whumph* and a weirdly luminous flame danced in the air above the coffin.

"My God," Thraxton muttered. "The human body rendered into flame. We literally become the phoenix!"

33

DEATH AND RESURRECTION

Robert Greenley staggered up from the horsehair couch and shambled stiffly to the small writing table. A week had passed but his face was still swollen and bruised from the beating he had received at the hands of Mordecai Fowler. He drew out the chair, wincing as he settled into it. He grabbed a stack of correspondence and began shuffling through the letters, reading the return addresses.

Knuckles rapped at the parlor door.

"Come."

The door opened and Thraxton strode in. Greenley looked up and saw who it was, but did not acknowledge him and went back to perusing the letters. Thraxton stood looking down at Greenley, waiting for him to speak. When it was clear he did not intend to, the Lord addressed him: "Mister Greenley, sir."

The older man gave no indication he had heard anything.

"You know what I have come here to ask you."

"The answer is 'no,' to any question or favor you may ever ask of me... no."

Thraxton seethed, but held his tongue, trying to compose himself. After a long pause Greenley seemed to feel the weight of his stare and looked up. "Oh, I have no doubt you feel I should be grateful to you, but it was your interference in our lives that precipitated this whole affair. Aurelia was coming to see you in wanton defiance of my express command. The other night—your daring rescue—changes nothing. I fully intend to seek satisfaction against you in the courts."

"Aurelia is not your property," Thraxton said, anger rising in his voice. "She is her own person, born with free will and her own mind. And you are not God to command her, me, or anyone else!"

The letters spilled from Greenley's quaking hands. "You dare to speak to me like that in my own house?" Greenley hauled himself up from the writing desk, snatched a poker from the fireplace and shook it at Thraxton. "I'll cut your black heart out! To think that you were creeping into my house, using my daughter for your whore while I was sleeping in my bed!"

"I cannot undo what has been done... but I can make it right."

"Make it right? You have stolen a flower from my garden. I should beat you to a bloody mass, but I know that dragging you through the courts will injure you more."

Thraxton faced him calmly. "Now I know who you are.

The quick fists. The explosive temper. The fact that there is no liquor of any kind in the house. You once were me, weren't you? At a younger age? A bare-knuckle fighter. A drinker. A whorer. You see in me everything you once were. That is why you hate me, because I am everything you despise in yourself. No, not despise... fear."

Greenley's face turned black with rage. "By God, I will smash you!" He lunged at Thraxton, swinging the poker, but Thraxton grabbed it. Greenley strained to wrestle it from Thraxton's grip, but the younger man held firm. Finally Greenley gasped, let go, and staggered back, glaring at Thraxton with pure hatred.

"She carries my child," Thraxton said in a quiet voice.

Greenley's head tremored, all color drained from his face as the words knocked the fight out of him. He staggered back and fell into an armchair, suddenly very old and frail.

Thraxton stepped nearer. "I know the man you were, because I was that man, also. But I have been changed by a woman who saved my life—your daughter. I understand your jealousy, because it is born of the love you have for Aurelia. But consider this, a woman once saved your life— Aurelia's mother. I ask now that you allow your daughter to save mine. Will you give us your blessing?"

Greenley's head had drooped as he listened to Thraxton's speech and now he shook it slightly. "Never!"

"Not even to protect the reputation of your own daughter, to spare her the disgrace?"

"No!"

"To ensure your grandchild is not born into the world a bastard?"

Greenley's hands shook as he covered his face.

"Will you give us your blessing?"

Greenley did not move or speak for several minutes, until he spoke a faint, barely perceptible, "Yes."

Thraxton swallowed and drew in a long breath. "Thank you."

He turned and left the room.

Greenley slumped in the chair for a long time, unmoving. But then his shoulders began to heave and a keening sound ripped from his lips as he broke down and wept.

Augustus Skinner's heart was about to burst. He had just hobbled up four flights of stairs, leaning heavily on his cane, and in his weakened state he was sweating and dizzy. Fortunately, some kind soul had positioned an old and lopsided chair at the top of the dark stairway and now he dropped heavily into it, gasping for breath as he waited for his heartbeat to slow. From the chair, he had a clear view down the hallway to the door of Doctor Garrette's office. Skinner had made the journey out of desperation, after the doctor had ignored his repeated summonses. Although his pride balked, Skinner's craving for laudanum was the stronger.

He would beg if need be.

Just then, the door opened and Silas Garrette stepped out into the hallway. He drew a key from his coat pocket and locked the door, then turned and walked straight toward Skinner. For a moment, the critic thought of calling out to the doctor, but something held his tongue and he leaned his face back into the shadows. Garrette walked straight past, oblivious to his presence and tripped down the stairs, settling the white top hat on his head. Long after he disappeared, a distinctive odor swirled in the air—a choking chemical whiff.

Skinner limped to the office door and stood looking at the name stenciled on the glass: Dr. Silas Garrette. Even though he had watched the doctor lock the door, he took hold of the knob and tried to turn it. Locked. He felt a surge of heat as the sweats overtook him. A single pane of glass separated him from the laudanum he panged for. A giddy notion seized him. He raised his cane, ready to smash the glass.

"Waiting for the doctor, are you?"

Skinner started, nearly fell, barely managed to get the cane beneath him. A large woman with a face like a bulldog and asthmatic breathing to match wheezed in the hallway next to him.

"Yes. I'm a tad premature for my appointment."

The porcine eyes rolled up and down Skinner, taking in the crooked stance, the way he leaned painfully on the cane.

"Bad leg, I see. Touch of the rheumatics?"

"Shooting accident," Skinner lied. "Quite painful."

"Ah, very regrettable." The woman chuckled inappropriately. "Can't help much standing about then, can it?"

"Especially after all those stairs." Skinner rubbed his right hip for emphasis.

The woman laughed again, eyes vanishing into slits in the doughy folds of her face. She nodded several times, and then seemed to reach a decision, producing a brass ring jangling with keys. "I am Mrs. Parker. I have the pleasure of being Doctor Garrette's landlady, don't you see? I am certain the doctor would not mind if I let you in. Therein you can rest your leg while you wait."

"Very civil of you, madam."

Mrs. Parker unlocked the door and led the way inside. She waddled around the office which bore all the trappings of the medical profession—a desk, an examination table, a skeleton dangling from a hook in the corner—having a damned good snoop, obviously as curious as Skinner to see the inside of the office.

"I understand the doctor mostly makes house calls as I don't ever recall seeing any patients come to the office. Do you not think that is... unusual?"

"Is that correct?"

"Yes. As a matter of fact, you are the only patient I have ever seen."

"How interesting."

The landlady chuckled, her eyes roving around, taking everything in. Finally she seemed satisfied that her premises were not being destroyed or dismantled and bumbled out, chuckling to herself. Augustus Skinner waited a few moments to be sure she was not going to return and then limped around the office, exploring for himself. It looked pretty much the same as any doctor's office he'd been in before, but then he noticed the smell: that same chemical aroma that clung to the clothes of Silas Garrette. His nose led him to a door at the back of the room. It was locked, but in his haste to leave, Silas Garrette had left the key in the lock. Skinner felt sure he would find medical supplies within, including the laudanum his body ached for. He turned the key and stepped into a dark room that reeked dizzyingly of chemicals. Fumbling in his pockets he drew out a box of matches.

When he struck the Lucifer, he was not prepared for the ghastly things the flame summoned from the shadows.

Dust motes twirled in shafts of supernal light filtered through the faces of saints and angels hovering on the stained glass windows. Tenuous wraiths of smoke from the many candles that burned twirled up to the vaulted ceiling to join the dance. The organ groaned into life and sprung open the church door, throwing in a slab of light. Constance Pennethorne stepped from the glare, dressed in a glowing gown of white shot silk fashioned by Worth in Paris, a bouquet of Night Angels clutched in her hands. The music swelled and the congregation surged to its feet as the bride glided down the aisle on the arm of Mister Wakefield.

The bridegroom, Algernon Hyde-Davies, waited at the foot of the altar, his blonde curls shining in the light. His Best Man, Lord Geoffrey Thraxton, stood by his shoulder. All eyes followed the bride's majestic progress down the aisle—all except for Thraxton's, which stole a furtive glance toward the rear of the congregation where somewhere, invisibly, Aurelia watched, marooned in the deepest, darkest shadows the church could offer.

"Constance looked so lovely," Aurelia said.

"Yes," Thraxton agreed.

Both she and Thraxton were seated in the shadowy interior of his brougham. Both side curtains were tightly drawn to shut out the brilliant day. Thraxton cracked his curtain slightly and peered out.

Constance and Algernon were just climbing into an open landau outside the church and waving goodbye to the throng of well-wishers.

Aurelia drew in a shaky breath and then spoke in a trembling voice—a speech she had obviously practiced. "Geoffrey, I release you."

He dropped the curtain and turned to look at her.

"Release me?"

"I... release you from any promise you might have made or implied... any obligation you may feel toward me."

"I don't understand."

"You belong in the light, with your friends. In the real world. I am condemned to live in darkness. I could never ask you to share my fate. I am sorry now that we ever met. It would have been better never to dream of happiness—"

Her voice strained to finish, but ended in a sob as her

composure collapsed and she turned her face away.

Thraxton took her trembling hand in his.

"Until you came along, I stumbled in the darkness for years. Now, you are my light." He pressed her hand to his heart. "For you burn like a candle... in here."

After a few moments, she dared to turn her head to meet his gaze.

"Aurelia... you and I are all the world we need."

"Really?" she asked in a tremulous voice.

Thraxton smiled. "Forever."

Silas Garrette was full of smiles as he entered the room. "I understand you are ready to move forward with the lawsuit?"

Greenley shook his head. "There will be no lawsuit."

Garrette's face dropped in disbelief.

"I fail to understand. I received a communication from you just this morning—"

"Circumstances have changed."

"Since this morning? How is that possible?"

"They are to wed. There will be no lawsuit."

"Wed? We are talking about the same man? Lord Thraxton? The blackguard? The seducer?"

Mister Greenley did not answer. He opened a strong box atop his desk and counted out a stack of bank notes, setting them on the desk top. "You will find here full payment for all your time plus an additional sum for your inconvenience.

Please consider this matter and our relationship at an end. I wish you a good day, sir."

Garrette did not move. He had not worked so hard to have Thraxton slip the noose this easily. "You are pleased about this marriage?"

"My daughter's happiness is my sole concern."

"I do not understand. Just the other day—"

"My daughter carries his child."

At the words, excitement stirred in Garrette's heart.

"But your daughter's condition…"

"An illness of the blood. Her mother suffered from the same malady. She cannot stand the touch of the sun and must live her life in a darkened room. In truth, she may not—" Greenley's voice broke. He cleared his throat. "It is unlikely she will enjoy a full life."

"I am familiar with such cases."

Greenley glared suspiciously. "You cannot be correct, sir. I have searched all of Europe for such a doctor. None exist. The condition is exceedingly rare—"

"Not in some parts of the world," Garrette interrupted. "I learned of the condition and of its cure while serving with the British army in Crimea."

Greenley gasped. After years of disappointment, hope was extending a hand toward him, but he was almost too afraid to take it.

"If so, then this is miraculous news!"

"Yes, it is a condition caused by an imbalance of the humors, remedied by a simple operation. However, the procedure must be carried out as soon as possible—before your daughter's pregnancy advances any further."

For a moment, hope danced in Robert Greenley's eyes before he reeled it back in.

"Operation? You speak of an operation?"

"It is a rudimentary procedure—one that requires no hospitalization—so simple it can be carried out in her room."

He turned and strode toward the door. "I must fetch my medical instruments and some additional... apparatus. After I return, your life and your daughter's will never again be the same."

Silas Garrette showed himself out and hailed a cab. As he settled himself on the leather seat he wore an expression of smug pleasure. He was giddy with thoughts of the life forming inside Aurelia Greenley. What a child that might be. He imagined it even now, pale and ethereal as the mother, a ghost floating in its amniotic darkness. Fate had just delivered a new sibling for his children and an opportunity to teach the insolent Thraxton an excoriating lesson on the respect that death commanded.

Silas Garrette clomped up the stairs carrying a large jar under one arm, an enormous bottle of chemicals under the other. He had to set everything down to unlock the door to his office. But upon turning the key in the lock, he was alarmed to find the door already unlocked. He entered and looked around, his spine stiffening as he noticed the door to the windowless room slightly ajar, and the glimmer of gas light within. He moved like a man walking against a hurricane as he approached and shouldered the door wide.

Augustus Skinner sat in the leather armchair. He was holding a black revolver, and now he leveled it at Garrette's chest.

"Come in, Doctor Garrette... or whoever you are."

Silas Garrette hesitated, then slid into the room. His eyes could not help but dart to one side, checking that his beloved brood still slumbered safely in their glass jars.

"Your so-called 'children' I take it?" Skinner mocked disdainfully.

Garrette said nothing. The Gladstone bag sat atop the bench. Inside, his medical instruments: bone saw, cleaver, and his wicked sharp scalpel. He eased a step closer. "I am a doctor. They are part of my studies—"

"Studies into what? Depravity? Tricksterism?" Skinner lifted his cane and pushed open the cabinet door. Inside, the two phrenology busts topped with theatrical wigs and whiskers.

"Wigs. Disguises. Who are you really?"

No response.

"I also found this pistol," Skinner said, brandishing the revolver. "Hardly something I would expect a man in the medical profession to possess."

"My army revolver. I was a surgeon—"

"In Crimea," Skinner interrupted. "Yes, you have spoken of it. Or is that another lie?" He gestured with the pistol. "Take off the hat."

Garrette seemed reluctant, so Skinner aimed the pistol at his face. "Go on."

As Garrette removed the white top hat, he noticed that he had left the bottle of chloroform on the bench, loosely corked. Next it to it was a white handkerchief. He casually reached to set the top hat down on the bench, pushing the bottle with the brim of the hat so that it toppled. Chloroform gushed around the loose cork, soaking into the handkerchief.

"Now the wig."

He eased off the wig, revealing a scalp traced with jagged red scars.

"And the rest—the full disguise."

Garrette glared hatefully. He peeled off whiskers, eyebrows, mustachios. The creature named Silas Garrette evaporated before Skinner's eyes, leaving a bald, gaunt face staring down at him.

"Doctor Garrette. My stalwart surgeon. You never did remove the pistol ball, did you?"

The doctor grinned morbidly. "No... and by now it is likely gangrenous."

Skinner shuddered at the man's venom. With his free hand he lifted a bottle of laudanum he had discovered, his hand tremoring as he fumbled it to his lips.

"You've imbibed a good deal of laudanum, haven't you, Augustus? I can tell by your pupils. You probably could not shoot straight if you tried."

Skinner flung the bottle at the doctor's feet, smashing

it, splashing laudanum across the doctor's trouser legs. He drew the hammer of the pistol back and centered the muzzle on his adversary's face. "On the contrary. I think I've had just enough to steady my aim. Shall we see if I can shoot straight?"

Doctor Garrette's lips tightened to a slit. The sickly sweet odor of chloroform billowed in the air.

"How many atrocities have you committed under the guise of healer?"

"The public would not understand my work." Garrette lifted one of the glass jars. Inside, his special child—Janus, the double-faced baby—nodded gently in its chemical currents. "As a surgeon in Crimea I probed the mysteries of death. With a scalpel I could tease apart the tissues of life until I cut away the fibers binding the soul to the body and liberate it. Now, I am probing the nexus where inanimate matter receives the quickening and is shaped by the forces of nature."

Doctor Garrette's voice trembled with passion as he spoke; his eyes gleamed in the flickering gas light.

"With those abominations? You truly are deranged!"

By now the aroma of chloroform, slightly sweet in small quantities, soured the air.

Skinner gasped, suddenly breathless. "What is that infernal smell?" He tried to rub his face with a clumsy hand but missed.

"The smell is chloroform. I tipped the bottle over and it is dripping into the white handkerchief next to where you sit. I am quite inured to breathing chloroform—a result of my addiction these many years—but I am sure that you are feeling its effects quite strongly."

Garrette's words seemed to rattle down a tin chute into his mind. Beneath it, Skinner became aware of a deep susurrant respiration—his own breathing. His eyelids seemed suddenly heavy and he realized with terror that he was on the verge of lapsing into sleep. He fought to stay awake, but found himself gripped by a dreamy paralysis. Although he fought it, the hand holding the pistol sank slowly into his lap. His eyelids drooped shut for what seemed like a moment but when he opened them he found the gun had magically vanished from his hand. His eyes fluttered and closed again. And this time when he opened them Doctor Garrette was seated on a stool in front of him, a scalpel clutched in his hand; unrolled on the bench next to him the leather holster of surgical instruments.

"To a surgeon," Garrette said in an echoey, underwater voice, "the human body is little more than a puppet made of meat: a collection of sticks, the skeleton, animated by the contracting forces of muscles working against ligaments and tendons. For example, if I sever the tendons behind your knees..." He leaned down, drove the scalpel into the back of Skinner's right knee and sliced upward, severing the tendons, and then did the other leg. "...you lose the ability to stand up."

Skinner's eyes widened. He realized with horror what was being done to him. He could feel pain, but only distantly. The outer limits of his body had dissolved, leaving him a passive observer—a balloon floating in a cloud of chloroform.

"And lastly, there's that tongue of yours, which is sure to begin wagging." The gaunt face swam up close, filling his vision. The reek of chemicals was gagging. He felt his jaws being spread as Garrette reached in and seized his tongue, drawing it out of his mouth, stretching it.

"Yes," Doctor Garrette said. "I'm afraid it's going to have to come out."

He caught the glitter of a scalpel and then his head jerked as the doctor sawed away at the meat.

Unfortunately, Augustus Skinner remained conscious, his soul trapped in its prison of suffering flesh for the duration of what proved to be a long and horribly tedious operation.

34

RIPPED FROM THE WOMB

The fist pounding on the front door launched Robert Greenley out of his chair. Despite his soreness, he rushed through the hallway, growing angrier with each painful step over the impudence of that impatient banging.

When he snatched the front door open, Doctor Garrette stood on the front step, the black Gladstone bag clutched in one hand. He held a large jar filled with a clear liquid beneath his free arm.

Greenley hesitated, then stepped aside and let the doctor in. As he brushed past, Greenley caught a whiff of the strangest odor clinging to the man's clothes, but assumed it was something related to his profession: powerful disinfectant, perhaps.

"I think it would be prudent to first consult with Aurelia's present physician, Doctor Fuller."

"That would merely delay things. To be effective, the

procedure must be carried out immediately."

"What exactly is this procedure—?"

But the doctor was already climbing the stairs. "I am a very busy man. Your daughter is upstairs?"

Greenley followed the doctor up the staircase. The odor really was quite overpowering. He knocked twice on the bedroom door before showing the doctor in. The room was dark apart from a single candle burning on the bedside table. Aurelia stood up from a chair, the novel she was reading clutched in her hand.

"Father?"

"This is Doctor…"

"Garrette."

"Doctor Garrette. You have already met my daughter, Aurelia."

The doctor stepped to the bedside and looked down at Aurelia, then took hold of her chin and turned her face first this way and that. In the quivering candlelight her skin shone luminous and pale, the eyes all pupil and uncanny. Silas Garrette shivered in anticipation: the unborn child she carried must be near translucent. "I will need to give your daughter a thorough examination."

"Of course."

"Including the more intimate aspects of her physiology."

"I beg your pardon?"

"Her feminine parts."

Discomfort rippled across Greenley's face. "Again? Is that entirely necessary? I am not sure I feel comfortable—"

"Of course, you may stay and observe if you wish."

Like most men of his time, Greenley was squeamish about such matters. He quickly excused himself and fled the bedroom.

The doctor flashed an unconvincing smile and instructed Aurelia, "Please lay back upon the bed."

Uneasy, she shyly complied.

Doctor Garrette set the glass jar atop the dresser, then opened his bag, took out his leather holster of instruments and unrolled them. He reached back into the bag and produced a stoppered brown bottle and a mesh face mask.

"Do you know what chloroform is?" he asked.

"Yes."

"I am going to sedate you. Do not be frightened. It will help you... slip away."

Doctor Garrette placed the mask over her mouth and nose and dripped several drops of chloroform onto it.

"Breathe deeply. Soon you will find yourself lost in the most interesting dream you've ever had."

Aurelia looked up with frightened eyes. She grabbed his hand, trying to pull the mask away, but he kept it clamped in place.

"Don't fight it. Let go. Fall into it... fall into it like death!"

Her struggles faded as the chloroform swept the light from her eyes. Aurelia's hand loosened, fell away limp. Her eyelids fluttered and closed.

Doctor Garrette stepped to the bedroom door and turned the key, locking them in and Robert Greenley out.

He returned to the bedside to find Aurelia breathing deeply, fully unconscious. He unfastened several of the buttons on the front of her dress, and then pushed it up onto her chest. Her abdomen was softly domed. She was maybe two months along. With scalpel in hand, he knelt on the bed and pressed his ear to her belly, listening.

Father... Father... came a tiny, distant voice. His newest child was there, sleeping just beneath the flesh, waiting to meet its new father. Just a few quick scalpel strokes away. His fingers trailed across the leather holster until they found his favorite scalpel. He drew it out, breathed upon its reflective surface and polished the blade on his sleeve.

In the downstairs parlor, Robert Greenley paced, ill at ease. The idea of a stranger, albeit a doctor, having unrestricted access to his daughter disturbed him. Especially this doctor. There was something queer about the man that disturbed Greenley the more he thought about it. For one, he wore a white top hat—not a fashion befitting the gravity of such a profession. And then there was the man's peculiar aroma, a scent that Greenley felt he had smelled before but could not place. When his unease peaked, he climbed the stairs to Aurelia's room and knocked softly on the door. No answer. Greenley waited a few moments, then quietly turned the doorknob and pushed. To his surprise, he found the door locked.

"Doctor?" he called, rattling the handle. No reply. He banged a fist on the door. "Doctor, what is going on?" A strange silence. Robert Greenley was a big man, so when he shoulder-charged the door the deadbolt tore loose of the casement on the first impact. Inside, he found the doctor, a scalpel in his hand, crouched over Aurelia who lay unconscious on the bed, exposed.

Greenley roared with rage and leapt on the doctor and the two men toppled off the bed, upending the table and flinging the glass jar into the air. It hit the wall and shattered. The doctor slashed at his attacker's face, but Greenley seized the hand with the scalpel and pinned it to the floor. The open bottle of chloroform was gurgling itself empty on the rug beside them. The doctor grabbed the bottle with his free hand and splashed chloroform in Greenley's face, who recoiled, bellowing, as the volatile liquid burned his eyes.

Doctor Garrette broke free and leaped to his feet. The jar was smashed. No time. He rolled up the leather holster and stuffed it into his coat pocket, then lifted Aurelia's limp form from the bed and flung her over one shoulder.

Groping, flailing, unable to open his eyes, Greenley caromed out of the bedroom and slammed into the wall at the top of the landing. He heard feet thunder down the stairs, the front door crash open and though he stumbled blindly after, he knew it was too late.

Aurelia had been taken.

35

THE STORM BREAKS

A late afternoon of turmoiled weather.

It was only four p.m., yet a weird twilight came and went. At times bright sunshine cast sharp-edged shadows. Minutes later, the world dimmed and gusting winds snapped the Union flags flying above Trafalgar Square. On the far horizon, a dark armada of towering storm clouds sailed toward London, threatening violence to come. The gloom, slowly suffocating the dying day, matched Thraxton's mood. After the wedding, he had dropped Aurelia at her home and then driven the brougham to Victoria Station. Here, he had said his last goodbyes to Algernon and his new bride before they vanished in a cloud of white steam as the Dover train thundered from the station.

Now Thraxton stared through stray raindrops streaking the windows of his carriage, his fingers restlessly twisting and untwisting the phoenix head of his walking stick as the blue brougham trundled through London traffic. By the time the carriage turned into Soho Square, the lamplighters were already making their rounds. When the brougham clattered to a halt outside Aurelia's house the front door yawned wide and then Robert Greenley staggered out, his clothing disheveled, his eyes squeezed tight, face contorted with pain.

Thraxton sprang from the brougham and ran to him.

"Mister Greenley?"

"The doctor! A scoundrel. An imposter. He has Aurelia! You must stop him!"

Puzzled, Thraxton looked around just in time to see a tall man bundle Aurelia into a hansom cab. The man jumped aboard and threw a retreating glance over his shoulder—his eye fixing upon Thraxton. He had on a white top hat and rose-colored pince-nez spectacles. Thraxton remembered seeing that face before.

Wimbledon Common.

Mist-shrouded fields.

The duel.

The confrontation with Greenley. The doctor had been there, also.

The world slowed and froze. The cries of costermongers, the rattle of traffic in the streets drained into silence. The man stared at Thraxton, the lenses of the rose-tinted pince-nez glowing red in the flickering gas light. A voice spoke in his ears, and Thraxton could not tell if he heard it or merely remembered the words:

Death will not be mocked, nor sneered at. And there are many doors death can enter by... as you will learn at your cost.

The brakes released and the world lurched forward, set in motion once again. Sound surged back into Thraxton's ears with a rush.

He ran to his waiting brougham and vaulted onto the driver's seat next to his servant. "Harold! Quickly, after the cab!"

Harold looked flummoxed, but cracked the whip over the horses' heads. The carriage lurched away, almost colliding with a goods wagon loaded with beer barrels. The driver screamed a mouthful of Billingsgate and shook his fist at them. Thraxton ignored him, straining through the failing light to keep his eyes affixed to the hansom. Traffic was heavy and wagons and carriages stretched as far as the eye could see. Still, through Harold's skilled driving and judicious use of the whip, weaving wildly past slower carriages, they hove within a dozen lengths of the black cab. But as the traffic squeezed beneath a railway bridge, a flock of sheep being driven to Smithfield Market flooded the roadway, stopping the traffic ahead of them, while the hansom they were pursuing managed to slip through.

"Damn and bloody blast!" Thraxton yelled and jumped down. He threw a desperate look up at his servant. "Harold, return to Mister Greenley's house. Take him to the nearest police station."

"What will you do, sir?"

"Follow on foot and hope the hansom will also be held up."

Thraxton left the stalled brougham and dashed on ahead, running pell-mell through the frozen traffic. He reached the milling flock and barged his way through the mindless press of baaing sheep. As he ran beneath the railway bridge a train roared overhead, showering soot and fiery cinders on everything below. He plunged out of the gloom of the bridge and was just in time to see the hansom turn onto Wellington Street.

He knew instantly where it was headed—the River Thames.

Minutes later, he arrived at Waterloo Bridge, breathless, sweat salting his eyes. He was in luck: it looked as though every carriage, brougham, omnibus and horse cart in London was trying to squeeze across the bridge. Traffic in both directions was at a standstill. He spotted the hansom cab, snarled with the rest and ran up to it, snatching the door open.

Empty.

"You there, driver!" Thraxton shouted up. "You had a fare, a man in a white top hat and a young lady. Where did they go?"

The cab driver pushed his bowler onto the back of his head.

"Got off at the steps, sir. Just before the bridge. Looked like they was headin' for the steamer dock."

At that instant a steam whistle shrieked. Thraxton ran to the bridge railing and looked out just in time to see a passenger steamer pull away from its pier and chug north up the river. As it passed beneath Waterloo Bridge, he could see passengers standing at the railing. Among them, a figure in a white top hat with his arm around the shoulders of a small figure in a black dress who slumped against him, head lolling. As the steamer passed beneath the bridge, the tall man looked up at him, raised his white top hat and waved it jauntily—Doctor Garrette.

Thraxton pounded down the steps. A small paddle-wheel steam-tug drifted a foot from one of the piers, smoke billowing from its stack. The boat's skipper, an abbreviated stump of shoulders and brawn whose physiognomy mirrored his vessel, stood gripping the tiller, smoke billowing from a pipe jammed in his mouth. Thraxton leaped from the end of the pier and landed sprawled on the deck at his feet.

"Sir," he said, breathlessly. "I need to hire your boat. A lady's life depends upon it."

The pursuit was short in distance, but prolonged in time. The steam-tug *Cricket* was powerful but slow. It trailed behind the larger steamer, which steadily drew away. But the captain of the tug knew where the steamer was heading, to Cadogan Pier just a few miles down the river in Chelsea.

They were drawing stares, and that was bad.

Silas Garrette knew that he and Aurelia presented an incongruous spectacle that pulled the eyes of the other passengers to them like iron to a lodestone: the tall, gangly man in the white top hat (which made him seem even taller than his six foot six height) and the pale-skinned, diminutive young woman who dangled in his arms, limp as a child's rag doll.

The couple standing at the railing had been watching them since they boarded. They appeared to be of the lower classes but were dressed up in their best finery: the woman in gaily colored dresses over crinolines and a flowery bonnet unseasonal for late October; the man in a bowler and scratchy tweed suit that stretched tight across his barrel chest, his muscular arms squeezed into sleeves too narrow. The man's mustachios were trimmed in a military style and Garrette guessed he was likely an ex-army man and probably very handy with his fists. His inkling that this could be a danger was confirmed when the man whispered something to the woman and then left his place at the railing and approached.

"Here," the man said. "What's your game, then?" He indicated Aurelia's limp form with a nod.

Garrette's right hand reflexively dipped into his pocket and fondled the cold smooth steel of his scalpel. His eyes focused not on the uncouth face but on the carotid arteries— swollen tributaries of blood pulsing in the man's throat. So readily accessible. A quick slash and the churlish oaf would bleed out in seconds.

"I am a doctor. This young lady is my patient."

Despite the authoritative tone of Garrette's voice, the military man remained skeptical.

"She looks drunk to me. Or maybe you slipped her somethin'?"

"Perhaps you should mind your own business."

Step a little closer, fool, Silas Garrette thought as he began to ease the scalpel from his pocket. *I'd laugh to see the look on your face when I open your throat.*

"I think this young lady needs help. I think maybe she is my business."

Aurelia's droopy-lidded eyes opened a little. She started to make mewling sounds of protest, but Garrette pressed the chloroform-soaked mask over her nose and mouth to stifle them, and her body slackened in his grip as she breathed in the vapors.

The man's eyes widened as he watched the mask press over Aurelia's face. The huge hands balled into fists and he took a step forward.

"She has the consumption. It is highly infectious. I would keep my distance if I were you."

At the mention of the word "consumption," the man's face paled and he stumbled backward. The other passengers sitting close also quickly vacated their seats and moved away. The military man took his female companion by the arm and drew her farther along the railing.

Silas Garrette allowed himself a smile. He was quick with the scalpel—a few seconds' work—but he needed to secure a new glass womb to supplant the flesh one he would rip his child from. He threw a look over the stern of the boat. He could see the tiny figure of Thraxton on the deck of the pursuing tug, but the slower boat was falling further behind.

What's more, they were steaming toward a place Silas Garrette knew it would be impossible for Thraxton to find them.

In the skies above London, daylight grappled with night. At times bruise-colored clouds swamped the sun, suffocating the light. At other times, the clouds tore apart, shafts of sunlight shot down and bright day returned. The air smelled like rain. Ragged scraps of dark cloud scudded low. Now and then the sky shook with a distant rumble, a premonition of stormy weather moving in. On either side, steamboats chuffed up and down the Thames, venting smoke like watery dragons.

"Can you go no faster?" Thraxton shouted above the rattle and wheeze of the steam engine.

"Not without risking the boiler," the captain replied. "The old gal's ailing of late."

By the time the *Cricket* drew alongside Cadogan Pier, the steamer had discharged all of its passengers. Thraxton jumped from the deck, dashed up the pier, and was just in time to see Garrette drag Aurelia through the gates of the Cremorne Pleasure Gardens. Now he understood the madness behind Dr. Garrette's method. The Cremorne Gardens was a popular public entertainment which featured park-like pavilions, dancing platforms, and acres of gardens, grottoes and tree-lined boulevards to promenade. Once lost amongst the thousands of Londoners that flocked to the place, it would be nigh impossible to find them again. As he sprinted through the iron gates, someone bellowed: "Oi! You there. A shilling for entrance!"

The uncouth voice emanated from the barred cave opening of a ticket kiosk. Thraxton scrabbled in his pockets, seized a handful of coins and flung them through the bars, then ran up the main pathway, scanning the crowd.

Doctor Garrette had found the perfect place to hide.

Everywhere men in top hats and frock coats walked arm in arm with ladies. But then, in the distance, Thraxton saw a single white hat carried along on a river of black toppers.

At the side of the path a wooden hand pointed the way above the words: *Pagoda and Dance Platform.* He could already hear the strains of an orchestra striking up. They were playing a waltz. Thraxton had visited the Cremorne many times, and had danced on the very same platform. Here the crowds were always the thickest. He hurried in pursuit.

In the gathering dusk all the gas lamps were lit; colored globes strung from trees and atop poles illuminated the grounds like a fairyland. Hundreds of dancing couples whirled counterclockwise around the circular dance platform. At its center, an orchestra played inside a brightly lit pagoda of the eastern fashion. Thraxton dodged through the crowd toward the iron railings that bordered the dance platform. Up close, he spotted a figure in a white top hat swaying to the music. But when he reached the spot, the man proved to be one of three drunken swells ogling the women and braying with laughter. Thraxton knew the man in the white top hat, or at least he knew Thraxton, for the man seized his arm and blathered, "Geoffrey! Come along and have a drink with your old friends."

A gap opened in the dancers and he glimpsed the man in the white top hat, who met his gaze, smiled and whirled Aurelia away, who sagged in his arms like a broken doll. Thraxton snatched his arm from the drunken swell's grip and pushed him away roughly. He barged his way in among the dancing couples, fighting the counterclockwise flow, earning himself angry shouts and slaps from some of the dancers, but the white top hat was moving toward him. He lunged through a gap in the dancers and seized the man's shoulder.

"What the deuce!" The alarmed face that looked into his was not Doctor Garrette. The woman was not Aurelia.

Stunned, Thraxton released the man and looked around just in time to see Aurelia being dragged off the dance floor. But by the time he had fought his way off the dance platform and back on the other side of the iron railings, Aurelia and her abductor were nowhere to be seen. Thraxton ran along the sylvan avenues, eyes scanning for a white top hat, but it was no use.

They had vanished.

Exhausted and despondent, he flopped onto a park bench, walking stick laid across his lap, his head in his hands. A thousand fears and recriminations tumbled through his mind.

Directly across from the bench, a brightly colored poster plastered on a wooden hoarding depicted a gas balloon rising against a night sky bursting with skyrockets. An elaborately flourished script announced: *Fireworks at dusk. Balloon Ascents Nightly (weather permitting)*. Beneath the balloon, a hand indicated the way. Something about the poster leaped out at Thraxton. He jumped to his feet and ran in the direction the finger pointed.

When he reached the large lawn from which the balloon ascents took place, a crowd of spectators milled. The balloon, filled with lighter-than-air hydrogen gas, was a royal blue color emblazoned with winged sylphs cavorting around its mid-section. Below the gas envelope a wicker basket large enough to accommodate five or six adults hung suspended and now paying customers clambered aboard, aided by the balloon pilot and his assistant. The flights were tethered. The balloon, once filled with passengers, was allowed to rise to a height of three hundred feet, providing a night-time aerial vista for adventuresome patrons before being winched back to earth.

Thraxton earned some cutting stares as he roughly pushed to the front of the crowd. His heart somersaulted as he saw a white top hat at the back of the balloon basket, a shorter female figure standing beside. The balloon was already lifting off. Thraxton vaulted the iron railings in time to catch hold of the wicker basket and climb inside. With Thraxton's added weight, the balloon sagged and bumped back to earth.

The balloon pilot was outraged. "See here! What the devil—?"

"Sir! That man has abducted my fiancée!" Thraxton shouted, pointing. "We must hold him and send for the police."

All eyes in the balloon turned to the man in the white top hat. With unnerving nonchalance, Silas Garrette drew a scalpel from his coat pocket and pressed the blade to Aurelia's throat.

A woman shrieked. Yells and shouts followed as passengers panicked.

Thraxton tried to push toward Aurelia, but was shoved back as people leaped and threw themselves over the sides of the basket. When the balloon pilot tried to grab Garrette, the doctor slashed his throat with one quick scalpel stroke, hurling him aside so forcefully he hit the side of the basket and toppled out. Suddenly unweighted, the balloon shot skyward, the handle of the unmanned winch whirring out of control as the tether unreeled.

The doctor kept the blade pressed tight against Aurelia's windpipe, who looked at Thraxton with sad, helpless eyes. "Shall I sacrifice her now?" he taunted. "So she can bleed to death in your arms like a slaughtered lamb?"

The basket jolted mightily as the tether reached the end of its windings and tore loose of the winch. Unrestrained the balloon continued to climb while a light breeze carried it over the Cremorne Gardens.

As the balloon drifted directly above the fireworks pavilion a fusillade of skyrockets whooshed into the sky and the air around the balloon exploded in starry bursts of fire. Buffeted by the blast, the balloon pitched and rocked, knocking them off their feet. Thraxton used the distraction to leap forward, snatch Aurelia from Garrette's grip and pull her behind him. In the struggle, Garrette dropped the scalpel. It slid along the floor of the basket and he lunged for it, but Thraxton kicked him in the face, rolling him away. When they both clambered to their feet, Thraxton now held the scalpel in one hand, his walking stick in the other.

Bam, bam, bam... KABOOM! They drifted through choking clouds of gunpowder smoke as more explosions detonated around them. The balloon shuddered as a skyrocket slammed into the ropes holding the basket and snagged, a fiery cone of sparks spraying from its base. Thraxton knew it would explode at any moment and knocked it loose with a blow from his walking stick; it sputtered away and detonated with a deafening bang, sending green and red fireballs whizzing around them, peppering their faces with hot gunpowder.

Through it all, Doctor Garrette laughed uproariously. "You mock death?" he shouted above the din. "We are in a balloon filled with volatile gas, surrounded by exploding fireworks. What a glorious way to die!" He said more, but his words were drowned as a second wave of skyrockets whooshed up from below and blew the sky around them into curtains of glimmering fire.

Their drift had stopped and Thraxton realized that if they remained at that altitude the balloon was doomed. He slashed the cord holding one of the sandbags with the scalpel, releasing it. As its weight fell away, the balloon surged upward. He cut loose a second sandbag and the balloon rushed higher until soon they were looking down on the fireworks bursting below. Climbing past a thousand feet, higher elevation winds caught the balloon and carried it east. The streets and smoking chimney pots of London drifted far below. They were above the lower level clouds now, in a sky lit by the ruddy sun dipping into the cloud tops. Afraid of a fight with Garrette over a sharp blade with Aurelia so close, Thraxton tossed the scalpel away to be rid of it.

"Very clever," the doctor said. "You have disarmed yourself." He smiled as he withdrew the leather holster of instruments from his overcoat pocket, unfurled it with a flick, and drew out a small cleaver. "I will carve you into stumps and use what's left of you as a pillow while I slice open the belly of your whore and take what is mine."

Thraxton thumbed the release catch on his cane and gave it a twist. He thought he was carrying the sword cane topped by the snarling tiger. Instead, the phoenix head came off in his hand and he found himself holding the slender glass tube filled with brandy.

Dr. Garrette laughed at his befuddlement. "How very chivalrous. Are you going to offer me a drink?"

Thraxton snatched the stoppered glass tube of brandy from the cane and then lunged forward and smashed it across his enemy's face. The glass tube shattered, its sharp shards slicing open the bridge of Garrette's nose and dousing his face and chest with brandy. He sputtered, reeling backwards, wiping brandy onto his sleeve.

Now he was furious and came at Thraxton slashing with the cleaver. "Time to jettison the useless ballast." Thraxton deflected the blow with his walking stick driving the cleaver blade into the edge of the wicker basket where it stuck fast. The two men wrestled, crashing from side to side of the basket as they fought, punching, kicking, clawing at each other's faces. The two were evenly matched and finally broke apart, gasping for breath. Garrette's disguise had been destroyed in the fight, and now his false whiskers and eyebrows dangled loose.

"Death is a gift," Garrette managed between panting breaths. "A gift earned through suffering that cleanses the soul and makes it worthy. I will make you worthy of death—both of you."

Meanwhile the balloon had continued to climb and now drifted toward the armada of anvilhead storm clouds, towering and mighty. As they passed beneath one, the hair on Aurelia's head stood on end as the air grew tense with static electricity. Suddenly a jagged bolt of lightning flashed just below the balloon with an almost instantaneous crack of thunder.

"Roar! Roar on!" Garrette laughed. "Death is awakened and has come for us all."

Aurelia pressed her face into Thraxton's chest, her small body trembling. "Geoffrey," she whispered, "I am ready to die with you… but I want our child to live."

Thraxton looked down into her face. "Our child shall

live. We shall live." He gently pushed her away and crouched down, gathered the pieces of his walking stick, and screwed the phoenix head back into place. Then he raised the stick to strike at Garrette.

"Geoffrey!" Aurelia called. "Look!"

When Thraxton turned his head, the brass phoenix was surrounded by a glowing ball of St. Elmo's fire.

Garrette unleashed a snarl and sprang forward while his adversary was distracted. The two wrestled for the walking stick, crashing from side to side, until Garrette pinned Thraxton to the floor of the wicker basket. With inhuman strength he pressed the walking stick into Thraxton's throat, crushing his windpipe.

"Life is weak, but Death is strong!" Garrette said. He shifted his weight until his thin knees straddled the walking stick. Thraxton's face purpled as his windpipe was crushed flat.

The doctor calmly snatched up his white top hat and settled it upon his bald pate. "Die slowly, Lord Thraxton. I do enjoy a good prolonged death."

"Geoffrey!" Aurelia screamed. She looked around the inside of the basket for a weapon but there was nothing. In desperation, she snatched the gold Ankh from her neck, breaking the chain, and flung it at Dr. Garrette. It hit him in the face. By reflex, he grabbed it.

"What's this?" he said, pulling the chain away and staring at it. "A pagan charm?"

Just then the tiniest of sparks leapt from the gold Ankh

and Dr. Garrette's clothes, splashed with brandy and permeated with volatile chemical vapors, ignited. He leaped up from the floor of the balloon and staggered drunkenly around the basket, yelling, hands beating at his face and chest which crawled with a weird blue flame. Aurelia rushed to help Thraxton sit up. By now, the doctor was fully engulfed. Realizing that the balloon would be the next to catch fire, Thraxton burst upward, slammed a shoulder into the doctor's stomach driving him up and over the side of the basket.

Silas Garrette fell earthward trailing a faint comet's tail of gray smoke. The white top hat, also burning, tumbled slowly after. He plunged through the top of a small black cloud and out the bottom, screaming all the way—a scream not of fear but of impotent rage. Thraxton watched the meteoric plummet until Garrette vanished from sight in the glimmering constellation of gas lights burning in the streets of London.

"Geoffrey!"

He pulled Aurelia into a crushing, desperate embrace. But now, suddenly loosed of the weight of a grown man, the balloon rocketed upward faster than ever. Above them towered a thunder cloud the size of a mountain. The base of the cloud concaved in a dome that could have swallowed St. Paul's Cathedral and a dozen more. The balloon began to lash and writhe as it hit the swirling vortex of air being sucked up into the cloud. The light turned a sick, ominous green, and Thraxton realized with dread that they were about to be drawn into a thundercloud from which there could be no survival.

"We are going to die, are we not, Geoffrey?"

"I had a life, but never lived until I met you."

Thraxton looked into Aurelia's violet eyes, bright and unafraid. "It does not matter... because I am here with you, and I shall never let you go."

"Promise?"

"I promise."

"And I shall never let go of you."

They were ascending at tremendous speed, sucked into the cloud's converging updrafts.

Their embrace tightened as the world turned opaque white, faded to gray and then black. For a time there was nothing but darkness and then a deafening concussion as the world exploded in a blinding white dance of luminous atoms.

36

A NEWSPAPER REPORT

THE DAILY DOINGS

MAD DOCTOR IN BALLOON MURDER RAMPAGE!

The Cremorne Pleasure Gardens in Chelsea witnessed one of the most heinous crimes in London history on Wednesday night. As the evening balloon ascent began, one of the passengers, a tall man in a white top hat produced a knife, seized a young lady, and threatened to cut her throat.

THROAT SLASHED

When the balloon pilot, Charles Green Spencer of Battersea, attempted to apprehend the man, he was brutally murdered by having his throat slashed. His body was then thrown from the balloon in full sight of the horrified crowd. Fearing for their lives, screaming passengers leaped from the basket, whereupon the lightened balloon quickly ascended, bearing aloft the helpless woman along with a gentleman who observers say claimed to be the lady's fiancé.

LIFE AND DEATH STRUGGLE

Witnesses on the ground reported seeing a tremendous struggle between the two men in the basket as the balloon drifted over Cremorne, narrowly avoiding being struck and destroyed by an aerial bombardment during the nightly fireworks display.

IMPALED ON RAILINGS

It is unclear what happened next in the balloon, which was seen to ascend to great altitude above the city of London in the midst of a violent thunderstorm. It appears that the madman was either struck by lightning or fell from the balloon's basket. His badly burned body was found impaled on railings in front of a private residence in Kensington. The condition of the corpse indicated that the body fell from a great height. The madman in question has been preliminarily identified by the Metropolitan Police as one Doctor Silas Garrette, although this identity is now in question following the discovery of a gruesome murder committed at the said physician's office in Hogarth Road. Here detectives discovered the grossly mutilated body of Augustus Skinner, a literary critic who wrote for *Blackwell's Gazette*. Police now speculate that the true identity of the man is Doctor Jonas Hooke, an army surgeon who served with the 34th Regiment of Foot in Crimea. The police are not revealing the specifics of what they discovered in the doctor's office, although one officer described it as "a scene of horror," and as "the lair of a truly diabolical mind."

CRASHED TO EARTH

The remains of the Cremorne balloon, the *Sylph*, crashed to earth in a farmer's field some one hundred and twenty miles away. The survival of the young lady and her male companion is currently in doubt. It is believed they perished when the balloon entered a thundercloud, although no bodies have been reported discovered along the presumed flight path of the balloon.

37

THE NEW SEXTON

Highgate Cemetery, London, 1869.

Algernon and Constance Hyde-Davies strolled along the paths of Highgate as their children, Nathaniel (aged ten) and Rebecca (aged eight), skipped through the leaf-strewn grass, hide-and-seeking behind the grave markers and stone angels, then springing out and shrieking as they surprised each other.

"Rebecca! Nathaniel!" Constance called out. "Mama wishes you to stay near!"

As they rounded the curving path, they noticed an elderly gentleman pushing a bath chair fitted with tight-shuttered curtains.

"Good lord!" Algernon said. "I believe I know this fellow."

The pathway was narrow and eventually the two parties converged. Although a decade had passed, Algernon instantly recognized the man, much older and grayer, the once-rigid back now stooped by time.

"Mister Greenley."

The man stopped upon hearing his name. His eyes flickered over Algernon's face. Recognition was instant. He seemed a little suspicious of meeting his former superior, but the presence of Constance and the children visibly softened his demeanor.

"Mister Hyde-Davies, sir."

The two shook hands.

"This is my wife, Constance, and my children, Nathaniel and Rebecca."

"Say hello, children," Constance said.

The girl clung to her mother's skirts, suddenly bashful while Nathaniel bowed smartly from the waist and said, "A pleasure to make your acquaintance."

"Do you have a monkey in the basket?" Rebecca asked, looking at the enclosed bath chair.

"Rebecca!" Constance snapped. "Where are your manners, young madam?"

The young girl looked hurt. "I am sorry, Mama."

Greenley unfastened and drew aside the curtain. The children peered into the dark bath chair and even Algernon and Constance craned forward.

Inside they saw a slender girl of around the same age as Nathaniel. She was very beautiful, if extremely pale. A delicate tracery of veins showed faintly at each temple. She had her mother's long auburn hair but the violet eyes were striking.

"I should like you to meet Hope Aurelia Thraxton,

daughter of Lord Geoffrey Thraxton and Aurelia Thraxton," Greenley said with deep pride in his voice.

"Hello," said the pale little girl. She smiled as her eager gaze swept over them. For both Constance and Algernon there was something uncanny about the young face.

"She is as beautiful as her mother," Constance said, her voice tight as a harpsichord string.

At her words, Greenley dropped his eyes and looked at the ground. "Aye, that she is."

"You and I shall be great friends," the pale girl said to Rebecca in her floating, ethereal voice. She turned her eyes next to Nathaniel. "But you shall break all our hearts."

"That's enough, now, Hope!" Greenley interrupted. "These good people don't want to hear any of your nonsense." And with that Greenley quickly recurtained the bath chair. "Begging your pardon," he muttered, "but we must be cutting along. She is very susceptible to the light."

Robert Greenley steered his granddaughter's bath chair around them, in a hurry to leave.

"One moment, sir," Algernon said.

Mister Greenley stopped and stood still, without turning.

"Geoffrey... Lord Thraxton. Do you know of his whereabouts? Since Constance and I returned from the Galapagos, we have lost touch. He answers no letters. I understand his London home was sold some years ago."

After a reluctant pause, Greenley admitted, "He sees Hope on the weekends. He is to be found here... somewhere."

Algernon stiffened at the words. "You mean... you

mean he's here? At Highgate?"

"Never leaves. Haunts the place."

Still brusque in his manner, Mister Greenley muttered a "Good day" and trundled his granddaughter away.

Algernon and Constance exchanged baffled looks.

"What does that mean?" Constance asked. "How can he live here? In the cemetery?"

Algernon shook his head in bewilderment.

"Why is that little girl so pale, Mama?" Rebecca asked. "Why does she ride in a bath chair? Can she not walk?"

"Shush, do not ask questions," Constance chided. "Inquisitiveness is impolite in young ladies."

They continued along the path, passing a gray-haired groundsman with a salt-and-pepper moustache raking leaves, a shabbily dressed fellow with a bowler hat and a stained jacket with the elbows nearly worn through. Algernon was tempted to ask him if he knew of a gentleman who visited the cemetery on a daily basis, but the question seemed ridiculous so he kept mum as they passed.

Around the bend they plunged into the deep gloom of the trees. Up ahead lay the Thraxton tomb. They found the tomb door unlocked and the latch lifted to Algernon's touch.

"You must be quiet, children," Constance hissed at her children. "This is a tomb. A place where the dead sleep. Be respectful." The children dropped their heads, suitably cowed, and Constance nodded for Algernon to enter.

The tomb was surprisingly bright. A great many candles burned here and there. There were two biers. One bore the name Aurelia Greenley. A single white bloom lay upon the tomb—a Night Angel apparently just left there by Robert Greenley. Constance laid a bouquet of posies below it, and caressed the cold lead casket with her slender fingers. "She was so lovely."

"Yes," Algernon agreed, but his own words—*a bloom that cannot abide the touch of man*— ran through his head as soon as he said it.

The bier stood next to another, this one empty, that bore the name Lord Geoffrey Thraxton.

The Hyde-Davies family left the tomb after a short, meditative stay. Neither husband nor wife spoke as they walked arm in arm back along the curving paths toward the cemetery entrance and Swain's Lane, although Constance did have to scold Nathaniel from time to time, who like any schoolboy, could not resist kicking leaves into the air from the piles raked into heaps alongside the paths.

They had to walk single-file to pass around the wheelbarrow parked in the path, which was laden with shovels, rakes, an adze and an object that immediately caught Algernon's eye: a walking stick topped with a golden phoenix bursting from the flames.

"I say," Algernon said, stopping. "I know that walking stick!"

The shabby groundsman was raking leaves a few feet away and Algernon shouted to gain his attention. "I say, you there, sir!" The man was raking with his back to them and showed no indication of having heard. Algernon kicked through the pile of leaves fencing him off from the verge and shouted louder.

"I say, excuse me!"

The groundsman stopped raking, looked around, and shuffled forward a bit, dragging the rake. "Sorry, sir," he said. "Deaf in one ear. Can I help you?"

"This walking stick. Would you mind telling me where you—"

As the groundsman took a step closer both men recognized each other at the same moment.

The shabby groundsman was none other than Geoffrey, Lord Thraxton.

For several moments, neither spoke. The two old friends simply stood looking at each other. Ten years had passed. Algernon, promoted to head of Kew Gardens and married to a wealthy widow, had risen in the world and his expensive clothes showed it. By contrast, Thraxton's clothes were stained, dirty and worn through with holes. For a moment, uncertain whether he had been recognized, Algernon thought about retreating, saving his old friend from an encounter that might cause him embarrassment. But it was too late: Thraxton had recognized him and knew, in turn, that he had also been recognized.

Thraxton took several more steps and eagerly reached out his hand. "My dear, dear, old friend."

Algernon grasped Thraxton's hand, reveling in the long lost feeling of flesh upon flesh. If both had not been Englishmen, they would likely have hugged. For his part

Algernon could make no reply at first, for his throat was clenched tight, his eyes pooled to overflowing. Thraxton's eyes sparkled, too.

"What happened to you, Geoffrey? Where did you go? We lost all contact after... after..." He could not bring himself to finish the sentence.

"I went nowhere. I remained here."

"Here?"

"At Highgate?" Constance asked.

"Yes, I am the sexton now. Old Charlie passed on. He's buried over there, next to his wife."

"But... but why?" Algernon asked. "Why did you drop out of society?"

"I made two promises to Aurelia as she lay on her sick bed. She made me promise to help those less fortunate, so I sold the London home and used the proceeds to establish a mission for fallen women. The Thraxton family estate, the title and the family fortune has been placed in trust and will pass to Hope upon achieving her majority."

Algernon spoke with a hitch in his voice. "So now you have nothing?"

But Thraxton smiled and shook his head slightly. "Now I have everything."

The look in the eyes of Algernon and Constance seemed pitying, as if to say: *You have everything except Aurelia.*

"No," Thraxton corrected, in answer to the unspoken question. "My beloved is with me always. I am keeping my second promise, to watch over her as she sleeps."

"You will be rejoined with her, Geoffrey," Constance said, gripping his hand solicitously. "We of the spiritualist movement truly believe that."

"But she has never left my side. We walk these paths together every night and lose ourselves in conversation."

The look that Algernon threw Constance was freighted with concern. He was hinting to let the matter drop, believing that his friend was delusional. Thraxton caught the brief exchange but said nothing.

"Mummy!" a girlish voice cried. "Nathaniel's being horrid!"

All three looked up to see the boy throwing handfuls of leaves at the young girl, who was vainly attempting to throw them back, giggling, her long blonde hair already entangled with leaves.

"Nathaniel!" Algernon said sternly. "Desist at once!"

The three turned their attention back to one another, but the moment had passed, as mere speech proved inadequate for emotions so profound. The sun had just slipped behind the cedar of Lebanon, and dark shadows crawled from the trees and bushes and sprawled lazily across the pathways. It was time for them to take their leave.

"Good to see you, old stick," Algernon said, pumping his old acquaintance's hand. "We are still friends, are we not?"

"Forever," Thraxton said, a melancholy smile settling on his face.

Constance kissed his cheek. Algernon wrung his friend's hand a final time, a hand now calloused with manual labor, and the family departed, leaving Thraxton standing knee deep in the golden splendor of a summer passed.

As per his usual routine, at exactly six-thirty p.m., sexton Thraxton clanged shut the iron gates of Highgate and padlocked them, then circuited the pathways to make sure none of the living had been locked inside with the dead. When he reached the place where he left the wheelbarrow parked, he sank wearily onto a nearby bench and set the Bullseye lantern on the pathway at his feet. He still had a backache's worth of leaves to rake, but a cemetery has nothing but tomorrows.

It was almost fully dark now; in the sky, rags of gray cloud snagged upon the sickle of a crescent moon before the wind ripped them loose, causing the light to fade and flare… fade and flare. A hawk moth shot past, then returned, whirling around his head in spin-dizzy circles. It alighted on his knee and trembled there a moment, antennae twitching, wings pulsing open and closed, then flitted away into the dark. The beam of his lantern spilled across the path. Atop a nearby tomb an angel perched, its face lifted to heaven, one arm outstretched, a crooked finger beckoning. As Thraxton watched, the angel's wings slowly unfurled, stretched full, then flapped. The stone angel rose from its pediment, drifted forward a few feet, then pointed a toe down and alighted gently on the pathway, its final wingbeats stirring the dead leaves in their piles. Thraxton stood up as the shadowy figure stepped into the light, illumining the form of a small angel with bright violet eyes and a mane of auburn hair.

"My inamorata."

"I am forgetting the way back. Each time I must come from further away. Maybe you should let me go."

"Never."

"Then maybe it is I who should let you go, Geoffrey."

"Please, let us not talk of these things. Not tonight."

"Why not tonight?"

"Because tonight is our anniversary."

"Anniversary?"

"The anniversary of the day you took my hand and led me through the streets of London. Through a world I barely knew existed."

"We found the party, remember? The grand house where they were holding a ball?"

"And we danced in the street."

"We sipped champagne and waltzed in the streets of London."

"Perhaps we should waltz again."

"But we have no music."

"No, we do. Listen."

Just then, wind stirred the treetops as the world snatched a breath. Somewhere, a wind chime clonged, its soft coppery tones resonating from afar.

Thraxton slipped a hand around the angel's waist, the stone rendered suddenly soft and warm. They grasped each other's hands and began to dance, sweeping along pathways ankle deep with crisp autumn leaves. An angel made flesh and a man resurrected. Their eyes locked, a smile on their faces.

In truth, Augustus Skinner had been right: Thraxton was never a particularly good poet, but in his devotion to Aurelia, he was writing a love poem with his entire life.

And though his feet never left the ground, his heart soared.

Acknowledgments

Thanks, once again, to my agent Kimberley Cameron for continuing to make my dream a reality.

Also, I'd like to thank my Titan Books Dream Team: my astute editor Miranda Jewess and my Titan PR gal Cara Fielder. Also a big thanks to designer Julia Lloyd, who produced the best imaginable cover for *Angel*.

I would also like to thank my friends and loyal cadre of readers: Cindy Thompson, Debra Borchert, and Nancy Coy.

Finally, thanks to all those fans who wrote terrific reviews of my earlier books on GoodReads and on Book Blogs, or who have written to me personally to tell me how much they enjoy my writing. In a business of constant criticisms and rejections, you provide a salve to my soul.

About the Author

Vaughn Entwistle grew up in northern England but spent many years living in the United States, earning a master's degree in English from Oakland University. He is the author of the critically acclaimed novels in the Paranormal Casebooks of Sir Arthur Conan Doyle series, *The Revenant of Thraxton Hall* (to which *The Angel of Highgate* is a prequel) and *The Dead Assassin*. He lives in north Somerset with his wife and cats.

THE REVENANT OF THRAXTON HALL

VAUGHN ENTWISTLE

Arthur Conan Doyle has just killed off Sherlock Holmes and is suddenly the most hated man in London. So when he is contacted by a medium who has foreseen her own death, he is eager to investigate. He travels to Thraxton Hall, accompanied by his good friend Oscar Wilde, where they encounter a levitating magician, a foreign Count and a family curse. Will they catch the murderer in time?

"Entwistle's absorbing first in a paranormal series featuring Arthur Conan Doyle finds the celebrated author having a "beastly day" after killing off Sherlock Holmes." *Publishers Weekly*

"A witty atmospheric tale featuring [a] unique detecting duo." Cara Black, *New York Times* bestselling author of *Murder Below Montparnasse*

"It's a treat to meet the Great Detective's creator... And partnered with Oscar Wilde - what a bold and wonderful conceit!" John Lescroart, *New York Times* bestselling author of *The Ophelia Cut*

THE DEAD ASSASSIN

VAUGHN ENTWISTLE

1895. England trembles on the verge of anarchy, terrorist bombs are detonating around the Capitol, and every foreigner is suspected of being an enemy agent. In the midst of this crisis, Dr. Arthur Conan Doyle and Oscar Wilde are summoned to the scene of a gruesome crime that has baffled and outraged Scotland Yard's best. A senior member of Her Majesty's government has been assassinated and the body of his attacker lies several streets away—riddled with the bullets that inexplicably failed to stop him from carrying out his lethal mission. More perplexing, the murderer is recognised by a detective as a man he himself saw hanged two weeks previously... Conan Doyle calls in his friend Oscar Wilde for assistance, and soon the two authors find themselves swept up in an investigation so bizarre it defies conventional wisdom and puts the lives of their loved ones, the Nation, and even the Monarch herself in dire peril.

"With a truly likeable detective duo, a very strong plot and a marvellous grasp of characterisation, The Dead Assassin is a marvellous read." The Book Bag

"I enjoyed reading this book... the overall impression is highly positive." SF Crowsnest

THE PROFESSOR MORIARTY NOVELS

MICHAEL KURLAND

A sweeping and eloquent detective series featuring Sherlock Holmes's nemesis, Professor James Moriarty. Aided by an American journalist Benjamin Barnett, and his infamous network of informers, criminals and 'specialists', Moriarty reveals himself to be far more than just "The Napoleon of Crime", working for both sides of the law, but always for his own ends.

The Infernal Device
Death By Gaslight
The Great Game
The Empress of India
Who Thinks Evil

"Michael Kurland has made Moriarty more interesting than Doyle ever made Holmes."
Isaac Asimov

"As successful as its predecessors at bringing fin de siècle Europe to brilliant life... the action veers and twists like that in a contemporary spy thriller." *Booklist*

THE ALEXANDER BRASS NOVELS

MICHAEL KURLAND

A charming mystery series set in 1930s New York, featuring newspaper columnist extraordinaire Alexander Brass and his long-suffering assistant, Morgan DeWitt. From blackmailing Nazis, accommodating nymphomaniacs and US senators, to missing confidence tricksters and the glamour of Broadway, Michael Kurland brings his inimitable style to bear.

Too Soon Dead
The Girls in the High-Heeled Shoes

"A smart, wide-eyed style that perfectly fits the time and place." *Publishers Weekly*

"Michael Kurland writes a brilliant period piece that fans of the the classic thirties mystery will simply devour… a fabulous whodunit."
Midwest Book Review

"Michael Kurland's fans know he's been the mystery field's best-kept secret or years; that status is about to change… An instant classic." Loren Estleman

For more fantastic fiction, author events, competitions,
limited editions and more

VISIT OUR WEBSITE
titanbooks.com

LIKE US ON FACEBOOK
facebook.com/titanbooks

FOLLOW US ON TWITTER
@TitanBooks

EMAIL US
readerfeedback@titanemail.com